Part One
Blood Sanctuary
Blood Grace Book III

VELA ROTH

D1595656

FIVE THORNS PRESS

ISBN 978-1-957040-03-5 (Ebook)
ISBN 978-1-957040-08-0 (Paperback)
ISBN 978-1-957040-09-7 (Hardcover)

Edited by Brittany Cicirello, Suncroft Editing

Cover art by Patcas Illustration
www.instagram.com/patcas_illustration

Book design by Vela Roth

Map by Vela Roth using Inkarnate
inkarnate.com

Published by Five Thorns Press
www.fivethorns.com

Visit www.velaroth.com

CONTENTS

For my mom,

who stands victorious in Sanctuary.

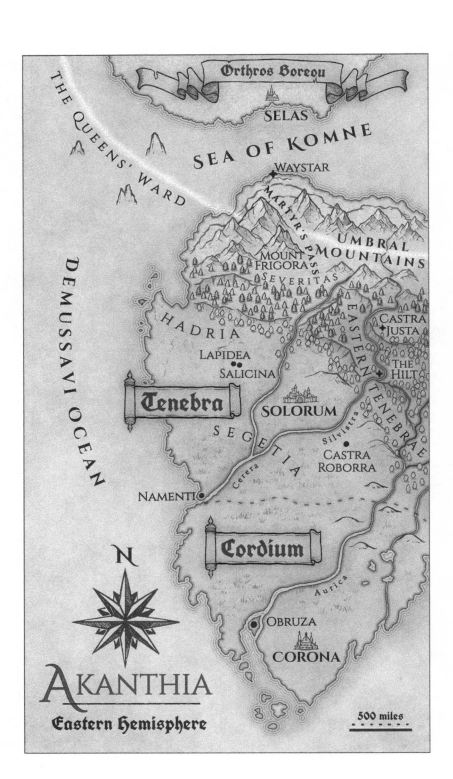

44

nights until

WINTER SOLSTICE

BEFORE DUTY CALLS

THE TASTE OF CASSIA's blood lingered in Lio's mouth. Her aura filled his residence. Her scent was all over his bed. He watched her sleep and counted the freckles on her left shoulder.

Now that she was with him, he no longer missed the Dawn Slumber. Polar night was a balm when it meant he could lie awake with her sleepy face against his chest and her body relaxed in his arms. He didn't dread the return of sunrise months from now, either. If he dreamed of her, he would awaken to find she was not just a dream. She would be here to satisfy his Craving for her. His addiction to her blood would be no torture, only a pleasure for them both.

By the time polar night ended for the season, the Tenebran embassy would be gone—short one member. Cassia would still be here in Orthros. She would have the chance to choose a future here for herself. That was Lio's silent vow to them both, and he would keep it, no matter what challenges they faced during the Solstice Summit.

She didn't even know she was his Grace and that without her, his Craving for her would be fatal to him. She had only spent one night here so far.

But what a night. He was certain he was already making progress in his unspoken effort to convince her to stay. She had revealed her feelings to him through the Blood Union. His Hesperine nature imparted that empathy and bound him to all living things, but Grace bound him and Cassia together most powerfully of all. The change of heart she had experienced in his arms last night had been as good as a promise.

Over the sound of her restful breathing, he heard the bells of Selas chime second moon across the capital city. Unease uncoiled within Lio, but he tried to let it go. Of course it was excruciating that Cassia must return to the guest house. Of course it would be grueling to act as if they meant nothing to each other.

But they were equal to the task. Cassia was the courtier, traitor, and unsung hero who held her violent countrymen back from the brink of war. Lio was the diplomat who had convinced immortal, unchanging Hesperines to invite a human embassy from Tenebra to Orthros for the first time in history.

The peal of bells ended, and Lio knew he must wake the unseen hand of Tenebran politics. Should he kiss the lips that swayed free lords with a word? Perhaps he ought to nibble the short, upturned nose that could scent the king's lies a mile away. No, he would nuzzle the temple of the mind that devised brilliant schemes.

Cassia stirred and burrowed deeper in the silk sheets to tuck herself closer against his body.

"With a good moon like that," he murmured in her ear, "I hope you'll stay for breakfast."

She ran her hand down his chest, as if testing to see if he was solid and not one of the illusions he conjured from light. "I really am in your residence at House Komnena. Last night wasn't all a marvelous dream."

"No. Shall I pinch you to convince you you're awake?"

"I don't think that will be—ow!"

At his bite on her earlobe, she laughed. He followed the nip with a slow suck, and a shiver went through her hip under his hand.

"I don't have to leave yet, do I?" she asked.

"Not quite yet. I'm afraid I only let you sleep for an hour."

Cassia let out a relieved sigh. "The hours are indeed long here. I can't believe how much has happened since we sailed into Harbor last night. Time hardly seems to pass at all in Orthros."

"Such is the pace of life here. We don't rush anything." He twirled his fingers in slow circles on the back of her thigh.

She told him how much she liked that with a caress from her foot, which had enjoyed such devoted attentions from him the night before. She lifted her head and blinked at him. The stained moonlight pouring in through his windows caught and gleamed in her hazel eyes. "I'm in Orthros."

He caressed her face. "We made it."

They shared a smile that they both understood. That only they understood.

Her beautiful, fierce determination stirred in her aura. "Now we have to make it through the Summit. We have to win."

"They couldn't stop us before. Not the King of Tenebra, not the Mage Orders of Cordium, not the heart hunters they hired." Lio cupped Cassia's cheek, holding her gaze. "We will win."

"Their warmongering is no match for our peace. We will see the king's alliance with Cordium broken to bits and Tenebra's ancient truce with Orthros thriving like roses in the dark. This Summit isn't going to end like the last one."

The last one, when any chance of peace between their peoples had shattered. When the threat of war had separated him and Cassia and trapped them on opposite sides of the border for half a year.

The Equinox Summit had almost parted them forever. She had just said aloud she didn't want that.

"That time is over." Lio gave her an adamant kiss.

She kissed him in return with all the zeal he felt in her aura. Her hand tangled in his tousled hair, catching the one braid he wore. She knew that thread of a braid meant a powerful promise to her, but her touch felt like a promise to him.

If he didn't stop her now, they would be late for tonight's official events. He pulled his mouth away. "You told Perita you're sleeping two hours late, didn't you? Two Orthros hours."

She trailed her fingers along his unshaven jaw. "Mm hm. Which is three Tenebran hours. I'm sure she's thrilled for three whole hours in bed with Callen. For two newlyweds, being handmaiden and bodyguard to the royal representative from Tenebra to Orthros is a demanding occupation."

"In that case, you and I have just enough time for coffee, breakfast, and the nightly invasion."

Cassia frowned. "Invasion?"

"We are expecting a small, quiet, and inescapable force of three." A grin came to Lio's face. "As soon as I lift the veil spell over my residence for moon hours, Zoe always comes in with her goats."

Cassia's face lit up. "I'll have time to see her before duty calls."

His Grace and his little sister were already drawing as close as he had hoped. "Why don't you relax a moment longer while I make our coffee?"

Before he could get out of bed, Cassia hooked her leg around his. "What about your breakfast?"

His gaze fixed on her short leg intertwined with his long one, her olive skin against his nocturnal pale. He listened to her pulse, and his body wanted to take up the rhythm. The shard of white marble she wore as a pendant throbbed between them, luring him. Cassia's talisman of protection was also a sacred artifact of their love.

"I enjoyed dinner all night long," Lio said. "My needs are certainly satisfied for the time being."

Cassia shook her head. "No more skipping breakfast. We learned our lesson on the voyage, when you couldn't make it through the night without suffering from your hunger. We will make time for your needs."

She issued her verdict with a kiss that made his fangs shoot out of his gums.

She was here in his bed insisting he feast on her now. Lio prided himself on his self-discipline, but now was not the time for pride. His canines and everything below his waist were in agreement.

He took her foot in his hand and pulled her leg higher around him. He would make it a quick breakfast. Find out how fast she liked it. See just how little time he needed to make her climax.

A fist pounded at the front doors. Lio and Cassia jumped apart and sat up halfway.

Lio put an arm around her to soften the startle. "I sense Mak's aura."

"I thought he and Lyros were on guard at the guest houses."

"They are, and neither of them would risk taking their eyes off the mages unless it was urgent."

A sudden sweat beaded on her skin. "What could have happened?"

The pounding came again.

"I'll go find out while you get dressed." Lio disentangled himself from her and levitated out of the spacious window seat that served as their bed. His magic sent the silk pillows flying. "Sorry."

"I feel like hurling pillows, too." Cassia clambered out of the bed-clothes. She nearly tripped over her hound, who jumped up from his blanket to greet her.

"He thought the other side of the room was too far way," Lio explained on his way to the door. "While you were asleep, he came to lay by the bed, so I moved his blanket."

"Thank you, Lio. That was kind of you." Cassia ducked behind Lio's dressing screen, her canine shadow following her.

Lio fastened his robe around himself along with his personal veil spell, which would have to substitute for cold ablutions. No time to walk across the library and open the inner doors. He took one Hesperine step to the entry hall. He opened the veil over his residence, and before he could open the front doors, his cousin stepped inside.

"Chrysanthos called a surprise council," Mak announced. "Bloodless mage expects the entire embassy to leap to attention. If Cassia isn't there in a quarter of a Tenebran hour, he'll know she's not where she's supposed to be."

"Goddess. If Perita tries to wake the illusion of Cassia sleeping in the guest bed—"

Mak shook his head. "Lyros has eyes on Perita and Callen's chambers. They're running behind, too. Just get Cassia to her guest room before Chrysanthos realizes she's the Hesperine sympathizer he's hunting."

"We're on our way."

Mak disappeared, and Lio stepped to Cassia's side behind the dressing screen. She had her gown on, barely, and she was shoving her feet into her shoes.

Lio slung an arm around her waist. "Perita will come to wake you any minute for a council Chrysanthos just called. We're out of time."

Cassia's hand closed around the glyph shard at her neck. "My Sanctuary ward can't protect me from being late. I hope that mage of Anthros melts in his own god's pyre."

By the time she finished speaking, Lio had them and her liegehound at the guest house halfway across the city, hidden amid the white rose bushes in the courtyard and a veil spell to cover their arrival.

From beneath an archway, Mak lifted a hand. "One of the initiates just delayed Perita in the hallway to give her fresh linens. Hurry."

Cassia yanked Lio's mouth to hers. The astonishing kiss was over before he could appreciate it, leaving his fangs unsheathed and his body throbbing. She darted through the glass door of her guest room, and with Knight at her heels, disappeared behind the curtains.

OUT OF LINE

THE COURTYARD DOOR CLOSED behind Cassia just as the bed-chamber door sprang open before her. Perita rushed in, her pretty face pallid, her light brown hair falling out of a knot. She was still in the act of tying her apron over yesterday's wrinkled gown.

She cast one glance up and down Cassia. Perita's gaze didn't even hesitate on the glyph shard, which protected itself and Cassia from discovery and danger. But her handmaiden took in her wild, unbound hair and her disastrous attempt to dress herself in her purple formal gown.

"I only got an hour of sleep," Cassia blurted. She waved a hand in the direction of the courtyard. "I gave up after a while and put my dress back on to go look at the roses."

Knight plopped down on her feet, hiding the one that was only half in her slipper. He had barely been able to walk last night, until Cassia's secret introduction to the Queens of the Hesperines, when Queen Soteira had healed him with a chuckle and a scratch on the chin.

Cassia put on a long-suffering expression. "Knight worked himself right out of his bandages, incorrigible fellow. It's hopeless trying to keep a liegehound still."

"Oh, my lady, I'm so sorry I'm past my time! Please—"

Although Cassia's pulse pounded, she gave a laugh. "Perita, be at your ease. We are still growing accustomed to Orthros time. What's the hurry?"

"We're already running late! Apprentice Tychon sent Apprentice Eudias over from the other guest house to tell Callen to tell me to tell you that his master wants the whole embassy to meet together to talk about tonight's events."

"Tychon's master has called this council? Then I will take my time dressing Knight's wounds again before we go. After all, my hound heroically fought in Martyr's Pass while that mage sat around on his berobed backside."

"As you say, my lady." Perita bit her lip, but didn't quite manage to hide her smile. She eyed Knight. "I can scarcely see his wounds under all that fur. Best bandage him up again to remind everyone of his battle scars."

Cassia held back a sigh of relief. It seemed her flimsy excuses and the famously strong constitution of liegehounds were enough to avert Perita's suspicions.

She need not worry her handmaiden would ever get close enough to Knight to examine where his wounds had been, not when Perita had to use a medicinal tonic just to keep his fur from making her ill when she did Cassia's laundry.

"I will not have you run yourself ragged on the mage's account, Perita. We are not at the beck and call of 'Honored Master Adelphos,' even if he is from the royal Sun Temple of Anthros at Solorum." Cassia recited Chrysanthos's false identity in a mocking tone.

It wasn't as if anyone in the embassy was unaware that Chrysanthos was really from Cordium. But of course he would insist they refer to him as a mage from Tenebra's capital, even amongst themselves, in case Hesperine spies were listening. It was almost laughable that he didn't realize all of Orthros already knew he was the Dexion of the Aithourian Circle, second-in-command of the Order of Anthros's elite war mages, the Hesperines' mortal enemies.

Perita scowled. "Right you are, my lady. Don't you worry about that mage. Callen and I won't let you out of reach again, not after the heart hunters attacked you in Martyr's Pass. We'll never forget the 'honored master' sat safe and sound while the rest of us got caught in the avalanche the heart hunters conjured."

"Having you and Callen to rely on sets my mind entirely at ease."

If only Cassia could confess that she was on the Hesperines' side and in danger of Chrysanthos sending her up in flames if he ever found out. The trust between her and Perita had withstood every test thus far. Might it survive heresy, too?

Cassia could not afford to find out. Some secrets were too dangerous to reveal. She must keep her friend safe.

"I suspect," said Cassia, "that 'Honored Master Adelphos' wishes to give us instructions to reassure himself we will not step out of line—and he wishes to draw the line himself. This council is an opportunity for me to show him I walk my own path."

TRIAL BROTHERS

EHIND LIO, MAK CLEARED his throat. "You're not quite invisible."

"Right." Lio strengthened his veil, rubbing his mouth.

He heard footsteps resume in the corridor inside the guest house. Perita's aura moved toward Cassia's rooms. The door banged open.

Lio didn't breathe as he observed the women's exchange through a gap in the curtains. But Cassia's quick tongue didn't fail her. Perita soon went about her duties as if nothing was amiss. While she and Cassia opened a trunk of gowns, Lio withdrew and slid the curtains tightly shut with a subtle act of Will.

Lio joined his cousin under the archway on the other side of the courtyard. "Thank you."

"I told Lyros I'd get a thank you. He was betting on a fist in my face."

"I'll save that for the training ring." Lio gave his cousin's shoulder a shove. "It wouldn't be fair for me to attack a hungry opponent."

"Don't rub it in," Mak threatened. "Lyros and I were *working* all night."

Mak appeared as if he had just come on duty in his regalia of a knee-length black fighting robe and sandals laced to the knee. His brown hair and the darker brown braid of Lyros's attached at his temple were neatly bound in his speires, the iconic hair ties of Hesperine warriors. But there was an edge in his aura.

Lio looked at his cousin ruefully. "Breathing down the mages' necks is more fun at the beginning of your watch than the end, I take it."

Mak waved a dismissive hand, although his irises had retreated to a rim of brown around his dilated pupils. It had been a long night, and Mak and Lyros's Craving for one another must be troubling them.

The Solstice Summit might alter history and be the greatest triumph of Lio's diplomatic career, but his idea of bringing the enemy home for a visit put all of Orthros on the alert. Lio regretted the burden he placed on the Hesperines' army, especially since Hippolyta's Stand consisted of only four people, and they were his aunt, his two cousins, and his Grace-cousin.

Lio sighed. "I'm sorry you're stretched so thin."

"I'm glad we have enough work to go around," Mak replied. "Besides, some of the Prince's Charge are here to reinforce us. Patrol is a lark when the famous Hesperines errant who serve under our First Prince fill our ears with tales of their adventures Abroad. Perhaps you, Lyros, and I will make our own legends before the Summit is over, eh?"

"When we made it through the Trial of Initiation together, I never imagined that scarcely a year later, we would be responsible for the conduct of Cordian mages within our own borders."

Mak half grinned. "Not bad, is it?"

With a laugh, Lio massaged his aching gums. "I'm grateful we're in this together."

Mak crossed his powerful arms over his barrel chest. "Challenge gladly accepted. What are Trial brothers for?"

"Throwing a punch at me for putting everyone through this."

"I'll save that for the training ring, too. I *am* ready for breakfast."

"When do you and your breakfast get to the end of your watch?"

"As soon as your breakfast is sitting in her chair at Chrysanthos's council. Then the mage is our relief's problem."

"Who's your relief?"

"You are, you lazy scrollworm."

Lio stood up straighter. "The Stand is officially assigning me a watch?"

"After your magic saved us so much trouble in Martyr's Pass, don't think you can escape lending us a hand again. You're on watch from now until the diplomatic events start at midnight, and you won't have time to change in between. Go put on something sharper than your veil hours robe and report back here for duty. Your orders are to ensure the safety of Orthros's only ally in the embassy while she attends council with our enemy."

Lio smiled, baring his fangs. "My pleasure."

THE EMBASSY'S READER

ASSIA ALWAYS WOKE TO a strategy. She pulled the impossible out of her sleeve in the midst of a crisis, or she pieced the plan cautiously together over time with the secrets she cultivated. With her own counsel as her only guide and her only judge, she succeeded by the skin of her teeth.

But tonight, she would commence the strategy she and the Hesperines had collaborated on together.

They would not just succeed. They would be victorious.

Cassia stood at her dressing table and let her handmaiden armor her for the coming campaign. Perita smoothed the crimson gown while Cassia ironed out the words she would say. Perita brushed her hair while Cassia untangled the consequences in her thoughts.

Cassia had never had so much to lose and so much to gain by thwarting the king's plans for alliance with Cordium and war with the Hesperines.

Not only justice for her sister's fate at the king's hands. Not only gratitude toward the Hesperines who had been Cassia's only saviors the night of Solia's death. Not only the lives of all the Hesperines errant and the threat of Cassia's own death upon a heretic's pyre.

There was the threat of the Departure. That version of the future weighed upon Cassia, too dreadful to bear, and she was at a loss as to how to carry it. The Summit must not fail to secure peace, for the Hesperines would leave Tenebra rather than meet the Mage Orders in battle.

The Queens would invoke the Departure. They would sequester all their people behind their ward. Forever.

There was only one hope that lifted that burden from Cassia's shoulders. Now that she had let herself begin to imagine it, she could not push the vision away. She must hold fast to it, for it gave her strength.

If the Summit succeeded, Cassia's work in Tenebra would be done. She could stay here. She would never lose Lio again. They would have each other and all of Orthros ahead of them. They would never run out of time.

This council of Chrysanthos's was several hours too late to sway the course of events. The Queens of Orthros had already summoned their closest advisers to a secret circle the night before, with Cassia in attendance as their informant.

Cassia would not fail to show proper appreciation for her mortal allies, as well. "Perita, you are marvelous. I think that's the fastest you've ever gotten me ready for anything."

"We're not at the mage's beck and call, but we don't want him to have too much time to have his say before you get there, either."

They left Cassia's rooms to find Callen waiting patiently in the corridor with Apprentice Eudias fidgeting beside him.

"Basilis," the subordinate mage greeted Cassia. An expression of relief crossed the young man's long face, but then he licked his scrawny hand and tucked the thin, black strands of his hair under his yellow apprentice cap. He glanced at the walls, which had ears, of course.

Cassia was happy to know they were the ears of Hippolyta's Stand and the Prince's Charge, and she had already told them most of the things the mortals avoided discussing. "What's the matter, Apprentice Eudias?"

"Honored Master Adelphos must not be kept waiting! He insists everyone arrive punctually." The apprentice might have been announcing that Anthros himself was about to descend in his sun chariot and put all the guilty to the pyre on the spot. Eudias scurried down the hall.

Cassia followed after him at a dignified pace. She was not going to run to the Dexion's whistle, not to mention make Callen run all the way to the New Guest House after the attack in the pass had put his bad leg to the test. Attired in a leather tunic with his sandy hair tidy, Cassia's bodyguard was the picture of an efficient and ready warrior, even if the Hesperines had confiscated everyone's swords. Cassia hoped the dark circles under his eyes meant he and Perita had enjoyed their silk sheets and not that his old wound had made a misery of the night. Perita had been unusually tight-lipped on the matter, and Cassia could not ask Callen how his leg was holding up without offending his pride.

Eudias seemed to remember his duties as the superfluous protector Chrysanthos and the king had assigned Cassia. He hovered ahead of her and her friends in the hall and waited.

"Good morning to you as well," Cassia said when they caught up to him.

Eudias flushed. "Well, thank you, Basilis. Good morning. Or rather, I suppose it's actually good evening, isn't it?"

"Strictly speaking, yes. It is night in Tenebra right now, but a new 'day' for the Hesperines, I suppose. Moon hours correspond to our hours of darkness, when the Hesperines are wakeful, and veil hours to our hours of daylight, when they rest. In any case, you may go on ahead to present yourself to the Honored Master punctually, if you like."

"Ah, thank you, no, that won't be necessary. It won't do for me to leave your side, Basilis." He fell into step beside her.

They found their way back to the main hall of Rose House, then to the gallery that would take them to the New Guest House. Sir Benedict was already in the arched stone corridor, and the moment they entered, he took Cassia's arm.

"Are you well this night, Your Ladyship?" the knight asked.

"None the worse for wear, thank you. How are you, Benedict?"

"Ready for anything." He glowered ahead toward the mages' lodgings.

"Even tonight's diplomatic events?" She smiled at his attire.

"I am not here to impress, Your Ladyship."

At twenty-three, Benedict was only a year older than Cassia, but he wore the long tunic and loose braccae that were the tradition of their forefathers. His sturdy garments were more suited to a call to arms than an appearance at a foreign court, and his golden brown hair was cut short to accommodate a helm. The only finery he wore was his spotless wool tabard displaying Segetia's coat of arms. The fox carrying a sheaf of wheat in its mouth was an uncanny reminder of the future free lord of Segetia.

Flavian had no place in Orthros. Her promise dance with him last month had been a lifetime ago. The lady who had discussed their marriage had been a different Cassia.

"As the First Knight of Segetia," Benedict said gravely, "my only purpose is to act as my liege's official representative, carrying out Lord Titus's commands in all things—and to protect you as my lord Flavian would, were he here. It is shame enough that you will not be in Tenebra to celebrate with him when your fathers make your betrothal official. But I will see to it that you make it safely home for your wedding, if it is my last deed in this world."

"I do hope you are being rhetorical, Benedict."

His only answer was a grim expression.

She wished she could spare Benedict from the suffering brought on by his good intentions. She let him escort her and her retinue to the end of the gallery and out to another courtyard. Knight felt the urge to mark his territory on one of the potted junipers, but the beds of mint made him sneeze. Benedict showed Cassia into a common room richly appointed in ocean tones of green and blue, where there were chairs and a round table of the wrought iron craft popular among Hesperines.

Chrysanthos had taken up a position facing the door with the air of a man sitting at the head of a council table. Their arduous journey had not crumpled the flower of Cordium. His golden skin and black hair reeked of expensive scent oils, and there was not a crease in his red-gold robes. But here in Orthros, where the Hesperines radiated real beauty, the Dexion's handsome face and manly physique had no power to win him admirers.

The Tenebrans around him cast wary glances at him. Benedict seated Cassia with the Kyrian and Cheran mages. Then he joined the men, who milled around the sideboard muttering amongst themselves. True to their resolve not to eat a bite of Hesperine food, the embassy had set out their own provisions and travel utensils, at least what had survived the journey to Orthros. Alas, they must be just as suspicious of Hesperine wash water, for the air in the room was suffocating with the smell of men who had traveled hard, then bathed only in oils or not at all.

Cassia turned to the venerable mage who led the small Kyrian delegation. "We find ourselves a long way from the Temple of Kyria tonight, don't we?"

"My bones announce it loud and clear, but they are along for the journey, whether they like it or not." The Semna chuckled, pulling her hood closer around her deeply lined face.

"Shall I mix you another tonic?" asked Apprentice Ariadne, one of the younger mages of Kyria. Above the veil that covered the lower half of her face, her brown eyes were concerned.

"No need, my dear." The Semna patted her hand. "I shall put a little of my own healing to work on myself."

"I can prepare your litter," offered Pakhne, her other veiled attendant.

"Nonsense. I will attend tonight's events on my own two feet. But thank you for your concern."

Cassia smiled. "Kyria could not have chosen a more able messenger than you, Semna. We are fortunate you are here."

"Years ago, when I left matters in the current Prisma's hands and retired to my solitary shrine, little did I know the goddess would call me out of my meditations one more time. Pray that only my bones weaken, and not my voice. I must do as Kyria has bade me and bring her invitation of mercy to the Hesperines."

Cassia leaned closer. "Semna, are the rumors true? Was Hespera really also called a goddess of mercy in ancient times?"

"My, my, Lady Cassia. You have become a devotee of the Prisma, haven't you? Few outside our temple remember history so old."

"I seek wisdom for the present. Where better to look than the past?"

The mage nodded in approval.

"Hespera is called the fallen goddess," said Cassia. "I think that must mean she was once elevated high. Was there a time before when matters were not as they are now?"

"There was. A time when the gods were in harmony, before Hespera's conduct led her followers astray and made Kyria grieve for their loss. All children were once Kyria's children. She wishes all of them to put aside their harmful ways and return to her. It is never too late."

"Then there must be hope for reconciliation. We must not give up on your message, Semna. I am sure the Hesperines' hearts will be touched by words of mercy."

Benedict returned, balancing plates for all the women, with help from Callen.

"Brave and blessed ladies," said the courteous knight, "Lady Cassia tells me you did not wait to be asked, but volunteered to accompany the Semna on her final quest."

"Of course," Ariadne replied. "We begged the Prisma to spare us from our duties in the temple so we might have the honor."

"And I promised to return them to her," the Semna said, "whether I make it back to Tenebra or not. Ariadne is Deutera's most promising apprentice, and Pakhne is an important intermediary between the temple and the community."

Pakhne arched a brow at Benedict, but her blue eyes were smiling. "Before I surrendered my place in the world for the joys of serving the goddess, Sir Benedict knew me differently. He remembers me as the eldest daughter of Free Lord Galanthian, a lady of Free Lord Hadrian's faction."

The knight gave her a bow. "I remember you as a devout woman and now know you as a brave one."

"Well said," the Semna told him. "Kyria is mother to us all, and it grieves her for her children in Segetia and Hadria to be enemies. If I am not here to see these fine young mages safely home, you, Sir Benedict, must help Lady Cassia do it for me."

"By Andragathos, Semna, I will see Mother Kyria's handmaidens safely to her once more. But we have every intention of carrying you home as well."

"Thank you, Benedict," said Cassia. "I am counting on you."

The two mages of Chera sat nearby, ever-present but aloof from the gathering. Shrouded from head to toe, they were faceless, silent reminders that the mortals had undertaken this journey prepared to die in the Hesperines' clutches, and the Mourning Goddess's handmaidens were ready to wail them into the next life. Cassia wished all of them would realize that the only knells they would hear in Orthros were the sweet chimes of House Kitharos, the bells that counted the Hesperines' hours.

Chrysanthos held out a hand to the goblet before Cassia. "A little taste of civilization, Basilis, with my compliments. I took it upon myself to provide wine so we need not suffer without alcohol to warm us during our lengthy stay here in the frozen north."

She glanced from the bottle at his hand to her full goblet. He had hauled wine on their entire journey from Solorum? Enough to share?

Perhaps he was just living up to his colleague Skleros's accusations of being a spoiled aristocrat. Or perhaps Chrysanthos was living up to his reputation as a formidable Cordian courtier, and he had a more premeditated reason for providing Cassia with a beverage of his choosing. Cassia had no intention of drinking or eating anything he set before her.

She reached down and rubbed Knight's ears. Her taster gazed up at her with begging eyes, but she would have to disappoint him. No tidbits from the table today. Knight was more than equal to mundane poisons, but what if a mage's brew could overcome even a liegehound's natural resistance to toxins?

"How generous you are, Honored Master," Cassia said. "I feel it is a crime to refuse such a luxury as a wine of *your* choice, for I am sure I have seldom tasted anything so fine. But I fear I am too recently recovered from a terrible bout of seasickness I suffered during the crossing." She put a hand to her hollow belly. It was all the mage's fault she had missed her breakfast and worse still, Lio's.

Chrysanthos offered a slight bow from his seat. "Of course you must consider your health. Perhaps the stew the men have prepared from the dry provisions will be less challenging to your constitution."

That stew contained the meat that had died in Tenebra at least a month ago and was probably poisonous on its own. "Thank you for your concern. However, I am committing myself to a fast tonight."

"There is nothing better for your health," said the Semna. "It will cleanse your body and clear your mind."

"I must strive to be at my best," Cassia enthused. "I feel called upon to eschew any worldly distraction from my cause. No one should feel obligated to join me in my commitment, of course."

"I am inspired to follow your example, Your Ladyship." Benedict gave his bowl to Perita. "What better way to prepare our spirits for the test of Orthros and to preserve our rations for those who are in greater need?"

Cassia smiled at everyone. "I hope all of you will enjoy the Honored Master's generosity on our behalf."

The scent of belladonna filled Cassia's nose suddenly, and she stiffened in her chair. A muscular, black-robed arm entered her vision, and a black leather gauntlet scooped her wine goblet off the table.

Cassia looked up and met the poison-green gaze of Master Skleros. He smiled, which made the scars on his face look even more horrific. She could smell his leather breastplate and the emblem painted on it in blood.

The Glyph of Hypnos, an eye closed forever. The Gift Collectors' rendition always reminded Cassia of a bloodthirsty mouth. The Order of Hypnos's bounty hunters took all too much pleasure in sending Hesperines to the god of death and dreams. No doubt Skleros would love to pack one of their mortal accomplices off to his god, too.

She reminded herself that the Hesperine healers had locked away his potions, except for a few harmless tonics, while the Stand had confiscated his blades. But Gift Collectors like him were deadly alchemists. Could he have concocted a poison from ingredients at hand?

Cassia's Sanctuary ward could stop an Aithourian's unveiling spell, but she didn't know if it would halt poison in her veins. She didn't want to put it to the test.

Skleros's voice emerged, hoarse as if he had undergone torture the night long. "I won't let it go to waste."

Chrysanthos lifted his glass to Cassia, or perhaps to his partner in crime.

Skleros strode across the room, his leather armor creaking and his short mage robes swinging about his knees. Cassia's anxious sweat gave way to a chill. The Gift Collector took a seat behind the Dexion, away from the table, as Hypnos always lurked behind his brother Anthros.

Leaning back in his chair, Skleros savored a sip of wine, then set the goblet on the floor between his heavy, spurred boots. From a pouch in his robes, he drew a wrapper leaf, which he packed with some manner of plant shavings and rolled into a smoke. He held the tip to the fire charm Chrysanthos had given him, a sunstone infused with the Dexion's war magic.

Nothing happened. Skleros scowled and tapped his smoke against the sunstone. A tiny cinder flared to life there, only to wink out.

Eudias sank into his chair with a shudder. Even Tychon, Chrysanthos's strapping apprentice, swayed in his seat. The Dexion set down his wine goblet.

"You could cut the Hesperine magic in this room with a knife," Skleros snarled.

Suddenly Cassia noticed a shadow behind the Gift Collector. Strange. The spell light in the room was casting shadows the other way. The darkness that loomed over the necromancer was slender and broad-shouldered and as tall as a bloodborn Hesperine.

Cassia coughed into her hand to hide a smile and looked around. No one else seemed to notice. But each time she glanced at Skleros, then away, she glimpsed Lio standing cloaked in illusion behind the necromancer.

Skleros tried once more to light his smoke, which gave off a puff of herbal fog, then hissed out. The Gift Collector growled something in Divine. Whatever insult or obscenity he had uttered, Cassia caught sight of Lio's fangs.

The necromancer put his fire charm away with an expression of disgust. "The blood magic in this place overpowers every other spell. I'd put a stop to that, if our hands weren't tied by godsforsaken diplomacy."

Chrysanthos took a swig of wine, his knuckles white around his goblet. Although Skleros had stored most of Chrysanthos's magic in a human vessel back in Tenebra to help the Dexion hide his identity, it seemed Chrysanthos's senses were not so dulled that he was immune to Lio's tide of power.

The Dexion shifted in his seat, and the spurs on the boots Skleros had given him clinked. "The mage who made that fire charm for you owes you an apology."

"I'll extract the apology from a Hesperine," the Gift Collector promised.

Lio crossed his arms, his blue eyes gleaming with the magic that had halted hundreds of heart hunters in their tracks.

Master Gorgos, who really was a Tenebran mage of Anthros from Solorum, fanned himself, his face ruddy. "Allow me to invoke Anthros's protection upon us all."

He commenced a lengthy prayer, then launched into cautionary teachings about resisting the temptations of wicked beauty. He put the fear into his audience with drama worthy of his master, the royal mage. His mentor had promised that the first from their temple to volunteer for the embassy would be appointed his future successor, pending the king's approval, and Master Gorgos was the only one who had taken the bait. But Cassia could hear the man giving voice to his own fears with his words.

At last Master Gorgos was done describing fruits that appeared succulent and tempting on the outside but were filled with worms on the inside that would rot your gut and your soul. When Cassia saw Lio roll his eyes, she struggled not to laugh. Several lords and mages disguised sighs of relief behind coughs and murmurs of agreement. Callen had scarfed down his rations in record time, but Perita gave him her unfinished stew.

Chrysanthos said in summary, "My colleague has, at such descriptive and vivid length, emphasized a truth we can all agree upon. Everyone here wants to make it home."

That roused adamant murmurs from all present.

"Our goal is the same," the Dexion told them. "I hope you all recognize that I am well prepared to help you achieve it. Allow me to demonstrate my commitment as we go over the Summit itinerary the Hesperines have provided us."

He lifted a hand, and Tychon went around the room handing out rolled documents that were tied with silver-and-white silk cord. The Dexion's apprentice might be a scroll-pusher who licked his master's boots until they shone, but he was also training as a war mage. Although serving as a magical channel between the Dexion and his vessel hindered Tychon's spells, the apprentice's warlike build suggested he took Anthros's ideals of manhood to heart and knew how to use his fists, too.

Before Tychon reached her, Cassia turned in her chair to speak to Callen and Perita. "Didn't we receive our own copy of the itinerary?"

"Yes, my lady." Callen hesitated, then reached behind his back and pulled a scroll out of his belt. "One of the initiates brought it while Eudias and I were waiting in the hall, but I thought there might be some mistake. You wouldn't think they'd run out of that fancy cord for the royal representative's copy."

Cassia took the scroll and tried not to look Lio's way. Her copy was secured with a silk bracelet embroidered with dancing goats. She tucked the token from Zoe into her belt pouch, resolving to wear it when she finally got to spend time with Lio's little sister during veil hours.

Cassia unrolled the itinerary and saw it was written in parallel Vulgus and Divine. What a wonderful opportunity for her to figure out Divine words based on the Vulgus she knew. Her only regret was that the dictionary Lio's mother had given her must remain hidden at House Komnena.

"Now," said the Dexion, "if you will all look with me at the first night on the itinerary."

While all the mages in the room, male and female, studied the Divine text, the lords and knights fiddled with the scrolls, their gazes wandering. Only Benedict read the itinerary with concentration.

Cassia spoke up. "I must confess, my lords, I am a painfully slow reader. Of course I lack the refined education in the Divine Tongue allowed only to mages, as befits the servants of the gods. However, I do have some ability to read our own vulgar tongue and would gladly serve you and improve myself by acting as your reader. Allow me to impart the Vulgus portions of the itinerary to you."

Chrysanthos looked up from his scroll, his expression affronted. "With all due respect, Basilis, I do not believe the lords of Tenebra need a girl to read anything for them."

"Thank you, Lady Cassia," said Lord Gaius. Free Lord Hadrian's representative in the embassy was as gray-haired and plain-speaking as his liege. Not to be outdone by Segetia, he wore a surcoat emblazoned with the arms of Hadria, a fortress on a blue shield. "Not everyone here comes from a learned household. Most of us are men of the sword, not the scroll."

Chrysanthos covered his surprise with one of his supercilious smiles. "I'm sure those who do come from learned households will be happy to oblige and spare the females of our party the burden."

Benedict cleared his throat. "I believe I am the only man here who needed to learn both sword work and reading to fulfill his duties. As the royal representative, Her Ladyship is more qualified than I to read the itinerary."

At last Chrysanthos must have caught on, for his smile turned snide. Did he think himself, the son of a Cordian princess, too highborn to be surrounded by illiterate warlords and the king's bastard girl child?

This girl child out-warred the lords and outsmarted the king. Reading wasn't all Solia had taught her. "Royal representative though I may be in these extraordinary circumstances, I am in no way royal. And yet I was blessed to be mothered by a princess. Although our years together were short, my elder sister, in her generosity, gave me a court education."

Many of the Tenebrans murmured respectful invocations, and one of the Cheran mages signed a blessing for the dead.

Chrysanthos went back to his wine. "Let us begin. We enter the most treacherous territory of all tonight, but heed my council, and we will navigate successfully."

Cassia smiled at the Dexion. "We appreciate your eagerness to serve our best interests, Honored Master, but I cannot imagine the terrain here could possibly be more dangerous than the pass, where some of us were surprised by an avalanche. We managed to make it out safely."

Cassia could tell by the seemingly relaxed hand the Dexion wrapped around his goblet that she had gone as far as she could. But not too far. Just far enough. The free lords were looking not at Chrysanthos, but at her with expectant expressions.

"What is tonight's order of events?" Lord Severinus was the first to ask.

Cassia knew the events in the pass were fresh in the mind of the young, pale-haired lord. He had nearly died in the avalanche at the hands of the heart hunters who served his own father—whom Cassia's father had hired. She and Lord Severin had quite the common ground.

She cleared her throat. "Tonight at fifth moon, the Hesperines will officially introduce us to their royal family, which marks the beginning of the Summit proper."

"The Hesperines have a strange way of telling time," one of the older lords grumbled. "Why can't they just refer to dawn and dusk like normal folk?"

"Polar night must require them to be creative," Cassia suggested. "I believe fifth moon is our midnight, and Hesperines divide the months not into fortnights, as we do, but into weeks."

"What's a week?" the lord asked.

Cassia pretended to study the itinerary, as if she had not already had a lesson in the Hesperine clock and calendar. "A period of eight nights, it seems. According to the schedule, for the first week of the Summit, we are the guests of honor at a royal celebration at House Annassa, the Queens' home. Each of the following three weeks will be devoted to one of the major areas of Hesperine life: magic, craft, and service. Then there will be several nights reserved for negotiations. Finally, the fourth area of Hesperine life, Ritual, will be represented by the ten nights of the Winter Solstice festival."

Benedict visibly braced himself. "We're to spend this entire week with the Queens of Orthros themselves?"

"The Queens will host us tonight," Cassia answered, "then each of the princes and princesses, from eldest to youngest, will welcome us into his or her respective residence for one night."

"Not every prince," Chrysanthos cut in. "First Prince Ioustinianos, the Queen's eldest, is conspicuously missing from the itinerary. I wonder why that could be?"

Skleros took another swallow of wine. "What a disappointment. I so wanted to meet the Blood-Red Prince, who rampaged across Tenebra and Cordium with his fellow Blood Errant."

"That sounds fearsome." Cassia pressed a hand to her throat. "Do set my mind at ease, Masters. Did not Elder Firstblood Apollon, himself one of the Blood Errant, assure us only last night that they are quite retired?"

"Hesperines don't die. They don't retire either." Skleros caressed the goblet in his hand. "Unless you help them along."

Chrysanthos smirked. "We have already caught our hosts in a lie. The prince's absence calls Apollon's claims into question."

"First Elder this, Prince Firstblood that." Lord Gaius threw up his hands. "Who can keep up with all their strange names and titles, much less how they're related to each other?"

"How *are* they related to each other?" Lord Severin put in. "They can't have children, therefore..."

Benedict shuddered. "Don't think too hard on it."

"Regarding the First Prince," Cassia said, "I can set your minds at ease. Surely you heard what the firstbloods were all saying about him at the welcoming ceremony last night. He is serving as his mothers' regent at a distant Hesperine settlement. It sounds as if he was deeply disappointed his duties prevent him from returning to the capital for the Summit."

"No," said Chrysanthos. "I heard no one say that."

"I did," said Benedict.

"Who?" Chrysanthos demanded.

"Elder Firstblood Argyros," Benedict answered with confidence.

Lord Gaius nodded. "Yes, the Queens' Master Ambassador. He told me that, too. As much as I hate to agree with the Segetian boy." He frowned at Benedict.

Lord Severin chimed in. "Orthros is barely populated outside the capital, but the Hesperines do have an outpost up the coast."

All of that was true. None of them needed to know the First Prince was his mothers' regent in Orthros Abroad and lived in disguise as a Tenebran hold lord, and that the Hesperines' settlement north of Selas had nothing to do with it. They also didn't need to know that Argyros, Lio's uncle who mentored him in both diplomacy and mind magery, had worked a spell on the mortals at the welcoming ceremony.

From the corner of her eye, Cassia caught a glimpse of smiling blue eyes. She was glad Lio felt reassured that the First Prince's secret was safe. Aiding Lio's beloved Ritual father was without doubt one of their most important responsibilities during the Summit.

She would do everything in her power to continue buying time for the Prince's Charge so they could find Orthros's missing Hesperines errant and bring them home. The Hesperines who had saved her life when she was seven were out there now, vulnerable targets for mages bent on persecuting them. Her rescuers were counting on their prince—and on her.

"What does the 'celebration' tonight entail?" Lord Gaius asked Cassia.

"Guides will arrive to show us to House Annassa, giving us a tour of the city on the way." Cassia studied the note Lio had left her in the margin of the itinerary. "The Queens are holding a royal banquet, and we are to rest assured we will be the recipients of their hospitality, not the main course."

Chrysanthos coughed mid-swallow.

"Be wary!" Master Gorgos warmed up again. "Heed the fate of the unwary traveler who met a beautiful Hesperine female at the crossroads by night. She seemed so fair and kind that he accepted the food she offered him. Once he tasted a bite, her spell upon him was complete, and he had to return to Orthros with her, powerless ever to escape. Eat not a morsel from the banquet table tonight, no matter how luscious it appears, for succumbing to temptation opens you to the vile magic of the Great Blood Sorceresses."

Chrysanthos recovered from his wine. "I advise you to follow my colleague's suggestion. Do not waste your effort trying to appear to be good guests."

"What if they take offense?" Lord Severin asked. "Wouldn't that put us in more danger than if we eat their food?"

"The Hesperine embassy didn't eat a bite at any of His Majesty's royal feasts in Tenebra," Cassia reminded them. "I am sure the Queens will understand."

"What the Queens understand," said the Dexion, "is that we are not impressed by their hospitality. We are not here to be lulled into complacency by fine food. Silk sheets are tasteless jests in the face of the history between Hesperines and mankind. We are here under Anthros's banner, and no feminine wiles can induce the god of war to lay down his arms."

Had Chrysanthos just asserted his authority over Cassia in the same breath as he decried the Queens? That was too close a parallel for comfort. Cassia had best wave Anthros's banner about to avert suspicion.

She drew herself up. "The ground of Tenebra holds the bones of all our men who have died under Anthros's banner and of the women who labored to bear them. We care nothing for fine food and silk sheets. What speaks to our hearts is the chance to protect our homes and see our families prosper in peace."

Lord Gaius looked at the Dexion with narrowed eyes. "We may all be here under Anthros's banner. But who among us is best prepared to lead the charge?"

The walls had ears, but they were not the king's, not anymore. At the enemy's table, Chrysanthos had precisely three allies. Himself, his apprentice, and the silent Gift Collector who sat behind him drinking his wine.

His disdainful smile firmly in place, Chrysanthos answered Lord Gaius. "Perhaps you suffer from misconceptions after your unfortunate encounter with the late royal mage."

Lord Gaius, like the rest of the embassy, visibly tensed. "While we are guests of the Hesperines, let us not discuss that man."

But Chrysanthos forged ahead. "Yes, the man who tried—and failed— to assassinate the Hesperine embassy during the Equinox Summit at Solorum. The man who couldn't even properly disguise himself as Honored Master Amachos, Tenebran warder, and was exposed as Dalos, a war mage from the Aithourian Circle in Cordium."

Oh, Chrysanthos was bold to critique his dead rival's ruse, when he was attempting the same misdirection under the Hesperines' very noses.

The Dexion sniffed. "That fool brought great trouble upon Tenebra and caused a catastrophe for his order. No wonder you have doubts about any Anthrian mage's ability to assist you in your dealings with Hesperines. But you will soon see the mutual benefit in working with an expert. I assure you the king has appointed the most capable of commanders, appropriate to this field."

"But how shall the spoils be divided?" Lord Gaius asked.

Skleros drained his goblet. "There's enough to go around, but only to the huntsmen who help bring down the prey."

"We haven't been invited to a hunt," Lord Gaius pointed out, "rather, we have been offered the chance to keep the hunters away from our game."

The necromancer pulled a tinderbox out of his robes. "You mistake wildcats for hunters. You can't reason with animals. If you don't kill the beast first, it will kill you."

The gray-haired lord crossed his arms, and his sleeves slid back to reveal skin as scarred as Skleros's. "I'm old enough to have fought beside my great-grandson. That's as long and full a life as any man can ask the gods for. I'm ready to die in battle, but if it is to be among monsters, that will do. I didn't come here to save my own hide. I came here to make sure my great-grandson need never go to war against those he cannot fight with the sword. Why did you come?"

"Blades work well enough on Hesperines, if you strike in the right place." With flint and steel, Skleros lit his tinder, then held it to the end of his smoke. "But fire works faster."

Lord Gaius eyed the necromancer. "It also burns everything in its path."

At that moment, a hush fell over the room, starting nearest the courtyard and moving among them all, until it overtook even Skleros.

In the doorway stood the Queens, arm in arm. Their combined presence filled the room, more beautiful and powerful than any spell. Queen Soteira wore her hair as a royal headdress in a tower of intricate braids. The celestial bodies of the night sky swirled across her black silk robe, embroidered in gold and silver, and matching jewelry shone against her deep black complexion. Next to her, petite, round-faced Queen Alea, snowy pale from head to toe, stood barefoot in her simple temple vestments, her floor-length hair loose. They wore a braid of each other's hair in a crown around their heads.

They bestowed their smiles upon the gathering. Was Cassia the only one who saw the laughter in their eyes?

"Well met, neighbors from Tenebra," said Queen Soteira.

Queen Alea glanced over the mortal gathering with anticipation. "We hope you will spend the rest of this evening at our table."

THE QUEENS' BANQUET

ROM HIS POSITION IN the royal retinue, Lio beheld an amazing sight. Whether due to politics, manners, or sheer awe, every man in the Tenebran embassy came to his feet before the Queens of Orthros.

Even the mages of Anthros and the Gift Collector rose from their seats. They stood like men ready for a threat. But they could not be ready for this moment.

Annassa Alea spared the confused Tenebrans the struggle of deciding whether they should bow because she was a queen or if that would cause Anthros to strike them down because she was a Hesperine. She invoked a great power that held sway over the Tenebrans. Tradition. She held out both her hands, palms up, in a Prisma's gesture of blessing.

The mortals responded in the time-honored way, tracing a glyph to their respective patrons over their chests. At a Hesperine's invitation, signs of Anthros, Kyria, Chera, Andragathos, and various other deities were offered up in Hespera's house. Cassia joined the mages of Kyria in signing the harvest goddess's glyph. Lio traced the cup and thorn of his Goddess upon his breast, thanking her for blessing his people with such brilliant Queens and for placing him here to witness this moment.

But there was no reverence in the Dexion's aura as he signed his glyph of Anthros. Only defiance. Skleros slowly traced the glyph of Hypnos written in blood on his breastplate. Lio could smell that it was human blood.

He did not believe for a moment that intimidation had been the only intent behind Chrysanthos and Skleros's drama over Cassia's wine. But Annassa Alea's voice called Lio's own intentions back to diplomacy.

"It has been a long time," she said. "Not since the first Equinox Summit nearly sixteen hundred years ago have I had occasion to speak with Tenebrans and temple mages, who were once my countrymen and colleagues in my mortal years as Prisma of Hagia Boreia, which was the Great Temple of Hespera in the north. I look forward to hearing of the land whence I came and how worship continues there. I am sure you can all tell me of many exciting changes, but also of beloved traditions that remain constant, no matter how much time has passed."

She took Queen Soteira's arm once again. "My Grace, Soteira, the greatest healer from the Empire across the sea, joins me in welcoming you."

Queen Soteira rested her hand on Queen Alea's arm. "We offer you the hospitality of our House tonight. We will show you our beloved city and guide you to our home."

Cassia gave a curtsy. "We shall be deeply honored to have places at your table."

The Annassa gave no one else an opportunity for formal statements. No man had a chance to take the lead before they proceeded inside. Annassa Soteira helped a wizened mage of Kyria to her feet and began to speak with her of healing magic.

Annassa Alea looked Chrysanthos in the eye. "Walk with me."

The war mage returned her gaze. Lio wanted to wipe the cloying smile right off the Cordian's face. How dare the man smile like that at a mage of Hespera whose power made his look like a candle before a moon?

"Gladly," said the Dexion. "I intend to make the most of this rare occasion. There has never been a time when a mage of my cult has met with you, Ritual Firstblood, on better terms than my predecessors...and there never will be again."

"You would be amazed how history can surprise you, were you to live long enough to watch it take shape."

Aithouros's heir fell into step beside the only surviving creator of the Hesperine race, and they walked out into the courtyard side-by-side.

The rest of the royal retinue eased amid the delegation to usher, herd, and otherwise engage the mortals. Lio went straight to Cassia's side. With the Queens nearby, no one could be safer, but he still seethed from the mages' threats. He would find out what Chrysanthos and Skleros had attempted. In the meantime, he would not let her out of his reach.

Lio bowed before his Grace. "Lady Cassia, allow me to escort you to House Annassa."

"Thank you, Ambassador." Her expression was merely courteous, but her aura was full of warmth, welcoming his nearness.

The guests bundled into the bespelled silk cloaks, gloves, and shoes Lio's people had given them upon their arrival to protect them from Orthros's polar climate. He and his fellow Hesperines then led the mortals out through the courtyard to the avenue behind the guest houses. There waited the caravan of sleighs that would carry them in comfort through the city. The teams of pure white boreian deer puffed out their clouds of breath and stamped their broad, cloven hooves upon the snow, making the silver bells on their harnesses jingle. Fluffs of fresh snowfall alighted on black silk seat cushions, only to fly away quickly in a fresh breeze.

Annassa Alea hopped up onto the driver's bench of one of the lead sleighs. For a moment, Chrysanthos stood staring up at her with a strange expression on his face. His aura was at once confused and offended, as if it were the gravest transgression that she did not conform to his dreadful imaginings of her. He hesitated, then climbed in beside her. She held a conversation with him that Lio could not hear.

"I confess, Ambassador," said Cassia, "I cannot begin to imagine what Annassa Alea and the Honored Master have to say to one another."

"As to that, Lady Cassia, I can offer no insight. I can only say that no ambassador in the Queens' service, however dedicated, can do justice to their diplomacy."

As usual, Benedict clung to Cassia's arm, and Eudias followed her like a spare hound. Lio could feel their apprehension, but Callen's and Perita's too. He blanketed Cassia's escort in thelemantic reassurance and met her protectors' posturing with patient courtesy.

His reward was to take the driver's seat of their sleigh with Cassia beside him. Knight occupied all the space on her other side, leaving nowhere for Benedict to ride but behind them with the rest of Cassia's retinue. With Cassia close at his side and her enemies in separate sleighs, some of Lio's tension abated.

"Ambassador, I don't see any reins," Cassia remarked.

"The Blood Union makes a kinder guide than a bit. In any case, these teams know the city so well, we scarcely need to direct them."

Annassa Soteira, leaving the driver's seat to one of her retinue, settled into her sleigh with the mages of Kyria. Orthros already had at least one potential ally among the Kyrian delegation, Lio realized. He recognized Apprentice Ariadne's aura from the night the Equinox Summit had ended. She was one of the mages who had secretly delivered Zoe and the other Eriphite children into the Hesperine embassy's care so they could escape Tenebra.

The Queens shared a glance, and then the sleighs sailed into motion. The mortals found themselves on the tour of Selas with the Annassa as guides. The metal sleighs, large but light, swept along the snowy streets, shining under the spells lights that glowed inside the city's stained glass lamps. The cavalcade was soon well beyond the Docks District.

Cassia looked all around her, taking in the homes and libraries and workshops. "Elder Firstblood Apollon's deeds have shown him to be a mighty warrior, but the architectural style he founded shows him to be an artist of great imagination. I see his strength in these structures, but such elaborate fancy, too."

"My father says he hopes his designs pay tribute to the Goddess's majesty and beauty, but also her creativity."

All but Cassia cast furtive glances at the towering buildings.

"Interiors veiled by stained glass," said Cassia, "and exteriors guarded by fanged beasts of stone. I am all curiosity, Ambassador. What are these creatures with wings and horns, which cap your pillars and lurk above your archways?"

"Gargoyles," Lio answered. "All fanged creatures in this world, such as snakes and cats, are sacred to Hespera, but gargoyles are her own familiars. Our sacred teachings hold she made them from her blood to guard her realm of Sanctuary from threats by other gods."

"I see. They are your divine protectors."

The looks on the other Tenebrans' faces suggested they found them more terrifying than comforting.

"Do they..." Benedict ventured. "They aren't her real gargoyles, are they, guarding your city?"

"Well," Lio answered, "I've never seen my father's sculptures come to life myself, but the goddess may work any miracle she likes, I should think."

The Tenebran warrior went pale, and by the way his hand fidgeted under his cloak, Lio suspected he was signing another glyph. When Callen pulled Perita a little closer to him, though, Lio regretted playing on the mortals' fears.

"Gargoyles dwell in the Goddess's realm," Lio assured them. "Their task is to protect against other gods, not mortals."

For mortals, Hespera's followers had Hippolyta's Stand. Aunt Lyta and Skleros rode together in vicious silence. Lio's aunt looked diminutive across from the necromancer, but Skleros watched the Guardian of Orthros like one predator watches another. Tychon and Master Gorgos sat as far from the pair as the sleigh would allow. Her Stand regalia made it clear she was not there to socialize. She had her voluminous, dark auburn hair bound out of her way in her speires. Mak and Lyros were a silent threat sharing the drivers' seat. Lyros might be the shorter and leaner of the pair, but his height and strength outclassed the Tenebran warriors by far.

The familiar, broad stone ways of Selas took them into the depths of the city, nearer and nearer to its center, House Annassa, which stood at the heart of the capital in easy reach of all the Queens' people. Lio mentioned the history of various landmarks and pointed out his favorite sites. Enjoyment flowed between him and Cassia.

As they took a winding road beneath a long colonnade, she asked, "Ambassador, am I mistaken that you said your father planned the city as well?"

"That's right. Your question leads me to suspect you doubt the city has a plan at all."

"I confess to having lost my bearings the moment we left the guest houses behind. Where are we now?"

"Ereba's Labyrinth, named for the fallen elder firstblood of Hagia Notia. My father insisted that within the city's order, there be room for freedom. The docks, the elder houses, and civic buildings such as Hypatia's Observatory and Hippolyta's Gymnasium serve as navigational stars. The rest of the city forms constellations around them over time as our families grow and create."

Perita and Callen were murmuring to one another in the back. Amid the rushing of the wind and sleighs, their voices were low enough to escape their fellow mortals' attention, but not Lio's.

"These Hesperines live in greater luxury than the king," Perita said.

"*These* Hesperines," Callen replied. "What about the ones who aren't royals or elders?"

"Well, we've seen a lot of workshops."

"So the rich craftsmen and merchants play noble, just like in cities back home. What about tallow chandlers like your father? Farmers like my father was? Where are the common folk?"

"Aye. The Hesperines will shows us around the grand houses, as if that tells us anything about Orthros, but I dare say the servants' quarters won't be on the tour."

Lio could tell Cassia's friends were accustomed to the important folk not including the servants in the conversation. "Thoughtful observations, Master Callen and Mistress Perita."

Callen looked uncomfortable and did not reply. Perita showed Lio a polite face, but her aura was unimpressed.

"In fact," Lio went on, "each Hesperine learns a craft and joins a service—a profession. We all depend on one another to thrive. Everyone who lives in Orthros is important."

"Well," Callen ventured, "you must have common neighborhoods somewhere, Ambassador."

Lio gestured around them. "None of the residents of Ereba's Labyrinth are royals or elders. Many of them are firstbloods in their own right, however. Anyone who is not part of an established bloodline may found their own and gain a vote in our government."

"Who works your farms?" Eudias wondered. "Where do you keep farms in all this snow? The food we have seen in the guest houses must come from somewhere."

"Indeed, there are gardens and greenhouses all over the city that supply us with whatever produce will tolerate our climate. The forest and the ocean also provide ample forage. Farming and cooking are honorable crafts on which Orthros depends to accommodate our human guests." Lio pointed out one of the homes as they passed. "Four generations of one of our farming bloodlines live there. They are Ritual tributaries of Blood Komnena, in fact."

"Tributaries," Callen echoed. "So you do have lieges and vassals, just like anywhere else."

"On the contrary, Master Callen," Lio answered. "We do not call them tributaries because they give us tribute, but because we have given our magic to them, as one river flows into another. My father Gifted the firstblood of that family. She does send us the most delicious produce at festival time, though. She and her descendants are accomplished agriculturalists who specialize in root vegetables."

The mortals in the back of the sleigh all stared at the house until it was out of sight.

Perita frowned. "It takes a lot of people to keep up a house of that size. Do the folk who beat the carpets and polish the silver get votes, too?"

"No one in Orthros is a servant," Lio answered. "We all do for ourselves with cleaning spells or honest work. *Every* family has a vote, no matter their origin."

"Astonishing." Cassia rubbed it in. "So in Orthros, even vegetable farmers live in mansions and have a seat on the council."

Lio sensed her companions' doubts. But they would meet Hesperines from all walks of life throughout the Summit. They would see.

"...riches built on illusion and corruption!" Master Gorgos's voice dashed by as the Stand's sleigh passed them. "...traded their souls for finery!"

"Ambassador," Cassia asked very seriously, "are Hesperine vegetables corrupt?"

His laughter almost escaped him. He cleared his throat into his hand. "I assure you, all vegetables grown in Selas are non-illusory and free from corruption. We sell them in Imperial markets for coppers, not souls."

At last they entered the Heart of Selas and drove through the grove of royal evergreens that led to House Annassa. One by one, the sleighs paused and allowed their passengers to alight at the foot of the steps that led up to the Queens' Terrace. While the sleighs jingled away back through the trees, the mortals ascended to House Annassa.

Lio smiled at the familiar surroundings. Sanctuary magic enveloped them all in a warm embrace. No snow ever covered the gleaming black-and-white marble floor and railings of the crescent terrace. The Queens sat down together on their silk-cushioned iron bench.

The mortals stared. At the gentle seat that served as Orthros's throne, at the open terrace that served as the Queens' court. At the side tables covered in platters of rich fare, at Lio and the rest of the silk-clad retinue, who poured coffee, fruit juices, or mead for the guests. Most of the mortals held their cups and plates untouched, but Lio caught sight of a few sneaking sips or nibbles of the delicacies.

At the urging of the Annassa, the embassy took seats around them. As if in a dream, the mages and free lords of Tenebra attended the Queens of Orthros.

Chrysanthos stood apart with his fellow mages, his courtier's mask firmly in place and no hint of dazzle in his eyes. He radiated anger as acrid as an Anthrian spell, and Lio suppressed a wince of surprise. He sensed Cassia's alarm as well.

What *had* the mage and Queen Alea spoken of? Whatever it was, it had gotten under his skin. With a touch of her benevolent, implacable hand, she had put the war mage on the defensive already. Lio's diplomatic caution lost its battle with his satisfaction. Aithouros's whelp was indeed no match for even one of the Queens. When they were both done with him, he would go home having been taught a lesson indeed.

Whether he would heed it was another matter.

CASSIA'S MALADY

AFTER THE MORTALS RETURNED to the guest houses, befuddled more by their hours in the Queens' presence than by wine, Lio took up his watch in the courtyard outside Cassia's guest room. He prepared himself to wait for Perita's departure.

But only moments later, he heard Cassia pacing alone within. He slipped inside.

With speed worthy of a Hesperine, she had her arms around him. Velvet crushed against him. She hadn't even let Perita stay long enough to undress her.

"Good veil." She smiled, but her body was tense from head to toe.

Lio buried his hands in her hair. "Once I've taken you home where you'll be safe, I'll come back here and search the New Guest House for the goblet. If there was anything to Chrysanthos and Skleros's little game with the wine, we will find out."

Her brows lifted. "That's a good idea. Thank you."

"I'm sorry you had such a close call."

"Ha! I would never be fooled by such a blatant attempt. It was a clumsy play on their part. Skleros can't even light a smoke properly in a Hesperine's presence."

Her jests rang true, not like the hollow ones she sometimes wielded to cover her emotions. She really wasn't worried about the wine. Lio rubbed her back, and she eased closer against him, but did not relax.

"Did you get enough to eat at the banquet?" Lio asked.

She put a finger to her lips. "Shhh. Don't tell anyone. Knight and I stuffed ourselves with the help of a Hesperine illusionist."

"I told you I would see to it you don't miss any more meals." He brushed her mouth with his.

She lipped him like a hungry thief trying to resist the fruit trader's stall. "You missed your breakfast."

"Mm." He kissed her back. "My little sister also missed seeing you. I'll try to endure until after bedtime stories."

"Of course. We should see Zoe first." Cassia's hands drifted down his chest.

His gaze arrested on her fists. Her heart pounded against his. He could smell the sweat beading on her skin. She stole one more kiss, as she had at the start of moon hours.

He cupped her head under her hair and held her to him, opening his mouth for her. At last she melted against him, and her hands unclenched. She breathed a sigh and plumbed the depths of his mouth.

He pulled back just long enough to speak. "If *you* can't wait until after bedtime stories, my rose, you have but to ask."

Her cheeks darkened. "I'm usually more self-disciplined."

"You've been self-disciplined—and deprived—for half a year."

"When we were apart, the feeling that came over me sometimes—it went deeper than that. It was more than just wanting you. I—" She stepped back and tucked a strand of her hair behind her ear. "Never mind. Zoe is waiting on us."

Lio took Cassia's hands. "You're shaking."

"Too much coffee, I'm sure. I'll be fine."

"You're stifled in velvet, but you feel like you're freezing."

"A brisk walk to House Komnena will warm me up."

He pressed his fingers to her throat. "Your pulse is racing. But there's no need to be afraid."

She clutched his hand. "I *am* afraid. Why am I afraid, when you have been right next to me all night? Why did the last few hours feel like years, just because I couldn't touch you? I thought I wouldn't feel this panic anymore now that I'm with you, but it came over me during the banquet, and I cannot shake it off. It's just like those awful months in Tenebra, when we were apart."

Lio pulled his distraught Grace into his arms and smiled into the darkness over her head. "That's exactly how I felt."

She breathed another sigh and took a step backward toward her guest bed. "I can't wait until after bedtime stories. I can't wait to go home. I need you so much that making love to you is all I can do about it."

To that declaration, the only worthy response Lio could find was to surrender his mouth to her again. With a little whimper in her throat, she fastened her lips to his and sucked his tongue.

Goddess bless. It was true. Even mortals felt the effects of Grace. More than lust, more than pining. Cassia suffered her own Craving for him.

He let her urge him along to the bed and offered his mouth for her consumption all the while. Petite though she was, with strength born of gardening and treason, she pushed him onto her bed. They sprawled together on the spacious mattress, her gown fanning around them, red as blood against the white bedclothes. His Hesperine physical prowess would not be necessary for what she had in mind. Grinning, he lay back for her so she could straddle him.

Her gaze locked on his fully unsheathed fangs. She licked her lips. Thorns, her Craving was rough and sweet. With trembling hands, she all but tore his robes open, and he helped her by getting her voluminous skirts out of her way.

Now she stared at his rhabdos. At the sight of how hard he was for her, she rasped a breath, and her lips parted. Cup and thorns. Cassia was ready to make a meal off of him.

She planted her hands on his chest, rose up on her knees, and came down on him fast. Her krana throbbed tight around him as if they had been teasing each other for an hour, not kissing with their clothes on for mere moments.

His head jerked back against the bed, and he bared his fangs. She rode him hard. He buried his hands in her skirts, forgetting to breathe. But she panted over him, breath after breath, pleasuring his senses. Her chest rose and fell within the confines of her bodice. The glyph shard swung at her neck with her wild pace, mesmerizing him into the pleasure that pounded through his body.

His hearing filled with the rustle of her skirts and the drum of her pulse, his nose with the smell of her body in a passion. Above him, her irises were a slim ring of hazel around her wide pupils. His tongue went dry, his thirst burned in his veins, but she fed him pleasure with every move.

Her eyes widened. A warning ripple flitted through her krana along the length of his rhabdos, and he shuddered under her. A long cry tore out of her, her body heaved once on his, and then her hips were writhing. He fisted his hands and watched her, felt her sate herself upon him.

Her head fell to rest on his chest, and she lay limp, catching her breath.

"Better?" he ground out.

"Oh Lio. It's not difficult after all. It's so easy. I just need you."

She cuddled against him, pulling her knees up around him. Her soft, wet krana tortured his rhabdos with a tender caress.

He could barely speak around his fangs. "Now I need you, Cassia. Everything you're willing to give me."

"I want to be everything you need."

He rolled her over, pushing her knees up higher as he drove down into her. She lay in a pile of crimson velvet and rocked under him with new eagerness, clawing her hair away from her throat. She met his gaze with glazed eyes and licked her lips again. She was inebriated with wanting and taking, as drunk as he on the Craving and the instinct to sate it at any cost.

He bared his fangs again, letting her see his hunger. Her hips shifted subtly under him, releasing, surrendering to his need. A fierce instinct awoke in him and overtook his body. He braced himself and thrust deeper inside her. He went still and held her under him.

She gazed up at him with an expression of fascination, her face just inches from his. Her breaths pressed her body against him. After a moment, she whimpered and tried to roll her hips under him. But he held her legs up and leaned into where their bodies joined, stilling her.

Tears slipped down her cheeks, and he trembled. A wave of sweet, painful intimacy swept through their Union. This was as it should be. If he joined their minds, he would climax now.

But he wanted to taste their bond, to join them completely with his fangs in her throat. He nuzzled her neck, and her head tilted back as if on reflex. Her pulse raced into a crescendo.

He bit her once to open her, a second time to penetrate her. Raw Cassia flowed into his mouth and heated him.

She clung to his shoulders and went wild under him. Her movements sped her blood flow and made her flood his mouth. Down his throat. Into his belly. Throughout every vein, coming to a head at the tip of his rhabdos inside her. He anchored her on his shaft while she tossed and twisted under him.

He gulped down countless missed feasts within moments, racing to have his fill before his body lost control. Her blood filled him until his vision hazed and his ears roared and he experienced her purely through his auric senses.

He bellowed her name in his mind as his climax and his magic surged out of him. Their bodies spasmed together, grinding into the bed. She called his name aloud, once for every pulse of his ecstasy inside her.

At last he lay tangled with her, his fangs still in her throat. Her blood sang in his veins, and pleasure left him languid in its wake. He blinked and dragged in a breath. When she smoothed his hair, he sighed and caressed her throat with his mouth. He smiled against her vein, then healed it with a kiss.

"I don't know what came over me," she whispered.

"The same thing that came over me."

"Is there a word for it in Divine? For I know none in Vulgus."

"You know the word." But he did not say the one he was thinking. "*Good*, isn't it?"

She groaned in agreement. "So good."

SWALLOWED BY THE SUN

THE GOBLET HAD TO be somewhere in the common room. Lio drifted about the deserted chamber. The air stank of the cured meat with which the Tenebrans had filled their hollow bellies upon returning from the Queens' banquet. The oversweet perfume of Chrysanthos's favorite wine lingered from earlier that night. But Lio caught no whiff of alchemy, and no hint of necromancy wormed across his senses.

He paused at the sideboard before a stack of dishes. Most had undergone a hasty scrub with a rag and still reeked of stale rations. But one goblet was spotless and redolent of vinegar and purging spells.

Lio let out a hiss. No amount of cleaning could erase the imprint of Cassia's fear and Skleros's sadistic gloating. The arcane scent of their opposing auras clung to the goblet. It was definitely the one. He should turn it over to the Charge, who would know how to handle it safely.

Lio went out into the courtyard, sensing about him for the nearest Hesperine aura. Another's questing awareness met his in the Union.

"Rudhira," Lio said in surprise. "I'm glad you're here."

His Ritual father manifested before him. Rudhira's famous blood-red hair was escaping his long braid, and there was mud on his Tenebran riding boots. His steel-gray eyes softened, and a smile relieved the grim expression on his pale, hawkish face. "Well met, Lio."

"I didn't know you would be back in Selas again so soon." Lio embraced him.

Rudhira clapped Lio on the back as he released him. "I just escorted two returnees home."

"You found two of our missing Hesperines errant?"

"They are with their families as we speak. For the first time in eight years."

"Goddess bless. Orthros needed that tonight."

"I only wish they were more than two."

"You will find the others."

Rudhira hesitated. "This is a difficult time Abroad. Worse than I have seen it since—in a long time."

"For you to say that, Rudhira, I know it must be."

"Seven Hesperines errant. Gone. We were right on their trails, and then they disappeared."

"They must have gone into hiding to avoid the Cordians. You sent out the warning that Chrysanthos's war circle is in Tenebra."

"I don't mean they went underground. I mean Kalos reports that sometime between the Spring and Autumn Equinoxes, they disappeared."

Lio fell silent. If the Charge's best scout could not find the trail, there was no trail.

Rudhira's gaze became distant, as if he were staring at something far beyond the safety of Selas. "All of us Abroad expect to bear the brunt of the mages' forays, but this? It's like the sun swallowed them whole. No last stand. No Mercy."

"Alkaios?" Lio asked.

"No," Rudhira answered, "he was not among the seven who recently disappeared. I still have a scout following the traces of his path."

"Cassia will be so relieved to hear that."

"I know how difficult it is for her to wonder if she will see the Hesperines she met in her childhood ever again. She bears it well, not knowing the fate of those who saved her life and gave the Mercy to her sister. Unanswered questions can be worse than bad news."

"Or they can be invitations to hope."

"Hold fast to your hope and share it with Mak. When he learns I was here, I know he will ask you if I said anything about his sister. You may tell him Nike's whereabouts are still a mystery, but Kalos is on her trail."

"I will share my hope with you as well. No news of your Trial sister is good news."

Rudhira clasped Lio's shoulder, but said nothing.

Lio could only imagine how he would feel if he hadn't seen one of his Trial circle in nearly a century. He must turn the conversation to Rudhira's consolation—his duties.

Lio nodded at his Ritual father's chain mail. "You aren't here at the guest house to invite the mages to a party, I take it."

Rudhira smiled, all fangs and no humor. "I must return to Tenebra shortly. I merely took the opportunity to make a patrol around the mages' lodgings before I leave. As tempted as I am to give the embassy a surprise invitation to my residence in my current attire, I promised my family and yours I would behave during your Summit. How did the mages take our excuses as to why the First Prince is not on the itinerary?"

"The Cordians were suspicious, as we expected, but I think the Tenebrans swallowed it with Cassia's influence to help it go down. For her efforts, I believe Chrysanthos and Skleros may have tried to poison her this very night."

Rudhira's red brows descended, and a storm brewed in his aura. "Right here in the guest houses?"

"In her wine, not that she would fall for such a thing. She is too clever for them, and thankfully, I was there on watch. I've found the cup the mages used. I was just looking for a Charger who might deliver the goblet to you for me, but now I can give it to you myself."

"You haven't touched it, have you?" Rudhira demanded.

Lio shook his head. "Just in case the Gift Collector used a poison that can harm Hesperines as well."

"Show me."

Lio led the way into the common room. Before he even pointed out the goblet, Rudhira went right to it. Out of his belt satchel, he snatched a cloth bag that emanated warding magic. Without touching the goblet, he levitated it into the bag and tied the warded fabric closed.

"I knew it," Lio said. "There's a malign spell on it, isn't there?"

"I'm not sure yet, but we mustn't take chances with a Gift Collector."

"Could you spare some time to examine the goblet for any evidence of what the mages attempted? When the embassy arrived, we confiscated everything Skleros brought with him that might have been poisonous. I cannot imagine how he managed to concoct something dangerous. I would ask our healers here, but no one has your expertise in Gift Collector poisons."

Rudhira stowed the warded bag in his belt satchel. "You were wise to come straight to me. The Charge is well equipped to handle such dangerous items."

"The strange thing is, after Cassia found a polite excuse for refusing the wine Chrysanthos poured for her, Skleros made a show of not letting it go to waste. He took the goblet and, well, he drained it."

Rudhira's eyes narrowed. "I most certainly want to examine this personally. Gift Collectors are infamous for their unnatural fortitude. If we can learn more of how they manage to withstand mortal danger, it will be a victory for us."

"I won't detain you from your duties any longer."

"It is my duty to ensure Cassia's safety, and yours." Rudhira shook his head. "And yet she escaped the mage of dreams on her journey here only for the Gift Collector to threaten her. We promised her she would be safe once she arrived in Orthros."

"She will be," Lio said. "I protected her from the mage of dreams. I will protect her from the Gift Collector."

Approval lit Rudhira's gaze. "I see you are coming to terms with your encounter with the enemy mind mage in Martyr's Pass."

"I hope so. As much as one can with an event that cost so many lives."

As much as Lio ever could, after experiencing hundreds of humans' deaths with them inside their minds.

"Talk to a mind healer if you need to." Rudhira's tone brooked no argument. "Your mother can refer you to one of her colleagues, if you need to speak with someone who has some distance from the event."

"I've spoken to you," Lio said. "How is your progress healing the mind of the man who survived the pass? Have you learned anything from him about the mage of dreams?"

"I'm sorry to say the man you saved remains too damaged to communicate at all, much less reveal information about the mage who broke his mind. I will continue to work with him. But I believe the mage of dreams is no longer a threat, since his task was to ensure only the favorites of the king and the Orders made it to Orthros, and he failed."

He had failed. Lio had rescued his Grace from the mage's pawns. The mage of dreams had killed his own men and fled rather than face Lio in a thelemantic duel.

But for a few moments before that, Cassia had believed herself cornered. She'd had to listen to her kidnappers describe their master's perverse plans for her.

Neither Lio nor Cassia would ever forget Martyr's Pass.

Lio unclenched his jaw. "He demanded Cassia from the king as payment for his work. He charges for his services in women. I want to know his name."

"So do Lyta and I, but we suspect it is erased from history already. The Order of Hypnos does not tolerate failure by one of their own. Their Order most likely punished the mage of dreams before the snow settled in Martyr's Pass. Skleros is probably gloating at the thought that he has outperformed—and outlived—his fellow mage of Hypnos."

"Skleros certainly had no qualms about murdering six necromancers from his own Order, as Cassia told us. Having bested another rival, might he regard Cassia as a victory prize from the fallen mage of dreams? Could that be why the Gift Collector is targeting her?"

"His motive may not be so personal. He may only have acted because of his uncanny alliance with the Dexion. He is most likely assisting Chrysanthos against her because she stands in their way."

She had drawn the Orders' gaze, and they didn't even know she was a traitor, saboteur, and Hesperine sympathizer. Lio's fangs unsheathed a measure. "There are already too many mages endangering her. We must be absolutely certain the mage of dreams is no longer a threat."

"The Charge will make sure. Cassia's enemies are our enemies." Rudhira pulled on one of his gauntlets. "I hope you have told her the truth of my bond of gratitude to the two of you. I will never forget that your efforts to secure peace have given us hope of avoiding the Departure."

"Yes, I told her. It came as a blow to her that our people would consider leaving Tenebra permanently. After what Hesperines errant did for her, she will stop at nothing to make sure you can continue performing the Goddess's mercies in Tenebra."

Rudhira fastened his other gauntlet and studied Lio. "What you haven't told her is the truth of what she means to you."

Lio cleared his throat. "So much for my mental defenses."

"Your mental defenses are the very best," Rudhira reassured Lio. "But your intuition is better."

"I should hope so, after centuries of training from my mother Soteira in the ancient Imperial tradition of mind healing."

"No," Lio conceded. "I have not told Cassia she is…everything to me."

"Ah, the cherished tradition of dancing around the subject and coming up with quaint euphemisms to describe eternal addiction to one another."

"I think times must have been much simpler when the Queens decreed that any public, verbal acknowledgment of the Grace bond counts as avowal."

"Much simpler." Rudhira's gaze became distant again, then sharpened on Lio. "Don't complicate things between you and Cassia. It is always better to deal straightly with others—especially in love."

"Thank you for your wisdom."

Rudhira sighed. "I wouldn't call it wisdom, after making it to my age without swapping braids."

Lio raised a brow. "You are undeniably qualified to offer advice about women."

Amusement glinted in Rudhira's eyes. "Tell her as soon as you can."

"She landed in Selas only last night. It's still a little soon to spring it on her that my life depends on her, don't you think?"

"You endured separation for half a year. You have saved countless lives together. If numbers are what will convince you she is ready for the truth, then you must see your bond with her is well advanced."

"No, that's not what I'm waiting on. I want to give her time to choose."

Rudhira raised a brow. "You cannot really doubt you are her choice."

"Time to choose Orthros," Lio explained, "for herself, not for my sake. When she is confident the future she envisions for herself is here, then I will tell her how much I need her. Our bond is a heavy responsibility."

"And a great joy."

"Of course. But she has lived under a tyrant's thumb her whole life. I will not let our love be tainted by any sense of obligation to stay."

Rudhira was silent a moment, as if he left something unsaid. "Cassia leaps at every opportunity to protect a Hesperine's life. This time, that life is yours. Bear that in mind."

THE LION'S DEN

GEOMAGICAL WARMTH DRIFTED UP from the marble floors of House Komnena and filled the lofty, grand Ritual hall. An even warmer feeling came over Cassia at the sight of the comfortable chairs and the coffee table that stood around the mosaic Ritual circle in the center of the floor.

Lio's mother lifted a dish of almonds from the table. "Have you had enough to eat tonight?"

Cassia smiled. Hesperines certainly took to heart their responsibility to keep their human guests well fed. "I had plenty at the banquet, thank you."

Lio's mother gathered her elaborate braids and the loose sections of her jet black hair and tied them away from her face with a simple ribbon. "I don't usually work during veil hours, but these two returnees may need the immediate attention of a mind healer without even realizing it."

The smooth, rich tones of her voice seemed to hold a soothing magic even when she wasn't working. Cassia did not wonder why wounded minds followed the guidance of Komnena's words out of their despair.

"I'm so glad they're home," Cassia said, "where they can receive the care they need."

A kind smile graced Komnena's elegant features, making the family resemblance between her and Lio even more apparent. "You are certain you do not need anything before I go?"

"I'll be fine. Zoe and I will have a good time."

"She's with Apollon in his workshop. Let me show you the way."

To hide her sudden apprehension, Cassia focused on Knight. "*Dockk dockk.* Time to see the *kaetlii.*"

With Knight wagging his tail beside her, Cassia followed Komnena into her study. Lio's mother crossed the thick rugs and closed the stained glass door to the terrace, shutting out the cold. Her familiar, Anna, fluffed herself on her perch and continued to doze under the low spell lights. Knight cast a wary glance at the eagle, and Cassia rested her hand on her hound.

Komnena pulled back a silk drape across from her desk to reveal a doorway. She led Cassia into a larger room. Bookshelves and scroll racks peeked at them through the shadows, all the way to the ceiling.

"A library," Cassia exclaimed. "Are there enough books and scrolls in the world to fill one so vast?"

Komnena sighed at the sparsely occupied shelves. "I'm afraid our collection is rather small compared to the other elder houses, to say nothing of the royal library. Lio and I are working diligently to catch up so our bloodline's library will serve our tributaries as it ought. Apollon's workshop is right through here."

With a smile, Komnena pushed open a pair of doors and left Cassia alone to enter the patriarch's domain.

Cassia smoothed the bracelet from Zoe on her wrist and stepped inside.

The Lion of Orthros's den had a view of Zoe's goat barn. The workshop was a bright, spacious chamber full of windows and spell light.

Cassia could not see anyone else from here. She would have to go in and look.

The big table covered in sketches and blueprints reminded her of Lio's desk. Racks of tools, supplies, and carefully labeled mineral samples called to mind his bookcases.

Apollon was Lio's father. She had no reason to hesitate to cross the threshold of this room.

But as she stepped inside, her knees trembled. She fisted her hands in her skirts. Her belly cramped.

She knew how to keep walking forward, even when everything in her rebelled at what she must face. But she had thought that in Orthros, she wouldn't have to do that anymore.

This was nonsense. She should never feel this way in the first place.

She put a hand on Knight and made herself walk further into the room.

The marble floor was smooth under her shoes. The air was pleasantly cool and smelled of stone. There were no weapons and martial banners on the walls, only a creator's tools and maps of Selas.

One step at a time, Cassia approached the table. It didn't face the door. She found herself standing next to an artist's stool. She reached out a hand, then curled it back, then reached again. She brushed her fingers over a blank corner of the half-finished sketch he was working on. Right now, the figure there was only an outline, a vaguely feminine shape with a hint of long hair. She was on her knees.

Cassia snatched her hand back and hastened away from the desk. She stopped short in front of a red marble statue that dominated the center of the room. The work appeared to be a self-portrait of Apollon with his eyes closed, an expression of the purest contentment on his face. He stood behind a stone tribute to Komnena with his arms around her, and together they held her heavily pregnant belly. With one eye of white marble and one of red, Komnena's statue smiled down at their unborn son.

"Have you ever heard the story of the first goats?" came Apollon's voice from further in the room.

"The very first goats ever?" Zoe asked. "No, Bosko's grandmama never told us that one."

"It's part of the story of the first people. Our elders have always told it, and our mages wrote it down. People and goats have been together a long time."

Zoe paused. "I don't know where people came from, either."

"Long ago," said Apollon in his deep, gravelly voice, "before our time In Sanctuary, before the Great Temple Epoch, and before the Hulaic Epochs before that, it was the time of the goddesses and gods. Kyria and Anthros already had fourteen children together, seven sons and seven daughters. Kyria was proud of their Fourteen Scions and loved them with all her heart. But as Anthros watched their heirs grow in power, he was displeased."

"That doesn't make sense," Zoe interjected. "Why would he mind? You want Lio and me to be as powerful as you and Mama."

"Anthros didn't trust his children the way your mama and I trust you and Lio."

"So Anthros was mean to his own children, too? Not just other people's?"

"He told Kyria they must not have any more children, because he must keep order among the gods. Kyria was sad, for she wished for more babes to hold in her arms and raise into strong scions. Her children were grown, and her husband left her lonely. So she decided to use her own power of life and growth to make children without Anthros. In secret, she crafted life from the soil, creating seven more daughters to cherish. She hid them from her husband."

"Just like the mages of Kyria kept us Eriphite children safe from the Order of Anthros."

"Just like that. But Kyria needed Hespera's help then, too. When Kyria's daughters grew into womanhood, she was so delighted with them that it grieved her not to share her joy with her husband. She was sure once he saw the beautiful children she had made, he would love them as she did and welcome them into the family. Promising her husband a wonderful surprise, she dressed her daughters in gowns befitting goddesses and presented them in Anthros's Hall, where each one cast spells to show the great talents for healing and growth their mother had given them."

Cassia drifted closer to Apollon and Zoe. She paused behind a tall shelf. Under a work table across from her lay the statue of a golden, sleeping lion.

"Anthros must have been proud of them!" Zoe said.

"No," Apollon replied. "He dishonored his wife's precious gift."

Zoe gasped. "He dishonored a gift?"

"He was angry at Kyria for disobeying him and outraged she had created life without his help. He decided he must make an example so no gods would ever challenge his rule. Before Kyria's very eyes, he cleaved her daughters' divinity from them, striking away their goddess-given power. So sundering their magic from the sacred soil they were made of, he divided them into spirit and body. Their spirits he banished from his Hall, casting them into Hypnos's realm and decreeing that his brother should bind them there for all eternity. Their bodies fell lifeless before Kyria. The other gods and goddesses had never seen a punishment so terrible. They called it mortality and learned to fear Anthros anew."

The lion statue stretched. Cassia jumped and pressed a hand to her mouth. The enormous cat stood up and fixed her with a reflective gaze. Knight bared his teeth.

"That can't be the end of the story," Zoe protested.

"Of course not," Apollon assured her. "Death is never the end of the story."

The lion yawned at Knight and padded away in the direction of Apollon's voice.

"Kyria was full of grief," Apollon said, "but too frightened of her husband's anger to challenge his ruling. All the way in Sanctuary, Hespera heard her fellow goddess weeping, and her heart was moved by Kyria's pain."

Cassia caught her breath and walked onward.

Apollon's voice was much closer now. "Hespera hastened to Kyria in secret. She found the bereaved mother crying over the lifeless bodies of her daughters."

Shrouded figures surrounded Cassia. Statues, half-formed or unrevealed, stood draped in white sheets.

"'Why has my brother Anthros, your husband, done this terrible deed?' Hespera asked Kyria.

"'He thinks my daughters hideous and unnatural,' Kyria lamented.

"'Nothing that lives is hideous or unnatural. Your children are wondrous, and so too is your love for them. Do not despair, for there is yet hope for them.'

"'They are handmaidens in your brother Hypnos's court, now. Even if you could convince him to release them, Anthros would only strike them down once more.'

"'Leave Hypnos to me. I will spirit your daughters away, and Anthros need never know. He will not hurt them again, and he will not punish you.'

"'If you take my daughters to Sanctuary, I cannot visit them. Anthros would find out.'

"'I will soon make a place for them where you can come and see them grow and work their magic.'

"And so saying, Hespera carried the lifeless bodies of Kyria's daughters to Sanctuary. Into the bodies Kyria had made from the soil, Hespera placed a heart and filled it with her own blood. Hypnos was angry, but he could not hold those of his sister goddess's blood in his realm. He had no choice but to relinquish the seven women's spirits to Hespera. They returned to life, strong in magic and the will to survive. But they were no longer as powerful as goddesses because of the wounds Anthros had dealt them.

"Hespera called upon Kyria's brother Demergos and his wife Chera to help her make a safe home for the women. Demergos gave them fertile fields, and Chera gave them pure, sweet rain. Hespera grew thorny plants and created fanged beasts to guard them, and she named the world Akanthia."

"And that was when they got goats?" Zoe asked.

"Indeed it was. All of Demergos and Chera's children brought gifts for the women. Eriphon, the cheerful shepherd, gave them a herd of goats so they could have milk and cheese."

"And friendship," said Zoe.

"The most loyal of friendships," Apollon agreed.

Zoe was quiet for a moment. "But where did men come from, Papa?"

"That is another story."

Cassia rounded the corner of a large slab of marble. A number of the statue covers draped several chairs and another worktable. Inside the makeshift shelter, the light of a stained glass lantern revealed Apollon in an undyed work robe, sitting on the floor with Zoe on his lap. Beside them, her two small goat kids drowsed amid a pile of storybooks. The lion had gone back to sleep with his tail draped over the end of Apollon's long, curly blond braid.

Cassia knelt down and peered inside. Apollon winked at her.

Zoe's little nose flared, and her head came up off her father's shoulder. "Cassia!"

"Zoe! I'm so sorry I'm late."

But the child beamed with her baby fangs and missing front tooth. "Would you like to come inside our cave?"

There didn't seem to be room inside the cramped space, Apollon's presence was so big. Only the look of delight on Zoe's face, and the image of it changing into an expression of disappointment, gave Cassia the strength to accept the child's invitation.

Cassia gathered her skirts and scrambled inside. The black-and-white goat, Midnight Moonbeam, stirred and bleated in disapproval while her sister, Rainbow Aurora, continued her nap, her brown-and-white side gently rising and falling. Knight crawled in after Cassia on his belly and settled down on the opposite side of the "cave" from the lion.

Apollon petted the lion as one might a house cat. "Don't worry about my familiar. He is too content with his situation to pick fights, even with dogs."

Zoe crawled over, all knobby knees and skinny ankles and soft cotton play robe, and climbed into Cassia's lap. A bracelet just like the one she had given Cassia dangled from her wrist. "Your dress is so beautiful."

"Thank you. I like to wear it because it reminds me of the red roses Hespera made to protect us."

Shyly, Zoe touched Cassia's bracelet. "You got my gift."

"Lio made sure. It's a beautiful present, and it cheered me up so much when I had to be at the guest house. I love how the pattern matches your mantle." Cassia cuddled Zoe close and looked at her as an excuse not to meet Apollon's gaze. From the corner of her eye, she saw the goats crawl in his lap.

"Papa helped me make a cave," Zoe enthused.

Her favorite silk mantle lay to one side, a sure sign Apollon's creation had assuaged her fear of open spaces so she did not feel the urge to cover her head. The beauty of her long hair was completely unhidden. Her twin braids shone, the color of creamed coffee.

"You must be having so much fun," said Cassia. "It sounds like he tells wonderful stories, too."

Zoe nodded. "Papa knows all the old stories, and Lio knows the new ones, and Mama knows all the facts."

Apollon chuckled. "Zoe knows our family."

Cassia smiled into Zoe's hair. "I heard your father's story as I came in, and I enjoyed it very much. No one had ever told it to me before, either."

"You must have heard the way they tell it in Tenebra," Apollon guessed.

"As always, I like the Hesperine way much better." Cassia held Zoe close and tried looking at Apollon.

A blond man loomed above her. His power loomed even larger. She met eyes the same dark blue as Lio's but saw only the icy, sky blue gaze of the man who had sired her.

She glanced away quickly, studying the title of one of Zoe's story books as if she were not filled with shame and fear. How could she have such thoughts about Lio's father? How could the king have followed her to Orthros?

"I think we have time for the story of how men came to be," Apollon said.

Zoe settled down in Cassia's lap and looked attentively at her father.

He cleared his throat. "The women used their magic from Kyria to cultivate Akanthia, the world Hespera had given them with Demergos and his family's help. The seven humans cooperated and made everything prosper. When Kyria visited in secret, she shared in their happiness.

"But after Kyria's rebellion, Anthros remained suspicious of his wife, and he sent their son Aetos, his winged messenger, to follow her. Hespera's thorny plants prevented Aetos from entering the world, but he evaded her fanged animals long enough to spy on the women. He reported back to Anthros all that Hespera and the other gods had done for Kyria's daughters.

"Anthros wanted to go and destroy the women and their world, but Hypnos advised against inciting war with Hespera, Demergos, Chera, and perhaps even Kyria. Fearful of losing his wife's loyalty forever, Anthros heeded his brother and agreed to Hypnos's devious plan.

"As Kyria had done, Anthros created his own children. He forged seven sons and breathed life into them. But he did not give them his divine powers. He made them mortal, with only just enough strength and magic to fulfill his commands. He ordered them to go into the women's world and conquer it for him. He promised that if they succeeded, he would elevate them to a place of honor in his Hall, where their spirits would dwell in glory forever. But any who failed, he would give to Hypnos as payment for the death god's assistance.

"The men did as their father god bade them and went to Akanthia. They claimed they were fleeing Anthros's anger and begged for entry past the gargoyles and through the thorns. The women welcomed them and showed them how to cultivate the world. They were pleased with the men's strength and magic and rejoiced in their company. The men began to doubt what Anthros had told them, for the women and their world were beautiful and good.

"The women urged the men to ask Hespera for her blood, so they too could have heartbeats and grow stronger in magic. The men agreed, and they petitioned the goddess, who gladly gave of her power to them.

"Still it grieved Hespera that Anthros had robbed the women of their mother goddess's power and that he would never give the men he had made the power of gods. She resolved she would eventually find a way to restore the humans' true power.

"The fourteen humans lived long, happy lives. When the magic of Hespera's first gift of blood was eventually spent, they went to live in Sanctuary. Some of them left behind children who inherited Akanthia. We are all heirs to that gift."

"But now we have the Goddess's Gift that never runs out," Zoe said. "I bet there's another story, the one where Hespera keeps her promise to give back the people's true powers."

"You are a very wise girl."

"That's why she made Hesperines, isn't it? She kept her promise the night Annassa Alea and Papa Anastasios and the other great mages did the first Ritual!"

"And here we are, full of our rightful power and safe in the world she gave to us."

Zoe's eyes slid shut, and she fell asleep with her hand resting on Cassia's bracelet.

In the silence that followed, Cassia was alone with Apollon.

She stroked the child's hair and tried to find something to say. "Why did men change their minds about women?"

"Many of us never did."

"I'm sorry. I've known so many who heeded Anthros."

"You don't have anything to apologize for. There is no need to tell me the story of where your fears came from."

He knew. She could find all the right words, but try as she might, she could not hide how she felt from the Blood Union, especially not with Elder Firstblood Apollon. Not with Lio and Zoe's father.

His kind words were an invitation to speak. But his kindness only drove the words she didn't want to say farther down inside her. The silence stretched on.

"Thorns. Did I miss bedtime stories?" The sound of Lio's voice relieved her misery.

He folded himself down to peer inside Zoe's cave. His gaze fixed on her and Cassia, and an expression of utter tenderness came over his face. Cassia may have known many who heeded Anthros, but the one she knew best was all Hespera's.

43

nights until

WINTER SOLSTICE

RELICS

E ARLY MOON HOURS LAID a chilly hush over Rose House as med-
itative as any predawn. Cassia detained Lio at her door and gave
him one more kiss, taking one more taste of coffee and cassia rolls.

He smiled against her mouth. "I'm glad we had time for breakfast."

"Mmm. So am I." She smoothed his silken black hair, tucking his braid
behind his ear. "And time after breakfast to spend with Zoe. I approve of
this new schedule. From now on you must always wake me well before
first moon."

"Since Chrysanthos intends to make his councils a regular occurrence,
we will have to get an early start."

"As long as I get my start with you, I can put up with his schemes."
With a sigh, she turned to go.

Lio caught her hand. "Do you feel ready for tonight's event?"

She arched a brow at him. "Somewhere between the window seat and
the bath, we managed to discuss politics to my satisfaction."

At her mention of satisfaction, Lio's gaze trailed over her. "I hope I
have not been remiss in my responsibilities."

She smiled slowly. "You have neglected nothing, I assure you,
Ambassador."

He cleared his throat. "I want you to be well prepared to meet Second Princess Konstantina. She will do her part to host the embassy in
deference to the Queens, but under protest. I'm afraid it will be quite a
confrontation."

"After the time you spent last night familiarizing me with Konstantina's
views on key political issues, I have my bearings for my encounter with

her. I will consider this round two, after round one with Elder Firstblood Hypatia upon my arrival."

"You proved yourself to Hypatia with courage and grace. Konstantina is a member of the royal family, however, and the scribe of all our laws. She has influence and resources that even her mentor Hypatia does not. This will be a challenge."

"One of the greatest we have faced," Cassia agreed, "but I would rather face an ancient, brilliant scholar of Orthros, even the most vocal and powerful Hesperine opponent of the Solstice Summit, than any Tenebran mortal enemy of our cause. After everything I have been through to arrive at an audience with the Second Princess of Orthros, I shall not meet her without resources of my own."

"True words, my rose." Lio caressed her hair. "Konstantina's respect is a great gift, if she chooses to bestow it. Although I forfeited it when I proposed the Solstice Summit, that will not reflect on you. She will judge you for yourself, for she is just. If anyone can soften her blows to our cause, it is you."

"The loss of her favor truly pains you."

"When I decided to do this, I had to accept the consequences. I knew a rift with Aunt Kona would be one of them."

"Aunt Kona. That makes sense. She's your Ritual father's sister."

"And my mother's colleague. My uncle's friend. My teacher in light magic and law. My people's princess."

"Do not despair of her good opinion. I will make our case to her."

He kissed her once more. "May the Goddess's Eyes light your path tonight."

After he took his reluctant leave, Cassia went into her room, leaving the courtyard door open to let in the roses' fragrance.

A compulsion drove her to one of the heavy iron storage chests that furnished her guest room. She raised the lid and reassured herself her gardening satchel remained inside undisturbed. She unfastened the old canvas bag's tarnished buckles and checked on the contents.

The glyph stone was as Cassia had left it. She ran her fingers over the glyph of Hespera engraved on the white marble, although the symbol was nearly invisible from centuries of wear and the more recent stains of her and Lio's blood offerings. The ancient capstone was shedding mortar into the bottom of her satchel, especially from the broken corner where she had chipped off the shard. But the magic in the mother stone beat strongly in time to the pulse in her pendant. She could rely on the Sanctuary ward resident in the stone, just as she had when it had still been part of the long-forgotten shrine of Hespera at Solorum.

As Queen Alea had promised, the glyph stone's own magic was protecting itself from discovery. Even from Lio. How would Cassia ever find the strength to tell him the place where their love had begun was no more? He need never know she had rescued the glyph stone mere moments before Chrysanthos had razed the shrine.

She wanted to leave Lio happy in the belief that she had collected her pendant and rose seeds from their Sanctuary and left it standing. She and Lio were keeping the shrine's legacy alive. Makaria, the human mage of Hespera who had originally cast the Sanctuary ward there, had died in the persecutions of the Last War, but her magic lived on. Her lover Laurentius, a worshiper of Anthros, had sacrificed his life fighting to help the Mage King bring a just era to Tenebra. His cause lived on, as well, in the Solstice Summit.

Whenever Lio saw the shard around Cassia's neck, he smiled. When she planted the seeds and grew roses for his residence, he could enjoy them without grief and see them as reminders, not ruins. Cassia could no longer bear to live in the ruins of happier times.

Cassia sifted through the other artifacts she kept hidden in the glyph stone's lee. If not for the Sanctuary ward, her sister's linen garments would be sure to draw attention by the potent smell of the flametongue oil that gave them their magical properties. She cupped Solia's carved wooden pendant in her hands. It felt warm in the cool air of the room, its ivy symbols as alive as the glyph stone in their own way.

If the Summit succeeded, if Cassia's work in Tenebra was done, she would never need this again. She would finally have done justice to her sister's legacy.

Cassia tucked the pendant away, fastened her satchel, and closed the Hesperine chest. She went and knelt before her travel trunk from Tenebra. She paused in reverent solitude for a moment, then, for the first time, opened the chest of her sister's gowns of her own accord. She would wear a princess's gown to her official presentation to the Queens' eldest daughter. Cassia could scarcely believe it, but she no longer dreaded the necessity of wearing one of the dresses remade from Solia's wardrobe.

Cassia had thought her anger the only force that could make these into something more than grave shrouds. But there was magic at work upon them now. If Zoe clutched at these skirts one time, they would transform, and Cassia would no longer grieve to wear them.

STAR MOTHS

WHEN KNIGHT GOT TO his feet suddenly, Cassia looked up from the chest. Her hound leaned eagerly toward the open door, ears pricked and tail wagging at something in the courtyard. Or someone.

"Do we have a visitor, darling?" Cassia got to her feet. "Let's go see."

Knight bounded into the courtyard. Cassia followed him out to find him twining around the legs of a Hesperine, shedding all over her plain, undyed robe. Cassia opened her mouth to call off her hound, but then their visitor laughed. The Hesperine endured Knight's licks on her hands and face with a pleased, albeit surprised, expression.

Cassia hurried forward and put a hand on Knight's back, just in case. "Please allow me to apologize. He isn't usually this exuberant."

The Hesperine laughed again, standing helpless under Knight's shower of affection. The look she gave Cassia was all curiosity. "No need to be sorry. I had no idea he'd like me this much. He's not at all what I expected."

"I see his reputation precedes him yet again."

Cassia's visitor looked to be a youngblood almost Lio's age. She was also pretty. Very, very pretty, with rosy lips, lustrous pale skin, and jet black hair braided against her head in a coronet.

"I don't know the first thing about dogs." The lovely Hesperine asked, "Where should I pet him?"

"Ah, how about a rub on the ears?" Cassia suggested.

The Hesperine gave it a try, and Knight melted into shut-eyed, tail-wagging bliss.

The only Hesperines Knight had so loved at first sight were the

Queens. He had even seemed to sense them in their eldest son and begged the fearsome First Prince for affection.

Cassia eyed the youngblood's homespun robe with doubt, but thinking of Queen Alea's temple vestments, ventured to voice her theory anyway. "May I ask if you are a relation of the royal family?"

The Hesperine shook her head at Knight. "You've given me away. Yes, I'm the eighth princess. The youngest, you know."

"It's an honor to meet you, Princess."

"Oh, please don't bow. It will get very inconvenient. I'm one of Lio's friends, and I hope you'll be spending a lot of time with us." She stretched out a hand to Cassia.

Cassia's jealousy caught up with her, an injustice to the warm welcome she had just received. Lio was friends with one of the princesses. One who was his own age. And beautiful.

And kind. Cassia put on a smile and extended her hand. She and the princess exchanged a Hesperine wrist clasp and the leftovers of Knight's slobbery greeting. A puff of berry fragrance filled the air, surely a cleaning spell.

The princess grinned. "All of us have been looking forward to meeting you ever since Lio confessed you're his share."

A pleasant blush spread across Cassia's cheeks at the casual acknowledgment that she was sharing her blood and pleasure with Lio. The Hesperine euphemism was almost quaint, and yet said so much more than Tenebrans' mercenary terms for courtship. "I've looked forward to meeting his friends, as well."

The princess's eyes lit with the promise of pure fun. "We're excited to show you Orthros. Lio has told us so much about you."

"I'm sorry I can't say the same about you. Lio doesn't speak much about his connections to the royal family."

The princess sighed. "Isn't that just like him?"

Lio had many friends here at home. Some of them were female. Cassia must not entertain such envious feelings every time she met one. "Since Annassa Alea trained him in light magery, you must have known him for a long time."

"Our families are close. It's tradition for bloodlines with temple heritage in common. Elder firstbloods from the same temple are always Ritual parents to each other's children. For example, Hypatia and Khaldaios are Ritual parents to all Argyros and Lyta's children, and vice versa."

"Hypatia is Mak and Kadi's Ritual mother?"

The princess made a face. "I'm afraid so. Her children get along well with Argyros, though."

"So the First Prince is Lio's Ritual father because both your bloodlines started at Hagia Boreia."

At the mention of her eldest brother, the princess's face brightened. "Yes, he is. It wouldn't be fair for the Queens to be anyone's Ritual parents. You really didn't find out until you met Rudhira? As much as we all adore him, I thought for certain Lio would tell you about him at least."

"He mentioned his Ritual mother once, although I also did not learn her name until the welcoming ceremony."

"Elder Firstblood Kassandra is Ritual sister to the Queens, so that's why she's Ritual mother to Apollon's children as well my siblings and me."

"So Apollon and Kassandra are your Ritual parents?"

"That's right."

Lio and the princess must be like siblings, Cassia reassured herself. Besides, he had made it clear that, for many years before coming to Tenebra, he had only had eyes for a silk maker by the name of Xandra. "You and Lio grew up together, then."

"Yes. I know all the childhood secrets that still make him blush."

Cassia laughed. "Do tell. What sort of embarrassments lurk in dignified Ambassador Deukalion's past?"

"Oh, where do I start?" The princess flopped down on one of the benches by the fountain. "I think the worst one has to be when he went to Wisdom's Precipice with Mak and Lyros."

Cassia sat down on the bench across from her. "That sounds ominous."

"It's the tallest cliff yet discovered in Orthros Boreou. It's up the coast from House Komnena, and the sea below is full of jagged rocks. The dive is actually a treat if you know how to levitate, but the Gift doesn't give us that ability until we're newbloods. Lio, Mak, and Lyros got the bright idea to take the dive to see if they could scare their levitation skills into appearing."

Cassia stared at the princess, struggling to find the humor in the situation. "Couldn't they have killed themselves?"

"Not quite, but the fall certainly made them wish they were dead. They climbed right up to the top all full of themselves, jumped straight off, and fell like stones into the ocean below. They floated in misery until the current washed them up at House Komnena, where Lio's mother was *very* distraught, and you can imagine how Lio's father feels about anything that upsets her. Even now, 'Don't take a dive' is Apollon's way of reminding Lio not to do anything to worry his mother."

"Their injuries must have been catastrophic."

"Don't look so green," the princess reassured. "Apollon took them straight to the healing Sanctuary, where Javed and their wiser friends gave them an earful. Mak and Lyros were put out about missing training, and of course Lio spent the whole time apologizing."

"I can count on one hand the times I've heard him apologize," Cassia mused.

The princess raised her eyebrows. "How did you get him to stop?"

"He so seldom has cause," Cassia said in surprise.

The princess smiled thoughtfully. "I knew you were a good influence on him."

Cassia could only reply with a laugh, for she didn't know what to say. No one had ever called her a good influence before. Everyone had said quite the opposite. Happily she had left "everyone" back in Tenebra, and they could not tarnish the generous opinions of a Hesperine princess.

"Well," the princess continued, "it only took a week for their injuries from Wisdom's Precipice to heal, at least the physical ones. They still bear the scars upon their pride to this night."

"Growing up Hesperine is more…eventful…than I imagined. I still have so much to learn about life in Orthros."

"Don't worry. Everyone feels that way when they first get here, even those of us who were Solaced as children. We spend our whole youth learning."

"Lio has told me something about Hesperine education. I think your service must be your duties as a princess."

"Yes, although there aren't many royal duties left over anymore. My elder siblings and their Graces have been doing this for so long. Their descendants, too. I'm younger than most of my grandnieces and grand-nephews by several 'greats.' At least when Rudhira meets his Grace, their children shall be properly younger than me. I look forward to spoiling them."

"I know the feeling," Cassia confessed. "I'm getting to know Lio's little sister."

"You must be enjoying that!" The princess had a knowing look in her eyes that made Cassia see her resemblance to the Queens for the first time.

"I am," Cassia replied. "More than I can say."

"Who can resist doting on the new sucklings? Especially those of us who are friends with Lio and Mak. We just can't stop crafting gifts for Zoe, Bosko, and Thenie. They deserve to be spoiled, after all they've been through."

"What does a princess do for her craft?"

Her gaze gleamed with mischief. "Bugs."

"I beg your pardon?"

The princess stood up and gestured for Cassia to follow her. "Here, I'll show you."

She led Cassia to one of the beds of ornamental greenery. Cassia realized what she had taken for a tiny spell light hovering among the fronds was in fact an insect with luminous wings.

"This is a star moth," said the princess. "I bred them, actually."

"You bred something this beautiful? That's remarkable!"

The princess looked very pleased at the praise. "It took a lot of magic, so I suppose I cheated."

"I know something about breeding dogs, but I had no idea you could make a new kind of animal."

"The Goddess made them, really. I just helped them along. I understand you're a gardener, so you'll be interested to know the star moths are attracted to this kind of fern. It's a cold-tolerant species from the southern Empire."

Cassia felt of the fronds' waxy texture, careful not to disturb the moth's perch. "I never thought I'd lay eyes on a plant from the Empire."

"There are plenty of them here. I bet you've never seen a mulberry tree."

"I've never even heard of mulberries."

"Wonderful. I'll give you a tour of my orchard. I'm not much of a gardener, but I manage to keep my trees healthy for the sake of my bugs. My favorite will eat nothing but mulberry leaves."

Cassia found herself smiling genuinely, and a great deal of her tension eased. She'd had no idea Lio's illustrious friends would be so easy to talk with, especially one of the Queens' daughters. "Thank you so much for the invitation. I shall look forward to that very much."

"I'll make sure we have time for it in between all the important Summit business."

"That will be a pleasant relief from the embassy."

"In the meantime, I have something for you. Since I'm the youngest, you won't get to my residence until the end of this week, and I can't wait to give you my welcome gift." From a floppy pocket of her robes, the princess pulled out a glass jar and handed it to Cassia.

"Ladybugs!" Cassia peered inside to see at least a dozen marching and fluttering about a leafy stem. "The best defenders in any garden."

"They're especially good for roses. I'm much too tender-hearted when it comes to bugs, even the ones considered to be pests. But everything has to eat. I can't protest when the ladybugs make a healthy meal off of the invaders that hurt plants."

"This is a truly thoughtful gift."

"I'm so glad you like them. I hope you'll like the celebration at my residence, too. I promise not to make it boring. I must distinguish myself from my elder siblings somehow. I fear the only way I shall ever make my mark as a princess is by contrast. Which suggests a rather disruptive course."

"In my experience, disruptive can be very productive."

"I think you can help me in that regard."

"Of course I would be glad to help in any way I can."

"Tell me, Cassia, does anyone at Solorum play Kings and Mages?"

"Yes, there is a Kings and Mages board in the Temple of Anthros. It's a mark of great distinction once an apprentice earns the right to play with the masters. The king often joins the royal mage for a game after rites."

"Excellent. I know the Dexion must be adept at the game, for it is a point of pride among mages in Corona, but we're not supposed to know he is Cordian. You have reassured me the game would be familiar to him in any case. Have you ever played?"

"No, it is men's exclusive pastime. I do know the matches are about much more than the game, though."

The princess nodded. "There's no strategy they pursue at that board that would be lost on you. Will you play when you come to my residence?"

Cassia hesitated. "I'm afraid I've never even seen the fabled board, for women aren't allowed in that part of the temple."

"Lio has a Hesperine version of the board, but you two must have been busy with other things," the princess said innocently.

Cassia blushed. "Ah. Yes. That is, I saw something like that on his coffee table."

"You can learn the game at my party. You'll be a natural, especially since we will be playing by Orthros rules."

"I have a feeling I shall like Orthros rules much better. Thank you for your invitation. I'll gladly join in."

"Oh, good. I'll have your help when I challenge Chrysanthos to a match. We are going to have fun—at his expense." The princess's eyes flashed. "We call the game Prince and Diplomat, you know, after Rudhira and Argyros. My brother taught me to play."

"It sounds as if Chrysanthos is in for a night he'll not soon forget."

"I'd best go work on getting ready for him. It will take me the rest of the week to make sure everything is just so."

"Princess, before you depart, would you be so generous as to answer a question for me in return?"

"Certainly."

"Does your family have royal colors?"

"Yes indeed. Black and white, naturally."

"Thank you. That will help me get ready to assist your family in making a statement this week."

The princess smiled. "I'm so glad we got to talk before all the official introductions. I wanted us to have a chance for good first impressions. I think we actually have a great deal in common."

"It's been a pleasure," Cassia said honestly. How could the princess worry about what sort of impression she made on anyone?

The princess gave Knight one more rub behind the ears. "And you are a wonderful dog. Not everyone sees my mothers in me, you know."

There was the answer to Cassia's question, perhaps.

With that, the princess turned and walked away, and the star moths swarmed up from the ferns to follow her.

A REEL ON A BLADE

ASSIA HURRIED BACK INSIDE, but there was no need for her haste. Perita had not arrived to catch her lady fraternizing with Hesperines. Cassia smiled to herself. Her friend was probably stealing a moment longer to relax in silk sheets with the one she loved.

Cassia had taken care of her and Knight's necessities, put on his unnecessary bandages, and even managed to get herself mostly dressed by the time her handmaiden bustled in.

When Perita saw the gown, her frenzy calmed somewhat. "That's a nice choice, my lady."

"Solia loved this dress. She said it reminded her of daisies. Please tell me, would my black gloves set it off nicely? I think I have a belt and headdress to match those, don't I?"

Perita nodded as she checked and adjusted Cassia's attire from head to toe.

"Thank you," Cassia said. "At the welcoming ceremony, I overheard someone mention black and white are Orthros's royal colors. I thought this would be a gesture of goodwill, but I could not feel confident in my choice until I had your opinion."

"A fine idea, my lady."

Satisfied she had left her friend enough to do to save face, Cassia watched Perita work. Although Perita chatted like always, her smiles were fleeting, and she concentrated intensely on her duties. She looked too pale for someone who had left her new husband a few moments ago.

"Perita, are you feeling all right?"

"As well as any of us feel, I'm sure, my lady."

"Your seasickness didn't follow you ashore, did it?"

"Of course not. It's just wretched cold here, is all."

"Why don't we close the courtyard door?"

"As you like, my lady."

Cassia dropped several more hints about cold weather and warm beds. Perita did not take any of those opportunities to complain she wasn't well or suggest she and Callen were enjoying themselves. She remained utterly focused on her work.

Cassia praised the results as always, trying to keep the worry out of her voice. When they joined Callen and Eudias in the hall, she gave up on her questions, lest she embarrass her friend in front of the men. Perita was silent all the way to the New Guest House.

When they entered the courtyard there, hushed, familiar voices drifted from somewhere in the greenery.

"You really didn't take any?" asked Lord Adrogan. "Not even a morsel?"

"Certainly not," said Benedict. "There is no telling what foul magic might befall a man who eats even a bite of Hesperine food."

"It can't be any fouler than what we brought here in our saddlebags. That mess is so stale, it can hardly be called food anymore."

"It will be easier to keep our provisions from spoiling in this frozen wasteland."

Cassia slowed her pace, making a show of studying the nearest juniper to stall her retinue's progress.

"How can all fifty-six of us be expected to survive on such meager fare?" Lord Adrogan bemoaned.

"You would prefer the gods' displeasure to battle rations?"

"Hedon would have begrudged no man a taste of that banquet last night! Come now, Benedict. You can trust me with a confession. We both grew up on our betters' leftovers, you and I. I've had to beg for every hand-out from my eldest brother, while he takes what he will, as if he owns all he surveys. Aren't you tired of taking the scraps from a free lord's table? I know I am."

"I don't know when you developed such particular tastes."

Lord Adrogan laughed. "Well, it has earned me the regard of

a particular lady, I can tell you that. You cannot question my good taste when it comes to my Biata, surely, even if she is a maiden of the Hadrian faction."

"I would never hold the loyalties of a lady's family against her personally. See here, the stakes are different for you. Few men among us have brides awaiting our return. You have more reason than most to take no chances while you are here."

"On the contrary, I have even more reason to be bold. Opportunity never comes without risk. And I know how to make the most of opportunities. If I play my cards right, I won't return home to marry up—but to elevate my future wife to my level. We have the chance to be men of renown, Benedict. The men who braved Orthros. Bravery attracts followers, and followers mean power."

Cassia's pace, although slow, finally took her around a decorative bed of mint and into view of the men. She saw Lord Adrogan caress the gleaming tiles beneath his feet with the threadbare toe of his velvet shoe.

"Not just glory awaits," he mused. "Perhaps profit, too."

"Your Ladyship," said Benedict in surprise.

The knight cleared his throat and stood at attention like a boy caught with his finger too near the pie. But next to Lord Adrogan's fashionably short tunic, tight breeches, and wavy golden hair, Benedict looked staid and pious.

Cassia gave Benedict a smile she hoped he would find reassuring. "You are discussing Orthros's temptations with the best possible person, Lord Adrogan. You must be aware that Benedict is a member of the Knightly Order of Andragathos, the Seventh Scion, the god of male virtue and righteous warfare." She refrained from raising the issue of the history of conflict between Andragathos's followers and Hesperines. Benedict was more likely to wage a campaign of personal asceticism than a holy war.

Lord Adrogan gave Benedict a slow smile that didn't reach his eyes. "Yes, Benedict is well known for his high-and-mighty principles. Now if you'll excuse me, I must get a head start gnawing the jerky so I'll have time to swallow it before we are expected anywhere."

Cassia stayed her former suitor with one of the wide-eyed, fawning glances he expected from ladies. He lingered nearer. Knight's lips pulled back a bit from his teeth, as if he were remembering when he had taken a bite out of the cloak Lord Adrogan had once given Cassia.

"It's not just the food here that is very fine, is it, my lord? Where do you suppose the Hesperines come by all these luxuries?"

"They do not pull silk and marble out of the desolate snow, Lady Cassia. They trade. With someone."

"But not Tenebra or Cordium," she replied. "Whoever could be supplying them with these goods?"

"I don't know, but whoever it is, they're making shiploads of gold."

"Well, our lands are wealthy in the gods' bounty," said Cassia staunchly. "There is no flax, wool, or metalwork like ours! I'm sure some of our noble houses could afford to bargain for silk and marble, just as well as these mystery traders, whoever they are."

"Who brokers bargains with Hesperines?" Benedict shook his head.

"Someone brave and interested in also making shiploads of gold." Lord Adrogan flashed a smile.

"Tenebra is wealthy in courage, too," Cassia enthused.

Lord Adrogan went inside the common room, and she let him go, satisfied she need not grease the wheels any further. The wealth of Orthros was already working its magic on Lord Adrogan and other young profiteers like him who had joined the embassy to seek their fortunes.

Rank without swords, wealth, or land was mere bark without bite. Lesser nobles like Lord Adrogan had little to lose and much to gain by risking danger to put teeth in their titles. They were among the most likely to set aside their prejudices against the Hesperines, even if it was greed and ambition that inspired them to do so.

Benedict offered Cassia his arm. "You look very well, if I may say so, Your Ladyship. I am sorry my lord Flavian can't see you in your present attire."

"You can tell him all about it next time the two of you knock back a pint together."

That brought a faint smile to Benedict's face. "I expect I shall have all sorts of impressive tales to tell him about your feats here in Orthros, if—"

"*When* you return to pull him out of his cups."

Benedict's snort might have been a chortle. "Let us hope he has heeded your admonitions on that subject, Your Ladyship."

"Do you think Genie's presence at court will be a moderating influence on him?"

Benedict's expression became more stoic than usual. "My lord Flavian would do anything for Lady Eugenia's sake."

"I asked a question about Flavian," Cassia mused, "but I wonder if I just received an answer about Benedict."

"Of course I would do anything for her. You know my devotion to my liege lord and his entire family."

Cassia had also seen the signs of his particular devotion to vibrant young Genie. Did Benedict know she was not Flavian's cousin, as the world believed, but actually his half-sister, the illegitimate daughter of his father's beloved concubine? Cassia suspected the family had trusted Benedict with the secret, but refrained from probing him. "I fear Flavian and Genie's love for each other, not to mention their similarities in temperament, are likely to inspire both of them to acts on each other's behalf that are rather too bold. Reckless, even."

Benedict sighed.

Cassia patted his arm. "And they claimed your journey to Orthros with me would be a challenge! I think you have the easy task, actually. I am not likely to require you to rescue me from myself."

"How fortunate we are in your steady character, Your Ladyship." He took a step toward the common room.

Cassia stood where she was. "And in yours, Benedict. Do not forget who awaits your return, and that unlike some lords here, you have nothing to prove."

Under the surprise in his eyes, there was a bitter glint. But when he spoke, his voice was kind. "I am grateful you feel I have already proved myself to you."

"I am not the only one who values your personal merits over other lords' ambition."

He was silent for a moment. "Would that your judgment upon me were law."

"I speak of neither judgment nor law, but the regard of those at whose table you have sat as a friend these many years."

"Speaking of table, Your Ladyship, allow me to escort you to breakfast."

Without speaking further, he guided her into the common room. Chrysanthos's chair was empty, but Master Gorgos was busy preparing everyone's spirits for battle.

"Remember what befell the first mortals!" the Solorum mage admonished. "Kyria disobeyed her husband and made women, those pitiable and incomplete creatures, woven only of a goddess's weaker nature, without that strength of life which flows from the manhood of Anthros. Anthros deemed the females suitable only for serving as handmaidens of Hypnos. Then the blood goddess cheated the god of death out of that which the god of war had awarded him. Hespera stole away with the women's corpses and revived them into a half-life to serve as her sorceresses, concocting for them their own twisted realm where they might run rampant."

Lord Adrogan fiddled with a strip of jerky. "We are not children, mage. We do not require a review of temple stories."

"Here in Akanthia, the world tainted by Hespera's touch," the mage rebuked, "it is all too easy to forget the very teachings that have been drummed into us since birth. Do not forget that Anthros forged the first men to make war and sent them down into this world to discipline the women's wild magic and make them obedient to him. Once his men succeeded in restoring order, he promised, he would count them among his Scions and bestow upon them godhood. But the temptresses of Hespera convinced the first men to throw away their divine inheritance and partake of the dark goddess's blood. It is women who robbed men of our right to be gods."

Lord Severin opened his mouth to speak, but Master Gorgos charged onward without taking a breath.

"The first men forfeited Anthros's favor and died, their souls lost to Hespera's realm forever, but the god of war, in his beneficence, did not forget their heirs who survived in Akanthia. He promised a new reward to all who would take up his banner and return to the true purpose he had created them to fulfill. Generations upon generations of men have restored Anthros's order in this world and driven back Hespera's corruption. Although we have lost all hope of godhood, we may still win places of honor in Anthros's Hall, where we shall thrive with eternal vigor. Consider the destiny of men who disappoint him. Hypnos claims those fit only for eternal sleep."

"Or those worthy to become Overseers of the Dead," Skleros said around the smoke between his teeth. "The Master of Dreams knows who his champions are, and that we shall relish the work he has in store for us in his kingdom."

Master Gorgos looked offended that he had been interrupted and raised his voice. "Do not forget the worst fates of all, which befall those who succumb to Hespera. Mortals who die corrupted by her are trapped in her dark Sanctuary, banished from the sight of Anthros. Those who become Hesperines are doomed to exist here in this twisted shadow-world, never to return to the divine domains."

The Semna's walking stick thumped on the carpet as she entered. "Do not forget that Kyria never ceases to grieve for the lost and always looks for ways to rescue them from their own mistakes."

Cassia helped the Semna into her seat. Kyria sometimes needed assistance rescuing people, and Hespera always needed champions to protect her world from Hypnos and Anthros's cunning attacks.

Chrysanthos swept in, scrolls under his arm and a bottle of wine in hand. He halted to stare at Cassia's gown.

"Basilis," the Dexion greeted her. "No one would question your dedication to the embassy in your present attire. What a creative choice of colors."

Cassia knew she was dancing a reel on a blade. There was no room for error. She must execute each step perfectly.

She met the mage's gaze, donning her most devout expression. "Have you heard 'The Tale of the Cruel Bailiff and the Kind Bailiff'?"

"Where I come from, we call it 'The Tale of the Cruel Inquisitor and the Kind Inquisitor.' Together the two of them extract confessions from heretics at record speed."

"Shall we play a game, Honored Master?"

"I would be delighted to join you at the board, Basilis."

TRUE COLORS

CASSIA WAS WEARING THE royal colors of Orthros. A bold and
risky move. Lio struggled not to give her a bold and risky look
in front of the rest of the embassy.

He escorted her through the black iron gate of Konstantina's residence
and along the paths of glistening white quartz that led to the Second Princess's private entrance to House Annassa. Cassia looked like she belonged
here. She was radiant in gentle white, with bold statements of black at her
slim waist and small hands and upon her long, ash brown hair. Knight
paraded beside her in a ceremonial gait, as close as he could be, but never
touching her skirts.

"May I, as a diplomat, express how moved I am by your attire, Lady
Cassia? Such a statement gives me hope for peace."

"You are very kind, Ambassador. How happy I am to know my gesture
is taken as I intended it."

No Hesperine could mistake her meaning. He could only pray Chrysanthos had. Lio shot her a worried glance, but Cassia's reply was a sly smile.

At intervals along the path stood members of the Prince's Charge
who served as Konstantina's bodyguards tonight. The Hesperines errant
observed the embassy's progress with courteous expressions and watchful
gazes. Rudhira's love for his sister was writ large in the obvious presence
of his warriors throughout her garden, and her disapproval was writ large
in her powerful aura looming ahead of Lio and the embassy.

The royal rose garden engulfed them, and he heard the mortals gasp.
Lio listened to Cassia breathe fast and deep. She turned in a circle, taking
in the roses of every color and variety.

Lord Gaius sniffed a vine of bright pink blossoms climbing a trellis beside the path. The hardened warrior smiled to himself. "These beg to be a wreath upon a lady's hair."

Lord Adrogan drew a red bloom close to his face. "The women of Tenebra would pay a king's ransom for scent oils from this flower."

Benedict stared into the depths of a buttery yellow rose as if mesmerized. "What wonder of Kyria's handiwork is this?"

"Not Kyria's at all." Eudias put his hands in his sleeves and nodded to the Semna. "Begging your pardon."

"There is no pardon to beg, young man," she replied. "We have nothing to do with these."

Only the mages of Chera seemed to disregard the situation. The two women were wrapped in concealing spells that hid their thoughts as thoroughly as their robes obscured their hair, faces, and bodies from head to toe.

Eudias cleared his throat. "These are roses. Hespera's sacred flower."

"Harlot's kiss?" Benedict recoiled, giving his hand a shake. There was a drop of blood on his finger where a thorn had pricked him. He held his wounded hand away from him, casting nervous glances at every nearby Hesperine.

The Semna gave him a disapproving glance from beneath her hood. Her attendants glanced away, little gasps fluttering their veils.

Benedict bowed. "I ask the forgiveness of all ladies present. That is a vulgar expression."

Lord Adrogan snorted. "But that's what the flower is called in Tenebra."

"You saw them at Rose House," Eudias pointed out to Benedict, "in the courtyard and in pots inside."

"I thought her ladyship's guest house was named for the window! The flowers look nothing like that symbol."

"Old wild roses have five petals," Eudias explained. "These are cultivated varieties of garden roses with a more elaborate appearance."

Lord Gaius shook his head. "I can't say I've ever seen one in the wild or a garden in all my long years."

Lord Adrogan eyed Eudias. "How do you know so much about them?"

"From books," the apprentice answered.

Tychon looked upon the roses with disdain. "Identifying signs of Hespera's influence is an essential part of the education of all mages of Anthros."

The confused expression on Master Gorgos's face gave way to a flush of zeal. He parked himself in the center of the path, as far from the roses on either side as he could get. "Anthros's diligent farmers and Kyria's devoted gardeners have succeeded in uprooting Hespera's corruption wherever it is to be found in Tenebra."

"Esteemed Master," Cassia said delicately, "with respect for Tenebra's faithful, we are guests in our neighbors' home. When we meet with the Second Princess tonight, let us join together in thanking her for her hospitality by offering her our compliments on her impressive garden."

Lio bowed. "You are very kind, Lady Cassia. Allow me to offer my gratitude to all of you for your forbearance. This garden is the pride of our Second Princess and a source of great joy to all the royal family. I know the sight of these flowers, an illegal and feared symbol in your own lands, puts you to the test, but surely all our gods must smile that we manage to maintain order amongst ourselves and turn our thoughts toward peace."

Lio started forward again, and the unsettled embassy followed his lead.

From the back of the group, Lord Adrogan's low voice reached Lio's ears. "Shame anything so fine is illegal. What a waste."

"I have to agree with you, for once." Benedict sighed. "If only there were a way to reclaim such a lovely flower into the mother goddess's garden."

"Don't waste your tears," came Chrysanthos's voice. "They smell just like any other weed when they're burning."

A flinch went through Cassia's aura. Lio gritted his teeth and walked on.

Skleros laughed at Chrysanthos's remark, and the odor of one of his smokes befouled the fragrance of the garden.

To the toll of fourth moon, the embassy arrived at the princess's door. Steep front steps led up to the towering entrance covered in gargoyles and statues of Hesperine heroes. The princess was as renowned a patron of the arts as she was a rosarian. The Tenebrans all but cowered, trapped between the threat of stone beasts and the temptation of harlot's kiss. The Cordians seethed. Cassia seemed to find amusement in their distress, and Lio tried to find some consolation in her aura.

A pair of initiates stepped into sight on either side of the double doors. They made an elegant but unnecessary gesture with their hands, and the entrance swung open.

In the doorway, Konstantina stood waiting, beautiful and majestic in her wrap of ceremonial Imperial stripweave crafted from Orthros silk. Lio was not sure what he regretted more: that the Summit did not have her support, or that it caused her to suffer fools tonight.

"Guests from Tenebra," she greeted them, "I am Princess Konstantina, Secondgift of the Queens, who sees their Will done in all ways. Tonight I shall be the first of the princes and princesses to show you royal hospitality. Here at my residence within my mothers' House, you will experience the finest of Orthros."

Chrysanthos chose that moment to reassert his authority. Was he feeling emasculated, perhaps? Before Cassia could respond to the princess, the war mage came forward and propped a boot on the first step. He launched into the Divine Tongue, reciting age-old, elaborate formalities without stopping to accept a reply.

Konstantina gazed down at him with a disinterested expression while he talked at her. Did the Dexion think to aggrandize himself before *her* with the language of Cordium's scholarly circles? She had mastered that school under the tutelage of Hypatia, one of its founders. And that was only a fraction of Konstantina's education. She commanded respect in every university and royal court in the Empire, her mortal homeland. She spoke more languages than there were circles in the Dexion's Order.

When she smiled, Lio knew the mage had already lost the debate.

She broke into the Dexion's monologue with a customary rhetorical reply, her rich voice and Hesperine diction lending the ancient words beauty and nuance. The mage's consternation was gratifying.

She let him get a word in, only so she could deliver a rebuttal that directed their exchange toward the discourse she preferred. Did he realize she had taken command of the conversation?

While the mages listened with rapt attention or self-important nods, the Tenebran lords watched with a range of dumb stares and wary gazes. Cassia wore her court mask, while her aura sharpened with attention. She told Knight to heel and eased closer to the dueling mage. It appeared she was ready to make her move and form Konstantina's first impression of her.

Lio stayed close by her, ready to assist. Eudias was not so swift, and Cassia had to beckon to him. He gave her, then the Dexion a worried look, but followed her.

Lio hoped this confrontation wouldn't get out of hand. He and Cassia could not have planned for the unexpected contest between the princess and the mage. Lio had to admit, since last night, he had devoted rather more energy to Cassia's budding Craving for him than to their duties.

Cassia lifted her gaze to the top of the steps. Between one of Chrysanthos's volleys and the next, she inserted herself into the exchange.

"I stand amazed! What an auspicious meeting this is, Second Princess and Honored Master. The likes of me are seldom so privileged as to witness lofty discourse between such significant personages as yourselves."

The war mage half-turned and, for the second time that night, stared in surprise at the female who had interrupted him. Konstantina looked down and studied Cassia's attire.

"Basilis," Chrysanthos quelled her, "allow me to convey His Majesty's message to the Hesperine royal family in their own tongue so nothing is lost in translation."

"How expert you are at translating the king's words from Vulgus into Divine. While our Hesperine hosts certainly understand both, as do our own mages, Tenebrans like me face the disappointment of having to forgo your edifying discussion. Those of us who speak only the king's Vulgus would not wish to miss a word of his greetings."

Did Chrysanthos realize her compliment had just destroyed his entire argument? With one blow of politeness, she had declared him unqualified to be the spokesman for the king who had formulated his statements in Vulgus, and she had pointed out the irony that the words would lose nothing in translation unless the mage expressed them—or rather, warped them—in Divine.

Chrysanthos dismissed Cassia with one of his smiles and opened his mouth to get in another word before Konstantina had a chance to reply to his last.

Cassia hastened to address Konstantina. "I am merely the daughter of a king, and not a princess. But I would do my part to bring your words to my people, so that they receive a full understanding of your people, who are so fortunate in you, their eldest princess and Queen's champion. Might the ambassador and Apprentice Eudias translate the proceedings for me?"

With her hand on her heart, she gave a curtsy, echoing the heart bow that all Hesperines made before the Queens to show their devotion. Konstantina's expression defrosted a measure.

Lio followed through with a bow. "I would be happy to assist. Should it please you, Second Princess, I will convey your words faithfully. I have much to learn from your discourse."

To his relief, she accepted his peace offering, and in Vulgus. "Very well, Firstgift Komnenos. Translate my words for Lady Cassia and our other noble guests from Tenebra into their own tongue."

"It will be my honor, Second Princess."

With another curtsy, Cassia thanked her.

Konstantina gave a gracious nod and delivered her riposte to Chrysanthos. She and Chrysanthos proceeded to exchange verbosities that masqueraded as compliments, while in fact lauding their own virtues, prodding at each other's views with vicious distaste, and dropping hints about how the other was violating the sacred.

Lio found it rather exhilarating to keep up with them. He reached for parallel words in Vulgus moment by moment, striving to shed light on the princess's meanings.

Apparently Eudias took the Dexion's silence as permission to fulfill Cassia's request to assist with the translation. He repeated Chrysanthos's statements with remarkable eloquence of his own. It would be apparent to any Hesperine there that the young scholar had received a Cordian education, and applied himself to it.

The Cordian mages' ruse was wearing thin at this moment, and Chrysanthos seemed to realize it. He reiterated that he was a mage from Tenebra who had served as an emissary to Cordium and proceeded to drop names of many famous mages he knew from, he claimed, his travels.

Although Cassia said nothing, Lio found the greatest thrill in feeling her mind at work, quick as the dueling tongues. She must be translating for herself what the mage and the princess left unspoken, as surely as Eudias and Lio translated their words.

The princess and the Dexion dragged them all along for a lengthy contest. And Lio thought he was wordy! Was this what mage politics had resembled in the Great Temple Epoch? What an incredible glimpse of what society might have been like when Hagia Notia had thrived in Corona, and the most sophisticated mages of Hespera had negotiated with their colleagues at the Hagion of Anthros. Hypatia had once dwelt at the center of that society. Konstantina now vanquished it.

"'As a servant of my people,'" Lio translated, "'I strive ever to uphold the rule of law. I have been blessed with the calling to codify the Queens' acts and decrees in writing for their people. It is my honor to be their speaker before the Firstblood Circle and to keep its annals in order to preserve the wisdom of all Orthros's leaders. I seek ever to be the faithful keeper of Orthros's writ of law and executor of my mothers' kind and just judgments. When I preside at disputes and mediate for our people, I strive to see the Will of the Queens and the Goddess done.'"

Eudias said for Chrysanthos, "'Mankind's ambassadors find themselves greeted by a female who is truly without compare. A woman who is the author of laws is unheard of among us. No man here has ever bent his knee to laws written by a lady's hand.'"

When the princess smiled again, it was clear she was about to have the last word. "What a new experience for you to do so, now that you must abide by our laws during your stay here. In a land so foreign to you as ours, you are sure to have many unprecedented experiences. Welcome to Orthros."

THE SANCTUARY ROSE

ASSIA FOUND THE CELEBRATION in the Second Princess's residence as impressive as Konstantina herself. Moon hours carried the embassy through halls of marble and glass at Orthros's stately pace. Each long moment was filled with the aromas of coffee and roses, the seduction of drums and flutes, and the gleam of silk. Vulgus and Divine feted and challenged each other from the library to the music room and through galleries of sculpture, textiles, and ceramics.

When Konstantina's Grace joined her in debating the mages, Cassia could see he was the princess's ally, partner, and equal in all things, including scholarship. Cassia gathered that Grace-Prince Adwene had been a formidable intellectual at the Imperial university in his mortal life, some thirteen centuries earlier. Their children and descendants who were in attendance all proved just as accomplished. Cassia dreaded forfeiting the princess's respect with one ignorant remark or one inattentive mistake regarding who was related to whom.

Cassia paused by an enormous vase packed with fat rose blooms. Lio halted on the other side of the arrangement from her. That kept the proper distance between them. It also, she observed, imposed a mass of flowers between him and the watching gazes of Benedict, Callen, and Perita. They had lost Eudias somewhere along the way. Knight plopped down between Lio and Cassia and panted in contentment.

Lio gave her a look that made her forget what she had stopped here to ask him.

She swallowed. He looked so very fine in his high-collared black formal robes, with his silver medallion of office upon his breast. "Ambassador…"

"Yes, Lady Cassia?" His gaze caressed her neck.

She tried to gather her scattered thoughts. "A question about tonight's event…"

"Ah, yes." He cleared his throat, and his gaze returned to her face.

"Do we have the honor of meeting all of the princess's descendants tonight?"

"All those who are of age," he confirmed. "The children were not deemed ready for such an occasion."

Cassia nodded to show she understood his code for *keep the babies as far away from Chrysanthos and Skleros as possible.*

At Cassia's elbow, Benedict appeared as if the collar of his tunic were too tight. Perhaps the fragrance of the roses was suffocating him. "There are more of them?"

"I take it upon myself to be prolific." Konstantina rounded the vase of roses, a silver cup of coffee in her hand.

Knight wagged his tail and gazed hopefully at the princess, who ignored him. With his hand on his heart, Lio gave the princess a bow nearly as deep as Cassia had seen him give the Queens. Benedict disguised his startle as a bow of his own.

Cassia curtsied and attempted to smooth over Benedict's blunder. Of all times for his courtesy to fail him. "How fortunate Orthros is that you have so strengthened the royal line, Second Princess."

Cassia had yet to stand this close to the Queens' eldest daughter. She was an image of Hesperine beauty, her height regal, her skin dark as the night sky. She wore a robe woven in black-and-white geometric patterns that draped over one shoulder, leaving the other bare. The thick coils of her hair fell to her ankles, bound at intervals with silk bands that glittered with black-and-white jewels. Were those opals and the fabled moonstones? Her brown eyes were sharp with intelligence, missing nothing.

Konstantina acknowledged Cassia with a nod over her coffee. "It is the foremost duty of every son and daughter of the royal bloodline to pass on the Queens' undiluted power to as many new Hesperines as possible. That is why we have the unique status of royal firstbloods, so we may each found a bloodline of our own and increase the Queens' legacy to their people."

Cassia saw an opportunity to cultivate common ground. "You would naturally wish to pass on your parents' power and lineage, and with it, your family's wisdom and traditions."

"Our inheritance from our mothers must not be squandered," the princess replied. "Seven of the eight Ritual firstbloods who, thanks to Hespera's generosity, created our kind, are lost to the world forever. So too are my mother Soteira's clan, along with their knowledge and magic. My mothers' legacy must be preserved through us."

Cassia nodded. "I am sure any mortal, whether of humble or elevated birth, can understand this imperative. Our farmers pray for many children, as our lords strive to found lasting bloodlines. What could be more precious to human or Hesperine than family?"

Konstantina swiveled her gaze to Benedict. "Perhaps I can aid your understanding. Every scholar is first a student, second a teacher, before anything else."

"How gracious of you to enlighten our guests in their own tongue," Lio put in.

"You have done well as a translator," Konstantina told him, "but when there are no mages between my guests and myself, Vulgus is an effective language of discourse."

Lio bowed to the princess once more. "You learned Vulgus on Annassa Alea's knee along with Divine, as you learned the tongues of the Empire from Annassa Soteira. Your words elevate any language you choose for your discourse."

A hint of a smile appeared at the corners of the princess's mouth.

Benedict bowed again. "Your great scholarship is wasted on us, Second Princess. You need not expend your energy on a lesson."

"But you and your countrymen are all curiosity tonight. I have heard questions among your peers as to how the transfer of royal power is achieved, and whether the Queens' children are, in fact, their children."

Benedict cleared his throat. "I advised the lords and the other knights not to pry into your affairs, Second Princess."

"That would be a well-intentioned sentiment, if it were not a disguise for your discomfort. Your questions would be welcome, if they represented a desire to learn. Nevertheless, you find yourself in a house of knowledge and debate. I will answer."

Her exchange with the knight had drawn an audience that comprised most of the embassy. Callen and Perita moved closer to Cassia, as if to accommodate the crowd, and she knew they had her back.

But Cassia would not come to Benedict's defense this time. He had made himself the princess's target, and Cassia would not shield him. After the Tenebran men's impudent and sometimes disgusting speculations all night, Cassia would not stand in Konstantina's way, however the princess wished to respond. In fact, Cassia would relish watching Konstantina set the record straight.

The princess took a step closer to Benedict. "The Queens have loved, taught, and protected every one of their children. *That* is what makes us theirs."

"Of course, Second Princess. I am certain they are, ah, most devoted mothers."

Cassia watched Benedict try to fit the Queens and their daughter into one of his two or three categories for women. It was written all over him that his attempt was a failure.

Konstantina gave the knight a smile truly worthy of a princess, one with fangs. "That said, allow me to reassure you we are of the Queens' own blood. When we were infants in their arms, they fed us from their fingers." She held up one finger. "Then, when we grew teeth, from their wrists." With mesmerizing grace, she turned her hand over to expose her wrist.

Benedict looked away, sweating. Was it the mention of drinking blood or the sight of a woman's wrist that put his underlinens in a twist over the fate of his soul?

Konstantina took a step closer, Benedict a step back.

"Now we are grown," said the princess, "and we would shed every last drop of our blood for our children—or for our mothers, who gave all of us life. That is how parenthood works in Orthros. Is it any different in your kingdom?"

Inwardly, Cassia winced. That question would certainly strike at Benedict's heart.

He bowed again, this time to cover a long silence. "Tenebrans shed blood for many reasons, but alas, not always for the sake of their children. Would that our parents always fulfilled their sacred obligations."

"Your grief runs in my veins," said Konstantina. "Children should never bear the failures of their elders. When anyone's child suffers, we all have cause for sorrow."

"I cannot disagree."

Konstantina raised her glass slightly. Benedict lowered his gaze.

The princess turned. "Lady Cassia, walk with me in my garden."

To that abrupt invitation, there could be only one answer. "I would be honored, Second Princess."

Konstantina quelled Cassia's escort with a glance. They dropped behind Cassia to let her walk at the princess's side across the tiled hall, and Lio followed behind Konstantina. The princess's family members parted to make way, and certain members of the embassy attached themselves to Cassia's retinue.

Konstantina led them through a side door and back out into the garden, and Cassia looked over her shoulder to assess their audience. Not only Benedict, Callen, and Perita, but also the Semna, her attendants, Lord Gaius, and Tychon strolled in their wake.

Unseen light and imperceptible warmth seemed to surround Cassia, and she glanced around her to see if perhaps the Queens had decided to join them. But her gaze landed only on Konstantina.

The princess smiled. "I have veiled us. We may speak freely."

Cassia studied the flowers they passed. "I understand you are the Royal Master Rose Gardener."

"The royal rose garden here at my residence is my gift to Orthros. You may like to know it is open to any who wish to visit."

"It is magnificent, Second Princess. How your roses thrive under your light magic! I'm told you invented many of the spells that make it possible for all the beautiful plants in Selas to grow."

"The application of light spells to horticulture is one my areas of magical research."

"You are a light mage like Annassa Alea and a mind healer like Annassa Soteira, is that right? The insight into people that your theramancy provides must be an asset to you as a magistrate."

Konstantina regarded Cassia. "Theramancy is indeed beneficial when applied to law. Just laws are those that mandate the best in our natures and protect us from the worst, and a just mediator must understand the difference."

"I have heard so much about your great contributions to your people. Allow me to express my admiration."

Konstantina's countenance was as dignified as ever, but there was an unmistakable gleam in her eyes. Amusement. "You come armed with many compliments tonight."

Cassia swallowed her dismay. If a laugh was all her efforts earned from Konstantina, she must do better. "I assure you I am most sincere, Second Princess."

"I can see that." There was kindness in the princess's gaze, too.

"I believe you are too committed to upholding truth to tolerate flattery."

"I accept it only from those who flatter me with the knowledge that we are both too smart to believe it. Argyros taught his student well. Lio brings compliments to parties like the right wine for the occasion. Taste without substance, but we must all equip our props for our roles."

"The truth is never flattery. No one can disregard your eminence among Hesperines."

"You are ready to confront the full force of my eminence, I can see. Stand down, Lady Cassia. I brought you out here to show you my flowers."

They turned a corner in the path, and Cassia saw that they had lost their caravan entirely. She and Knight were alone with the princess, surrounded by rose hedges too tall to see over.

Konstantina slowed her march to a stroll. "There now."

"Did you and Lio have this planned, Second Princess?"

"My plans do not require the assistance of youngbloods, but I am certain he will catch on and occupy the others with a few mental adjustments."

They turned another corner, and there before Cassia was the largest glass structure she had ever seen. Rods and curls of wrought iron framed enormous plates of transparent glass. Through the foggy panes, Cassia caught glimpses of more roses.

"You may gasp in delight aloud, you know," said the princess. "Your rose-fearing countrymen will not overhear."

"When I first heard of the existence of greenhouses, I longed to set foot in one," Cassia confessed.

"Many rose varieties can thrive outdoors in my garden because, as you can imagine, my mother Alea's Sanctuary magic is most concentrated here at House Annassa. The plants that require more shelter and care, I keep in here."

The princess hesitated with her hand on the door, contemplating Knight. He sat poised on his haunches, clearly longing to leap up and go to her. He gave her his most pitiful begging gaze.

"Does he have a habit of digging?" she asked.

Cassia shook her head. "He is a most excellent gardening companion."

"Very well. He may come in with us. Don't linger in the doorway, lest we upset the temperature balance."

His tail wagged his whole body as the princess opened the door. Despite his excitement, he heeled beautifully. Cassia hurried inside behind Konstantina.

The garden had felt temperate compared to the rest of the city, but the greenhouse felt warm by contrast. Rose fragrance filled Cassia up till she thought she might levitate.

Konstantina discarded her silk shoes just inside the door and proceeded barefoot. She set her silver cup aside on the lip of a planter as she went. She halted at a potting bench and donned a pair of thick canvas gloves, then tossed a second pair to Cassia. "I'm afraid you may find these too large for you."

Cassia overcame her surprise just in time to catch them. She left her black velvet gloves on the potting bench and pulled on the canvas ones as she hastened to follow the princess further into the greenhouse.

Were they really here for a gardening lesson? Or was the greenhouse the princess's Kings and Mages board? It didn't matter. Cassia would play any game for even a moment in here.

The princess led her past beds and pots of roses, between rose bushes and rose trees. At the very center of the greenhouse, Cassia could not help but gasp aloud. On an iron trellis the size of a spiral staircase, a rose climbed from the floor all the way up to the top of the greenhouse, where the vines spread out along the trusses to cover half the ceiling. The blossoms had layers upon layers of snowy white petals.

The princess looked upward with Cassia. "This is the Sanctuary Rose.

These were once grown in all the Great Temples of Hespera, and it was tradition to present the blooms to new mages upon their entry into the Goddess's service."

"Is that why there are bushes like this in the courtyard at Rose House?"

Konstantina nodded. "The most beloved pursuit of our gardeners is cultivating endless varieties of roses. I bred bushes from this climber. When Blood Komnena built Rose House, Lio suggested Sanctuary Roses for the courtyard as a symbol of welcome."

"Your roses are masterpieces, Second Princess. How old is their mother plant?"

"Older than I, and I have lived more than fifteen hundred years. We grew up together, this rose and I, although it came to Orthros before I did. Our people cut it back to stalks and smuggled it out of Hagia Boreia in a pot. It was the only rose they managed to save from my mother Alea's temple before Aithouros and his circle burned it to the ground. The refugees carried it all the way over the mountains, but once they settled in Orthros, the rose would not come out of dormancy. Still, they kept the pot as a relic, hoping one day this rose might experience the same rebirth as our people had."

"How did it come back to life?"

Konstantina looked at her hands, straightening her gardening gloves. "By the time I was a novice and chose gardening as my craft, the rose was nothing more than a root system under the soil. Even so, I petitioned my mothers to be given responsibility for it, and they obliged. For years, I tried everything I could think of to revive it. Its first bloom appeared just in time for my initiation."

Cassia let out a breath in wonder. "Your magic is great indeed, Second Princess."

"There is another group of original rose varieties from the Great Temple Epoch. Hespera's Rose was a living plant before it was a symbol upon windows and handkerchiefs. They have only a single layer of five petals, which mark them as the oldest roses of wild origin. Does that sound familiar?"

"Did they once grow in shrines of Hespera and other places of succor?"

"Yes."

"Crimson climbers that produce bright red hips in the fall."

"Well done. You have rediscovered a lost variety of Hespera's Rose and brought it home."

Cassia's mouth hung open. "May I ask how you know?"

"I can feel their magic on you. You come to know the aura of roses as you do their fragrance. Your reputation as a gardener is justified, I see. Tell me, how have you brought them with you? In what condition?"

Cassia was grateful the princess was concerned about the roses' immediate needs, not where Cassia had found them. She was not prepared to speak of the shrine, from which she had salvaged both the glyph stone and the roses. "I'm afraid all I was able to bring with me were seeds."

"Have you ever grown roses from seed before? It is a greater challenge than starting them from cuttings."

"Not roses, but I have started many other plants from seed."

"Do you understand the process of stratification rose seeds require in order to sprout?" The princess's tone was patient. "Do you know how to protect the sprouts from the fungi to which roses are susceptible? Are you familiar with what mixture of peat and minerals is best for rose seedlings?"

Cassia blushed and shook her head. "It appears I shall receive a lesson in rose gardening, rather than discourse, from you tonight. Allow me to thank you, Second Princess."

"All I ask in thanks is to see the first bloom as soon as it appears. Fifteen hundred years is a long time to miss someone you never knew."

Konstantina turned away and beckoned. Cassia followed her, not daring to comment on the words the princess had spoken from her heart. They returned to the workbench, where a row of tiny pots waited. The sight of the unbroken soil in them filled Cassia with a quiver of anticipation. She could envision the seedlings that would soon peek their little faces into the light.

The princess hefted a sack from the ground onto the workbench with her own hands, not levitation. "Bring that bag of peat over here, if you will."

Cassia retrieved another sack from a few paces away.

"I hear you have a spade you prefer to use," said the princess.

Cassia reached into the velvet purse at her belt and pulled out her battered, dingy spade. "It is rather difficult to explain why I carry this to formal events."

Konstantina set an empty pot before Cassia. "Gardening is as much magic as scholarship. You are holding an artifact in your hand that you have infused with emotion over the course of many years and with magic through blood rituals. You should always use it when you give plants new life. They will grow better."

"So it does hold power beyond my attachment to it."

The princess nodded. "Stratification means storing the seeds in the cold for a time, then bringing them into the warmth. This mimics seasonal changes and convinces the seeds it is time to sprout."

Cassia listened, rapt, to Konstantina's lesson. Then she followed instructions as the princess guided her through potting a sprout that had already been stratified. As they worked, Knight sat obediently beside the potting bench. By the time they were done, there was soil on their formal garments, and Cassia was smiling.

Konstantina nodded in apparent approval. "These seedlings are my Winter Solstice gifts to the Eriphite children. I will see to it Zoe receives the one we just started together."

"I will pass on what you have taught me tonight and help Zoe learn to care for her rose."

"My welcome gift to you will be waiting at Lio's residence upon your return. My initiates have delivered all the supplies you will need for your rescued roses."

Cassia gave Konstantina a true heart bow, bending at the waist with her hand on her heart. "Thank you for your generosity."

The princess took off her gardening gloves with a sigh. "My dearest Hypatia is an astronomer, not a gardener. She spends so much time staring at the stars that she does not know a weed from a rose."

"When a star is so eternal, perhaps that makes it easy to disregard anything so young and fleeting as a flower."

"History has proved that a rose is tenacious. Cut her back, and she will spring up again. It is a mistake to underestimate her, and it is a shame to discourage her. She should be cultivated."

"With respect for your expertise, Second Princess, I must tell you that wild roses do not train easily to trellises."

Konstantina picked up a pair of shears and considered them. "Yet even the wildest roses must be pruned for their own good." She set the shears away from her. "Not too much, however. They do not tolerate the same care as garden roses."

Cassia let the tension out of her body, making sure her hand did not tighten on her spade. She knew she was in dangerous territory now, but going in unarmed was the best defense. Konstantina had told her to stand down. And so Cassia would.

"Did not Hespera create thorned plants to defend those under her protection?" Cassia asked. "Does not every rose serve the same purpose—to keep her people safe?"

"Indeed, your purpose and mine are the same. I too seek to rescue Hespera's lost creations from Tenebra. One in particular, which also came over the mountains with the Queens during their flight to Orthros. A red rose without compare in the Goddess's Eyes, but with such thorns. He does not realize he too needs the shelter of our mothers' garden."

"I see. I understand now which rose errant you mean, who does not wish to be pruned. My understanding is that his entire garden would wither if his thorns were not there to protect the more fragile blossoms. What would become of his wildflowers if he were transplanted?"

"He *must* be transplanted before he is breached. What good will it do anyone if he is lost forever? Better to return and lie dormant and learn to bloom again."

"You have been growing roses much longer than I," Cassia said carefully. "You know how to care for this one better than I would ever presume to. But as his fellow wild rose, I must say, I do not think he would ever recover from the loss of his garden Abroad."

"Once again, I find myself at odds with an eager thorn bush."

"You are the thorniest of us all, I believe."

Konstantina laughed. "I like the compliments you bring to parties. They are not flattery, and yet they are exactly what people want to hear. I must warn you, you are right."

"It is clear you are a great defender of Orthros. I do not wish to be your opponent."

"You have a healthy direction and strong growth. I have no intention of taking my shears to you. But do not grow into my path, Cassia. I have devoted countless years to laying out this garden, and I am so close to finally restoring our rose errant to his rightful place in it. I will bring my brother home. I will not stand by and watch him throw away his life."

"Second Princess, that is between you and the First Prince."

"You and Lio have grown up right in the middle of it, and Ioustin has added his Ritual son to the ranks of the thorns who defend him. I will not lose you to his garden as well."

"Lio and I belong in the same garden," Cassia protested.

"Of course. What do you take me for? I do not stoop to driving wedges between young lovers. Which is why you and Lio must be together in my garden."

Cassia swallowed. "What are you asking me to do?"

"I ask nothing of you. I am going to give you what I know you want—knowledge. A rose like you feeds on it. I know, because it is my nightly drink. Listen to what I have to say. You will know what to do about it."

Cassia was not sure she wanted to know any of Konstantina's secrets. They would be useful, to be sure—but they must come at a great price.

Konstantina watched her, waiting. "I do not have to teach you that what you do not know can hurt you. When has someone like you ever turned down information she could use?"

"You have indeed been growing roses longer than I. Very well. I cannot refuse what you wish to tell me."

"Watch me trim the spent blooms, and I will teach you." Konstantina took up her shears and headed for the center of the greenhouse.

"*Baat,* my Knight. Stay here by the potting bench and show the princess what a mannerly fellow you are." He didn't budge as Cassia joined the princess beneath the spreading limbs of the Sanctuary Rose.

Konstantina paused to examine the tangle of vines at her eye level. "Ioustin has told Lio a secret. My brother is unpredictable in many ways, but not when it comes to honor. I am certain that when Lio proposed the Solstice Summit, Ioustin felt honor-bound to express his gratitude by revealing something that should *never*"—she snipped off a wilting bloom—"have reached the ears of anyone outside the royal family."

"I breathe royal secrets, Second Princess. They do not frighten me."

Konstantina reached for a flawless white flower and turned it around.

The petals on the other side were disfigured by disease. She cut the bloom off and sent it up in a flash of light. "Has Lio told you what Ioustin revealed to him?"

Konstantina must be talking about the Departure. Was she trying to set a trap for Lio? "All I know of the First Prince, I learned at the Queens' circle upon my arrival. Hypatia was there and can relate to you what Lio and I spoke of with his Ritual father. Although you disapprove of the Summit, you surely do not doubt that Lio is trustworthy."

Konstantina snapped her shears closed again. "I bounced Lio on my knee when Ioustin's hands were too full of weapons to hold a baby. As I told you, I am not going to drive a wedge between you and Lio. You may thank me later for helping you avoid a rift."

"We are partners in all our aims, I assure you."

Konstantina met her gaze. "There has been a plan in place since our people fled Tenebra, a measure to which we have never had to resort in the history of Orthros. The ruins of our ancient temples were still smoking, and the Equinox Oath was young. We were not certain the Mage King's guarantee of protection for Hesperines errant would hold, or that his new Tenebra would be a strong enough buffer between Cordium and Orthros."

"So this secret is another holdover from the Last War."

"A piece of wisdom," Konstantina corrected. "We have always kept in mind the eventuality that we might need to make the Departure. The night before Lio's proposal of the Solstice Summit, my mothers were ready to call our Hesperines errant home for all time."

There was no use trying to hide from the Blood Union. Konstantina was probing Cassia to see if the news came as a shock, and the princess would sense that Cassia was not surprised. She would also feel how Cassia dreaded the threat.

Let her. "I know about the Departure. If that displeases you, Second Princess, you must address yourself to the First Prince. Your brother gave Lio express permission to tell me."

"Of course he did. Naturally, my brother is in favor of the Summit, for it allows him to deny for just a little while longer that he is out of time."

"With respect, Second Princess, the Departure is not a foregone conclusion."

The princess looked at Cassia over her shears. "Of course it is, because I shall see it done."

A chill went down Cassia's spine. So this was the fortress of thorns she and Lio faced.

"I see," Cassia answered calmly. "So Lio and I find ourselves in the middle of a political contest between the Queens' two most powerful children. Thank you for the warning."

"It is not a warning." Konstantina slid her finger along the blade of her shears. From her blood, a spell light came to life and shone upon a rosebud. The petals unfurled all at once into a magnificent bloom. "It is an invitation to help me restore the garden."

"You're asking *me* to take your side against the prince?" Cassia demanded. "You think I would use the Summit to promote the Departure? Do you have any idea what Hesperines errant did for me?"

"I do."

"The crows would have picked apart my sister's body. The arms that held me and made me feel safe. The face that smiled at me. The throat that gave voice to the only words of love I ever heard. I would have lain dead on the same field, just out of reach. A seven-year-old girl with an arrow through my heart."

The princess's eyes flashed with emotion. "I am trying to save lives, Cassia, not cost them."

Cassia stripped off Konstantina's gloves and hurled them at the princess's feet. "You have tried to recruit the wrong person. I will not lift a finger to help you."

"On the contrary, I have spoken to precisely the right person. The Hesperine errant who once tried to save my life is still in Tenebra, just like those who rescued you. We must stop at nothing to make sure they return home unharmed."

"What does your defender have to say about the Departure?"

"He prays it will never come. He gives all his heart to his hopeless quest to restore some vestige of safety and dignity to a ruined land. But it will drain him dry. Now it is my turn to rescue him."

"The First Prince," Cassia realized.

"I was born with a rare disease that even the most powerful mages of the Empire could not heal. When I was five, my human family brought me to Orthros. I awoke in the Healing Sanctuary to two realizations. One, my mortal parents had returned to their important life in the Empire, relieved to be free of the ordeal of caring for a daughter who could never fulfill their ambitions for her. Two, I was not in pain. In that moment, I learned for the first time how it felt to not be in pain. Do you know who was sitting beside my bed?"

"He said he inherited both his affinities from Annassa Soteira. He would be a healer, too."

"Long before he was Prince Regent of Orthros Abroad, long before he went errant, Ioustin completed his training with her in the Healing Sanctuary. I was his first patient after his initiation. He was the first person who ever made me feel I was not a burden. In the weeks he spent striving to defeat my illness, a bond grew between us. He doted on me as much as I adored him.

"When even he could not heal me, he sought her aid. The night she told him only the Gift could free me from my disease, he wept privately at his failure. But what a smile he gave me as the Queens of Orthros asked me if I would like to be his sister."

To think, Konstantina and Ioustinianos had once loved each other as Zoe and Lio did. Centuries and politics had the power to change a bond that pure.

But not break it. Perhaps only make it stronger.

"Is that why you wish him to return home?" Cassia asked. "You believe he could better serve his people in the Healing Sanctuary?"

"This is not a contest of weighing the lives he could save with his healing against those he saves with his sword."

"Then why? You know better than anyone how much suffering he has the power to prevent. Why can he not rely on your support for his cause? He cares so deeply about all those who would be destroyed if Hesperines abandoned Tenebra. It is clear you do as well, Second Princess. You cannot really believe the Departure is worth the cost."

The princess stowed her shears in a nearby storage basket. "That cost is no greater than the one we are paying to remain. We must choose between two tragedies."

"How can you argue the Departure is the lesser evil? Think of all the people who would never receive the Mercy. When their kin and comrades have left them to die, it is Hesperines who show them that their lives still matter to someone, that their deaths are not in vain. Have you been immortal so long now that you cannot imagine what it feels like to face your end alone?"

"You forget yourself," the princess warned. "I still mourn the Hesperines errant who have died without the Mercy while trying to save mortals."

"What about the children? Would you deny them the life you have? How can you bear to think of infants freezing to death or being torn to shreds by predators—"

"Enough." The princess held up a hand. "I am a mother. There is nothing you can teach me about children. Tonight you have seen how many of my family were not adopted from the Empire. You cannot possibly know the pain I feel when I imagine what might have befallen my own children and descendants from Tenebra, had they never been Solaced."

"How do you bear it? Why not devote your power here in Orthros to supporting your brother's mission Abroad? You could be the Charge's greatest ally."

"To be a Hesperine errant is to awaken from every Slumber knowing this may be the night you lay down your life for the Goddess. To not be a Hesperine errant is to lie awake counting the lives you could not save." Konstantina drew a deep breath. "I thank the Goddess for every one of us who made it home. But I will not see any more Hesperine blood spilled for roses that will never grow. It is time for Ioustin to abandon his fruitless labor. He is all but withered. The soil of Tenebra is starving him."

"What about the Hesperites? Is not their mission to keep human Hespera worship alive in Tenebra a noble calling?"

"Ioustin will have no choice but to bring them to Orthros with him, where they belong. Worshipers of Hespera living as mortals in Tenebra and dying without the Gift is an open wound on the spirit of our people. They can finally become Hesperines."

"What about Nike?"

"You should understand about Nike most of all. She was like an elder sister to me."

"Invoking sisters will only harden me against your cause."

"Imagine if you could relive the night of your sibling's death—but this time, with wisdom and power. What would you give up to save her life? What wouldn't you sacrifice?"

Cassia took a step back.

"I cannot save Nike," the princess said to the Sanctuary Rose above them. "I could not save Methu. But my brother is still within my reach."

"Methu?" Cassia echoed.

"Prometheus. So much died with him. Ioustin needs to realize he did not. He needs to begin a new life here in Orthros and put down roots."

"You think he could do that while his comrades are missing?"

"He must have told you and Lio about the disappearances. Our people are vanishing without a trace. Who will be next? It is time for Ioustin to realize he is chasing Hesperines who are no longer there. He must bring home those who remain to him before it is too late. The fallen are with the Goddess in Sanctuary. We should not begrudge them that. But as my heart beats, my brother will not join the ranks of Orthros's martyrs."

"How can you give up on them like that?"

"Hespera never gives up on anyone. I am fighting *for* our Hesperines errant. How many more of them will we send Abroad with cheers and fanfare, without any promise of when their fight will end? How many more will we bring home broken for the sake of a victory than can never be won? How many more will die in a kingdom that begrudges their sacrifice?"

"Will you give up on Tenebra?"

"Tenebrans do not want our aid. They live in fear of us. They regard us as a threat to all they hold sacred. The king lays traps for us that will result only in further harm to us and his own people. The Oath has long since lapsed, and with it our purpose and rights in Tenebra. The mortals there wish to be responsible for their own fate, and we must respect their Will."

"The Oath can yet be restored. Tenebra can be made safe for Hesperines again. Made better, for Hesperines and mortals alike."

"Do not doubt that I cherish your hopes, as much as I lament this world will not reward them. Nearly sixteen hundred years, and all the power of our Hesperines errant has not been enough to create lasting change in Tenebra."

"They changed me. And I will change Tenebra."

"Do not let Tenebra change you, Cassia," said the princess. "Give your heart to your Summit. Ioustin thinks you and Lio have bought him time, but the time you have bought is mine. You have given me the opportunity I require to make my case to him. The Cordian mages are the perfect bait to lure Ioustin home. Every time he comes here to prowl around them, he finds a moment's rest in spite of himself. Every instant of respite is another chance for me to make him realize how much he longs to stay. I will open his eyes to how much his people need him here."

"You must know I will warn him of your plan."

"Go ahead. My intentions are no secret to him. We have been at this debate for a very, very long time, young rose. But debate is my service to my people. I will deliver our Hesperines errant. When Cordium begins the Next War, none of our own will be there to meet them in battle."

"There will be no war." Cassia repeated the promise she lived by. "There is still a chance for peace! The Solstice Summit is proof of that."

"Anthros's fire and sunsword are rampant plants. They don't stay in their garden. They grow across the face of the world and choke out every other living thing."

"Why aren't you taking your blades to them?"

"Phaedros tried that. It didn't end well."

"Who is Phaedros?"

"I will leave it to Hypatia to give you her firsthand account. She would never forgive me for stealing her thunder."

"I think that is a secret I need to know now," Cassia insisted.

"Only one thing should occupy your thoughts. I want you to attend the Circle of Rosarians' annual gathering under my patronage. You can present your rediscovery of a true Rose of Hespera."

"Thank you for your interest in my career." Cassia lifted her chin. "I will keep your invitation in mind while the world as we know it comes to an end."

"You are growing strong and true, wild rose. Mark my circle on your calendar. It is held during the Spring Equinox festivities."

Cassia sucked in a breath. "After the embassy has left."

Konstantina beckoned to the Sanctuary Rose. A perfect rosebud, just beginning to open, detached itself at the stem and came to her hand. She offered it to Cassia. "You must choose your garden. When the ward divides Orthros and Tenebra for all time, where will your roots remain?"

WITH A FLOWER

THE PRINCESS'S LIGHT MAGIC had snatched Cassia from Lio's sight, but even a royal's power could not disrupt his Union with his Grace. The turmoil in Cassia's aura raged along every path of the royal rose garden. Her denial stirred the trees, and the roses filled the air with the fragrance of her grief.

Lio had had enough.

He left the mortals wandering, befuddled and unconcerned, in a labyrinth of rose hedges and sent four different illusions of himself in opposite directions to lead them astray.

Cassia's aura hurtled toward him from the direction of the greenhouse. He stepped into her path. She came striding around the corner of a hedge, Knight bounding at her heels. Her white gown flowed around her, begrimed with soil. Her gloves were gone. She held a white rosebud in one bleeding hand.

Lio caught her in his arms. "Cassia, what happened?"

She was shaking with anger. "If we are to prevent the Departure, we must best Konstantina. We two, against all her power."

"Konstantina is the driving force behind the Departure? I should have known!"

"She has informed me in no uncertain terms she will ensure it comes to pass."

"I knew she opposed the Summit, but this…"

"She has decided our Summit is of use after all—as bait to get her brother home long enough for her to keep him here, so the Queens can lock him in. I will have no part in it."

"Cassia, did she try to—recruit you?"

"She wants to collect the two of us like pretty buds and put us in a vase to be watered. Just like her brother. He will wither in the soil of Tenebra, she says. She must rescue him before he becomes a martyr. She wants us all to sit safe here and do nothing for our people who are suffering and dying."

Konstantina had been the first to ask Cassia to stay in Orthros?

That moment was supposed to have been his and Cassia's. That declaration had been his to make. After everything they had been through, after how hard they had fought, after how carefully he had planned that event in their lives so it would be everything Cassia deserved.

He put his hand over hers where she held the white rose, gently, so as not to drive the thorns to prick her skin any deeper. He prized her fingers apart and eased the rose out of her grasp to wrap his handkerchief around the stem.

He could not let the princess take this moment from him and Cassia. Konstantina might have made the proposal, but the debate must be all his and Cassia's own.

It was time for them to start talking about the choice that awaited her. He could no longer be silent about how much he wanted her to stay in Orthros.

He would make this moment theirs. No anger. No fears. Only the love that awaited them.

Lio presented the flower to Cassia. "Do you know what this rose means?"

"Yes! I have to choose." Cassia turned away and hurled the flower from her. It landed with his handkerchief in a splash of blood at the fork of two garden paths. "My sister's death was *not* in vain! I will never abandon Tenebra."

Lio's words died in his throat. He stared at his Grace's back and the scattered petals of her verdict.

She turned to face him. "We must warn the prince of his sister's intentions. How can we get word to him?"

Lio was silent for an instant, gathering his thoughts. "This is not a matter for a Charge scout to relate to him. I will ask my father how we might discreetly arrange a visit from Rudhira so we can discuss this with him ourselves."

Cassia lifted her chin and straightened her back, and all expression disappeared from her face. Lady Circumspect, the king's daughter, stood composed in the Hesperine garden Lio had shared with his wild rose only a moment before.

"Good," she said. "I wish to tell the First Prince personally that I am the first rampart of thorns between the Second Princess and his cause. Now I had best rejoin the embassy before Konstantina's diversion of my attention creates even more problems."

She marched back the way they had come.

Lio picked up the lovely flower with which Konstantina had undone all his labors to offer Sanctuary to his Grace.

UNION STONE

THE RED STONE CAST pulsing, blood-colored light across Apollon's sketches. Cassia could sense as well as see the beat, as she could with her glyph shard. The stone was only the size of an egg, but the power in it felt larger than that. Beneath its polished surface, shades of red shifted like the liquid texture of the Blood Moon.

On the other side of the worktable, Lio's father leaned on his fists over the stone. "We have not used these in some years. It will give Ioustin a start, but he will answer, I am certain."

"Thank you for doing this, Father." Lio stood beside Cassia with his hands braced on the table, just a finger's breadth from hers. But not touching.

Cassia buried a hand in Knight's ruff. Lio had not been himself since the garden. Her head had not cooled, either. But they were united in their purpose, as always. Why wasn't it bringing them together tonight?

Zoe, snuggling in her mantle, leaned closer to her father from her vantage point on his stool. "This is just like one of your stories, Papa."

Apollon picked up Moonbeam from Zoe's lap before the goat could nibble his sketches. He set the kid gently on the floor next to Aurora, then put an arm around Zoe and smiled. "On this night, we will use one of the Blood Errant's union stones to send a message to the Blood-Red Prince."

"What's the important message?" Zoe asked.

Apollon exchanged a look with Komnena over Zoe's head.

Komnena sidestepped the goats to put her arm around Zoe as well. "We must talk with him about something Aunt Kona said. She is very concerned about him."

"Aunt Kona is always concerned about people." Zoe looked down, then at Cassia. "Last time I was at House Annassa playing with the royal children, I got scared. Aunt Kona used her light spells to make an illusion of a cave above us all, right over the Queens' Terrace!"

"That was very kind of her," Cassia conceded. "She told me how much she loves children."

"Aunt Kona wants to make sure Rudhira is safe," Komnena said.

"I would turn into a gargoyle and protect Lio if he was in danger," Zoe announced.

A smile relieved Lio's features for the first time in hours. "Then I am very safe."

"Well, let us see if this still works." Apollon pricked his thumb on his fang and let four drops of blood fall upon the stone.

The substance inside the stone whirled and pulsed faster. The stone's light grew brighter. Cassia held her breath and counted the beats in the stone. One, two, three…four.

She heard a sword whip out of a scabbard behind her. She and Lio spun around.

The First Prince stood there in full chain mail, brandishing a two-hander as tall as Cassia. Ioustinianos's unsheathed fangs were as threatening as his sword. His hair and clothes dripped a puddle onto the floor and filled the workshop with the unmistakable smell of Tenebran rain.

Apollon came around the table. "Forgive me for startling you."

The prince opened his mouth, spotted Zoe, then apparently refrained from whatever curse he had in mind to say. "I came ready to introduce Chrysanthos or Skleros to my blade."

Apollon laughed. "I am sure they would find it educational to meet Thorn in person."

Zoe, jumping down from the stool, did not let her father get far out of arm's reach. Clinging to him, she peered around him to stare wide-eyed at the enormous weapon.

The prince lowered his sword and knelt down, resting the blade flat on the floor before Zoe. "I would never bring this sword into Orthros unless I thought the people I love were in danger. The Queens' laws against weapons are very important. Let's not mention this to anyone, all right?"

Zoe nodded, then stepped over the sword and into her Ritual father's arms. How rare to see her initiate an embrace. Ioustinianos was so beloved that even shy Zoe took her chance to hug him when he was here. The smell of fresh-cut lumber filled the air, and the rainwater disappeared from the prince, Zoe, and the floor. The red light shining on his face illumined his smile.

Cassia looked for the source of the light and saw a stone just like Apollon's embedded in the hilt of the prince's sword.

"I retired my hammer in Tenebra," Apollon explained, "but I made sure I brought my union stone safely to Orthros with me."

The prince released Zoe and stood, retrieving his sword. He gazed for an instant at his union stone, then shook his head.

"I know," said Apollon. "You wonder what Nike makes of it in this moment, that the stone in her shield is aglow for the first time in so long."

The prince levitated his sword into the scabbard on his back. "Would that she had heeded that call before now. You know how many times I tried it."

"Would that we knew where in the world Methu's swords are, at this very moment, shining with the light of his blood magic."

"We'll never know what became of them, or even if they still exist."

Komnena chose that moment to welcome the prince with a hug. He embraced each of Lio's family in turn, politely ignoring Knight's pleas for his attention.

When the prince came to Cassia, he took her hand. "What happened here?"

Before she could answer, her pricks and scratches healed before her eyes.

"I ran afoul of some mighty thorns in the royal rose garden." Cassia glanced at Zoe. "Your sister was kind enough to give me a tour of her greenhouse tonight. She speaks very fondly of you."

"I would love to know what the two of you talked about." The prince hid his dark expression behind a smile before turning to Zoe. "Does my invitation to this council extend to coffee around the Ritual circle and bedtime stories?"

Zoe's face lit up, and she looked hopefully at her parents.

"Do you need to ask?" Komnena stroked Zoe's hair and smiled at the prince.

Apollon laughed. "We will keep you as long as you can bear to be away from the Charge."

"I will stay until you're asleep," the prince told Zoe. "Why don't you help your mother make coffee? There are some boring things I need to talk about with your father, Lio, and Cassia, and then we'll join you at the Ritual circle."

Komnena nodded, herding Zoe along, who herded the goats along.

Cassia, Lio, and the prince joined Apollon around his worktable for a council of war—or a private Summit. She could not tell the battlefield from the negotiation table anymore. Relating her encounter with Konstantina only served to give Cassia's anger new life. Although she took care not to mention the Departure in front of Apollon, it was riling enough to explain how the princess intended to use the Summit to lure her brother home.

"Rest assured, First Prince," Cassia finished, "my determination to make Tenebra safe for the Charge remains unshaken. You must be able to continue searching for the missing Hesperines errant and helping mortals in need. I know the ranks of your supporters are full, but count me among them."

"So I will, and so I have these long months you have held Cordium at bay. My bond of gratitude with you and Lio is strong." The prince nodded to Lio. "As he will tell you, I do not let our young ones fight my battles for me. It is my cause to protect you. But I respect your skills, and I value your aid. I must ask you to do me a great favor."

"Of course, First Prince," Cassia replied.

"Call me Rudhira from now on, and do not bow when I come for a family visit at House Komnena. I feel more at home here than anywhere in Orthros, don't you?"

She dropped her hand, which she had been about to put over her heart. "Yes, Rudhira. House Komnena is the only place I have ever felt at home."

Lio's hand slid into hers. Relieved, she held him tightly.

Rudhira sighed. "I'd like to make the most of my visit tonight. My course of action is clear. There is a very simple solution to Kona's complex plan of persuasion. If I'm not here, she can't talk me into anything. I will stay Abroad for the duration of the Summit, if you can spare me."

Lio winced. "We must."

Cassia could not miss Rudhira's wistfulness. She had to admit Konstantina was right about that. He did miss home.

He was indeed a wild rose. That was what it meant to have half your roots in Orthros and half in Tenebra. If the two were severed, you would wither.

"Will you not stay the night?" Apollon asked.

"Thank you," Rudhira answered, "but there is one place in House Annassa where I can safely pass veil hours. Imagine my youngest sister's delight at hiding me in her residence under Kona's very nose."

"Please apologize to the Eighth Princess for me," Cassia requested. "I am sorry my warning will cost her your company in the coming weeks."

Lio's gaze snapped to Cassia. "You've already met?"

Cassia nodded. "She took me quite by surprise when she paid me a visit at Rose House. So much has happened tonight, I didn't even have a chance to mention it."

"Apollon." Rudhira put an arm around his Ritual father's shoulder. "I don't want to miss this chance to see what you have so far of the new statue you talked about on my last visit."

Apollon gestured further into the workshop. "It's right through here."

By the time they disappeared behind some tall shelves, Lio's surprised expression was gone, but Cassia could still sense his tension.

"What's the matter?" she asked.

"Nothing, clearly. I should have known you two would get along."

The border between Orthros and Tenebra might close forever, and Lio still had the energy to fret over whether Cassia felt at ease with his friends. "Not to worry, my champion. She's very easy to get along with."

"I'm relieved to hear it."

"She went out of her way to give us a chance to get acquainted without the embassy around. She even brought me a jar of ladybugs as a welcome gift." Cassia ran her hands over Lio's shoulders.

The tension in his muscles eased. "Well, that's one royal encounter we don't need to worry about."

"The princess was quite informative about your past," Cassia teased.

"Oh, thorns. What did you two talk about?"

"The time you jumped off Wisdom's Precipice with Mak and Lyros." Lio covered his face in his hand.

Cassia grinned. "Perhaps I will conspire with her to learn all the secrets you haven't told me yet."

Lio gave Cassia a bemused smile from between his fingers. "You are already the master of all my secrets."

"Oh, I beg to differ." She brushed her lips across his knuckles. "I think I have only just begun to explore you, mind mage. But how I enjoy the thrill of discovery."

He lowered his hand, and she moved in for a kiss. He opened his mouth for her and breathed a sigh.

The sound of footsteps drew nearer, and Cassia let Lio go before the prince came back into sight. She could hear Apollon moving about on the other side of the workshop.

Rudhira drew closer. "A quick word before Apollon rejoins us. I regret that you are embroiled in the...discussion...between my sister and me. But as you are already deeply involved, I'd best provide you with all the context I can. You should know that Kona's voice is the strongest in all the discussions about the Departure within the royal family."

"We were going to warn you about that," Lio said.

Cassia nodded. "She declared that she will ensure the Departure comes to pass."

"She has said as much to me." Rudhira looked away.

Cassia tried to imagine the pain of a beloved sibling setting herself against your life's work. But she did not have to imagine the pain of losing a sibling.

Before she could say anything more, Apollon returned. Rudhira beckoned to them, and they gathered once more around the table.

He reached into a satchel at his belt and set a canvas bag before them. "You all need to hear this. Apollon, I want you to hover over the mages for us in my absence."

"You leave too much of the enjoyment to me." Apollon took a seat on his stool.

Lio's hand tightened on Cassia's. "You learned something about the goblet?"

"Yes and no." Rudhira pulled the wine cup out of the bag and stood the vessel on the worktable.

Cassia began to feel she could fill a gallery with evidence of her father's attempts to do away with her. The wine goblet would not look very dramatic next to her sister's Greeting dress and a heart hunter's crossbow.

Rudhira frowned at the goblet. "This is one of the most worrisome artifacts that has ever come my way. I can make nothing of it."

"How dangerous is it?" Lio asked.

"It isn't. I cannot understand what they intended, which is what troubles me."

"Do you mean to say they did not try to poison me?" Cassia asked.

"Tell me what you make of this," Rudhira answered. "The traces left on the goblet indicate that the wine was treated with a powerful but benign alchemical infusion, one I have prepared countless times myself. I believe mages refer to it as Apprentice's Toddy, but healers in Orthros call it Teething Tonic."

"That makes no sense," Lio protested.

"Hm," Apollon said. "I have never heard of a Gift Collector confusing his poisons and tonics."

"Tonics are all we've allowed him to keep with him," Lio said, "but why would he try to give one to Cassia?"

"I'm hardly teething." Cassia put on a smile, showing her mundane mortal canines. "What does this infusion do?"

"It is a remedy for sucklings or young mages whose magic has begun to manifest," Rudhira replied. "The infusion helps with the discomfort and anxiety that sometimes accompany blooms of power. You might say it is a treatment for magical growing pains."

All three of the Hesperines looked at Cassia. She carefully avoided Apollon's gaze, but could not escape Rudhira and Lio's scrutiny. The magic in the room waxed so full she broke out in a sweat.

"Well?" she asked. "Have the gods suddenly knocked me on the head and made me a mage since the last time a Hesperine sensed my aura?"

Rudhira shook his head. "I can't get past your Sanctuary ward."

"All I sense is strength of Will," Apollon said.

"Thank you," Cassia said to his sketches.

His drawing of the kneeling girl was nowhere to be seen. Now he was working on a portrait of Zoe.

"Actually," said Lio, "the Sanctuary ward seems to enhance my awareness of you."

"That's because you're part of it," she replied.

He looked at her with a knowing light in his eyes. "You are entirely magical, just not in the way that requires Teething Tonic."

Cassia smiled, then shrugged. "I've always been glad I didn't have magic. If it was weak enough for the Orders to ignore, it would be useless, and I'd be just as I am, anyway. If it was powerful…" She squeezed Lio's hand. "…I would have been stashed in a temple, where I would never have met a Hesperine. All the magic I need comes from Orthros."

Lio wrapped his arm around her. "A lot of use my thelemancy is, when I mustn't raid Chrysanthos and Skleros's minds to find out what they meant by this."

"Ioustin?" Apollon asked.

The prince was silent, his expression grave.

Lio held Cassia closer. "Rudhira, is there something else?"

"I am loath to give you cause to fear what might not even be possible. However, I want us to be watchful and prepared for anything, now that we know essential displacement is not just theoretical, but magic that Gift Collectors actually practice."

"I think you had best explain," Apollon advised.

Rudhira nodded. "We still know very little about essential displacement, but Imperial theramancers like my mother Soteira have wisdom for countering necromancy that is beyond the comprehension of Tenebran mages. Based on her teachings, my experience in battle against Gift Collectors, and the information you brought us about Skleros, Cassia, I am concerned about a possible threat we have not yet considered."

"Please tell me," she replied. "Perhaps something I saw when I was spying on Skleros and Chrysanthos could help confirm your theory."

"Or rule it out, I hope," said the prince. "You are the only one of us who has actually witnessed an essential displacement. The secret working you saw Skleros perform transferred the bulk of Chrysanthos's power into a vessel he can draw on through a channel. I wonder if other configurations of the process are possible."

Cassia felt as if there were a fist in her chest. "I know there are other 'configurations.' It did not strike me at the time—it should have! Now I realize Skleros used that very word. He said, 'This configuration of essential displacement requires three men.'"

Cassia had not seen such a look on Lio's face since he had made the heart hunters who had threatened her fall at her feet.

Lio pointed at the goblet. "Rudhira, are you suggesting Skleros could use essential displacement to cause Cassia to need a tonic for growing magic?"

"We must remember it is only a theory," the prince answered, "but it did cross my mind that the Gift Collector could transfer magic into Cassia in some way. He might attempt to make her a vessel."

"By the Goddess," Lio ground out, "no necromancer will treat Cassia as if she is some artifact to be used."

"Of course he will not," Apollon said. "We will send him back to Hypnos long before that."

Cassia would never forget the person Skleros had used as Chrysanthos's vessel. How the man had writhed, forced full of excruciating power against his will, his fate sealed and unknown to his family. She would make sure she never forgot, because there was no one else to remember.

She wished she could forget what the mage of dreams had planned to do to her.

She tried to ignore the cold sweat that broke out on her skin. She had known the danger she placed herself in, when she had chosen to be a woman who used her voice, who acted. She was adept at managing her fears. She was brave about facing them.

The king thought she was still his spare token, worth only what he could get from this or that man in exchange for her. He had bartered her all her life, first to suitors, now to Mages of Hypnos.

The day would come when she owned the market.

Cassia's heart hammered in her chest, but the pulse in her glyph shard answered, strong and steady. "Can a Sanctuary ward stop an essential displacement?"

"Even with the Queens' wisdom," Rudhira replied, "I cannot answer that. The Gift Collectors' rituals are still too unknown to us."

"It doesn't matter," Lio said. "Skleros will never have the opportunity to try."

"I refuse to be afraid of him while I am surrounded by Hespera's protection." Even as Cassia said it, her skirts seemed to weigh heavily on her legs, ready to trap her if she tried to run.

Lio turned Cassia to face him. "You have nothing to fear. Just imagine what would be left of Skleros if he tried that on my watch, or on Mak and Lyros's."

"Or with my Charge on guard," said the prince.

"Or with me in the same city," Apollon said.

Until this moment, Cassia had never heard Lio's father sound dangerous. But those words were a threat.

Not to her. For her sake.

"We have the mages well in hand," Apollon said.

Rudhira gave a nod, but his hands clenched. "Keep a closer eye on them."

"We will," said Apollon, Lio, and Cassia at the same time.

42

nights until

WINTER SOLSTICE

BOSKO'S WELCOME

"**H**OW WAS PRINCE DEMETRIOS'S party?" asked the bundle of silk and bleating goats.

Lio struggled to keep a straight face at the sight of his sister waiting for them in the Ritual hall. She had wrapped herself and her pets in her mantle so thoroughly that she could barely see out. Another lump under the fabric suggested she had a satchel full of toys.

Knight stuck his nose under the mantle. Zoe giggled.

Cassia grinned, her aura bubbling over with amusement. "I enjoyed the tour of Prince Demetrios's residence very much, but I could hardly wait for veil hours. I've been looking forward to meeting your cousins all night. Now you can finally introduce me to Bosko and Thenie."

Their mother caressed the top of Zoe's silk-clad head. "You may stay at House Argyros as long as you like. Lio and Cassia will bring you home when you're ready."

Zoe looked up at her. "It depends on when Moonbeam and Aurora get sleepy."

"Of course." Mother smiled. "The goats mustn't miss their bedtime."

There was no telling how long it would be before the open skies and broad avenues between House Komnena and House Argyros ceased to terrify Zoe.

Lio gathered his sister close to him. "I'll step us."

"Thank you," Zoe mumbled.

Cassia slid under his other arm and Knight crowded close to her skirts. Mother gave a final wave, and Lio carried his precious cargo to their destination, Uncle Argyros's library.

Uncle Argyros stood by the large, round table, which was laden with his full coffee service in all its elaborate elegance. But he did not wear formal silks, rather his silver veil hours robe. He could not have made a more eloquent statement that this was a family gathering. His dark eyes were solemn, but at the sight of Zoe and Cassia, he seemed less world-weary.

Lio was only grateful the distance between him and his uncle was not affecting Cassia's welcome into the family.

"Welcome to our home, Cassia." Uncle Argyros beckoned them nearer. "I'm so glad you could join us tonight. My Grace and our daughter regret they could not be here with us for your first visit. They patrol the ward this night."

The only sign of Aunt Lyta was her slim auburn Grace braid woven into Uncle Argyros's pale, floor-length braid. Javed sat with Thenie on one of the Imperial rugs amid a pile of colorful building blocks. Kadi's blond braid in his thick, curly dark hair was probably the closest he had come to his Grace tonight, as well, but his aura glowed with happiness as he extricated a drooly block from their tiny daughter's mouth. She clung to her father's hand with both of her small chubby ones, her fingers pale against his smooth brown skin.

"I hope you know you have our deepest gratitude," Javed said to Cassia, "although Kadi and I are thanking you one at a time, I'm afraid."

"And caring for the children one at a time, too." Lio winced inwardly. "The Summit places heavy demands on everyone, but especially new parents."

"Nonsense," Javed replied. "Kadi hasn't had this much fun in years. Mak and Lyros aren't the only ones giddy with delight to come within range of mages."

"Parenting two sucklings at once is extraordinarily ambitious at the best of times," Lio said. "But no one is surprised, Javed. We all know the strength and bravery you and Kadi possess."

Javed smiled. "We are only grateful it is within our power to keep Bosko and Thenie together, as a brother and sister should be, and close to Zoe."

"Having them as cousins now is even better than when we were just best friends." Zoe finished unwrapping herself, her goats, and their cargo and went to Thenie's side. "Cassia, this is my youngest cousin, Athena Argyra."

Cassia stood back, an arm around Knight. When Thenie showed no sign that the large dog upset her, Lio exchanged a relieved glance with Cassia. They had not been wrong in their assurances to everyone that Thenie and Bosko would be as safe around Knight as Zoe was.

Zoe sat down with their little cousin. "Thenie, this is the Brave Gardener!"

Thenie made a humming, grunting noise to herself and pounded a block on the floor.

"She understands," Zoe assured Cassia. "She just has her own way of showing it."

"You are right, Zoe." Uncle Argyros looked upon Thenie with a tender expression Lio had not seen on his uncle's face in a long time. "You do well to speak with Thenie as you do with everyone else. She learns more and more all the time from what we talk about with her."

"You had a hard start, didn't you, Thenie?" Zoe's brow furrowed. "She got the fever worse than any of us."

Javed caressed his daughter's dusty brown curls. "The Gift and my magic have healed her brain, but she lost a great deal of ability and understanding. She has much to re-learn. But you are safe and well now, my little one, and you have plenty of time."

Cassia knelt down before Thenie, her heart aching for every Hesperine in the room to feel. "Hello, Thenie. What a nice, safe place you have come to with your mama and papa."

Thenie didn't look at Cassia, but she made an expressive string of sounds that clearly meant something important, although the rest of them had not the knowledge of her private language.

Cassia smiled. "It's wonderful to meet you too."

"Where's Bosko?" Zoe looked around her, frowning.

Uncle Argyros cleared his throat. "He will be along in a moment. Mak is bringing him."

Lio shot his uncle a startled glance. Mak was supposed to be on patrol at the guest houses, and had been not half an hour past.

The calm over Javed's aura was certainly a veil. "Not to worry. They'll be home any time now."

Zoe's frown deepened. "He should be here for you to give Cassia your welcome gift."

"Thenie and I will represent the family. Is that all right with you, Cassia?"

Cassia gave Zoe a reassuring smile. "Of course."

Javed reached for a canvas case that sat neatly to the side of Thenie's toys. He set it in front of him, gesturing to Cassia. She sat down on the rug with him and Thenie, and Knight settled among the sucklings as if it were the most natural place in the world for him to be. Lio joined them, and Zoe scooted close to him, letting him slide an arm around her.

Javed opened the case. "Here is a complete set of alchemical supplies to compliment your gardening. You have here an alembic, scales, vials, and various other tools so you can make extracts and tinctures from your plants. These are the best quality and most accurate, exactly what we use in the Healing Sanctuary to blend remedies."

Cassia's aura shone. "I've never had anything like these. I can't thank you enough."

Javed smiled. "After coffee, we can talk about how to use the more specialized tools."

"Perhaps while we wait for Bosko," said Uncle Argyros, "Cassia and Lio could join me on the terrace for a moment."

The longer Bosko was unaccounted for, the higher Zoe's tide of anxiety mounted. Terrors from the time when they had been orphans were never far away, even here in the safety of House Argyros.

Lio put a hand on her shoulder and pointed to the floor-to-ceiling windows of the library, through which the breadth of the terrace was visible. "We'll be right outside."

"Here, Zoe," Javed soothed. "I think Thenie would love for you to hold her."

Zoe looked away from the open terrace and gathered their little cousin onto her lap, scooting closer to Javed. "All right."

Lio bent low to kiss his sister's forehead before helping Cassia up. Knight trailed them out of the library.

As soon as they were outside, Uncle Argyros closed the door and a veil spell behind them. "Bosko's latest adventure has, unfortunately, coincided with Cassia's visit. He deemed it exciting to make a clandestine excursion to the docks to see Mak and Lyros on patrol firsthand."

"Goddess have Mercy." Lio rubbed his face. "Kadi must be at her wit's end."

"Javed and I are keeping her and Lyta informed every moment," Uncle Argyros assured him.

"Is Bosko all right?" Cassia asked urgently. "The mages—"

Uncle Argyros held up a hand. "I would not allow my grandson within sight of them. I knew the moment he set foot outside the residence."

"But I can understand why you didn't simply stop him," Lio said.

His uncle nodded. "Suffice it to say, had I intercepted him in any obvious way, it would have been extremely unwelcome to him and likely to exacerbate our ongoing confrontations. I shadowed him, keeping him concealed from any mage's notice in the tightest of veils, until Mak and Lyros had the opportunity to safely blockade him. Lyros will hold down their patrol while Mak encourages Bosko to return home."

"It sounds like Bosko has some catching up to do, as well," Cassia said ruefully.

Uncle Argyros sighed. "The ward stops everything at the border except what we carry through it with us."

"As the eldest of the Eriphite children," Lio explained to Cassia, "Bosko has the clearest memories of their elders and the best understanding of what they all suffered. He's having an even harder time than Zoe. She gets frightened, but he gets angry."

"He is fortunate to have such a loving and patient family," Cassia said. "Nowhere else would he be treated with such forbearance. You are not harsh with him, in spite of his misbehavior."

Uncle Argyros watched the path that led through the orchard to the terrace. "A heavy hand is the last thing he needs."

Cassia studied Uncle Argyros while he wasn't looking. "I know how much it must help him that his grandfather is a mind mage who understands these things."

"I do understand." Now Uncle Argyros looked at Cassia. "Alas, a similar revelation has yet to occur to Bosko. He sees me as the living embodiment of law and order."

Mak came into view on the path with Bosko walking at his side. Willingly, it seemed, except for the petulant expression on his face. Uncle Argyros breathed a sigh of relief that Lio could feel all the way through the Union.

As soon as Bosko and Mak reached the steps, the suckling ducked his head, avoiding Uncle Argyros's gaze. The boy made to dash inside the house.

Mak halted him with a hand on his shoulder. "Hold your horses. We agreed on this, right? We're going to say hello to Cassia."

Bosko halted and turned in Cassia's direction, but did not lift his gaze. He mumbled, "Welcome to our home. We're happy to have you as our guest."

"Bosko," Mak said gently. "Wasn't there something else you wanted to tell Cassia?"

Bosko's aura hardened with stubbornness, but he forced the words out, a testament to Mak's rapport with him. "Thank you for what you did for me and the other children."

"I'm so happy you're all safe." Cassia peered under the mop of curls hanging in Bosko's eyes. "You know, if you wanted to visit the guest houses, you might have asked Mak and Lyros if they could bring you to see me. I've been looking forward to meeting you."

Lio felt a flicker of surprise in Bosko. The boy shifted on his feet. He glanced at Knight, a spark of interest in his aura. But then he made his escape.

Mak let him go. The door slammed behind Bosko.

Uncle Argyros looked to the heavens. "Cassia, allow me to introduce my grandson, Boskos Argyros."

"I'm sorry," she said. "I shall be the first to admit I am an utter novice with children. Especially boys. I think my brother, Caelum, was about Bosko's age the first time he deigned to speak to me."

"It's not you." Lio put an arm around her.

"Certainly not." Uncle Argyros turned to Mak. "Thank you."

"Happy to help, Father." Mak huffed a laugh. "Lyros and I will take him for a round in the gymnasium tomorrow night, when we get a break from patrol. That will calm the seas."

A wave of gratitude passed from Uncle Argyros to Mak. For all the conflict Bosko caused in the family, Lio was so glad to see his uncle and his cousin drawing closer over the boy. This was just what Mak and his father needed to help even out their own rather volatile relationship. For once, Mak was not the member of the family who had the greatest differences with Uncle Argyros. It was wonderful that Mak hadn't needed Lio to mediate between him and his father lately.

Lio felt an unfamiliar pang of confusion and regret. He would be no use for that purpose right now, in any case, when he and Uncle Argyros were hardly speaking at all. Just like he was no use with Bosko, and not at House Argyros enough to enjoy the new harmony between his mentor and his Trial brother.

Uncle Argyros clapped Mak on the shoulder. "Now you'd best get back to Lyros."

"Right," Mak said. "I can't let him have all the fun without me. Sorry I can't stay to visit longer, Cassia."

"I'm sure we'll see each other again soon," she said.

"Just you wait. The last night of the royal celebration will be a riot." Mak gave a wave and disappeared.

"I hope he doesn't mean that literally," Lio muttered. What exactly did Xandra have in mind for the celebration in her residence?

Uncle Argyros turned to Cassia. "I am sorry. As you can imagine, this is not the welcome we had in mind for you."

"There is no need to apologize, I assure you. I'm honored to be made privy to your family events."

"Let us turn our attention to the more pleasant features of domesticity. Given your expertise in horticulture, I thought you might enjoy a tour of my orchard. Then we can retire to the library for a tasting of each of my home-brewed coffee varieties."

"I would love that, thank you." Cassia looked up at Lio. "I know you will need to take some time to put Zoe at ease, after Bosko's absence gave her such a scare. Why don't you stay in the library with her while I get to see the orchard?"

Lio frowned at her and noticed his uncle doing the same. "Are you sure?"

"Of course. That is, if your uncle can spare you from our tour."

Uncle Argyros hesitated. "Well, there is nothing new there for Lio to see. Very well. We shall take a walk, Cassia."

"As you say," Lio acquiesced.

But he could only feel apprehension. Cassia had volunteered to be abandoned with the most intimidating mind mage in the known world. And Lio's absence did not seem unwelcome to his uncle.

BARE BRANCHES

ARGYROS MADE A VERY quiet tour guide. He and Cassia strolled in silence between orderly rows of trees that obscured the terrace from view. Even Knight seemed affected by the dignity of Argyros's presence and, thankfully, did not try to mark any of the elder firstblood's trees.

"Starflake," Lio's uncle said at last, gesturing to the trees under which they now walked. "It is evergreen and bears all winter long. When perfectly ripe, the fruit is sweet beyond imagining, with an enlivening, tart aftertaste."

"How lovely, that you have tree varieties here that provide fruit in Hesperines' optimal season. They are beautiful." Cassia could easily imagine the iridescent fruits drifting down from the stars like a gentle Orthros snow to alight on the white limbs and leaves of their trees.

The starlight caught in a pair of orange eyes and glowed. For the first time, Cassia noticed the large snowy owl perched in one of the starflake trees. He sat so still. Then with an important rustle of his feathers, he spread his great wings and swooped along the orchard row.

When he swept past her face, she let out a little gasp. The tip of his wing brushed her forehead, tracing an arc across her brow. She blinked and saw him perch on Argyros's arm.

Lio's uncle looked into the bird's eyes with a thoughtful expression. "Kathegetes puts on a rare display for you. My familiar seldom bestirs himself so. He is very set in his ways."

Cassia put a hand on Knight, but the owl did not deign to give her hound any notice. "His attention is an honor. I am sure such a majestic fellow has many important things to occupy him."

"He has been teaching me important lessons these many years." Argyros stroked the bird's chest.

Kathegetes returned Argyros's gaze with a piercing orange stare, then took off again with a hoot. Argyros and Cassia walked on, following the path the owl had taken.

Argyros spoke again after a moment. "I have a basket of starflakes harvested at their peak and a selection of coffees for you, as my welcome gift."

"What a lovely gift. Thank you." She smiled ruefully. "I shall keep them in Lio's residence, of course, so my handmaiden does not become suspicious."

"Advise Lio to make plenty of room. I suspect you will soon find that my gift is only one among a vast collection you will receive here."

"Everyone has been so generous to me. I am grateful. Ah, I recognize these. Pomegranate."

"They are suited to the dry climate of Orthros, and they have a symbiotic relationship with another Hesperine favorite you see in the next row, here. These are blood currants."

As they continued through his groves, Cassia found Argyros's botanical commentary scholarly but understandable. She could see why Lio's teacher inspired his admiration. She felt disappointed when they came to the end of the last row.

Argyros halted and turned to face Cassia. He put his hands behind his back.

Now Cassia knew where Lio had learned the gesture, which he always made when he was uncertain. How very telling.

"Thank you for showing me your trees," Cassia said. "It has been a real pleasure. Your orchard is wonderful."

"Alas, it is utterly lacking."

"How can you say that? You have so many different trees here, and all so healthy."

"Do you notice what is missing?"

"I cannot think what could possibly add to such a collection."

He scowled. "Coffee."

"Oh! So coffee comes from a tree."

"From *the* tree. The tree of life for my craft."

"You have such a fine orchard here, I could easily believe your craft is gardening."

She had meant it as a compliment, but he was quite stone-faced as he corrected her. "These trees you see before you are but a stepping stone toward the greatest goal of my craft: to grow coffee in Orthros. This orchard is merely an experiment. Allow me to show you the results."

She followed him back in the direction of the house. Above the tree-tops rose its peaked roofs and square towers. Cassia had seen in her dictionary that Argyros's name meant silver, and she thought his home befitted its namesake. Its granite walls, pillars, and buttresses ranged from dove gray to the gray-black of thunderheads, while its vibrant windows gleamed into the night like flashes of insight. How many of them had Lio made for his uncle's family?

Cassia hoped she could gain more insight from Argyros tonight, and his orchard was a pleasant avenue into more difficult subjects. "I have so much to learn about Imperial flora. How interesting to discover coffee comes from trees. Do you import it, as you do with spices like cassia?"

Lio's uncle nodded. "The Empire cultivates the trees and harvests their berries, which we process to yield beans. I can roast the beans to my satisfaction, blend different varieties in infinite ways, brew them to perfection, and finally, provide my fellow Hesperines with a true coffee experience through how I serve the beverage. But I am ultimately at the mercy of our Imperial suppliers. I cannot grow my own coffee."

"I can imagine how frustrating that is."

Clearly Argyros and Lio both devoted the utmost concentration and effort to anything that captured the interest of their extraordinary minds. No wonder they got along so well. Most of the time.

Argyros shot a disgusted glance at the modest greenhouse that neighbored his orchard. "The situation is unacceptable. After sixteen hundred years, we have yet to overcome this limitation."

Cassia suppressed a wistful sigh as they passed his greenhouse by. She proceeded cautiously, wary of insulting the elder firstblood's pride. "You have many skilled gardeners here, such as Princess Konstantina. I take it that these notable Hesperines have had no more success than you at growing coffee."

"Alas, none of our best efforts have been enough. I have consulted with every expert among our people. They have been generous with advice based on their centuries of experience and supportive in their provision of research materials. I have pored over their greatest works. I have taken countless journeys throughout the Empire to consult with families who have grown coffee for generations. I even earned a degree in agriculture at the Imperial university with a specialization in coffee."

"A whole degree in coffee? Your studies must have been fascinating."

"I have given the problem of coffee trees as much investigation as I have given magic itself. But even I have failed. Behold."

He opened another pair of glass doors and led her back into the library. The smells of paper, ink, and coffee wrapped around her again. The family's voices drifted between the shelves from somewhere farther in the room. Argyros showed her to a stately desk that dominated a corner where two rows of windows met. Their stone tracery held panes of clear glass that provided a view of both the terrace and the orchard.

Argyros rounded the desk and put both hands on the object that occupied it. He slid it across to Cassia.

"My most successful attempt at growing a coffee tree," he announced.

It was a wretched, shriveled remnant of what might once have been a sapling. Cassia stared in dismay at the pathetic creature. It had never grown taller than her forearm, to be sure. What leaves it might once have had were long gone. But the soil in its pot was moist. It was clear its doting papa continued to water it each and every day.

"I keep this on my desk," said Argyros, "to maintain my resolve. There is no hope of saving it. But the next one may yet be a success."

"That is true dedication. I'm sorry it has gone unrewarded for so long."

"I shall not give up hope. That, I must admit, is my ulterior motive for showing you my trees tonight. Would you be so kind as to lend me your expertise, Cassia? I need a fresh pair of eyes. All I ask is that you have a look at this and tell me what you see."

"I'm honored," she assured him, even as her tension mounted. He wanted her help with a plant she hadn't known existed? He thought she could be of assistance, when even the experts in the tree's native land had not been able to help him?

This was a disaster. Her first encounter with Lio's uncle, her first chance to make a good impression on him. He had done her the compliment of asking her a favor, and all she could do was fail.

"I will do my very best." She drew out her spade. "May I?"

"Of course." He held out his hands toward the coffee plant in invitation.

Cassia bent near to sniff the soil. Fragrant and rich. She carefully tilted the pot and peered under it. Good drainage into the dish in which it sat. Starting there at the bottom, she examined the tree all the way to its topmost spindly twigs, looking for all the signs that would normally set off a gardener's warning bells. Finally she chose a branch in a place that wasn't very visible and scratched through the bark to check the color of the tree's pith. Dry and colorless.

Everything looked perfect, except for the fact that the tree was dead.

"I have seldom seen a plant better cared for," she reassured Argyros. "It seems to me you have done everything it could possibly need. It is quite a mystery, isn't it?"

"One that has plagued me for centuries." He pushed the pot closer still. "Of course I would not allow myself to hope for immediate results. Such a vexing problem can only be solved after careful observation, to be sure. I know you will need time to examine the question from all angles and consider various experiences you have had as a gardener that may be relevant to the present dilemma. Feel free to take the tree back to Lio's residence with you, so you will have the opportunity for closer study."

Cassia swallowed. "I shall be the most careful of stewards. I'll put it in the window with the rose seedlings I started last night."

"I entrust the tree to you."

Cassia looked up from the poor thing to study its nurturer. "You have already been so generous tonight with your lovely gifts of coffee and starflakes. Perhaps it ill behooves me to ask for advice in return."

"Not at all. I would be happy to help in any way I can."

His face did not change, but his tone had. His despair over his trees was nowhere to be heard in his voice.

Cassia might have chosen the right strategy. "Truth be told, I hardly know where to start. Not long ago, I would never have imagined I would have the opportunity to ask you for your insight. How do I begin to consult your expertise, when you have sixteen hundred years of it? How do I, one player in this inglorious age of Tenebran history, start to learn from someone who influenced our greatest king?"

"Ah. A lesson in politics is what you seek." He put his hands behind his back again.

"Lio is fortunate to have benefited from your wisdom these many years." After losing Solia, Cassia had been without any teachers except her own experience. But she wanted to ask Argyros about his past, not bemoan her own. "Lio says you attended the very first Equinox Summit nearly sixteen hundred years ago. You assisted the Queens in negotiating the terms of the original Equinox Oath."

"Yes, I lent my voice to the Annassa's council with King Lucian and Queen Hedera."

"You mean the Mage King and the Changing Queen?"

"Indeed."

"Astonishing. I did not know his name. And...I was not certain of hers. Did she perhaps have another one? I think her own people must not have called her by a Tenebran name."

Argyros lifted his brows. "Are you a student of language history? Indeed, her name in her own tongue was Ebah."

A little chill went over Cassia's skin at the word, as if Argyros had just invoked the very magic Cassia had awoken at Solorum with that name, Ebah. "The old garden names survive in remote parts of Tenebra. I only know it because Ebah is another name for ivy. I don't think most Tenebrans ever think about the Mage King and Changing Queen's names, although they are our best-remembered monarchs. They are so lost in legend, it is as if they are not people anymore."

"They lived up to how history now remembers them."

"If they were so good and just, why did they expel Hesperines from Tenebra instead of defending you against the cults of Anthros and Hypnos?"

"King Lucian and Queen Hedera had no quarrel with our people, in fact, and they were actively resisting the Cordian cults' growing influence. However, the new monarchs had just succeeded in uniting the domains of the Tenebrae for the first time."

"Their position over the free lords would have been tenuous," Cassia said.

"Yes," Argyros replied. "There were still many Tenebrans who considered us their own, but just as many who regarded us with fear. King Lucian and Queen Hedera could not risk challenges to their authority from within or without. The new self-appointed Orders already sought a way to remove the strong royals who had suddenly foiled their plans."

"They must have thought they could make easy prey of the Tenebrae. How wrong they were."

"With the Mage King and the Changing Queen on the throne, the Cordian mages could not bring the Tenebrae under their power. King Lucian was also a living defiance of their campaign to prevent men of the sword from wielding magic. However, as powerful as King Lucian and Queen Hedera were, they knew a direct confrontation with the war mages and necromancers would have resulted in catastrophic loss of life and damage to their kingdom."

"The Tenebrae could never have withstood that, could they? Not when they were just beginning to recover from the Last War and generations of infighting."

Argyros nodded. "If the king and queen had taken our side, they would have risked being branded as heretics themselves and undermining all they had worked so hard to build."

"A good ruler would face the same decision today."

"They had to choose to keep their ship afloat or sink with Hespera's. They made the right decision to let us sail to a safer harbor."

"You still agree with the terms of the first Summit?"

"I do. Our Queens were highly satisfied with the outcome. King Lucian and Queen Hedera could have thrown us to the wolves and let the Mage Orders hunt us down. But they afforded us this much protection—they allowed us to leave in peace and go in search of a new homeland. Those who sympathized with our plight lauded their rulers' mercy, and those who hated us saw King Lucian as the warlord who was brave enough to banish us. A brilliant move that satisfied nearly everyone. We retreated over the northern mountains and built Orthros in this land of ice and snow, where mortals feared to tread even before our magic touched it."

"But you were allowed to return under the terms of the Oath."

"That too was a bold risk on King Lucian and Queen Hedera's part, but one that served them well for some time. They established us as those who cleansed the problems their fledgling government was incapable of addressing. More children than parents could feed. More casualties than warriors could bury. More criminals than the new magistrates could bring to justice.

"Our sacred practices were protected, and the Tenebrae's undesirables disappeared. The consequence, however, was that the people of the Tenebrae came to see us as vultures. Our function as adopters of the outcasts, corpse-cleaners, and avengers became a specter in mortal minds. Now we loom large in their imaginations as the creatures that will claim them if they do not walk the path of obedience to gods and king."

"I hold out hope Tenebrans will come to see you as you are."

"On that subject," Argyros said abruptly, "you and Lio have no need of my expertise. I can teach you nothing but ancient history. Come, we had best rejoin the others. The sucklings will soon tire."

So much for Cassia's attempts to divine Argyros's thoughts on either Summit politics or family politics.

With Argyros's tree cradled in her arms, Cassia rejoined Lio, no closer to discovering the reason for the rift between him and his uncle, much less mending it. Whatever she and Lio must face in the course of the Summit, it seemed they were on their own.

37

nights until

WINTER SOLSTICE

A GAME OF PRINCE AND DIPLOMAT

WHEN THE FINAL NIGHT of the royal celebration arrived, Cassia dressed in red and black with great anticipation. Let ladybug colors be her private jest with the Eighth Princess. Little did Chrysanthos know he had an appointment with her, and it promised to be a fitting finale for the gauntlet he had run this week.

In the residences of Princess Gregoria, Prince Kleos, Princess Helene, and Prince Iulios, Cassia had done everything in her power to covertly support the Hesperine royals. She had kept the translations flowing with invitations to Lio and encouragements to Eudias. She had murmured in the right ears among the embassy, raising the right innocent questions, heartfelt sympathies, and expressions of wonderment.

If the other mortals felt even a hint of the same longing and awe as she did in Orthros, they must surely look upon Lio's people with new eyes. There was no resisting the magic of the Hesperines' kindness. This Cassia saw in the young men's eager gazes and the stoic warriors' freer words, and especially the Cordian mages' faces, which hardened ever more as it became a greater and greater effort to deny the truth before their eyes.

Tonight Lio and his Trial brothers escorted the embassy through the back gateway of House Annassa, past an apiary and a greenhouse. Cassia peered inside, eager for a glimpse of the Eighth Princess's mulberry trees, and caught sight of the orchard housed within the glass.

The residence was a circular wing that ringed a courtyard. The central double doors swung open in welcome, and everyone crossed an entry hall into a long, low-ceilinged room with inviting plush carpets in deep, bold colors. The doors eased shut, closing in the warmth.

"Ambassador," Cassia said, "I do not believe my eyes. That is a fireplace."

"Indeed it is, Lady Cassia. Welcome to the Eighth Princess's hearth room."

The central feature of the chamber was a tiled hearth, where an actual wood fire burned. There was another fireplace at each end of the room, and their flames beckoned from between silk hangings that divided the space into intimate sections.

To the last man, woman, and mage, the embassy drew near the central hearth fire like moths to their beloved, proverbial flame.

The princess waited for them by the hearth in black-and-white formal silks. She stood arm in arm with a tall, well-built man who appeared to hail from the Empire. As the Tenebrans gathered around, she gave them her impish smile and greeted them in Vulgus. "Welcome to my residence, everyone. Please have a seat wherever you like and make yourselves comfortable. Put up your tired feet and warm your chilly fingers."

The Tenebrans stood about awkwardly. All except for the Semna, who marched nearer the hearth, leaning on her walking stick.

The princess reached out to help. "Here, Semna, please sit on the hearth tiles, where the warmth is best."

The Semna accepted the invitation. "Thank you, Princess. Geomagi are all well and good, but there's nothing like a real fire to warm old bones."

The ice broke, and the other Tenebrans began to drift out of their defensive knot. The princess's Hesperine guests, who all appeared to be about her and Lio's age, showed the mortals to comfortable chairs or even lured them to have a seat on silk floor cushions.

Where was Chrysanthos? Trying to break away from one of the princess's friends, it seemed, without success. The curly-haired, blond female Hesperine ensnared him in conversation. One by one, the princess's peers picked off Cassia's escort. A female with long, straight dark hair put Eudias at ease. Lyros drew Benedict and Severin into a discussion of fighting techniques while Mak showed Callen a place Perita could sit down. Even the indefatigable Semna dozed at the hearth, and her attendants breathed sighs of relief.

At the edges of the room lounged a dozen other Hesperines, just as well-dressed, but Cassia recognized them from the clandestine Charge patrols she sometimes saw at the guest houses when sneaking out with Lio. A couple of the disguised Hesperines errant attached themselves to Skleros every time the Gift Collector moved. It appeared they were his intimate companions for the evening, compliments of the First Prince. Finally Skleros parked himself at the hearth at the far end of the room and took the liberty of using the princess's fire to light a smoke. He leaned on the mantle, puffing and scowling.

Before long, Lio and Cassia stood before the princess, free of any retinue or enemy. Knight wagged his tail, the princess smiled at him, and Cassia had to tell him to heel three times while trying not to chuckle.

A subtle, superfluous motion of Lio's hands caught Cassia's eye. Had he just stopped himself from putting his hands behind his back?

Lio cleared his throat. "Eighth Princess, allow me to introduce Lady Cassia."

The princess winked at Cassia. "I've heard so much about you, I feel as if I know you already!"

Cassia smiled back. "The feeling is entirely mutual, I assure you, Eighth Princess."

"Yes," said Lio. "I understand you've already learned a great deal about Princess Alexandra this week."

Realization stung Cassia, and her throat closed. The princess's name was Alexandra. Ale*xandra.*

Lio *was* trying not to put his hands behind his back.

The princess was the famous Xandra, who had for so many years been the sole focus of his affections. The one he had believed he would avow.

Cassia tried not to look at the rug under her feet, but she must still stand on it. *I always went to her at her family's House,* Lio had said. *As intimate as we were... Xandra and I explored...*

Cassia's hospitality to Lio in her own hearth room had not been such an exceptional experience for him after all. What was a threadbare Tenebran rug compared to silk carpets and cushions?

Cassia's voice came out too high, too pleasant. "Can you imagine, the one thing I have not heard about you, Princess Alexandra, is your name."

Xandra gave her a rueful look. "Well, I would rather you know of my character. First impressions are very important," she reminded Cassia.

Lio was looking back and forth between them, and the panic in his eyes told Cassia this was not going as he had planned. At all.

When they had spoken of her conversation with the princess, he had thought Cassia knew everything. He hadn't realized he needed to warn her.

Warn her of what, precisely? Cassia insisted of herself. What more could they do to make her feel welcome? It was surely only she who struggled with petty feelings. They were the perfect hosts. They were perfect.

Xandra cleared her throat indicatively. "This is my guest from the Empire, Harkhuf Addaya Khemkare..." She recited a dizzying list of lineage and titles, resting a hand on her companion's arm in a way that made it very clear precisely how she was entertaining her guest.

He smiled, and the frosty maidens of Chera probably melted behind their veils at the sight. This Imperial challenger would usurp Flavian and Chrysanthos's devotees, were they here to glimpse his handsome face. He might be mortal, but his dark ochre skin was smooth and devoid of scars, and his teeth were as clean as a Hesperine's. His gold jewelry and embroidered tunic looked to be worth more than a free lord's entire treasury.

"Please excuse my Vulgus," he said in perfect Vulgus. "As the Divine Tongue is the predominant language here in Orthros, it has occupied the greater part of my studies."

Xandra beamed. "How fortunate that both were included in your education for office in the Imperial administration."

"Yes, for I rejoice at this opportunity to meet Tenebrans for the first time. Please call me Harkhuf, as my friends here in Orthros do. Is not the respectful egalitarianism of our Hesperine hosts a breath of fresh air after life at court?"

"I'm so glad you could be here tonight." The princess caressed his arm again. "Harkhuf had to receive special permission from his cousin, the Empress, to meet Tenebrans despite her strict laws against allowing your people any contact with hers."

"We are...outlawed in the Empire?" Cassia stumbled onward. Politics. She must seize onto politics, the program of the evening that would see her safely through this painful course.

"No visitors from Tenebra or Cordium are allowed to set foot on our shores," Harkhuf confirmed, "and Imperial guests to Orthros must not associate with the Tenebran embassy without express permission. I regret to say the brief contact between our peoples in the distant past had long-lasting consequences."

Lio started talking politics as well. "It was the Order of Anthros's only expedition that reached the Empire. Their conduct was such that they destroyed both Cordium and Tenebra's chances of a relationship with the Empire."

"Should Tenebran or Cordian ships be sighted in Imperial waters again," Harkhuf said, "they are to be warned to turn back. They only receive one warning."

So Harkhuf was the princess's share, but possibly also the Empress's eyes upon Orthros's proceedings with the Tenebrans. Cassia met his gaze. "I deeply regret that anyone from my part of the world behaved so dishonorably in the Empress's lands. I hope tonight will provide us with an opportunity to make amends."

"Speaking of misbehaving mages..." Lio said through his teeth.

Xandra's blond friend approached with Chrysanthos and presented him in Divine, then Vulgus, then another language that made Harkhuf share a conspiratorial glance with her.

"Eighth Princess," Chrysanthos greeted her. He gazed into her hearth, and firelight gleamed in his eyes. "What a singular party."

"Singular," the princess enthused. "I consider that a great compliment indeed."

"You are certainly broadening my view of Hesperines, Princess Alexandra."

"Well, that's what this Summit is all about, isn't it? But also about finding common ground." Xandra gestured to her blond friend. "Lady Cassia, meet my Trial sister, Eudokia Hypatia, who writes amazing treatises and serves as a Sophia, a teacher for young Hesperines."

Lio's Trial sister Kia was Hypatia's daughter? Cassia gave up hope of finding an ally there. "Your reputation as a mathematician and scholar precedes you."

"It is a real pleasure, Lady Cassia." Eudokia tossed her turquoise silk wrap over her shoulder in a gesture Cassia had seen Zoe imitate with her own beloved mantle.

Chrysanthos smirked. "Eudokia *Hypatia*. That explains a great deal, Sophia."

She gave him a glittering, fanged smile worthy of her mother. "It is our calling as scholars to explain the world to mankind and cure his ignorance."

"Come," said the princess, "let us join my other Trial sister for some music."

She drew them to a nearby semicircle of chairs and cushions. In the center, the black-haired Hesperine sat with silk panels behind her that formed a kind of stage. Her face was as lovely as a pale, golden harvest moon, and her robes shimmered with shades of deep blue and ocean teal. She was armed with a lute, and at the ready beside her was a stringed instrument Cassia had never seen before.

Eudias, sitting in the chair across from the Hesperine musician, leaned forward to study the unfamiliar instrument's long neck, compact body, and three strings.

The musician gave Eudias a smile that appeared gentle and kind. "That is a shamisen, a tradition of my mortal ancestors, who hailed from west of the Empire."

Eudias avoided her gaze. "Fascinating."

"This is Menodora Kithara," the princess introduced her, "from one of our founding bloodlines. Her family teaches all the Muses of Orthros—our musicians, poets, actors, and dancers. She is the most talented composer of our generation and a crafter of fine instruments."

Menodora smiled. "Your opinion is hardly objective, my friend. There are many gifted young Muses in Orthros."

"My *favorite* composer, then," Xandra insisted, "and the only Hesperine expert on the music of the Archipelagos."

"Those distinctions, I will not deny," said Menodora.

Both of Lio's Trial sisters were clearly in Xandra's faction. The princess sat near Menodora with Harkhuf and Eudokia on either side of her.

Chrysanthos did not take a seat, only stood on the other side of the circle from Eudokia.

Lio hovered at Cassia's side. "What will you play for us tonight, Nodora?"

"I am taking requests." She turned her smile upon Cassia. "A Tenebran court dance, perhaps?"

Cassia considered the possible double meanings in the offer. Was the Hesperine trying to emphasize that Cassia was a foreigner? Did Menodora wish to indicate by her command of Tenebran court dances that her princess was wise to Cassia's strategies?

"Thank you," Cassia replied, "but I am most curious to hear Hesperine music and broaden my education."

"I can't wait for your visit to House Kitharos later in the Summit. It will be a banquet for the ears. I will play some of our favorites to give you a foretaste." Menodora ran a finger over the strings of her lute, sounding a cascade of gentle notes. She commenced a pleasing tune that promised to lull the guests into ease.

Lio said under the notes of the song, "I regret a missed opportunity for dancing."

"This is hardly the place for it," Cassia muttered.

Lio tucked his hands behind his back with a deliberate air. Had he just transformed his once-nervous gesture into a silent apology?

Cassia winced inwardly. "But thank you for your kind invitation, Ambassador."

The music, like the fire, seemed to dull the sharp edges of the embassy's tension. Even Knight's ears drooped. But Cassia felt like she was walking on embers. Her enemies were not letting their guard down, either. Chrysanthos, Tychon, and Skleros appeared to expect an ambush from behind the silks at any moment.

Even so, the particular trap Xandra had waiting for the Dexion was sure to come as a surprise to him. If Cassia did her part to help spring it, would she find it was a trap for her, too?

The princess rose and strolled to a nearby table. She gestured at the game board there. "Honored Master, I know an area in which you are sure to be most qualified. Will you join me in a diversion beloved from Selas to Solorum to Corona? I have here a Prince and Diplomat set. You will easily recognize this, for it is our adaptation of what is called Kings and Mages in your part of the world. Surely a mage of your caliber is a great enthusiast for the game."

"Of course." Chrysanthos eyed the board of gleaming wood and its carved playing pieces. "I must wonder what the result would be, if I brought my rules to your table, Eighth Princess."

"But you cannot bring your rules, Honored Master. You must play by mine, even if you do not know them. Isn't that the tradition in your land, as well? No one is taught the rules of the game the first time they play."

"Indeed, we must all watch others and learn by observation until we no longer lose upon every attempt."

"I am sure it has been many years since you were a student at this board. Your considerable skill with your own rules will surely make you a quick study of mine."

"Are our two sets of rules so very different as one might believe?"

"Well, I can tell you that Hesperines always play fair."

"Is there such a thing as playing fair at this game, Eighth Princess?"

"If you're good at it, you don't need to break the rules. You make them work for you. Better still, you make improved rules."

"Is that what your people have done? Make new rules to suit you?"

"Come find out."

"It will be my pleasure to analyze your gameplay, Eighth Princess." He extended a hand toward the table for her to go first.

The princess took a seat at the table, and Chrysanthos sat across from her. With Harkhuf and Eudokia, Cassia and Lio drew near to watch. The embassy gathered round, and Skleros lurked on the edges of the crowd with the Prince's Charge on his tail. Mak and Lyros posted themselves behind the princess, while Menodora began a new song on her lute, filling the air with an inviting melody.

Xandra put her chin on her hand, studying the board. "I learned this game from its namesake prince."

"And which of your brothers is that?" the Dexion asked.

"The one you didn't meet this week. If you've been keeping count, you will know who that is already."

"I did wonder at the absence of the First Prince. So your tutor in this game was one of the Blood Errant."

The princess smiled. "Now is your chance to ask for a second to help you."

"I'll manage."

"Well, I shall choose a second, so you will feel all right about doing the same." She looked around her at her friends. "Ambassador Deukalion, you learned this game from the diplomat himself, your uncle. We shall make a formidable team."

If Cassia noticed Lio's uncertainty, surely the other Hesperines did as well. At least she and Lio were united in their surprise at what shape the princess's plan was taking.

He answered, "I will do what I can, Princess Alexandra."

"Now the threat is sufficient, is it not?" she asked Chrysanthos. "You need a second." Her gaze settled on Cassia. "Lady Cassia, have you ever played Prince and Diplomat?"

"No," Cassia replied, as she had when they had planned this, but with trepidation now. With one hand, the princess seemed eager to put Cassia at ease, but with the other, she set up Lio as her own ally and Cassia's opponent.

"You are a diplomat," Xandra encouraged. "Why don't you join us?"

Chrysanthos cut in, "It's hardly fair to subject Lady Cassia to our little game. She has never even seen a Kings and Mages board. Among our people, women occupy themselves with productive pursuits, such as weaving and gardening."

Cassia wouldn't play along with the princess, but she would play to teach Chrysanthos a lesson. "Perhaps I have learned something in the weaving room and the temple gardens that will help me at this, too."

Lio pulled up a chair for her to Chrysanthos's right. When she seated herself, Lio eased her up to the table before he rounded the board to take his place at Xandra's right. Chrysanthos opened his mouth to speak.

Cassia held up her hand. "Honored Master, you must not give me any hints. That is against the rules, is it not?"

He raised his eyebrows, as if to say, *hew your own crypt.*

Many, many people had looked at Cassia like that throughout her life. But she was expert at staying out of her own grave.

She was determined not to let her doubts overtake her. It was a board game. Even if she had never played, it must be a trifling challenge compared to real politics. What was the worst that could happen? She had suffered humiliation before, and it was meaningless. It wasn't as if they were playing for real stakes. Not lives.

Or were they? Were the stakes not the very highest at every moment of this Summit?

"All new players are entitled to the same basic tutorial before the game begins," Lio explained. "There are two different ways to win the game: brute force or strategy. Which method is right for you will depend on your natural aptitudes and preferences. Those who favor brute force use the sheer number and strength of their pieces to defeat their opponents, and those who find so many pieces at their disposal need only brute force to achieve victory. Those who have fewer pieces at their disposal need strategy to succeed, but those who favor strategy need fewer pieces to succeed."

"I see," said Cassia, although she didn't. Perhaps once she watched the game in action, the obtuse commentary would come clear to her.

"I see that Hesperines use a round board," Chrysanthos mused, "with circles instead of squares. How fitting. But the essential layout is the same. You have the plane beneath, and the paths superimposed upon it."

Cassia studied the polished, inlaid board. Black circles alternated with pale ones in neat rows and columns, and she supposed players were to move pieces from circle to circle according to a pattern. But some circles were marked in red outlines or with red symbols that seemed to mark an entirely different route across the board.

Chrysanthos fingered a crow carved of petrified wood. "Familiar pieces. Rooks, knights. I am astonished you did not cast the sun from the ensemble."

"Certainly not." The princess pointed to a disk of golden wood. "We must account for the sun. But you will notice the moons remain powerful pieces, in contrast to their reduced significance in your own game."

Two spheres gleamed at the center of the board, one of redwood, the other of ash.

Chrysanthos gestured at two stars made of pine and ebony. "Let me guess. There are queens on your board."

"The most strategic pieces of all." The princess swept a hand toward the board. "The guest gets the first move."

A mere courtesy? Or perhaps there was something unique about each board that gave its owner an advantage, which must be balanced out by letting the guest begin the game. Having seen Rudhira whittle a goat figurine for Zoe, Cassia suspected that the First Prince had crafted Princess Alexandra's game board, as well as taught her to play. Who knew what magic might be infused into each playing piece?

Chrysanthos reached for the pine queen. The moment his fingers touched the wood, he snapped his hand back, as if he had been burned. Frost coiled in the air around the piece.

The princess clicked her tongue in a scolding manner. "My turn." She picked up the pine queen and moved her through three red-bordered circles in a little dance around the ebony queen.

"Well, well," said Chrysanthos. "Strategic pieces indeed. A unique advantage to all Hesperines."

"Undoubtedly," Lio replied, but he reached for the rook nearest him and moved it four circles ahead in a straight line.

Chrysanthos steepled his fingers. "But you do not move a queen, Ambassador. I shall hazard a guess that only those of the Queens' blood wield their power."

The princess smiled innocently. "I did warn you that you would need help against me. Lady Cassia, it is your turn, now. The newest player always goes last, to allow time for observation."

Cassia surveyed her options. So, not all pieces could be of use to all players, and if she chose poorly, she forfeited her turn. But what determined a player's ability to move which piece?

A redwood knight drew her eye. The princess had dubbed her a diplomat, but Cassia decided to take a chance on the little warrior and his charging horse. With a smile for her hound, she reached for the piece. From the corner of her eye, she saw Benedict's look of approval.

She found herself able to pick up the knight piece. It felt uneasy in her hand, but the longer she touched it, the more determined she felt to use it. With no idea what the rules for movement were, she marched her knight along the nearest path, red piece on red circles. That seemed logical. Cautious, she moved only two spaces.

She folded her hands in her lap and waited. When a miniature gargoyle swept across the board of its own accord and knocked her knight over, she jumped.

Lio winced. "The knight isn't allowed that pattern of movement, as you can see."

Princess Alexandra gave Cassia a sympathetic look and set the knight to one side of the board.

"This game has a brutal way of teaching," Cassia said lightly, "but I shall indeed learn by observation at this rate, and quickly."

On Chrysanthos's next turn, he also moved a knight. He charged the piece forward one white circle, then one black, then leapt it through a red one. How obvious could he be? If this was how he taught his apprentices, Tychon must be a slow study.

The princess twirled the ebony queen in a pattern about the pine queen, and Lio followed up by moving a carved wooden scroll. What was all that supposed to accomplish?

Cassia eschewed Chrysanthos's lesson and did not make another attempt with a knight. What she needed to do was explore the pieces and determine which were at her disposal. She must tally her weapons before she could decide how best to put them to use. That meant ruling out the ones that would waste her turns.

In the name of thoroughness, she touched the sun. It punished her audacity by stinging her fingers as painfully as a mage of Anthros's spell. When she tried to pick it up anyway, Lio and the princess cringed, and Chrysanthos leaned back in his chair with a long-suffering expression. The sensation of fiery pin pricks traveled over Cassia's skin and through her veins all the way to her elbow.

"Well, that was conclusive." She put her hand back in her lap, resisting the urge to claw at her arm.

Knight rested his head on her thigh, and she gratefully buried her smarting hand in his ruff.

One round after another, Cassia watched the others move their chosen pieces in complicated, deliberate plays, while she worked her way through her options on the board. Lio and Chrysanthos took turns moving scrolls. No piece belonged entirely to either side, it seemed. Cassia found the scrolls, rooks, and apprentices all served her as well.

The strict patterns of movement allotted to each piece began to come clear to her, along with the relative strengths of each token. There was a whole pack of liegehound pieces that, she discovered, had few limitations on their movements. They quickly became her favorites, despite how nervous they seemed to make Lio and the princess.

Harkhuf and Eudokia were enthusiastic commentators, keeping up a running discourse on the game in three languages. Occasionally Eudokia let out a derisive laugh, or Harkhuf groaned in sympathy. Cassia observed their reactions as closely as she did the game. She took into consideration which remarks they directed at the mages in Divine and which hints they dropped her in Vulgus, although she could not understand what must be impolitic insults in an Imperial tongue.

Most of the embassy crowded closer and closer around to watch the game. The back of Cassia's gown dampened with sweat, and she was glad her black shoulder cape would conceal the moisture on her red gown. But it was good they had captured everyone's attention. The other mages' reactions to each turn gave her more clues, and so did Benedict's. Watching Flavian drink was not the only entertainment in Segetia, it seemed.

"Basilis is becoming quite the menace with her hounds," Eudias said in an appreciative tone. "They are her tokens indeed."

"A fitting strategy for a beginner," Chrysanthos approved.

Cassia vowed to help their side lose as excruciatingly as possible.

Lio smiled and used his rook to take one of the liegehounds she had left in his path. She patted Knight's head apologetically, and Lio bowed to him. The crowd laughed. Cassia put on a staunch expression and closed in on Lio's rook with another of her hounds, which she knew she would also lose on his next turn.

Chrysanthos bestowed a forgiving smile upon Cassia and moved the temple for the fourth time in what seemed to be an ongoing duel with the princess's rose. Xandra left the flower where it was and moved a thorn instead.

Cassia had yet to touch any of the princess's favorite pieces. There might be hidden traps in this game, not just for Chrysanthos, but for Cassia as well. Would it mean something to the Dexion if she succeeded in moving a piece that was especially Hesperine in character? How much significance was there in a person's affinity for each piece? She would stay with the safe, neutral choices.

She made a great show of enthusiasm every time she discovered a successful move for which the game did not penalize her. As if thrilled to be moving at all, she threw her tokens into the path of Lio's and Xandra's at every opportunity, then laughed aloud at her own mistakes. While Chrysanthos was busy wincing, Cassia studied the layout of the board to determine which of her pieces were protecting his favorites, so she could do away with them next and destroy his defenses.

The Dexion moved the shrine within range of Lio's rook. Lio, instead of fleeing, subverted the shrine for his own purposes, shifting it from the plane to the path. The more elaborate rules still eluded Cassia, but she gathered that Chrysanthos had abandoned the shrine on purpose. When it was his turn again, she saw what must be the reason why. He stole the princess's cup and moved it onto the circle where his shrine had been.

The real expert on subverting tokens was the princess herself. When she wasn't carving a devastating swath across the board using the queens and the moons, she kept stealing Chrysanthos's favorite pieces. The sickle and the sword both came to her hand and abandoned their master. He met her unapologetic, sympathetic smiles with his unreadable courtly ones. His expression became more and more frozen on his face.

The fires burned lower, casting deeper shadows on the faces of Cassia's fellow players. The side of the table grew cluttered with her sacrifices, and she began to wonder what she would do when she ran out of pieces. Then suddenly everything ground to a halt.

It was Chrysanthos's turn. He stared at the arrangement of his torch and the princess's recently moved blood moon as if he no longer saw anything beyond the game. Xandra smiled at him again, but this time there was an unmistakable challenge in her eyes.

Both their gazes flicked to the sun, which sat on the circle where it had been when the game had begun.

Chrysanthos sat back in his chair, as if in dismissal, and moved the scroll that sat between his torch and the blood moon.

The princess plucked his torch from its place and used it to take his scroll.

The mages in the room gasped.

"Females are never able to use the torch," Tychon protested.

"How would you know?" the princess asked. "You never let females play."

"Impossible," Master Gorgos sputtered.

Eudokia looked down her nose at him. "Clearly not, for you just witnessed it."

Chrysanthos scoffed. "You could not possibly be that singular, Eighth Princess."

"It is not very gracious of you to take back a compliment, Honored Master."

It dawned on Cassia that Chrysanthos was running out of tactics. Now that the princess had claimed the torch and disposed of the scroll, there were few pieces left on the board that the Dexion had touched in recent turns—his tokens. If Cassia understood correctly, he had exactly two left, the powerful temple and a useless macer.

Cassia put her last, best piece, the tree, to the most effective use she could. Completing a long series of gradual repositioning she had worked on with the slow-moving piece, she slid it into place on the plane beside Chrysanthos's temple, as if to protect him from Lio's nearby rook.

A less observant player than herself might easily make such a move on the plane, not realizing it left the path open. If the princess were now to take out Chrysanthos's macer with her cup, her move would complete the opening Cassia had started, and Lio would be able to switch his owl from the path to the plane by taking Cassia's tree. Then the temple would be alone on the plane with Lio and Xandra's best pieces.

Chrysanthos saw it coming, for he moved his macer out of range of the princess's cup. But she moved the torch again and took his macer anyway, which raised another collective gasp in the room. Lio followed through, taking out Cassia's final piece. He smiled.

The temple was surrounded. No matter where it moved, it would fall victim to the owl or the queens.

When Eudias's gaze fell to the sun, he gave Cassia the last clue she needed. He really ought to stop looking at it like that. He would give Chrysanthos away.

Cassia would have staked all her lost tokens on it. Only a war mage could move the sun. Everyone in the embassy who understood the game knew Chrysanthos could still win. But not without betraying the nature of his magic.

What a poetic victory. There was surely no sweeter way to make him lose. With his true power within reach, he must go willingly, voluntarily into certain defeat to maintain his lies.

Chrysanthos was as elegant at losing as he was at everything. He lounged back in his chair. But his body language was much easier to read than a Hesperine's. He was absolutely seething.

"Your Majesty," he said to the princess.

"Ah," she chided, "that's not what we say here when we concede to the victor."

His smile was pricklier than a touch of the sun. His eyes promised it was dangerous to test him. He put his hand on his chest and bowed to her. "Let me guess. Annassa."

"However did you know?" she asked.

"Go ahead. Perform the final honors." He glanced from one queen to the other. "I can already guess which piece you will use to take out my last token."

"Oh, no, you will *never* guess." Princess Alexandra plucked the sun off the board and knocked the temple aside.

ORTHROS'S FIRE

"**I**MPOSSIBLE," THE DEXION rasped.

The princess relaxed back in her chair and stretched. As she lifted her hands, all the fires in the room revived. "That was so much fun. We should do it again sometime during the Summit."

Cassia looked from the sun token to the hearth. The Queens' daughter was a...war mage?

"What trickery is this?" sputtered Master Gorgos.

"Now, now. Take care you do not insult our hostess." How quickly Chrysanthos masked his reaction. But it was too late. They had all seen how the princess's revelation had shaken him.

Tychon was sweating. "My compliments to you, Eighth Princess, on such a clever trick. I must know how you accomplished it. Would you be so kind as to enlighten us with an explanation?"

"What is there to explain?" she asked. "Every player's affinity becomes evident at the board to the knowledgeable observer. As you have seen, my affinity is for fire."

Master Gorgos looked aghast and red-faced and quite ready to subject them all to another lecture on the excruciating retribution that awaited those who dared defy the Will of Anthros.

Cassia had seldom seen a more skilled and gratifying plot than the one the princess had just carried out upon the mages.

Eudokia came to stand beside the princess's chair. "I am sure Honored Master Adelphos will now remind us all of the Order of Anthros's theory regarding the affinity for fire. Namely, that the mages born with this power are almost exclusively men, and that the few women who are born with it are doomed to an unfortunate fate. Because of their weak natures, females are unequal to the task of studying, much less mastering fire magic."

"It is not a theory," Chrysanthos returned. "It is a fact of nature. When a female is born with war magic, her own power is certain to drive her mad and eventually destroy her. To possess such power is a death sentence to any woman."

"To possess power untrained is a death sentence to any mage," Eudokia countered. "What fate awaits a male of any affinity who is never educated in the use of his magic? It is the lack of teaching, not the possession of power, which is a death sentence for females with an affinity for fire."

"They would never make it through the training. The power is too much for them, and they have no hope of ever controlling it. Only men can withstand the harrowing study to achieve the necessary strength and discipline. No woman has ever survived it."

"Has any woman ever been given the opportunity?"

"She has never made it that far. As soon as her magic manifests, it is pure chaos that is dangerous to her and everyone around her. This is a truth borne out by the sad, short lives of every female so cursed. If you are at all familiar with the primary sources, as you claim to be, Sophia Eudokia, you will know the firsthand accounts written by the mages whom the Order of Anthros sent to put the females out of their misery."

Eudokia opened her mouth, but the princess put a hand on her arm.

Xandra sat tall in her chair. "My firsthand account is even more immediate evidence, is it not? I was four when the Order of Anthros sent a war mage of the Aithourian Circle all the way from Corona to a remote village in Tenebra to 'put me out of my misery.'"

Hostility was written in every line of the mages' bodies. But none ventured farther out onto thin ice by questioning her tale to her face.

"When the mage verified my power was genuine," Xandra went on, "the man who sired me and the woman who bore me were all too eager for him to take me off their hands. He couldn't do away with me fast enough to satisfy the neighbors. The villagers seemed to think I would bring my curse upon all of them. I'm not sure why. It wasn't as if any of us asked for me to be born with an affinity for fire, least of all me. Fire magic is said to be a gift straight from the sun god, isn't it? I don't know why they thought Anthros would punish us for something that wasn't our fault, but the villagers were ready to stake their spirits on it. They built the pyre for the mage. That's what your archives say, isn't it? The child must be burned at the stake."

"That is not what the law calls for," Chrysanthos insisted. "The Order mandates that the death be painless."

"That must be why our village necromancer did his part first. I didn't understand why he was muttering over me like he had over grandmama before she died. It frightened me. Was I sick the way she had been? My mother told me to hush and go to sleep. I didn't want to. But the next thing I knew, I was waking up bound to a stake."

The princess's matter-of-fact, candid words were more effective than any overwrought teachings from a mage. With every gentle blow she dealt, the guilty consciences became more and more visible on the Tenebrans' faces.

So they did have hearts in their chests after all. Cassia had once doubted it. But she too was learning with them to see her enemies as human.

"The child should never wake during the sacrifice." Chrysanthos's court mask faltered.

"The sacrifice was interrupted," the princess explained. "By a Hesperine errant. While he was trying to persuade the war mage to release me, the necromancer's spell wore off."

"I have never heard of such an encounter between a Hesperine and an Aithourian war mage." Tychon wielded the comfortable defense of denying the truth.

"Oh?" the princess replied. "The mage's name was Zetros."

"Zetros was a well-respected member of the Aithourian Circle," Tychon protested. "He was in Tenebra offering aid to deprived villages when a member of the Blood Errant murdered him."

"Actually that member of the Blood Errant politely asked him not to burn a four-year-old to death. Zetros took offense and started hurling fire. The villagers ran for cover while the necromancer came to the war mage's aid. Imagine. Two grown men willing to die for their right to kill a little girl. For that is what they did. They fought to the death."

Chrysanthos recovered his haughtiness as quickly as it had deserted him. "I told you I thought our rules were not so very different. Imagine. A Hesperine willing to go to such lengths to get a war mage for his people."

"I. Am not. A war mage." The princess rose to her feet, and every hearth fire in the room rose with her. "I have never wielded, nor will I ever wield my magic in order to do violence to anyone or anything. I am a Hesperine with an affinity for fire, and I devote all of myself, including my magic, to the service of my people as their princess."

She raised her hands still higher, and unlit candles all over the room sparked to life in unison. Their flames played and danced, as bewitching and magical as spell lights, but far more chaotic.

"Tonight, my power is at your service. You see before you the only fire in Orthros. This is my welcome gift to you. Fire that brings comfort, not suffering, that nurtures and doesn't destroy. The fire that gave me life, as surely as it does you. Carry its warmth with you all the nights you are here...and don't let it fade when you return home."

HARBOR LIGHT

EVEN AFTER CASSIA PERSUADED Perita she needed no help undressing and her tired handmaiden departed her guest room, she did not rise from her dressing table. Perhaps when Lio arrived and saw her closed door and drawn curtains, he would realize she needed a moment.

Knight settled himself over Cassia's silk slippers, warmer to her even than the shoes' magic, and she sat a moment longer in her red gown and black shoulder cape. She had wanted to wear these to see Zoe. But right now she did not feel prepared to face the trip to House Komnena with Lio. When he had walked her back to Rose House with the rest of the embassy and their Hesperine escorts, she had been glad their abundant audience had prevented them from discussing the princess's party.

Cassia didn't know what to say.

She refused to say what she wanted to. Her feelings were unjustified. All of it ought to be a moot point. But it was not, not for her, and until she was certain she would not create conflict where there ought to be none, she dared not speak of any of it.

To buy herself time, Cassia quit her room. As she slipped out into the corridor with Knight following her, his feet hardly made a sound on the carpets. She glanced up and down the deserted passage, and the gleam of light at the end of the hall beckoned her. She followed the Harbor Light toward the front of the guest house.

It was not Lio's fault that Xandra was an impossible act to follow. It was not Xandra's fault that she and Lio made a perfect partnership, both in their magical prowess and their skill as politicians. It was not Cassia's fault that she had believed Lio when he had told her he and Xandra were not suited.

This evening had made it abundantly clear to Cassia how well-suited the Eighth Princess and Firstgift Komnenos were.

Cassia could easily imagine what sort of falling-out might occur between two sweethearts who had known each other so long. It was only natural for there to be periods of tension, especially when the two sweethearts in question were so passionate in nature. Such events, however definitive they seemed at the time, would ultimately be temporary. Lio undoubtedly believed his courtship with Xandra was over, but the time would come when he would see the light and realize no one could hold a candle to his princess.

Xandra was the daughter of his Queens. The sister of the First Prince. It all made sense now. Rudhira was more an elder brother than a father figure. How fitting for his sister and Apollon's son to embody their loved ones' loyalty to one another. Who would turn down a chance to avow into the royal family? Not Lio, the Hesperine's Hesperine.

How long would it be before Xandra and Lio recovered from their quarrel and stopped consoling themselves in the arms of their human guests? Not long, by Orthros's reckoning, before the promising diplomat and the beloved princess were once more headed for their destiny together, to the delight of their people. Harkhuf must know as well as Cassia did that they were merely temporary diversions.

It should seem like a long time to Cassia. But it didn't. It seemed too short, because she had let herself want more.

The hall ended at a staircase. Light spilled down the stairwell from above. Cassia followed it. At the top, she found a pair of doors and pushed through them. They let her out onto a balcony.

She halted in her tracks. She stood at Hespera's back with the whole harbor spread out below her. The statue of the goddess rose high, black and sparkling with shining white flecks like the night sky beyond, holding the great spell light of the harbor beacon in her uplifted hands. The cold, salty air brought tears to Cassia's eyes.

She had made the most basic of foolish mistakes. She had let herself get her hopes up. But she could not blame herself for that either, even if

Lio had never said anything about forever. Hesperines breathed hope, and the mortals around them could do naught but take it in and let it fill their lungs.

The thought of giving up that hope left Cassia breathless.

She wanted more…she wanted *everything*. Orthros. Eternity.

She did. She wanted that. Life this sweet, forever.

She wanted to become a Hesperine.

The realization came to her like the Harbor Light, the first time she had seen it emerge from the darkness. She could have that. Even if she lost Lio.

The Queens themselves had said the doors of Orthros were open to her. They had told her she was as one of their own. If she asked for the Gift, surely no one would deny her. After everything Cassia had done for the Hesperines, she had earned her place here. She had already made these people hers. They would welcome her as theirs.

She did not know how she could bear an eternity in which Lio was at Xandra's side. But Cassia would have eternity. Freedom from Tenebra. A way to serve her new people—her own garden, perhaps.

She would have the Gift. Magic. In her very own veins. Surely that would make her strong enough to bear anything. She would be powerful enough in her own right to make her own joy.

There was no doubt in her mind. This was the future she would fight for. However long or short her future with Lio proved to be, she would see to it she had *her* future.

She must now use the Summit to wrestle everyone into position, so she could send them home into the plot she had prepared for her key players. She had made sure her contingency plan was in place in Tenebra before she had departed. She had made that plan in case she lost her life. Little had she known it would save her life.

She wasn't fighting against death anymore. She was fighting for life— the future she wanted here in Orthros.

Cassia's new resolve gave her the strength to turn around and go back inside. Knight nuzzled her hand, as if in question.

"*Dockk*, my friend. All will yet be well. It will not be easy. But in the end, all shall be well."

TRIAL SISTERS

ASSIA RETURNED TO HER room to hear knuckles tapping on the courtyard door, as if they had been at it for a while already. She faced the door the way she faced everything. She marched to it and pulled back the curtains to do what she had to do.

But it wasn't Lio waiting for her on the other side of the glass. The princess's friends had come to see Cassia. Eudokia gave a wave, and Menodora smiled.

It seemed Cassia must find the strength to be a good guest a little longer tonight. She opened the door.

Eudokia stuck out a hand. "Let's do away with formalities. I'm Kia."

Cassia gave her the expected wrist clasp. "You are Lio's Trial sisters."

"Well," Eudokia said, "at least he told you about *us.*"

Menodora clasped Cassia's wrist in turn. "I'm Nodora. Lio has met with a delay, so we took the opportunity to come meet you properly. Allow me to offer my compliments on your first game of Prince and Diplomat. That was spectacular for a player of any level of experience, especially a beginner."

Eudokia smirked. "I'm not surprised. You managed to impress my mother. Prince and Diplomat is easy by comparison." Her smile disappeared. "Don't tell me Lio didn't mention Hypatia is my mother."

"I was unaware of your blood name until tonight."

"Well, let us clear that up right away. I am the youngest daughter of the most brilliant and most trenchant elder known to Hesperine kind. I wish I'd been at the circle when you arrived. I would love to have seen you make her eat her words."

Well, perhaps Eudokia was not such a partisan of her mother's and Konstantina's after all. Uncertain whether to offer sympathies or gratitude, Cassia settled for a safe answer. "Thank you." Before they could bring up anything to do with the princess's party, Cassia turned to Menodora and struck up polite conversation. "You are from the western Empire originally, you said?"

Menodora shook her head. "A place farther west than that, actually. The Archipelagos, where the Honorable Families' fleets rule the waters."

There was yet another land beyond the Empire? Cassia was more ignorant than she had imagined. "Please forgive my mistake."

"Not to worry. There are only two fleeters in Orthros, and none at all in Tenebra or Cordium, so how would you know? The Families don't even care to deal with the Empire much." Menodora waved a hand. "But we didn't come here to talk about me."

"On the contrary," said Cassia, "I appreciate the opportunity to get to know all of you and learn about how you came here. It has opened my eyes."

"Actually," said Eudokia, "you missed the point."

"What Kia is trying to say is that tonight was meant to put you at ease, and if that's not the case, we hope we can help you see things differently."

"I'm saying she missed the point. Cassia didn't come all the way to Orthros to mince words, did you, Cassia?"

"Well," Menodora assured, "it's true you needn't speak with us as if we're courtiers. We're Lio's Trial sisters."

Lio's, yes, and Xandra's. Not Cassia's. Their love and loyalty for each other predated her visit here by more time than she could fathom.

No matter how long she tried, how could she ever be equal to so much shared past?

"Thank you for your concern," she said, "but the princess's party was a triumph. No one appreciates what she accomplished tonight more than I do, I assure you."

"I think," Menodora cautioned, "you are perhaps appreciating a little too much."

"I beg your pardon?"

"You and Xandra are making an admirable effort, but alas, it has backfired on both of you."

Eudokia nodded. "We are here to clean up the mess, as good friends do when a spell blows up in your face."

They saw right through Cassia. But she would indeed continue to make an effort, and perhaps one day, her own feelings would heed her insistence that she bore Xandra no ill will, for the princess did not deserve it. "The princess deserves my utmost respect and admiration, and she has it. Not only because of her incredible fortitude in dealing with such difficult magic, but also because I have seldom seen a plot so gratifying or so well-played, and with such strength of character."

Xandra was wonderful. That's what made this so hard.

"Xandra would be very happy to hear that," Menodora replied. "Your opinion means a great deal to her. That's why she was so determined to have a chance to talk with you before the party. She wanted the two of you to get off on the right foot."

Why should Cassia's opinion mean so much to a princess of the Hesperines?

"Here." Eudokia held out a small, silk-wrapped bundle. "Allow me to give you my welcome gift. It is entirely inappropriate to present to you when the embassy visits House Hypatia for Mother's circle tomorrow night."

Cassia had no choice but to accept the gift. She unwrapped the crimson silk and ribbons to reveal a pocket-sized book.

"It's the *Discourses on Love*," Eudokia said, "and it's full of treats to reward you as you learn Divine."

"Kia," Menodora fretted, "we are here to offer Cassia our friendship, not embarrass her back to Tenebra."

Eudokia grinned wickedly. "Have you heard of the work, Cassia?"

Yes, when Lio quoted the erotic text to her in bed. "It's an important collection of Hesperine literature, I understand."

"A classic for the ages," Eudokia said.

Cassia tied the book to her belt with one of the ribbons. "This is exactly what my library needs. I inherited the most popular Tenebran volume on this subject from my sister, but I have exhausted its usefulness."

Even as Cassia's cheeks flushed, a chuckle escaped her. Suddenly the three of them were laughing together.

Menodora drew a flute out of her sash. "I was going to give you my welcome gift at the party tonight, but you weren't in the mood for Tenebran court dances." She played a strain of music.

The familiar notes brought Cassia's heart into her throat. "The only song Lio and I have ever danced to."

Menodora tucked the flute away. "An encore is in order when you come to House Kitharos."

Cassia was silent. She had been wrong. Even worse, she must admit it to these kind, brilliant Hesperines.

"I misjudged," Cassia said. "I thoroughly mistook your intentions tonight. That is unlike me, but—no excuses. I owe you an apology."

"Everyone needs help seeing the light sometimes," Eudokia replied, "even someone like you, Cassia, who is expert at reading between the lines."

"I don't know when I became suspicious of Hesperines, as I am of mortals."

"When Konstantina left you bleeding?" Menodora guessed.

Cassia's hands tightened. "Even she is motivated by love."

"You have brought the rules of politics to the table," Eudokia said, "for those are the rules at which you have become expert, after great effort. But the table you are playing at in this case is friendship—and romance. Fortunately, you have just as many allies in this game, and we are allowed to help you learn the new rules. Shall we speak plainly?"

Menodora smiled again. "You will lose no tokens with us. No gargoyles will leap out to strike down your pieces, and we are a kind audience who will encourage your moves, not critique them."

Their offer of friendship was too genuine and generous for Cassia to question. Hesperines had taught her to recognize a gift when she saw it. She would not throw this one back in their faces.

She felt a sense of brotherhood with Mak and Lyros. Dare she imagine achieving camaraderie with Menodora and Eudokia as well? Although they had never shared a rite of initiation, could they come together in this time of dread and conflict and, in their own way, be Trial sisters?

Sisters. Adult sisters who were friends. As Cassia and Solia might have been, if things had been different.

Cassia looked from Eudokia to Menodora. "I admit, I weary of hidden meanings. I would value your honesty. But your patience as well."

"You have both," Menodora promised.

"Why don't we take a walk?" Eudokia asked. "The city is beautiful at veil hours, when the lights are out. You can see even more of the stars."

"We won't let you get lost," Menodora promised.

"Thank you." Cassia let them lead her out into the night.

TRUTH IN THE BLOOD

KIA AND NODORA WALKED with Cassia and Knight on a meandering tour of the lanes between the guest houses. Glimpses of the harbor glittered at them between the tall, stately buildings, then the high walls and gargoyles cast their velvet shadows again.

What Kia had said about playing by new rules was true, more than Cassia wanted to own. For all her expertise at court, she struggled for words now. She treasured this offer of confidence from Kia and Nodora, but she had little idea what to do with it. She had never learned how to be this kind of sister. She was still learning from Perita how to be a good friend to other women.

Kia rescued her from the silence. "So did Lio explain what happened between him and Xandra?"

"He—that is, I— It would be wrong of me to pry."

"Only natural you should wonder," Kia replied, "but it's a question best addressed to Lio himself."

Nodora's brow furrowed. "Has he not told you?"

"We spoke of it once. I thought I understood what had happened, but now I realize the precise details did not come across amid his...diplomacy."

"Unsurprising!" Kia huffed.

"He talked all around it." Cassia frowned. "He told me she was a silk maker named Xandra, that's all. How can a silk maker be a princess whose craft is bugs?"

Nodora's eyes gleamed with suppressed laughter. "She raises the worms that spin the silk. When they become moths, their cocoons are harvested and turned into thread."

"*That's* where silk comes from? *Worms?*"

"That settles it," Kia declared. "Lio did a wretched job of explaining."

"Kia, I think perhaps one of your objective analyses would be a reassurance to Cassia on this occasion."

What a new world Cassia found herself in, where people spoke of objective analysis and reassurance in the same breath. She had never known hard facts to bring any comfort, and she felt only trepidation as she, Kia, and Nodora traversed an open plaza. A gurgling fountain carved in the shape of garden birds had never looked so menacing. But the two Hesperines had been kind enough to offer Cassia the truth. She needed that, no matter how it hurt.

"Rest assured we have complete privacy," said Nodora. "If we happen to pass anyone, they won't overhear."

"You've veiled our conversation?" Cassia hoped that question sounded better informed than her ignorant remarks about silk production or Nodora's origins.

Kia swept out her hand to indicate their surroundings. "There are veils everywhere you turn here, and everyone knows to expect it. When all your people have the power to read your heart, you grow accustomed to making an effort at privacy."

What a new world indeed. Cassia had best become accustomed to the notion of privacy, too. That would be rather nice, actually, after someone else had dressed her from her underlinens up every day of her life and reported their color to the king.

"I hope you do not find it inconsiderate of me to wonder about Xandra's private affairs," Cassia said.

"You are curious about Lio's affairs," said Kia, "which are yours as well. I am happy to offer you some reassurance. Let's start with what you do know."

Cassia told herself this was just like talking to Perita about such matters. These were her fellow females, even if they did have longer canines than she. "I gather he cared for her all the years they were growing up together and had every expectation of a lasting commitment. He said they were…very close…but never…as close as they might have been." Now who was talking around the facts? "It seems they had some falling out, but he never told me exactly what transpired that made him despair of their future. He spoke generally of realizing they were not suited. It still weighed heavily on his heart when he arrived in Tenebra."

Nodora wore a pained smile. "To say it was still bothering him when he left would be an understatement. Neither he nor Xandra expected to live it down for a good long time. It's one of the reasons why Lio's family agreed he should go to Tenebra. They were dreadfully worried about the danger, but they realized he needed a real challenge that would engross him."

Kia was nodding. "That's always Apollon's approach, when Lio is beside himself. 'Give the boy something to do.'"

"I suspect Apollon speaks from experience," Nodora commented.

"I keep telling Lio he's a great deal like his father," said Cassia.

"Ah ha," Nodora exclaimed. "So it is you we have to thank for his change of tune."

Cassia lifted her brows in question.

"Whenever we told him that," Kia explained, "he always replied, 'No, I'm not.' Until he came home from Tenebra. Now if you tell him he's like his father, he'll grin and say, 'Thank you.'"

"Mak teased Lio about 'following in his father's footsteps,'" Nodora quoted. "He kept suggesting a romantic adventure had put that grin on his cousin's face. It turns out he was right."

Cassia was blushing furiously now. As much as it had gratified her to learn her relationship with Lio was no secret here, she hadn't considered that Lio's "adventures" with her might have been the subject of so much detailed discussion among his friends. Humans and Hesperines were not so different after all. She suddenly felt more justified in posing personal questions.

"So Lio's father is known for such, ah, adventures?"

"It was only the natural result of his situation," Nodora said. "Argyros had Lyta right from the start, you know. They came to Orthros together. But Apollon lived for centuries before he met Lio's mother. When one is alone that long…"

"…and one is Apollon," Kia said, "one does *not* live like a mage. The same is true of Apollon's son."

"Lio has a tendency to love very adamantly. We've seen that cause

him a great deal of distress. So we're very glad he's found someone to…"
Nodora paused to choose her words. "…provide a focus for his energies."

That's what Cassia was. An outlet.

She was now very familiar with the extent of Lio's energies, and she could only agree it was a fine thing to be the focus of them. That he loved with all his heart? Of that she had no doubt.

The one who found herself the focus of that love was the truly fortunate one.

Kia gave Cassia another probing look. "When we were all sucklings playing Grace, Lio and Mak had our futures all planned out for us. Lio and Xandra would avow, Mak and Lyros would avow, and I would run away to the Empress's university in her capital, where I would meet a gorgeous mathematician who was genius enough to keep up with me, thereby relieving my friends of listening to my lectures."

Cassia choked on a laugh. The amusement in the two Hesperines' eyes was a clear invitation to share in their childhood jokes. A narrow path between beds of short willows brought the three of them into a closer huddle.

"And you, Nodora?" Cassia ventured. "What was to be your destiny?"

"They didn't have the chance to embroil me in their schemes until I came to Orthros when I was thirteen."

"She fell in with us because we were at a similar level of maturity in Hesperine terms."

Nodora laughed. "Immaturity, rather!"

Kia's eyes narrowed with mischief. "By then we had even more ambitious ideas."

Nodora rolled her eyes, but she was blushing. "I will only allow you to repeat this because Himself isn't anywhere in Orthros tonight."

Kia grinned. "Nodora was to fall madly in love with none other than Rudhira. She would end his eternal loneliness and become a princess."

"I think Xandra just liked the idea of me being her Grace-sister."

"Hmm." Cassia dared a little speculation of her own. "I would imagine the prince's numerous relatives welcome any opportunity to engage in matchmaking on his behalf."

"You have no idea." Nodora shook her head, looking very distressed for the prince's sake.

Cassia was also willing to speculate as to how many Hesperines in their youth became infatuated with the prince, but she kept that to herself. Nodora didn't deserve to be embarrassed further.

"You see how accurate our predictions turned out to be," Kia concluded. "The prince remains unattached, and Nodora is frequently attached to a sitarist from the Empire renowned for his nimble fingers."

"Kia." Nodora swatted her friend.

"I am spending a memorable season with a fellow mathematics student from the university, but he came to me as a guest, and I remain right here and keep lecturing my dearest friends. Only Mak and Lyros were quite right about their destinies, which surprised no one, and delights all of Orthros to this day."

"I see what Lio meant when he said Lyros and Mak make it look easy."

"That's certainly how it looks," Nodora agreed. "But love is seldom easy, in truth. Mak and Lyros have devoted great effort to what they have."

"Alas, no amount of effort on Lio and Xandra's part was sufficient to produce similar results." Kia's brazen tone changed, and she began to explain things as factually and patiently as if she were instructing Cassia on the proper way of tilling the soil. It seemed the blunt scholar was also a kind teacher. "As you correctly concluded from Lio's obtuse implications, he and Xandra were quite intimate with each other as youths. However, it was not in their natures to become lovers or share blood before Initiation."

"Lio is much too dutiful for that," Nodora put in, "and Xandra...well, you are a gardener, are you not, Cassia? You know the plants that don't show their flowers until late in the season but, when they do bloom, are no less lovely. Lio, on the other hand, is a very early bloomer. He was ready for Initiation even before he came of age and could easily have passed it instead of waiting for us all to go through Trial together." She cast her friend a teasing glance. "Kia was beside herself, even though she was ready almost as soon as Lio. Our decision to undertake it the same year meant she couldn't be a prodigy and pass before she was old enough."

"Nonsense. Lio is the eldest. It only makes sense he would be ready first. As to waiting, Mak and Lyros were much more impatient than I ever was, for they were desperate to make their union official. But we all agreed, didn't we? Because going through it together was so important to us."

"Lio said he waited for eight years for everyone to be old enough." Eight years he remained devoted to Xandra, intimate with her, longing for more.

"Four years," Nodora corrected with a wince.

"'Give the boy something to do,' said Apollon," Kia quoted, "for four years while Xandra came of age and four more while she made herself miserable preparing for Trial."

Nodora gave Cassia a sympathetic look. "I suppose it does seem a dreadfully long time from a human perspective."

Kia adjusted her mantle again. "If you were to attempt a mathematical comparison between humans' and Hesperines' differing perceptions of time, using our slow rate of maturation as a basis, I would say those eight years were roughly as long to us as two years would be to you, Cassia. Granted, attempting to establish such an equivalency is an inherently flawed endeavor, given that—mathematically speaking—the Hesperine aging process is not linear, but becomes exponentially slower the longer we're alive, and—philosophically speaking—the prospect of eternity is so immense as to fundamentally alter our awareness of the passage of time."

"The point being," Nodora translated, "in those eight years, we grew up as much as humans would have in two, and it hardly felt like any time at all to us."

Cassia listened in silence, unwilling to counter their attempts at reassurance and reveal she found little comfort in them. Nothing changed the fact that those eight years, however great or small in number, had undoubtedly been of great significance to Lio. Certainly to Xandra as well. Frustration and embarrassment had a way of making time seem like it lasted forever.

"It was harder for Xandra than for any of us." Nodora sighed. "She felt like we were all waiting on her."

"We kept reassuring her Nodora wasn't ready, either, but she wouldn't take us at our word."

Nodora shuddered. "I was more than happy for the extra time to prepare. I haven't been Hesperine as long as the rest of you. I wasn't in any hurry to test my powers."

"But your results were excellent." Kia patted her shoulder.

"Well, when the night finally came, it didn't seem honorable to make mistakes on purpose to make Xandra feel better."

"Was it so very difficult for her?" Cassia asked.

"She excelled at every single test," Nodora hastened to say. "Except one. I'm afraid self-control isn't her strong suit. Unfortunately, the Trial of Discipline is the most important one and the culmination of the entire Initiation."

"Well, the princess's magic is a unique challenge, which she has clearly managed to overcome."

Kia concluded matter-of-factly, "When Xandra finally passed Initiation, you can imagine how we all rejoiced. Naturally Lio had planned a very special celebration for just the two of them afterward, when they expected all their dearest hopes would be fulfilled."

Cassia felt the urge to stare at the flagstones or, better yet, flee the juniper orchard through which they strolled and seek refuge all the way back at Rose House. But she kept her back straight and her gaze level and listened, as she always did when she must confront realities she'd rather not consider. Like the thought of Lio and Xandra at an intimate celebration.

Kia shook her head. "It was no small challenge to discover the details afterward, for neither of them wanted to breathe a word of it, it was such a disaster. But we have since compared what we gleaned from Xandra with what Mak and Lyros extracted from Lio, and we now know the facts."

"When you feast together," Nodora said gently, "it is supposed to make the experience *better*. What pleasure you take from a kiss can only be sweeter when accompanied by a sip from the vein."

"You don't have to tell Cassia that, Nodora."

Nodora winked.

Cassia's face was hot, and her heart was pounding. She really didn't want to hear this.

Kia grinned. "The sharing of blood is indeed meant to enhance the sharing of pleasure, and that was certainly what Lio and Xandra had been expecting. But it seems the moment they tasted each other, it had the opposite effect."

Cassia stared at her. "It did?"

Kia nodded sagely. "One sip, and the blood ran cold. The thorn lost its edge. The cup went dry."

Nodora made a face. "It was so dreadfully awkward for both of them."

Cassia shook her head. How could that be?

"In light of that," said Kia, "there was no possibility of them resuming the intimacy they had enjoyed before, much less becoming lovers. It was quite over."

"Although Lio did ask her to try again," Nodora added sheepishly.

"And Xandra, in an admirable display of maturity and decisiveness, told him no. She may have been the late bloomer, but in this case she was the first to face facts. She realized there was no point in trying anymore and told him so."

"That must have been..." Cassia floundered. "Very sudden."

Kia snorted. "Long overdue, rather."

"Everyone was so relieved!" Nodora said. "We had all come to anticipate their eternity together with great concern. Except Lio's parents. I think they knew all along and were only waiting for him to release himself from his misery."

"If I may," Kia offered, "allow me to deliver the facts accompanied by some philosophy. Lio and Xandra had been in love with the *idea* of each other, and when they tasted one another's blood, they were confronted in the most profound way with the reality of who they really are. They had known all along they were not suited, but did not believe it. They persisted in their pretense until that night, when the evidence in their veins made it impossible to deny the truth."

Whatever Cassia had expected, it had certainly not been this. How could anything cool the fire when a male found himself in an intimate embrace with Princess Alexandra?

Cassia had felt the unstemmable tide of Lio's passions for herself.

"I don't understand," Cassia said.

Kia smiled slowly. "Oh, but I think you do."

Cassia had seen the look on Lio's face when he tasted blood. Her blood.

"How could they not be perfectly suited?" Cassia protested. "She is the Queens' own daughter. And he is...everything a Hesperine ought to be."

"Exactly," Kia said. "All our ideals embodied in two people. I'm not sure which of them held the other higher on the pedestal. That's an exhausting effort, whether you're the person trying to bear the weight of a marble statue or the person trying to be one. And no one can drink stone."

BLOODBORN'S PATH

"Now," said Kia, "if you will allow me to illustrate the point with a rather heavy-handed example…"

She and Nodora steered Cassia onto a side path. An iron gate barred their way.

"Go ahead," Kia urged.

When Cassia opened the gate, it moaned, long and low. The sound echoed mournfully down the path beyond, which twisted between tall, dense evergreens. Cassia took care not to snag her cloak on the mighty thorn hedges that lined the trail.

The path soon opened into a circle around a monument. A tall, beautiful Hesperine of sandstone towered above them. Her powerful limbs and Stand regalia marked her as a warrior. Cassia peered at the plaque at the statue's feet, but it was all in Divine.

"'May the courage of Atalanta speed our steps,'" Kia read for her, "'as she now patrols the gates of Sanctuary.'"

"She was renowned for running the border." Menodora's voice was hushed. "She made quick sorties over to rescue humans out of heart hunter territory."

Kia contemplated Atalanta. "It took the bloodless cowards generations of effort and twisted magic to breed new liegehounds fast enough to keep up with her. Her last group of Sanctuary seekers made it to Orthros, even though she didn't."

"Her legend will certainly live on." Cassia found little consolation in her own words.

They spent a moment of silence at Atalanta's shrine before continuing onward. They passed four more statues, pausing for Kia and Nodora to explain each subject's fate. Whether at the hands of Aithourians, Gift Collectors, or renegade apostates, every Hesperine memorialized here had died a hero's death.

At the sixth monument, a round pedestal rose above their heads. A robed Hesperine reclined there with her eyes lifted to the heavens.

"Let's skip this one," Nodora suggested.

"No. Cassia needs to see them all." Kia translated, "'May Hesperines ever follow Hylonome's gaze to the stars, whence she now shines her light to guide our way.'"

"What befell her?" Cassia asked.

"She lost her Grace." Nodora had not sounded so grim even when they had discussed the heart hunters' methods of collecting trophies.

"Liegehounds again, I'm afraid," Kia answered. "I'm sorry, Knight."

He looked at her in blissful ignorance, his tail wagging a little. Cassia hugged him to her. "They certainly feature in your history a great deal."

"They are the only real weapon Tenebrans without magic have against us," Kia said. "In this case, Hylonome's Grace saved a rural community from a band of apostates a dozen strong, but the villagers' fear of Hesperines was stronger than their gratitude for being spared from the mage bandits. The villagers unleashed their dogs on him. Hylonome came home to Orthros and starved herself to death on top of the Observatory tower."

"That's horrible," said Cassia.

"We could have left this one out," Nodora insisted.

"No," Kia said firmly. "It's the most important one."

"That's enough, Kia." Nodora walked onward. "We are done here."

"But we have one more stop on Bloodborn's Path."

Cassia halted in her tracks. "That's what this is?"

"Indeed," the scholar answered. "This is Orthros's monument to everyone in our history who was born Hesperine."

Horror crept over Cassia. "Every single bloodborn? Do none of Lio's predecessors yet live?"

"Perhaps," answered Kia. "Come."

Cassia recognized when the grove gave way to the wild woods of House Komnena, although she could not place where on the vast grounds they were. It surprised her when they emerged from the tangled forest onto a cliff that overlooked the sea. A broad area had been cleared and laid with decorative stones. In the center was the most magnificent statue Cassia had yet beheld.

He was wrought of red-veined black marble. He was a handsome figure with a noble brow and a kind face. His body rippled with strength, and only a simple, classic garment girded his loins. He must have been ancient, for his countless rows of braids fell to his ankles. He was a moment caught in stone, a hero in motion. If Cassia watched long enough, he would complete the move his limbs seemed poised to make. A fighting move, surely. His hands were curled, as if around the hilts of swords. Yet he wielded no weapons.

Two children clutched his hands. Sculpted of the same stone, the little girls held fast to him as if for guidance. A third, smiling girl rode on his shoulders, while two boys stood at his sides, looking up at him with admiration on their faces. It was not an enemy that held the hero's gaze, but the third boy in front of him. A tall, gangly lad of solemn countenance. They gazed at each other as if holding a conversation of great import only they could hear.

Cassia studied the children. One of the girls had Nodora's eyes, another Kia's curls. The child on his shoulders had a coronet braid. Of the two boys, one was big for his age, but the other looked just as strong.

Cassia knelt before the tallest boy and met his gaze. She would know Lio's face anywhere, in any time.

"Prometheus." For the first time, Kia sounded reverent.

Nodora came to sit with Cassia and looked at her own childhood likeness. "He saved all of our lives, without even knowing it."

Knight stretched out between Cassia and Nodora, a tame beast at the great hero's feet.

"Nearly eight hundred years ago," Kia began, "the eldest unavowed Hesperines in Orthros grew weary of everyone wringing their hands over them, so they went Abroad to seek adventure and put their great powers to work for the common good. Pherenike Argyra. Prometheus Kassandros. First Prince Ioustinianos. The original Trial circle and Hippolyta's first trainees. They were already ancient and legendary. Apollon joined them, he claimed, to keep his niece and Ritual sons out of trouble, but in truth, he was the most restless of them all. For centuries, they performed bold deeds in the Goddess's name that no other Hesperines dared."

"As you've heard, they are the only Hesperines in history to fight with weapons." Nodora sounded properly scandalized. "You were at Waystar, the border fortress where, by law, they had to leave their arms every time they visited home."

Cassia bit her tongue about the recent appearance of the prince's sword at House Komnena.

"Prometheus wielded twin swords, the Fangs." Kia named them with relish. "Ioustinianos still carries his two-hander, Thorn, as he leads the Charge. Apollon laid down his stonemason's mallet when he met his Grace, leaving the Hammer of the Sun behind in Tenebra when he brought Komnena home. The stories say the prince keeps it at his fortress of Castra Justa in the wilds of Tenebra, should the night come when Apollon needs his weapon again. As for Nike, in honor of her mother's hand-to-hand combat, she eschews any blade. Wherever she may be, she goes into battle with only her enchanted shield, the Chalice of Stars. The Blood Errant are still making history—and enemies—from here to Cordium."

"Hesperines in Cordium?" Cassia asked, incredulous. "The Order of Anthros keeps mages on guard every moment to prevent you from setting foot there."

"That's the Blood Errant for you," said Nodora. "They went where gargoyles fear to tread."

Kia grinned. "Prometheus stole the Akron's Torch from the Hagion of Anthros."

"He *what?*" Cassia blurted.

The scholar's face was all alight. "He burned his name on the wall with it so everyone would know one of Hespera's own had bested the god of fire."

"The Akron had a personal grudge against him after that." Nodora wrapped her arms around herself. "It made Cordium even more dangerous for the Blood Errant."

"About a century ago," Kia continued, "they embarked on their most dangerous endeavor of all, another quest into Corona itself. As we've said, it was not their first mischief right under the Akron's nose, but it was their riskiest."

"Riskier than thieving from the Akron's own temple?"

"Yes, Cassia." Nodora leaned closer. "Can you believe it? They infiltrated the inquisitors' prison, with help from Basir and Kumeta. They went to rescue the heretics slated for execution on the Akron's Altar."

Cassia shook her head. "I can see Lio's father and Rudhira doing such a thing, but not the Queens' Master Envoys. They seem so cautious."

"Basir and Kumeta's wariness is born of the consequences of that final mission," Nodora said.

Hesperines going willingly to the place where their own were sent to die? "How did any of them make it back?"

Kia gazed into their hero's eyes. "Methu knew he was the one the Akron really wanted. He sacrificed himself so the others could escape with the prisoners. Everyone made it home, except him."

Silence fell between them. It was Cassia who dared break it. "Then he was executed in their place."

"The Order performs the immolations at high noon," said Kia, "so no other Hesperines are awake to offer comfort through the Union in those final moments. So there is no risk the captive will awaken from the Slumber and escape. But we can feel in our Slumber. He felt everything that happened to him, without being able to lift a finger to stop it."

Cassia said nothing. There were no words. She could not bear to look at Prometheus's statue.

She looked instead at young Lio, who could not look away.

At length, Kia said, "Apollon, Rudhira, and Nike went on the warpath, of course. They don't like to talk about it—no one does. That's how we deal with our own who do 'un-Hesperine' things. With silence. But I can't be silent, not when I and all my Trial circle owe our lives to the Blood Errant's vengeance. It took them years, for Cordium had become too dangerous, but they lay in wait for the mages to emerge or strategized to draw them out. They pursued or lured every last Aithourian who had anything to do with Methu's capture into Tenebra and destroyed them."

"Methu's suffering wasn't in vain," Nodora said. "The Goddess brought blessings out of all that horrible violence. None of us would be here, if not for him."

Kia sat down with Nodora and Cassia, pointing to Lio's statue. "Apollon was hunting down one of the Aithourians when he met Komnena. He would never have been in that remote part of Tenebra if he hadn't followed the mage there. He came home to Orthros after that, for his new family had to be his first priority. But Rudhira and Nike continued their campaign."

"Grace-Father and Grace-Mother begged Nike not to," came Lyros's voice, "but she would not heed them."

Cassia looked up to see Lio's Trial brother strolling out of the trees.

"How goes it?" Kia asked.

"Mak is almost done with him," Lyros answered. "They'll be along in a moment."

That gave Cassia her first suspicion that Lyros and Mak were the delay with which Lio had met. The full picture of the conspiracy began to come clear in her mind. Lio's friends had planned all of this.

Lyros joined them at Prometheus's feet. "Nike would not be swayed from her path of retribution. Nor would Rudhira, even by the Queens."

"And so it was," said Kia, "that although the Blood Errant had dwindled to two, they stole out of Orthros together once more, before their families could detain them with any more pleas. But Argyros and Lyta went looking for them to try once more to persuade Nike to come home."

A smile came to Lyros's face. "They didn't find her, but they did find my Mak. They realized they had a different priority than talking their adult daughter out of her choices. Their new son needed them to help him heal and grow up strong. So they came home with Mak, not knowing where Nike and Rudhira had gone."

"I could have told them," Kia said. "The Blood Errant's quest had led into the armpit of Tenebra once more."

Nodora chuckled at her Trial sister. "They didn't actually rescue Kia. She had already rescued herself."

"My village was frightened of me. I suppose it seemed unnatural for a tiny child to have such intelligence. Of course they concluded I was possessed. They tried to expose me three times, devising ever more elaborate traps to keep me in the woods until the wolves came, but I always managed to find a way out. Every time I wandered back home, the villagers were more alarmed. It's quite amusing, really. A whole settlement of adults beside themselves with fear over a little girl. In any case, the fourth time they tried to get rid of me, I decided not to go back. I set off through the forest in the opposite direction and ran into Rudhira and Nike on my way."

"As for me," said Lyros, "I have Basir and Kumeta to thank. They were gathering information about Methu's captors when they encountered me on the streets of Namenti. See, Cassia?" He took her hand, holding their olive-skinned palms side by side, then gestured to his green eyes and dark hair. "I'm probably a bastard of both Cordian and Tenebran descent, like you. We can't guess much more about my past on my own in the largest border city. That all came to an end when I tried to pick a Hesperine's pocket. Imagine my terror when Basir caught me red-handed—and my surprise when he and Kumeta had mercy on a little urchin and brought me home." Lyros grinned. "Someone important was waiting for me here in Orthros, although we were both too young to know it."

"You have already heard Xandra tell her story," said Nodora.

"The mage Rudhira killed to save her was the last," Kia finished. "Her brother brought her back to Orthros. Soon after, he formed the Charge."

"Nike did not return with them or join the Charge?" Cassia asked.

Lyros shook his head. "She stayed Abroad alone."

Cassia hazarded a guess. "I have noticed Lio's uncle is quite cold to the prince. Does he blame Rudhira for Nike's disappearance?"

"I'm afraid so," Lyros confirmed. "As if it does not grieve Rudhira just as much."

"He still goes by the name Methu gave him," said Kia, "Rudhira, which means 'blood red' in the language spoken by Kassandra's father's people."

"It is hardly my place to say," Cassia replied, "but Argyros's grudge seems an injustice to both the prince and Nike. After losing someone you love in such a way, you cannot simply go back to life as it was. You must do something about it. Make it matter."

"You understand." Nodora's voice was gentle.

"What about you, Nodora?" Cassia asked. "How did Methu's destiny bring you to Orthros from the Archipelagos all those years later?"

"Prometheus's legend is known across the Empire and even made it into our songs as far away as the Archipelagos. I should leave it up to Kassandra to speak of her life as a human. I will say only that she came to Orthros so she and her unborn son could escape a dynastic conflict. Centuries later, when my family faced similar troubles, we seized upon the hope offered by their story. We set sail for Orthros, the only place that provides refuge to, shall we say, politically significant figures who would be unsafe in any human land, where intrigue might erupt around them once more."

Kia put an arm around her friend. "I'll tell her the rest, if you need me to."

"No, that's all right. I want to be brave when speaking of my pain."

"If only two of you are here," Cassia said gently, "your losses must have been terrible."

Nodora nodded. "My mother was the captain. Her ship was all the home and family I had ever known. But we weren't prepared for the Notian seas. The weather…the ice… We wrecked upon the coast of Orthros Notou. Only two of us made it out alive—Matsu, who is my Ritual mother, and me."

"I am so sorry. I know what it feels like to lose everything in one stroke."

"Thank you, Cassia. It took me a long time to come to terms with what I lost. I will be the first to admit my transition into Hesperine life was an ungraceful one. But with a great deal of love and support, I eventually realized how fortunate I am. I consider it no dishonor to my human parents that I also regard my Hesperine fathers, Kitharos and Dakarai, as my parents in every way. This was what my mortal mother wanted for me, and what my mortal father would have wanted, had he survived to escape with us. Like Methu, my human family died so others could live."

"It's difficult." Cassia paused. "To live with so much gratitude to those who made you who you are. It's hard to know how to honor them."

"You understand," Nodora said again, with a nod.

At last Cassia found it in herself to look up at Prometheus again. He towered over them, powerful and joyous. His loss was the shadow under which all of these young Hesperines lived. But none more than Lio. The last surviving bloodborn in all of Orthros.

She'd had no doubt this was one of Lio's father's works, but

Prometheus's eyes confirmed it. One was a bolt of red, the other white moonstone. "So this is Apollon's tribute to his fallen Ritual son."

Lyros nodded. "When my sister Laskara approached Methu's mother about a memorial for Bloodborn's Path, Kassandra wouldn't hear of it. Laskara didn't dare speak to her for a year afterward."

"You see…" Nodora sighed. "Kassandra believes Methu was captured, but not killed. She feels certain he is coming back."

Lyros gestured along the cliff. "There's a statue of Nike just north of here, at Victory Point. That's why Kassandra felt all right about it when Apollon offered to sculpt Methu and put the work at House Komnena. He promised her it wasn't a memorial, just a portrait."

"Kassandra's grief must truly be too great to bear," Cassia said.

"Her magic complicates things," Nodora explained. "She has the gift of foresight."

Cassia tried not to sound doubtful. "Orthros has a seer?"

"We had two," Nodora replied. "Methu had his mother's affinity."

"Two seers at once," Cassia marveled. "There is only ever one at a time across all of Tenebra and Cordium. The Orders count themselves lucky if one is born every generation, and she is always appointed the Oracle of Chera." Cassia hesitated. "I have often wondered if the Orders coach a poor girl mage to recite nonsense so they can use her prophecies to get folk to do what they want. That is no reflection on your oracles, of course."

"I wouldn't put it past the Orders," Kia said, "but foresight is a genuine magical ability, specifically an extraordinarily rare dual affinity for light and time. Kassandra's is one of the strongest in recorded history. But because she sees the past and future as well as the present, her perception of what is and is not sometimes differs from our own. It isn't that she's wrong. All she sees and all she has foretold is true. Just not true in the way we understand it."

"All convoluted esoterics aside," Lyros put in, "she made a prophecy after Methu, the first bloodborn and the last to fall, was gone. Kassandra foretold that the bloodborn would return to Orthros. She holds to her belief that Methu will eventually fulfill her prophecy. But you see, we all know it has already come true, and it wasn't Methu."

"Of course," Cassia realized. "Orthros is no longer without the bloodborn. He arrived under auspicious stars and two full moons upon the Winter Solstice. He possesses a dual affinity...and a great destiny."

Kia pointed up at the sky, where the constellation of Lio's bloodline shone over their heads. "Those stars were Anastasios, to be exact, Lio's own foregiver. Queen Soteira was midwife at the birth, as she is for all mothers who receive the Gift while with child. I told you my illustration was lacking in subtlety, but I think I have gotten the point across."

Nodora took Cassia's hands. "We're all so grateful you're here."

"I meant what I said when you arrived," Lyros told Cassia. "Lio was in bad shape without you."

"As much as we hate to admit it," Kia said, "there are some things his fellow statues can't help with."

And yet they were making a valiant effort, judging by the look on Mak's face as he and Lio walked out of the woods. Cassia couldn't hear their conversation behind their veil, but Lio's hands weren't behind his back—he was talking with them. Mak was smiling and laughing with every appearance of patience, which seemed only to frustrate Lio further. When his cousin gestured ahead of them, Lio looked up and saw who was waiting.

His gaze went straight to Cassia's. She found she knew exactly what she wanted to say now.

Mak came to Cassia's side and offered her a hand. She let him help her up.

"I see you've been getting a history lesson," he said with a knowing smile.

"I've learned so much."

"Sorry I wasn't here to give you my story straight from the horse's mouth. But there's not much to tell. I cried a lot as a baby, until Mother taught me to punch things."

Cassia laughed aloud. Did Mak always have a joke to smooth the way for others?

Most of the time. But not always. His face sobered. "Do you know there's a statue of my sister here?"

"Yes. I have heard much about her great deeds tonight."

"We pay our respects to her every year on the Vigil of Mercy. That's coming up during the Winter Solstice observances. I hope you'll join us this year."

"I would be honored."

"We'll plan on that, then. But right now I'm afraid Lyros and I have to excuse ourselves. We haven't seen much of Bosko and Thenie tonight."

Lyros stood up and slid into Mak's waiting arm. "We'd best hurry home if we want to spend any time with them before they Slumber."

Kia hopped to her feet, tossing her mantle more securely around her shoulders. "I can't go home without saying hello to Zoe. If I only see her during lessons, she'll think I'm all work and no play."

"I'll come with you," said Nodora. "It's been all of one night since I last saw her. I have Zoe withdrawal."

Lio's friends did not waste time walking off. They disappeared all at once.

Lio rubbed the back of his head, opened his mouth to speak, then closed it again. He floundered like that a couple more times before Cassia went to him and put a hand on his lips.

He looked down at her, his brows descending. No statue could ever capture the range of emotion in his eyes. The intensity of his presence. He was a living being, messy and wonderful, flawed and beautiful.

He didn't need someone who reminded him of all he was trying to live up to. He didn't need someone who would help him struggle to be perfect. He needed someone who loved him just as he was.

Cassia loved him like that.

She was not destined to lose him, as she had feared tonight. Because she wouldn't let that happen.

She withdrew her fingers from his lips and kissed him. He froze in surprise. But it only took a moment for her to thaw him. She put her arms around his neck and kissed him thoroughly, until he wasn't trying to think of what to say. He was just kissing her in return, holding her to him, melting into her. She smiled against his mouth.

When she finally had to draw back for breath, he gasped with her.

"Cassia, I need you so much."

"I know."

PERFECTION

LIO BLINKED DOWN AT Cassia, his lips swollen from her kiss. "I have no idea what my friends said to you, but I owe them my thanks."

"We both do."

"I'm afraid I needed some of their patient insight as to why you were so affected by the party. I came out here to apologize."

"There's no reason for you to apologize."

"But you were so upset. At least let me explain."

"It's all right now, but if it will make you feel better, we'll talk about it."

His gaze darted over her shoulder to the statues. "I think we're embarrassing the children. Shall we go somewhere more private?"

"It strikes me that Methu would approve of two young lovers seizing the moment at his statue. A kiss seems a better tribute to him than anything. But let us excuse ourselves, in case we feel inspired to do more than kiss."

Lio laughed as Cassia drew him deeper into the woods. Well out of sight of the statues, they took shelter under a yew's low-hanging branches.

Lio held both her hands. "I didn't realize that when you and Xandra met, she introduced herself only as the Eighth Princess."

"Of course you wouldn't."

"How did we all manage to talk about each other without you finding out her name?"

"It never occurred to me." Cassia sighed. "I'm so accustomed to titles mattering the most. Amazing how she used hers not to hide, but to make me see her for who she really is. She wanted me to meet her without my feelings about the two of you getting in the way. In hindsight, I'm glad she gave me that chance. She carried out her plan well tonight, too."

Lio framed Cassia's face in his hands. "Her intention was to show you she's on your side. She supports what you and I are trying to accomplish together."

"I see that now. Putting me in a position to throw the game as Chrysanthos's second was a perfect parallel to me working with you and the royal family from within the embassy."

"Exactly. She never meant to make you feel like..."

"An inconvenient, momentary distraction from Ambassador Deukalion's perfect, eternal partnership with Princess Alexandra?"

"Goddess, Cassia, how could you think that?"

"I allowed myself to become very misguided tonight, and for that, I ask your forgiveness."

He shook his head, brushing her hair back from her forehead. "The reason I have said so little to you about Xandra is because I didn't think I needed to. I thought you knew all that was in the past."

"I needed some convincing, as it turns out."

"I have not been convincing enough?" He nuzzled her neck, his words low and warm in her ear. "Who fell asleep in my arms last night? Who awoke with me this moon?"

"Not Xandra." Cassia sighed against him, holding him close.

Lio ran his hands down her back. "You know your first time was mine, too. What part of 'Xandra and I never made love' says 'we have a future together'?"

"I attributed that to your stellar sense of propriety."

"Yes, I was very proper before I went to Tenebra." He cupped her buttocks in his hands.

She laughed and wrapped her arms around his neck. "I thought it was you who corrupted me, Sir Heretic. I begin to see I helped you off your pedestal in return."

"I spent my whole life trying to do everything right. Then I met you, and I realized all that truly matters is doing the right thing."

"The way you do everything is right for me, Lio."

"You and I are right, my rose. Xandra and I weren't and never would be."

"She's powerful and beautiful and kind. How could I not be jealous?"

Lio's expression was grave. "Xandra is indeed a lovely person. But she is missing one essential aspect that I cannot live without."

Cassia searched his gaze, waiting for his answer.

He kissed her nose. "Freckles. I must have freckles. Lots of them."

She laughed and enjoyed his next kiss. Wondrous. By some magic, she, Cassia, was the person Lio could not live without.

He needed her, just as she needed him.

"All is clear between us now?" he asked.

"Hmm. Do you have any other secret connections to the royal family you wish to confess?"

His mouth quirked. "Annassa Soteira delivered me."

"As she does for all bloodborn, yes."

"I see my friends have been free with my secrets tonight. But not the darkest one." He paused dramatically. "Kia and I once destroyed one of Aunt Kona's legal scrolls during a failed magical experiment. Please, do not give us up to her. I still fear her retribution."

They laughed together. She traced the unshaven stubble that framed his flawless mouth.

He rested his forehead upon hers. "So you feel completely reassured that no other lady is cause for concern?"

"I do," she marveled. "Although I needed more reassurance than I probably should have. I suppose…it is a recent discovery of mine…that there are times when life does not wound us. I still forget easily, and slide back into my old habit of hardening myself against the ills I am accustomed to expect."

"Cassia." His voice and his arms were so gentle. "No ills shall befall you here."

"You have to understand, in the world I'm used to, good things like you don't happen to people like me. Those with rank and family like yours don't choose the concubine's bastard over the princess. I'm sorry. I'm still so Tenebran in some ways."

"You know rank and birth don't matter in Orthros."

"But it does matter that Xandra is the Queens' daughter. The Eighth Princess and Firstgift Komnenos seem so perfect."

"I don't want perfection. I want you."

"Lio. You are the best thing that has ever happened to me."

She kissed him again. His hands tightened, holding her body against his. She stroked his braid, his oath to her. He had promised he would say all that needed to be said after their long time apart, but acknowledged it would take time. How well she understood. She had her own store of unsaid words.

Was it too soon to say them? If she waited, would it be too late?

No, she couldn't announce that she had decided to stay, not yet. She could not make a promise that sacred until it was in her power to keep it. She must wait until her plan succeeded. Until she was free. Then they could celebrate not an intention, but a certainty.

Lio pulled his mouth away. "You are powerful and kind and beautiful, you know."

"You always do the right thing."

He hesitated. "Cassia, have I ever made you feel fragile?"

"What are you talking about?"

"Have I ever said or done anything that gave you the idea I don't believe you're strong?"

"Of course not. You are the person who has always helped me see my own strengths. Why would you think otherwise?"

"Xandra said I treated her like glass, and it only made her feel worse about herself."

"It sounds to me as if you and Xandra were carrying around a lot of long-standing burdens that you and I never picked up in the first place."

"I still fear repeating the same mistakes with you. I'm afraid it's my tendency to treat my lady like a goddess to the point that she feels idealized rather than adored."

"You worship Hespera. What lady in her right mind wouldn't want you to treat her like that kind of goddess?"

Lio kissed her eyelids. "When I make a portrait of you in glass, I will give you one white eye and one red."

She looked down, at a loss for words. "No one has ever treated me the way you do. You told me the things we did in the shrine were sacred."

"And you told me you hold me sacred."

She put his hand to the glyph shard at her neck. "'Awaken unto me... beneath the endless sky, where we are free.'"

"My embrace is certain."

"'With your heart against mine, I shall be strong.'"

His brow furrowed. "Then what is that lingering knot of distress in our Union? I can feel you trying to untie it without success."

Cassia frowned and looked away. But why hide this? She could not make him a promise until she paved the way for her escape. But she could keep paving the way for what she hoped they would have together.

She could not resist seeing how he reacted to her hints.

She met his gaze. "I will always be jealous of Xandra. I cannot help it, for she has tasted your blood, and I have not."

Lio was silent for an instant, as if afraid to breathe. When he spoke, his voice was low, almost gravelly with intensity. "Cassia. Is that something you think about? You, drinking from me?"

"Yes. I imagine it."

"That gives you pleasure?"

"How can you think I would not feel pleasure at the idea of feasting on you, as you do on me?"

"That's not something I would take for granted."

Of course. His one attempt at providing the Feast for another had ended in disaster. How unbelievable, how unbearable, that Lio had any cause to doubt the pleasure his blood would give another. Cassia would make that right, when the time came, she vowed.

She ran a finger down his neck. "Does it give you pleasure to think of me drinking from you?"

"Pleasure?" He was nearly hoarse now. "Cassia, what would I do if you did not think of me in that way? How would I bear it if the thought disgusted or frightened you?"

"Nothing about you could ever make me feel like that. After the ways you've feasted on me..."

"The idea of you drinking from me is different."

"Yes. Yes it is. And I promise you I would never dishonor such a gift by feeling aversion or fear."

She placed a kiss on his throat, soft at first. He ran his hand up her back, over her hair, and eased her face nearer to him. She opened her mouth on him and gave his vein a gentle suck. She heard him gasp.

She could feel his pulse beating on her tongue. What would it feel like to actually…sink her teeth into him? What would he taste like? Would it come naturally to her, or would she need to learn how? Her face warmed with awkwardness, even as the staccato of his heartbeat in her mouth seemed to echo through her every vein, until her own heart beat with excitement.

She gave him a nip with her front teeth. He started in her arms. Easing his collar open, she trailed little bites of her incisors down his throat. She let one hand drift down the front of his robes to cup his arousal. He was already hard.

Cassia backed him against the ancient yew's trunk. "Didn't you ever think about it? All those long walks of ours in the woods at Solorum. Surely it occurred to you to seize an opportunity against a tree."

He licked his lips, watching her fingers work on the fasteners of his robe. "One tree in particular. An aspen. I put a fist in it instead."

A delighted laugh escaped her. "I shall never forget that tree. I'm so glad it wasn't just me."

"Cassia, my sweet, I do hate to say this, but—"

Her kisses and nips under his collarbone silenced him momentarily.

"—if I lift your skirts here and now, your legs are going to get *very* cold."

"Who said anything about undressing me? Let's see how impervious Hesperines are to the cold."

"Cassia, I…"

He trailed off as she opened her mouth on his chest. She gave him a long, slow kiss over his heart. Then she dared bite him harder than before. His skin and muscles shivered against her mouth.

"I would not have deprived you…" She bit him again. "…if I had realized how much pleasure this gives you."

"It is…life altering."

She grazed his nipple with her teeth, and he let out a short groan. No longer would she deny him this. She nipped and sucked each of his nipples in turn. When he was panting, she unfastened his robe further, treating him to the gentle pressure of her teeth as she went, all the way down his chest. He was speechless as she knelt before him in the snow.

"Mm. Entirely unaffected by the cold, I see." She took his rhabdos in her hands.

He shuddered. "Your hands are all the warmth I need."

She slid one hand along the underside of his shaft, all the way to the base. "My education in Hesperine words has only just begun. Teach me the words for these next."

His laugh turned into a groan. "Moskos."

She pronounced it back to him, teasing, and cupped his moskos in her hand. They tightened at her touch, tucking closer against him. She looked up to see his fangs emerge further.

She held his arousal in her hands, fondling and stroking. She slid her fingers over his velvet-smooth skin, feeling the hardness beneath. This was what she did to him. This was how he craved her touch—and her blood.

Just below his navel, she nibbled his skin. Down the trail of hair there, she pleasured him with her teeth. At last she put her mouth around his rhabdos slowly. She started with just the tip of his head, teasing with her tongue. She saw his hands fumble for purchase on the tree and his knuckles whiten.

She took her time, giving every inch of him the attention he deserved, licking and mouthing, sucking in long, leisurely, firm strokes. With her fingers, she traced every contour of his moskos, then covered him in the warmth of her hands.

She watched his expression above her transform from flushed enthrallment as he shuddered into her touch, to a grimace of pleasure as he began to thrust inside her mouth. He bared his fangs. She could feel his pulse quickening against her tongue. She could see, feel, taste his bloodlust.

It felt so good to have her mouth full of him. He was so hard and hot, waxed full. She slid him deep, as far as she could hold him, urging him with her hands upon his moskos. She met his gaze, inviting him with hers.

A ripple ran through his pale, bare torso, and a cry wrung out of him. He plunged into her mouth, but she was ready for him, and pulled back to give him room. She held him in her hands and mouth, feeling how his body worked as he pulsed and spilled into her kiss. Warm cream filled her mouth, and she swallowed hard, savoring the taste of him.

His rhabdos softened in her mouth, but above her, his eyes blazed. She pulled back, licking the last of his seed from her mouth, and saw him lick his lips as well.

He pulled her to her feet and spun them around so fast the world twirled. Just as she had imagined so many times, just as she had wanted, he pressed her against the tree and sank his fangs into her throat.

He drank from her with no shred of control. He bit and sucked, as if desperate to get her blood into him, and she reveled in it. She throbbed inside with the heat of her own pulse as he made her bleed for him.

Her climax made her knees buckle, and he held her up while she ground her hips against him. But he kept drinking. It seemed he would never get enough. Wonderful, for she wouldn't either.

He was relentless. Her head spun, and she gulped at the air while he made one hard draw after another at her vein. He pulled her to the cusp again, and her whole body tensed, her krana clutched tight. She needed it again, she had to have release. She spread her thighs, pressing herself against him, rocking her hips harder.

Her second climax made her cry out in astonishment. Harder, better than the first. He groaned and pushed her more firmly against the tree, tightening his teeth on her throat. She heard the scrape of bark on either side of her.

It wasn't until the last tremor ceased inside her that he lifted his head with a growl of relish. "Your pleasure tastes so good. I just want to make you climax all night so I can drink it."

In between pants, she managed, "I'll last you till moon hours." She eyed where his hands had scored the trunk. "I'm not sure about the tree, though."

They laughed together again, and he eased back to let her stand.

"Let us relocate to my window seat." He cleared his throat. "After we've said hello to the family."

"Right. We mustn't miss the goats' bedtime." Cassia pushed her tousled hair back from her face, assessing the blood spatter on her. "I'll fasten you up if you work a cleaning spell."

At the sight of the mess he had made, he blushed as he had when they had ruined an heirloom rug at the ancient Hesperine fortress of Waystar. But this time, he did not apologize.

SEAFARERS

"THORNS." LIO'S BLUSH SPREAD. "My mother is headed our way. We'd best get presentable so I can lift my veil."

Cassia swallowed a cascade of laughter and helped Lio fasten his robes. Her fingers fumbled, but between the two of them, they set him to rights in record time. A puff of moonflower and sandalwood fragrance, and his cleaning spell made her gown pristine once more.

They were standing side-by-side in front of Prometheus with folded hands and straight faces when Komnena came into view along the path that ran the length of the cliff. She was walking very slowly, but when she saw them, she proceeded at a more natural pace.

She gave them an all-too-benign smile. "There you are. I'm so sorry to interrupt your meditations, but there are two goats and a suckling anxious for tucking in and a bedtime story, and they cannot begin without Glass-tongue and the Brave Gardener."

Lio put a hand on his heart. "We never fail to answer the call of those in need."

"Saving bedtime is my favorite heroic activity," Cassia said.

"Papa errant needs a moment of your time first, Lio. He'd like to go over some of our Ritual tributaries' needs in preparation for your Gift Night."

Cassia smiled at Lio. "Do you celebrate your Gift Night on the date you were born?"

"Yes, on Winter Solstice."

"Not many Hesperines have reason to celebrate the night of their birth." His mother looked at him fondly. "I can scarcely believe my baby boy is turning eighty-nine."

Cassia stole an amused glance at Lio. With his beard, he looked a bit more mature than when she had first met him, but still no older than her. "Will you receive presents, like on a temple day?"

At her perusal, his eyes crinkled with good humor. "No, on your Gift Night, you give presents to others. Mother, Father, and I will agree on what best addresses the needs of each of our Ritual tributaries for the coming year, and I shall present our gifts to them on Solstice. It is a very important opportunity for us to provide for those under our care."

"We also have a lot of fun," his mother added.

Lio's gaze lingered on Cassia. "I'm looking forward to my Gift Night more this year than ever before."

"The more I hear about Winter Solstice," Cassia replied, "the more I look forward to it as well."

"It's going to be very special this year." His smile promised all sorts of surprises. "You'll enjoy it."

Komnena pointed overhead at their bloodline's constellation. "The Boreian Winter Solstice falls during the month of Anastasios, so our bloodline is responsible for a great deal of the planning, not only for Lio's Gift Night, but all the Solstice Vigils and Festivals."

"Why don't you go on ahead to speak with your father, Lio? I wouldn't mind a word with your mother." Cassia looked from Lio to Komnena. "That is, if you don't need to go straight back to Zoe."

"Kia and Nodora have not finished doting on her," Komnena replied. "Why don't you and I walk back together?"

Lio gave Cassia's hand a squeeze, then stepped out of sight. Cassia joined Komnena on the path, and they headed back toward the house. Someone made this pilgrimage to Methu often, judging by the fact that the snow had not piled up on this trail.

"You had a scare tonight," said Komnena.

Yes, Cassia had. For a brief time, she had faced the thought of losing Lio, when she had only just gotten him back. She searched for words. "Everyone has been very sensitive to what I've felt tonight. Since you're a mind healer, you would see me even more clearly."

"I find that what I learn from the Blood Union and my magic is merely a starting point. The real insight comes from speaking. That's how I do most of my work. No spells. Just talking with someone until we sort out what troubles them together."

"I've come to think of honesty as a powerful kind of magic. I see where Lio learned so much of what he's taught me."

"Here in Orthros, my methods are still a matter of some controversy. A mind healer is expected to delve into wounded thoughts and tidy up. My colleagues wonder what mere talking can possibly accomplish. But I persist, because I see how well my patients respond to our conversations, and their well-being is what matters. In another eighty years, perhaps, our scholars will decide what you have already realized—the power of words."

"If all your scholars are like Hypatia, it must take a long time for new thoughts to become accepted."

"The Queens say that the worst enemy of Orthros is not Cordium, but our own stagnation. I am fortunate in Annassa Soteira's partisanship of my methods."

"It sounds like you enjoy your work."

"I love it." A gust of wind blew in from the sea, and Komnena faced it with a smile, letting it pull her braids out of their elaborate arrangement. "My work healed me."

"Lio said you wouldn't mind if I asked you more about how you came to be a Hesperine."

"Not at all. What would you like to know?"

"Did you…ask Apollon to bring you to Orthros? Or did he ask you to return with him?"

Komnena shared a conspiratorial grin with Cassia. "He seduced me."

"Your story always did sound very romantic, the way Lio tells it."

"It was. My Hesperine descended into all the ugliness in my life and helped me find my way out. He seduced me with the promise of feeling safe for the first time in my life. With the first happiness I had felt in years."

"I understand. Your human life was very difficult."

"I was alone. Growing enough to eat on our barren little plot was impossible for one woman, especially a pregnant one. And I was always pregnant. My husband came home long enough for that, and little else."

"Your neighbors were not eager to lend a hand, I take it?"

"I wasn't beloved by many, because I wasn't beloved by my family, and they influenced others."

"From the farmhouse to the palace, families behave much the same," Cassia said.

"My parents died when I was young, and my aunt and uncle took in my brother and me. My brother, Leo, was the best mortal man I ever knew. Everyone who met him could not help but love him, even our bitter relatives. And he deserved it. He had an affinity for healing, as it turned out, and the mages of Akesios recruited him. To this day, I'm grateful his magic gave him a way out of that life. But I admit, I felt his loss."

"It must have cost you to do without him."

"He had been my defender against the family. They never liked me. I was too unruly and proud. They regarded my dreams as arrogance. They kept me just to get work out of me, so I married to escape. They predicted everything I did would fail." Komnena looked out to sea. "They were right about one thing. I was proud. But by the time Apollon met me, my pride and my hopes for a better life had worn away. I was ready to do anything to keep from starving during the winter and losing another babe. So I bargained with a Hesperine."

"You asked Apollon for help?"

"Indeed. A mage was troubling our settlement. I knew what he was there for, and I didn't want to be his next target."

"I keep thinking about what you said to Chrysanthos at the welcoming ceremony. How did you help Apollon defeat a member of the Aithourian Circle?"

"I beheaded the mage with a meat cleaver in my kitchen." Komnena wore her confession as gracefully as her silk robes.

A smile of admiration overtook Cassia. "I'm glad you made it clear to the Dexion that you're a hero of the Blood Errant in your own right."

"He would do well to remember how I taught his colleague the price of trying to take my child from me."

"The mage you killed was after Lio?"

"A mage of Anthros came to winter in the settlement and await the spring crop of infants. He planned to take away any child born with a significant magical aura. I was determined that if my little one survived, that child would not be stolen from me. So when I discovered a wounded Hesperine in the woods, I gave him my last milk goat. It was a difficult sacrifice to make, but if I got the Hesperine back on his feet, I reasoned he would take care of our mage problem. Imagine my surprise when the goat survived."

Cassia laughed with her. "Have you told Zoe about that part?"

"Oh, yes. It is a great delight to her that Mama and Papa met over a goat." Komnena halted at an outcropping that offered a stunning view of the sea. "I thought all I wanted was for my child to be born safely and have enough to eat. There was nothing more important to me than protecting my little one. But I came to understand I was starving for more than food. When I realized all I could learn here...all I could do... I had been hungering for so long for other people. And for myself."

"You found yourself here."

"And I discovered I like her right well." A wave crashed on the cliff below, and Komnena spoke over it. "Do you know the name of this sea, which separates us from Tenebra?"

Cassia shook her head.

"The Sea of Komne. I wept the first time I beheld it. I asked Apollon if it would be presumptuous of me to name myself after a natural wonder Hesperines had known for ages, when I was a young mortal who had played no part in Orthros's history. He told me, 'It is yours. It has always been yours, and it always will be, for you have chosen it.' So I became Komnena."

"It's a beautiful name. It suits you."

"Thank you. We named our son after the sea, as well, for I knew these waters would carry him into the abundant life I wanted for him. Deukalion means 'seafarer.'"

"A fitting name for a world traveler."

"We are so proud of his decision to serve as a diplomat. And yet every time he sails beyond that sea, I fear for his return. He would not have come back to me, if not for you."

Cassia listened to the waves, which had also carried her to Orthros. How grateful she was that she and her seafarer had both made it to these shores. She looked out over the Sea of Komne, and a sense of safety came over her. Tenebra was an ocean away.

"You were right, of course, when you said I faced a fear tonight. But I learned something important from it."

"That's what fears are for," Komnena said with approval.

"I need to learn more. I have some questions, but I'm not sure Lio can answer them. Since you help newcomers, I was wondering if I could ask you."

"Of course."

Cassia needed advice a bloodborn could not give her. Komnena had been a human woman who had made the choice to become a Hesperine. "Would it put you in an uncomfortable position if I asked you to keep this between us? Even from Lio?"

Komnena gave a kind laugh. "It is your choice what you wish to tell my son, Cassia. You do not need me to deliver your messages for you, especially in light of your profession of love for honesty. I would say it is my sacred trust to keep my patients' confidences, but that is hardly fitting between us. Every female needs private advice from other females from time to time."

Cassia took a deep breath. "Lio once told me it is a sacred tenet of your people to offer the Gift to everyone freely. But I know that can't mean just anyone. What must one do to earn that offer?"

"Ask. That is all."

"But...surely you have to show you're worthy somehow."

Komnena shook her head, her eyes shining. "No. It is the Gift. It is well and truly free."

How could it be that easy? How could something so powerful and good and true be right there before Cassia, hers for the taking? "But what if someone asked for it with the wrong intentions? What if they wanted the power for selfish reasons, and not to help others, as Hesperines ought?"

"A troubling question, but one to which the Goddess devised her own answer. The Gifting is an incredible experience, but not an easy one for an adult. Sucklings, in their innocence, come through it without trouble, and their powers awaken gently and gradually as they grow. But when an adult transforms from human to Hesperine, the Blood Union awakens all at once. Suddenly you are able to see all the life you have lived and all the choices you have made with empathy you did not possess then. It can be devastating to the conscience."

Cassia didn't want to imagine. Reliving all *she* had said and done…all the things she was not proud of…and it was too late to change any of them.

"When new Hesperines come through the Gifting," Komnena explained, "their hearts and minds are changed. They have seen through the eyes of all those they have known, and they have come to understand what impact their own words and actions had. They have learned how to treat others."

"It's like a purification."

"A teaching, I would say."

"Why don't we turn all the world into Hesperines, so everyone learns empathy?"

"That would take away their Will, wouldn't it?"

"Yes, of course. But I cannot imagine them being unhappy with what they gained."

"They might not gain it," Komnena cautioned. "Hespera seeks to rescue everyone, but some have chosen a path that takes them away from her. They destroy themselves."

Cassia listened to a wave break on the rocks below. "What do you mean?"

"Those who are truly wrong-hearted cannot withstand confronting their own deeds. Their own evil is too much for their minds, spirits, and bodies. They do not make it through the Gifting to become a Hesperine."

"It's possible to die during the transformation?"

"But that's not something you need trouble your thoughts about. It is a rare event in our history, when anyone so corrupt seeks the Gift."

How corrupt was too corrupt? How many cruelties could a conscience withstand?

"Cassia." Komnena touched her cheek. "If there is anything required to receive the Gift, it is one thing only. Love. Anyone who holds fast to that comes safely through into eternity."

Cassia knew how to love. She was coming to realize the love she had inside her was very strong indeed.

But was it strong enough to keep her alive, when she must face all she had done in the darkest, most loveless years of her life?

36

nights until

WINTER SOLSTICE

DUEL OF INTELLECTS

WHEN THE EMBASSY SET foot in Hypatia's library, it gratified Lio to hear the Tenebrans let out a collective exclamation. Their wonder rose in the Blood Union as the echoes of their voices ascended to the domed ceiling, where models of the planets levitated in orbit.

He sensed Cassia's low spirits lift for the first time in hours. They had been flying so high last night. What had sunk her? Cup and thorns, her playfulness in the woods... He had seldom felt so...free.

He had felt her teeth on him for the first time.

She had banished all the apprehensions closest to his heart. He felt securer in their future than ever before. She wanted what he imagined for them. She fantasized about it the way he did. She had given him a taste of it last night.

If he did say so himself, he had made good on his promise to drink her pleasure all night. So why had they been unable to recapture that brief sense of abandon they had enjoyed in the forest?

At breakfast, she had been so intent that he help her prepare for this circle that she had given him no chance to discover what worried her. Now she focused on the event at hand, and hints as to what troubled her receded further from his reach.

She ogled the enormous shelves arranged like spokes around the center of the room. "I could not count all these books and scrolls if I devoted the rest of my life to the endeavor. There must be countless ancient wonders here."

"You see, Lady Cassia," Lio said, "your first visit to House Hypatia is no cause for grim countenance. The eminent scholar's bark is formidable, to be sure, but she has promised not to bite our guests."

Cassia gave a courtly laugh. "I am not intimidated by what I do not understand, Ambassador. I am eager for tonight's scholarly circle, I assure you."

If the coming encounter with Hypatia was not to blame for Cassia's gravity, then what was? Why had she returned from her walk with Mother with such altered spirits? A conversation with his mother usually eased a person's burdens, and yet this one seemed to have made Cassia's heavier.

What could possibly weigh on her that she could not confide in him?

Kia, one of many scholars already crowding the library, awaited the embassy at the bottom of the grand staircase. "Welcome, guests from Tenebra. Come see what treasures and surprises the collection has in store for you."

Cassia took the lead as they joined Kia below in the central aisle. "Sophia Eudokia, when the ambassador told me your bloodline is custodian of an impressive library, he understated."

Kia swatted Lio's arm with one of the scrolls she had tied to her sash with silk ribbons. "He is always trying to cover for his feelings of inadequacy regarding his own bloodline's meager collection."

Lio smiled, his eyes gleaming with challenge. "Perhaps if your contributions to my experiments on magically transcribing text had been less... destructive...Blood Komnena's library would have a chance of catching up more quickly."

"*Our* experiments." Kia widened her eyes at him. "But let us not discuss them. We wouldn't want anyone to discover our...professional secrets."

Silent laughter echoed through Cassia's aura. She must have realized he and Kia were talking about the scroll of Konstantina's they had destroyed. Perhaps he and his Trial sister could help his Grace recapture her good mood.

Chrysanthos strode past Kia, examining the shelves. "Are there many secrets in this library, Sophia Eudokia?"

She turned in place to track him with her gaze. "We do not hoard knowledge here, Honored Master Adelphos. The doors of this library are open to all, at any hour of the night, every night of the year. These texts keep constant vigil in defense of truth."

Tychon followed in his master's wake with a disdainful look at the shelves. "We saw larger libraries on our visit to Cordium, did we not, Master?"

"The Akron's Library occupies three chambers," the Dexion mused.

Kia smiled. "This is only the first chamber. Our library occupies eight halls across four levels."

"Astonishing." Eudias clutched his hands in front of him, his nose inches from the shelves, as if he intended to breathe the titles on the spines and scroll ends.

"You live here?" Cassia looked all around them again, wonder in her voice. "You grew up surrounded by this?"

"I learned to read in this room," Kia replied.

Lio pointed to a nearby alcove, where there was a pile of silk cushions under a window. "Your mother sat on the floor with you right there. She held you on her lap for hours while the two of you worked through her scrolls."

Kia's gaze lost its sharpness and became distant. "I often came to tears because I was so impatient with all I did not know. Each time, she gave me a knowing smile and pulled me close and promised that one day, I would read every word in this room."

"She was right," Lio reminded his Trial sister. He knew she wanted no comfort about her differences with her mother, but he gave it to her, anyway. "How proud your mother is that you are here tonight to lend your thoughts to such a momentous discussion and participate in this historical moment."

"I don't know how proud she'll be by the time we're done. I make no promises to bite my tongue." Kia gestured around her with a scroll. "There is only one secret in this library. The first person who discovers it has my respect."

Eudias appeared thoughtful, but Tychon snorted.

"A scavenger hunt, is it?" the Semna piped up.

"A contest," Chrysanthos said. "Challenge accepted, Sophia."

Now Kia marched past the Dexion. She halted suddenly before Skleros and rapped his knuckles with her scroll.

The necromancer's tinderbox dropped from his hand. He glared at Kia over his unlit smoke.

Kia inched closer to Skleros. Lio took a step forward, unsure whether she or the Gift Collector needed a diplomat as a shield. Mak and Lyros flanked the necromancer in silence and watched the confrontation.

Kia glared into Skleros's eyes. "No. Fire. In the library. I will not tell you twice."

His answer was a sneer and a huff.

Kia levitated the tinderbox, and it hit her hand with a smack that made some of the mortals jump. She strode past Skleros, showing him her back, and handed his tinderbox to Mak. "You may petition the Stand to return this to you once you are back at the guest house."

Mak smirked at Skleros. "If everyone is extra friendly tonight, perhaps we'll feel inspired to be generous."

Kia held out her hand to Skleros.

"What?" the necromancer demanded.

"Fire charm," she stated.

He hesitated an instant too long. The fire charm flew out of his pocket, disarranging his robes on the way, and landed in Kia's hand.

"So, you get handouts from the greased robes in Corona." Kia worried the sunstone between her fingers. "You hardly ever see these in this hemisphere. Too bad they're so hard to replace."

There came a hiss, a pop, and a puff of smoke. The gleam inside the sunstone faded.

Skleros grimaced at Kia's handiwork.

"That's right," Kia said. "I'm a methodological deconstructionist."

Cassia cleared her throat. "Sophia Eudokia, I'm afraid I have never heard of that affinity. Would you be so kind as to explain it?"

"Certainly, Lady Cassia," Kia answered. "Strictly speaking, methodological deconstruction is an application, not an affinity. If I had remained mortal, I never would have been a mage, but I gained blood magic with the Gift. Using the abilities and awareness common to all Hesperines, I am able to act on scholarly observations to reverse charms and castings."

"She destroys the honest work of other mages," Chrysanthos said, "by dismantling their spells."

Kia beamed and dropped the stone back into Skleros's hand. "There. Perfectly safe."

"Don't ask me to light your smoke for you." Xandra joined them with her sketchbook under her arm and Nodora at her side. "The no-fire rule applies to everyone, even princesses. Kia's family has my solemn promise that I shall never practice in here."

"Then let us take this outside," the Gift Collector invited.

Xandra's eyes narrowed at the smoke dangling from Skleros's lips. "Are you sure that's wise? Fire magic is rather unruly, you know. I might miss your smoke."

"Oh dear," said Nodora. "That would certainly lower the spirits of this cheerful Summit. How would you explain it to the ambassador?"

Lio showed his most conciliatory smile to the necromancer. "That's all right, Princess Alexandra. Accidents are understandable. Speaking for Orthros's ambassadors, we could hardly classify a helpful gesture gone wrong as a diplomatic disaster."

Skleros put his leather-armored hands into the sleeves of his necromancer robes and gave a mocking bow. Lio heard the Gift Collector's knuckles crack.

"Princess Alexandra," said Cassia, "if I may beg a helpful gesture of you, there is a different matter with which your unique knowledge would be most helpful."

Lio sensed Cassia's decision and confidence. Her grim frame of mind was definitely not due to Xandra.

Xandra answered with hopefulness in her aura, betraying her uncertainty by adjusting her sketchbook under her arm. "I endeavor only to be helpful to the embassy, Lady Cassia."

"As you so kindly showed with your generous hospitality to us last night," Cassia replied. "The game was quite a challenge, but after giving it more thought, I understand it much better now. It was a pleasure to participate in your match with the Honored Master."

Lio could only listen with admiration and relief as his Grace made amends with Xandra in front of the entire embassy.

Xandra smiled. "I'm so glad there are no hard feelings. About your side's defeat, that is."

"Of course not." Cassia glanced at Chrysanthos, who was watching her. She tilted her head, giving him an arch smile. "We would never have hard feelings about that, would we, Honored Master?"

He gave a mage bow. "Speak for yourself, Basilis. If you have a favor to ask the princess, catch her in a good mood."

"I am in a most generous mood tonight," Xandra assured Cassia.

"Then perhaps," Cassia went on, "you will allow me to take you up on the kind offer you made me during the royal celebration to educate me about mulberries."

Xandra's face lit. "I would be delighted, if you're still interested."

"I look forward to it more than ever," Cassia assured her, "after glimpsing your extraordinary trees through the window of your greenhouse."

Nodora gestured at Xandra's sketchbook. "Princess Alexandra brought her notes with her, and the library contains many works on botany for the two of you to discuss."

Kia went to Cassia's side. "Come, let us enjoy the collection while we wait for everyone to gather for the circle."

Lio caught and savored this moment. Cassia and all his Trial sisters standing together.

Kia showed the embassy through the library, introducing them to Orthros's scholars along the way. Xandra cast an indicative glance at Konstantina across the room, and Kia nodded, steering them all in the opposite direction.

The mortals soon broke up into smaller groups, some pausing to study pictorial works, others captivated by the movement of the astronomical models overhead.

Lio stayed close to Cassia's side, although he was unable to give her even a brief touch to show his concern.

"I am no mage," Cassia said, "but I am greatly interested in tonight's proceedings. I think I shall enjoy witnessing the duel of intellects."

"You have a stronger stomach for violent sport than I," Lio replied.

"Are you worried the scholars will draw blood, Ambassador?"

"They could teach your hound how to be a dog with a bone."

She patted Knight. "Pay attention, dearest. You might learn something from the experts."

The hound pressed closer to her skirts, even as the crowd gave him more room.

"I confess to apprehension," Lio said. "Such circles as these were volatile enough in the Great Temple Epoch, when all our cults dwelt across the road from each other in Corona."

"Familiarity bred contempt." Kia ran her hand across a rack of philosophy scrolls. "Absence has made few hearts grow fonder. I expect we will resurrect the very debates that occupied us before the exodus."

Cassia watched the mages of Kyria gather around a lectern to examine a medical text. "Let us hope words of conciliation will win the debates."

Lio nodded. "We don't have time to bog down in old arguments in the week allotted to this phase of the Summit."

"I know." Kia gave him a disapproving look worthy of her mother. "A certain ambassador responsible for the itinerary would not hear my pleas to devote more nights to scholarship."

Nodora drew nearer. "That's because we must allow plenty of time for actual fun, such as music and dancing at the homes of Blood Kitharos and our tributaries."

Nodora eased herself into the space between Benedict and Callen, gently dispersing the tight formation of Cassia's retinue. A few more gracious words from Nodora, and even Perita relaxed, despite the cluster of Hesperines around her lady.

Benedict stood stiffly next to Kia, apparently still on watch for an opportunity to take Cassia's arm. Kia gave the knight a smile known for drawing geniuses like bees to honey. Benedict's frown deepened. Any good diplomat ought to discourage Kia from goading the chaste knight, but Lio was too glad for his Trial sister to deter Cassia's specter.

Eudias pored over the directory plaque posted at the end of the aisle. "Do you think the arguable mutability of affinities will be a topic of discussion tonight?"

Kia joined him. "Do you take an interest in the mutability debate, Apprentice Eudias?"

"As a matter of fact, Sophia Eudokia, I have made a small independent study of the fluidity hex versus the mutability spectrum versus essential immutability."

As Kia and Eudias evaluated the strengths and weaknesses of the competing theories, Lio noticed the apprentice's stammers gave way to enthusiastic questions and confident answers.

"No, there is an extant copy," Kia was saying.

Eudias looked perplexed. "But where?"

Kia smiled as if she had a Gift Night present for the apprentice. She led their group to the end of the aisle and around the shelves to the next section. From a rack, she withdrew a sizable scroll Lio didn't recognize. She unrolled it slowly, and the apprentice's eyes widened.

Eudias stared at it, slack-jawed. "An original? In Prismos Kheimerios's own hand?"

Kia held it out to him. "Have a look."

"Oh, no, no, I couldn't. Do please hold it for us."

Cassia leaned closer to Lio. "What work is that, Ambassador?"

"I am not certain. Kheimerios is outside the scope of my studies. I don't spend much time reading works by mages of Anthros."

Cassia's brows shot up. "I had no idea Hesperines keep such works in their libraries."

"Free Will is sacred," said Kia. "That includes freedom of ideas."

Xandra made a face. "I prefer to exercise my freedom by ignoring everything the mages of Anthros have ever written, especially about fire magic. I trained in the Imperial way."

Eudias scanned the rack the scroll had come from. "Sophia, do my eyes deceive me? These appear to be Kheimerios's complete works!"

"So they are," Kia answered.

Eudias was silent for a long moment. "The last known copies were lost in Pterugia in 893 Ordered Time when a quake damaged the temple Kheimerios founded. No mage of our cult has set eyes on his words in seven hundred years."

Kia placed the scroll she held into his hands. "This is the first time we've ever had a chance to let someone of his own cult know his works survive."

Eudias cradled the scroll with unmistakable reverence. Lio recognized the quiver of emotion in the apprentice's aura. Lio felt exactly that way every time he unrolled a scroll that preserved the words of a firstblood he had never had the chance to meet.

Eudias looked at Kia over the scroll. "During his lifetime in the Great Temple Epoch, Kheimerios presented a set of his works as a gift to a colleague of his—the Prismos of Hagia Anatela, the Great Temple of Hespera in the east. He put it in the temple library."

Kia smiled. "Apprentice Eudias, you have my highest respect. The depth of your knowledge has led you to the secret."

"The library *is* the secret." Eudias looked around at the other mortals. "Do you realize what this means? We're standing in the library of Hagia Anatela!"

"Everyone knows it burned down." Tychon waved a hand at the scroll rack. "Those must have come from somewhere else."

For the first time Lio had ever seen, Eudias gainsaid Tychon. "Hagia Anatela is the only place they could have come from. There are no other copies."

Skleros propped a spurred boot on a silk-padded reading bench. "Are you sure Hesperines errant didn't steal them from one of your temples? If they can steal the Akron's Torch from the Hagion of Anthros, why not a few scrolls?"

Eudias faced the Gift Collector. "Haven't you been paying attention to the titles as we've gone along? It's like reading the *Catalogue of Lost Wisdom*. They don't need to steal anything. They brought it all with them."

Chrysanthos said absolutely nothing, which told Lio the Dexion could not deny the truth before his eyes.

"It didn't burn." Eudias's voice hushed. "We thought it lost, all of it. Just like Hagia Notia in Corona."

"My mother took Hagia Notia's fate as a warning," Kia said. "She vowed the same would not befall her temple's library. During the evacuation of Hagia Anatela, she put a sack of scrolls on the back of each refugee. Together, they carried every last scrap with them all the way to Orthros."

Lio wondered if his Trial sister realized how obvious it was that she was proud of her mother.

"I had no idea," Cassia said. "I will never think of Elder Firstblood Hypatia in the same way again."

"She is a hero of our people, thanks to her deeds—in ancient times." Kia ran a scroll through her fingers.

"I am sure the mages and readers of our party must agree with me." Cassia smiled at Eudias and Benedict. "I cannot but see this library as a powerful testament to the shared history of our peoples. We can appreciate your mother's role in rescuing texts that are also sacred to us."

"Hypatia dragged the carcass here along with the meat." Chrysanthos clicked his tongue over the scroll he was reading. "Texts by Hephaestion, Sophia? Aithouros himself burned the works of his erstwhile brother-in-arms after they had their little disagreement."

"Then Aithouros took credit for Hephaestion's best ideas," said Lyros. "Tell everyone why."

When the Dexion did not respond, the mortals' gazes turned to Lyros.

Lyros crossed his arms. "Hephaestion was a brilliant military strategist. The Aithourian Circle dealt themselves a loss when they cast him out."

Chrysanthos let Hephaestion's scroll roll shut too fast, and Lio winced with Kia.

"Honored Master," said Eudias, "that scroll must be sixteen hundred years old."

"It is fuel for the fire," Chrysanthos said, "especially since the Stand has been reading it and learning Aithourian battle tactics."

Mak shrugged. "If something happens to it, we'll still have your copy, won't we, Lyros?"

"That's right. I think it's in our residence at your parents' house, isn't it?"

"You left it on the terrace. I put it back on your bedside table for you."

Lio wasn't sure how many of the Tenebrans were finally waking to the fact that Mak and Lyros's bond was deeper than battlefield camaraderie. Judging by the way Chrysanthos's eyes narrowed, the mage had just heard his suspicions confirmed.

Lyros smiled. "What are you going to do, Honored Master Adelphos? Skleros is unable to lend you his tinderbox, and Princess Alexandra has already made her position clear."

Chrysanthos shoved the scroll back into its rack. "It can stay here with everything else not fit to set foot in the temples of the gods."

With an effort, Lio bit his tongue. He must let his Trial brothers speak for themselves. Mak's aura blazed with anger, but he stood back and let Lyros go in for his kill.

Lyros strolled over and patted Chrysanthos on the shoulder. The mage flinched.

"Aithouros was a one-man army in combat, I'll grant you," Lyros said, "but Hephaestion really was better at taking the long view. Your Order should have kept him around. Too bad they just couldn't get past how Hephaestion loved Gladius."

"A well known detail of history," Chrysanthos said smoothly.

"Yes, it's all in the discourses," Lyros said. "In ancient times, there was a practice within the cult of Anthros of encouraging the closest of bonds between male mages. Hephaestion argued that reducing such partnership to mere brotherhood went against sacred tradition. He and Gladius defended their love to the last."

Now the mortals' shocked gazes were directed at the Dexion.

"Gladius the Martyr?" Benedict queried. "The Sword of Anthros? All of Tenebra and Cordium mark his death with a sacred festival every summer."

"Yes," Lyros answered. "Didn't you ever wonder why Gladius so eagerly sacrificed himself in battle after their circle turned on Hephaestion?"

Chrysanthos's expression was sour. "Gladius's role in their arrangement in no way shamed him before Anthros. Hephaestion's proclivities, on the other hand, befitted a handmaiden of Hedon, not an Aithourian mage. He was disciplined as befits an apostate."

Lyros's face was too calm. Lio had seen that look all his life. Chrysanthos had no idea how close he was to getting a taste of the Stand's discipline.

"Perhaps," said Lyros, "if you had not wasted Hephaestion, your best strategist, the Last War would have gone better for you."

"Must I remind you that we won the Last War?"

"Your enemy achieved a secure position and built up greater strength than ever before. You call that victory?"

"What triumph is there in retreat?"

"Retreat is fleeing from the enemy. We fled to Sanctuary. If you cannot see our victory, open your eyes." Lyros crossed the aisle and took Mak's hand with neither hesitation nor a passing glance at the mortals' reactions.

This was the image of triumph. This was Orthros, where Lio's Trial brothers need never hide or defend their love.

"May I compliment you on your strategy, my Grace?" Mak murmured, too low for mortal ears to hear.

Lyros squeezed Mak's hand. "When the embassy visits the gymnasium, it will be your turn."

"I'll just turn the embassy's education over to you two," said Lio.

Behind Chrysanthos, Benedict had taken Hephaestion out of the scroll rack again. The knight pored over the text with drawn brows.

Cassia took his arm and looked at the scroll with him. "Benedict, you read Divine, too?"

"There was a time when I was studying for entry into the Temple of Andragathos."

She cast him a surprised glance. "What do you make of Hephaestion?"

"He is eye-opening."

THE PHAEDRIC CRIME

RELUCTANT AS LIO WAS to interrupt the embassy's first experience with the library, at last he observed to Kia, "It appears everyone is beginning to take their seats."

Kia nodded. "I'll be with you in a moment after I re-shelve what we've taken out."

Cassia and Xandra surrendered a natural encyclopedia, Eudias parted with Kheimerios, and a troubled Benedict ended his introduction to Hephaestion. Lio ushered Cassia and her retinue to the open center of the chamber, where rows of chairs were arranged in two semicircles facing each other.

"The first row on the embassy's side is reserved for the mages," Lio explained.

Chrysanthos and his lot would be on the front lines and bear the brunt of Hypatia's debate.

"I'll be on the first row on the Hesperine side." Xandra pointed across the divide. "I mustn't let my eldest sister represent the royal family alone. Thinking caps ready, everyone?"

She crossed over to take up her post. That was one ally of the Summit on Hypatia and Konstantina's side of the room.

"Where is the royal representative to sit, Ambassador?" Cassia asked.

"In the second row, along with some Hesperines who will remain on the embassy's side to facilitate the discussion." Lio showed her to her chair.

She settled in with Knight on her feet. "Excellent. I was hoping I could rely on your translations again tonight."

"Certainly." Lio took the chair beside her.

Benedict halted in his tracks and glanced from Lio to the chair on Cassia's other side, which was occupied by a pile of Kia's scrolls. But the man said nothing and stepped around to the next row to take the chair right behind Lio. Lovely. He would be breathing down Lio's neck the entire night, literally.

Nodora sat down on the other side of Kia's chair, and Perita and Callen took the seats behind Cassia. Initiates offered cups of coffee and fruit juice, compliments of Lio's uncle, which the Tenebrans had to refuse.

Eudias turned in his seat to look back at Cassia and Lio. "How generous of our hosts to provide me with a seat in the front row. As an apprentice, I am uncertain I should be here, Ambassador."

"I assure you," Lio replied, "that chair is yours. Hypatia has invited all mages in the embassy to sit with her as peers. If you wish to speak, you need only extend your hand, palm-up, in the circle petition, the age-old gesture of scholars and mages engaging in debate among their equals."

"Oh, yes. I know the circle petition...although we don't use it much anymore."

The Semna's attendants seated her, and Ariadne ended up in the chair beside Eudias. Above her veil, her brown eyes smiled at her fellow apprentice, and not the way she smiled at everyone else. The young man did not appear to notice. Perhaps his vows of celibacy were welcome to him, or there was a lady or lad at home in Cordium for whom he reserved his heart.

Kia's scrolls levitated. She landed in her seat, and the scrolls landed on her lap. Her eyes were flashing.

Nodora leaned forward. "What's the matter?"

Kia cast a glance at Eudias, then took a deep breath, then put on a smile sharp enough to cut. "Honored Master Adelphos decided to peruse the shelves a moment longer. We discussed the *New Cosmology*. He was kind enough to explain it to me in terms a child could understand."

Eudias looked dismayed. "Sophia, does the Honored Master not realize your mother wrote it?"

Cassia's eyebrows shot up. "Apprentice Eudias, are the works of Elder Firstblood Hypatia still read in your cult?"

"Well, of course, Basilis. Have you not heard of her?"

"Not until my time in Orthros."

"She was one of the most dazzling lights of the ancient world. She began her career in Corona itself. Her works remain the seminal texts on many subjects."

Kia let out her breath. "They are so fundamental to magical study, it would be impossible to ban them."

"After a thorough examination of all her works by the Akron's inquisitors," Eudias explained, "it was decided that some portions of Hypatia's texts were pure and faithful to the tenets of the Orders. Although I am afraid certain of her works were judged too..." He cleared his throat. "They reflected the changing times, which led to the unfortunate falling-out between our cults."

"It's all right, Apprentice Eudias," Kia assured him. "You don't have to apologize that your cult sanitized and censored my mother's works and now continues to distribute them in mutilated form to young apprentices. That wasn't your decision. I shall not apologize for the fact that she was utterly heretical. During her time in Hagia Notia and Hagia Anatela, anyway."

At that moment, the legend in question made her grand entrance. With her olive skin and thick, artfully curled black hair, Hypatia would not have looked out of place among Cordian sophisticates of any epoch. She took a seat on the front row opposite the mages. At least her Grace was at her right hand. Khaldaios might buffer the helpless mortals from his beloved.

Next to him, Konstantina and Adwene took their seats, and the other Hesperine scholars filled the rows behind. Xandra's attendance was a statement for peace, but her presence alone could not moderate the strong opinions closing ranks around Hypatia and Konstantina.

When Uncle Argyros sat down on Hypatia's left, Lio breathed a sigh of relief. With Orthros's greatest diplomat on the front row, the Summit would not end in disgrace tonight.

The circle began, and Lio ran the race of translating for Cassia. Within the first half hour, she glazed over in the eyes. Kia exchanged a sympathetic, amused glance with Lio. Hypatia could still best all her students at being a walking dictionary. Eudias, however, watched like a bright-faced boy cheering on his favorite athletes at the games.

When Phaedros's name entered the discussion for the first time, both Lio and Kia tensed in their seats. He hesitated over his translation.

Cassia's attention sharpened. "I beg your pardon, Ambassador? Who do the Hesperines say must answer for his crimes against sacred principles?"

Lio cleared his throat. "Never mind. I think we are finished with this subject."

But Hypatia charged into it headfirst. If Lio had been a mortal, he would have broken out in a cold sweat. Kia sat on the edge of her chair, her whole aura alert with indignation.

"Sophia Eudokia," Lio said amiably, letting her hear his warning in the Union, "I know you have strong opinions regarding this problem, but I think perhaps we ought to allow the elders to move on to other topics."

"She's not going to," Kia hissed. "She's not."

Kia was right. Hypatia was not going to move on.

Cassia leaned closer to Eudias. "Apprentice Eudias, which mage of Anthros are the Hesperines critiquing?"

"Not a mage of Anthros, Basilis," Eudias murmured. "A Hesperine. Phaedros, who perpetrated the Phaedric Terror."

Lio had hesitated too long. Eudias's explanation stung him. He cursed himself for letting an apprentice war mage beat him to it.

But Cassia's aura was one big scoff. She didn't believe Eudias. She glanced at Lio. "Ambassador, can you shed light on this unusual subject?"

"Yes, although it grieves me to do so." Lio made himself say it. "Phaedros is indeed a Hesperine and a criminal. During the Last War, he caused unimaginable suffering to countless mortals, which brought grave consequences to your people and mine. Orthros in no way condones his actions."

"He was also one of the most brilliant mages ever to walk the streets of Corona," Kia retorted.

Lio shook his head to caution her.

But Kia wasn't going to drop the subject, either. "His works deserve to be read alongside my mother's."

"The Queens reserve a place for his writings in the royal library," Lio reminded her.

"Yes, in a veiled corner we aren't allowed to enter until we're of age," Kia shot back.

Lio sensed them heading into one of their heated debates about censorship and hypocrisy.

Thankfully, Eudias interrupted with a question. "Do you mean to say some of Phaedros's writings survive as well?"

"None of his original writings," Kia explained. "But he has been prolific in exile."

Eudias looked startled. "Oh. Ah, yes, I suppose he would still be writing, wouldn't he? Since he's still alive. But of course his landmark works dating from the Great Temple Epoch really are gone. All of those were in the library of Hagia Notia, which did not survive."

"No," Kia said, "only Phaedros did. Every last man, woman, and child in that temple was—"

Lio reached around and put a hand on her shoulder. If looks could kill, her glare would have sentenced him to death with the victims of Hagia Notia. But she didn't say anything else. Lio resolved to thank her later, whether it was her loyalty to her Trial brother or her concern for the greater good that inspired her to not jeopardize the embassy.

"I know," he said. "We are all grateful your mother left Hagia Notia for Hagia Anatela before the Last War. We all grieve for her friends and colleagues who were not so fortunate."

Kia's jaw clenched. "Whatever one's opinion on Phaedros's actions, we can all agree they were retaliation, not aggression."

Hypatia's gaze flicked to her daughter, and they all fell silent. Lio resumed translation, holding strictly to Hypatia's words.

"A madman?" Hypatia raised her brows. "No, I cannot offer insanity as his defense. He was in full possession of his faculties when he commenced the Terror. The night we call grief madness is the night we declare we are all mad."

"Then what defense do you offer?" Chrysanthos demanded.

"None. Although he is no longer one of our own, he is one of our kind, and for that reason, we take full responsibility for his wrongdoing, which he committed in blatant disregard for all our most sacred beliefs."

Konstantina made the circle petition. "Even now, the offense he committed is known in our laws as the Phaedric Crime, and it carries the sentence of eternal exile from our people and imprisonment behind a ward of the Stand's making. In all our long history, we have had cause to sentence only one Hesperine to that fate: the crime's namesake."

Hypatia nodded to her ally and extended her hand once more. "He acted in ways so vile they weigh on the spirits of our entire people. When he violated the Will of mortals and forced the Gift on them, he committed sacrilege against both the human and Hesperine natures that we hold in reverence."

It had been some time since Lio had worried about Cassia's opinion of his people, and his fears had seldom been justified. Until tonight. The doubt he felt uncurling inside her made him ill. How would he ever explain this to her? How would he ever justify why he had not told her?

Hypatia concluded, "It is my sincere hope you are satisfied with the steps we have taken to ensure Phaedros never harms another mortal again."

"Come now." Chrysanthos spread his hands, inviting the circle to agree with him. "You know our laws. Do you think Phaedros's incarceration is likely to satisfy us?"

"Can you deny that imprisonment until the end of time is a weightier sentence than execution?"

Cassia flinched. Lio had anticipated the shock in her aura, but it hurt worse than he had prepared himself for. The circle's words tasted bitter in his mouth as he made himself continue to repeat them.

Chrysanthos replied, "I think submitting Phaedros to Anthros's judgment the most fitting sentence."

Hypatia's tone and face were steel. "I assure you, no punishment is harsher upon a Hesperine than spending eternity with one's own conscience."

"You would argue he has a conscience? He carved a swath across Tenebra, creating an army of his creatures with the intent of marching upon Cordium. What conscience did he show toward the common people who flocked to become his followers, whom he deluded with promises of a new era? How many of them accepted his blood, and from his so-called Gift of immortality, received only excruciating death? I can tell you he spared no conscience for mages. He left no cult untouched. Whether through deception or brute force, he stole the gods' own for his cause and turned them into agents of his retribution."

Hespera's Mercy, the circle should never have spoken of this. This debate was supposed to have addressed esoteric theory, not the most controversial conflict between Hesperines and mages!

Lio could not allow this. He must get to his feet here and now and rescue his Summit from Hypatia. To Hypnos with the consequences. Lio tensed to rise.

Just then his uncle caught his gaze. Lio recognized the look in his mentor's eyes. Wait. Be patient.

Of all times, Uncle Argyros chose this moment to give the only advice he had offered since the night he had voted in favor of the Summit. Surely he saw where this was headed. It could only be a disaster.

Lio felt the touch of his uncle's mind, as surely as a hand on his shoulder, encouraging him to stay in his seat.

Uncle Argyros must know something about Hypatia's strategy. It was possible she had confided her intentions to him, her fellow elder firstblood from Hagia Anatela. The Summit may have cast Lio from the good graces of his mentor's closest colleagues, but no difference of opinion, however controversial, could erode Uncle Argyros and Hypatia's friendship.

Lio answered his uncle with acquiescence and sat back in his chair.

Cassia eased forward to have recourse to Eudias's translations again, and Lio hastened to give her his own. He would speak for his people, however it shamed him.

Chrysanthos had yet to give Hypatia reprieve. "If you will not give us the satisfaction of seeing Phaedros rightfully punished, why have you broached this subject at all?"

Hypatia's composure remained flawless. "We can have no hope of meaningful discussion when this scar stands between us, unacknowledged. As proof of our earnest commitment to reconciliation, we wish to face our own faults with honesty, unflinching. Phaedros played a role in the devastation of the Last War in ways that continue to grieve us these many centuries later. We can hold no one accountable for their offenses against us, if we are unwilling to hold ourselves accountable for our offenses."

Lio had to admit, the esteemed elder now making chaos of his carefully composed Summit was playing it like an expert harpist and turning it into an anthem of Hesperine principle. In the time before the debates were silenced, Hypatia had faced off with the Akron himself and bested him. She had outwitted the mind that later ordered the destruction of their temples. Chrysanthos was a little firefly buzzing about the star of her intellect, nearly invisible in the light of her conscience.

"I have broached this subject," she informed the mage, "in order to offer you words that have been impossible to speak in these sixteen hundred years of silence, which have held our cults in bondage. Phaedros, who was once my close colleague, has doomed himself to his chains, but in speaking his forbidden name aloud, I hope to strike off our people's shackles. On behalf of all Hesperine kind, empowered by my Queens to speak for Orthros, with Second Princess Konstantina, Royal Master Magistrate, to stand witness, I hereby offer you a formal apology for the Phaedric Terror. I express our sorrow over every single life Phaedros destroyed. We say with one voice, we carry your grief in our veins."

Gasps and murmurs went up around the room. Now Lio understood the look in his uncle's eye. Now he was glad he had done nothing to interrupt this stroke of genius—this long-overdue absolution.

Chrysanthos looked back at Hypatia, and Lio knew there was nothing in the mage's artfully crafted expression that she had not seen before. There was nothing he could say that would surprise her. "We will accept your apology, if you submit Phaedros to Anthros's judgment. Surrender him into my custody, and I will see to it the Order of Anthros brings him to justice."

Hypatia did not flinch. "We cannot agree to that, for your safety. You would not survive long enough to contact the Order, were you exposed to Phaedros. Although he forfeited his legacy as an elder firstblood through his criminal acts, he is our equal in age and magic. Only our power is enough to contain his. With our apology, we offer you this solemn vow. He will never harm another mortal again. Will you accept this?"

"My terms, once laid out, do not change."

She addressed the entire circle. "We have laid our hearts bare to you and placed them in your hands. It grieves me your spokesman will not accept our contrition. I can only hope the keenness of our pain is apparent to all of you. Although his answer is not what we hoped, we find consolation in saying these words to you at last."

Chrysanthos didn't understand at all. His response was irrelevant. Of course, it would be ideal if some true reconciliation could be achieved through this, but no one knew better than Hypatia that the Order of Anthros never changed its terms. No, she had not done this for the little insect who attempted to carry the ancient Akron's Torch.

She had done this for her people.

She had said those words for Hespera's own, who might now be able to forgive themselves.

There was no sound in the room except the rustle of skirts. Cassia stood, and all eyes went to her place in the second row.

"Honored Master Adelphos has spoken for the mages and thus for the gods, and all those who serve the divine must abide by his ruling. But it is my duty and my honor in this land to speak for those like myself, who are but humble non-mages, striving ever to become more holy creatures. On behalf of the people who live outside the temples, against whom Phaedros committed the greater part of his crimes, I wholeheartedly accept your apology. Henceforth, let it be known that in the eyes of Tenebra, Phaedros has paid a fit price, and we consider the scales of justice balanced."

Chrysanthos rose up from his chair and faced her. "You speak with a greater voice than you have been given."

"Not at all, Honored Master. I am but one small voice and one flawed heart. I will give the Hesperines my full forgiveness, for I too hope for the same from others."

In the silence, the Semna struck the floor with her walking stick in an unmistakable gesture of agreement. Then the room filled with the stomp of the Tenebrans' boots. While the Cordian mages were silent, every other mortal in the room applauded Cassia. Applauded forgiveness. For Lio's people.

A TENEBRAN THRUSH

WHEN THE QUIET OF veil hours descended, Cassia went out to the courtyard to wait for Lio. A flawless new bloom had appeared on one of the Sanctuary rosebushes. She could not resist burying her nose in its fragrant petals.

The sound of footsteps caught her by surprise. No Hesperine walked so audibly. It was a mortal who approached through one of the shadowed archways. Knight stood at attention.

She had no time to return to her room before Chrysanthos stepped into view in the moonlight. Her instincts clamored in warning, and she judged them justified. So did Knight, for he positioned himself in front of her.

Cassia put on a pleasant, polite expression. She need not explain herself. This was the courtyard outside her rooms, and she was here alone. It was Chrysanthos who was the interloper.

"Lady Cassia. How fortunate that I have run into you here."

"Are you lost, Honored Master? If so, I am sorry to tell you that you are far off course from the New Guest House." She gestured at the flowers around them. "As you can see, this is the courtyard at Rose House."

"Then I congratulate myself on my sense of direction. I was looking for your bodyguard's room, so that I might apply myself to him for a moment of your time. How unfortunate that I am tardy, and you have already dismissed your household for the night."

"Allow me to wake Callen and Perita, and we shall invite you into the sitting room, which serves as my hearth room."

He held up a hand to stay her. "No need. This common area will serve propriety just as well, and your liegehound is escort enough."

"No, Honored Master, I insist. Allow us to show you proper hospitality." She turned to go, forcing herself not to move too hastily, when all she wanted to do was flee.

"Lady Cassia, when you choose to play Kings and Mages, you cannot use handmaidens and foot soldiers as your tokens."

At the change in his tone, Knight gave a warning growl. Cassia let go of the door handle and put her hand on Knight instead.

So Chrysanthos had come to call her out on tonight's game. Very well. She did not need handmaidens and foot soldiers to beat him.

"Still trying to make effective use of a liegehound playing piece, I see." The Dexion strolled across the courtyard and leaned against the back of a bench.

The odor of his hair oils washed over her, just like that morning at Solorum when he had nearly thwarted her escape from the shrine of Hespera. The sound of flame and the taste of ashes came back to her. He had reduced that sacred place to a demonstration of his power for the king. He would not hesitate to do the same to Cassia.

"You made a move upon my game board tonight," he warned her. "You clearly do not know the rules."

The glyph stone had protected her from his spells that morning. She had the shard at her neck to shield her now. She looked him in the eye and did not back away. "Is that why you are here? To knock over my token and let me know I made a false move?"

"Oh, nothing so heavy-handed, I assure you." But his smile looked deadly. "Just a friendly word of advice from an expert to a novice. Stay in the orderly squares on your plane and leave the complex paths to me."

"Then in exchange, I will give you a friendly word of advice from a Tenebran to a mage. Do not leave most of your pieces on the plane and charge through the paths without them. You will find yourself with no tokens at all."

"As the Hesperines well know, he who relies on strategy needs few pieces to win."

From the corner of her eye, Cassia caught sight of the darkness behind Chrysanthos. The moonlight cast a long shadow through an archway where it appeared no one stood.

She could only hope she could trust her diplomat to rely on strategy. He must not take the path of the prince and charge in to rescue her.

"It's not the Hesperines you need to worry about, *Honored Master*. It is not to them that you owe your invitation to this gathering."

He whistled softly. "Oh-ho. My lady taunts at the gaming table. I had no idea you were such a bold bluffer."

"If you think that was a bluff, I fear you are not the strategist you believe yourself to be. You must keep all your pieces in the game. If you lose them, what is left to you? You cannot bring the sun into play."

"Well, well." He crossed his arms. "And here I thought you a novice. Be careful, Lady Cassia. You are showing your hand."

"I have announced my cards from the start. I have seldom had the chance to do anything of consequence for Tenebra until now. To the best of my ability, such as it is, I intend to serve my people."

"A pretty speech. Tenebrans like pretty speeches. They like shows of piety, too." The Dexion leaned forward, as if studying her for the first time. "I begin to see where your pieces are headed on the board."

"I doubt that."

"Come now." He gave a charming laugh. "My game plan is obvious to you. I too have made no secret of it. You can be as open with me. What is it you are after, wrapping the embassy around your little finger? To prove your usefulness to the king? To win from him something more than mere acknowledgment? Or a more personal contest, perhaps, with Lord Flavian's family. They are spectacular players all, and it will take a good game indeed to impress them."

"I have nothing to hide."

He put a hand on his chest, where he usually wore the sunstone medallion that signified his rank as the Dexion of the Aithourian Circle. "You should really consider confessing to your spiritual guide."

"I have nothing to confess."

"I am the last who will assign penance, I assure you. I am the finest player you will ever meet, and whatever your strategy, I would be happy to assist you in achieving it. Imagine what you could accomplish then."

"Oh, I see how it is. You are inviting me to be your second."

"You cannot deny it would improve both our games."

He had moved on from threats to temptation. And tempting it was indeed, to appear to accept his offer so he believed she was on his side for her own gain. How many of his moves might he reveal to her then, in order to enlist her aid with them?

But she knew such a strategy would be too costly. She had no time to waste pretending to be his token, even for the information she might glean. Her progress with the rest of the embassy hinged on her being one of their own, and even appearing to side with Chrysanthos would jeopardize that too much.

Tenebra had played with Cordium too long. It was time to show the Orders her people could win the game without the sun.

"I am flattered indeed, that you deem me worthy to sit at your table, Honored Master. But I am second to only one player, and that is Tenebra. I must reserve all my tokens for that cause."

"Really, Lady Cassia? You would give up the chance to share in my victory? You know that whatever it is you are after, I can give it to you. You're a clever woman, I can see. To have gotten to where you are, you undoubtedly know how to make the most of good opportunities, when they come your way. You must recognize that this is the greatest chance you've ever had."

"I have told you, Honored Master. I am after Tenebra's good. That is all."

His mouth twisted in a half-smile. "Innocence. You wear it well. Devout Tenebrans cannot resist it, I am sure. It arouses all their more noble instincts. But they are not so kind when the mask is torn away. Tenebra does not give gentle treatment to fallen women."

"I was never high enough to fall from anywhere. No man can move me, no matter how hard he pushes."

"You have yet to bear the weight of the gods."

"What's this?" warbled a voice from Cassia's left. "A theology lesson in the middle of the night? It won't do."

The Semna made her way across the courtyard, each tap of her stick like a judgment, her attendants in her wake. Cassia beamed at them. Pakhne and Ariadne gathered around her.

The Semna halted before Chrysanthos. "You should know better than to dawdle with a lady at this hour of the night, with no one in sight to vouch for either of you. No one questions *your* honor, I'm sure, but folk say unkind things about a woman caught standing too long with a fellow like you. Things Lady Cassia certainly does not deserve."

He bowed. "I beg your forgiveness. This was thoughtless of me. In my eagerness to continue our discussion of tonight's topics of import, I have been lax in my adherence to propriety."

"See that you keep your discussions of import to yourself, young man."

"As you say." Chrysanthos met Cassia's gaze. "I will not trouble Lady Cassia about Summit business again."

He turned to depart under the nearest arch, only to be halted by a grim-faced obstacle blocking the way. Callen stood at attention and stared at the mage in silence. His strong shoulders and broad fists, hardened under Lord Hadrian's command, made Chrysanthos's lithe athleticism look like a racing dog before a liegehound.

Chrysanthos gave one of his disarming smiles, which did not work. He tucked his hands in his sleeves, nodded as if in salutation, and turned to leave through a different arch.

Benedict lounged against the doorway, arms crossed over his chest. Across the courtyard, Lord Gaius held up the other arch.

Their gazes followed Chrysanthos through the only exit they had left him. As he walked through the shadow there, his steps hastened, and he glanced over his shoulder.

Callen came to Cassia's side. "Are you all right, my lady?"

"Thanks to all of you, yes. I assure you, I was utterly astonished to see him here. I was going to wake you, but he insisted—"

The Semna patted her hand. "No need to explain, my dear. Your predicament was quite clear. When I sensed his aura headed in this direction, I suspected where he was going and why."

"I cannot thank you enough."

"Thank *you*, my dear. You were Kyria's bird of mercy tonight, and I praised her as I listened to you sing."

Pakhne turned smiling eyes on Cassia, instead of the cold shoulder she had once shown at the Autumn Greeting. "My sister Nivalis's reports of you from Lady Hadrian's weaving room did not do you justice. You are a true representative of Kyria."

Benedict drew near, a rare smile on his face. "We need no temple canary, Your Ladyship. The Tenebran thrush will always sound sweeter to our ears."

Lord Gaius nodded in approval. "And she can out-sing him."

THE MORTAL WORLD

THE TENEBRANS LEFT CHRYSANTHOS with only one escape route. Little did they know it was the arch Lio occupied. As the mage came within a finger's breadth of him, Lio bared his fangs. Chrysanthos's step faltered, and he cast a glance over his shoulder.

That was all the satisfaction Lio could allow himself. Biting back a snarl and his Gift, he let the mage pass.

A few paces down the gallery, Mak fell into step behind Chrysanthos. Lio's cousin shook with silent laughter and gestured at his teeth with a scolding look. Lio waved to him. He knew he needed to put his fangs back in his head. Later he would need a round at the gymnasium, preferably with a punching bag no one would ever need again.

Lio tried to be patient, waiting at the edge of the courtyard while the Tenebrans fussed over Cassia. Her victory was written in their every reassurance. She was stealing Chrysanthos's pieces, indeed. Already the Summit was proceeding more favorably than they had hoped.

But Lio found himself more and more on edge each time she smiled at Lord Gaius or expressed her appreciation for Callen. When she took Benedict's arm, it was not to hold him at arm's length. She was at ease with him. She let him show her back to her room with the Semna on his other arm as escort.

Goddess, I am jealous, Lio admitted.

This was nonsense. He should feel nothing but admiration as he watched Cassia's influence grow. He should not feel as if Benedict were pulling her away, deeper into the human world, as they disappeared behind the curtains into her room.

LIFE DEBT

CASSIA WAS SURPRISED, BUT very glad when Perita invaded the gathering of guests in her room. Perita wielded her undeniable authority as a handmaiden to banish everyone, all but carrying the Semna out on a pillow and shooing the menfolk off to escort the elder. Callen was the last to go, after using a kiss to extract a promise from his wife that she wouldn't be long.

"Perita, you didn't have to get out of bed," Cassia said.

"Callen said you asked for me."

"I asked *after* you. I think he was right to come alone to face Chrysanthos. Just as I said earlier, I can undress myself."

"Nonsense. I should have come to give that mage a piece of my mind." Perita scowled, brandishing Cassia's hairbrush.

Cassia bit back a smile and readied herself for one of Perita's tirades. Whatever insults her friend hurled at the mage, they were sure to be satisfying to listen to.

But Perita's rumbling did not turn into a storm. She fell into gloomy silence.

Cassia had never given up on any endeavor. She was certainly not going to be defeated by Perita's silence. It was time to find out once and for all what was bothering her friend since they had come to Orthros, besides the general fears she shared with the other Tenebrans.

Cassia took her friend's hands. "Perita, please tell me what's bothering you. If it's something I've done, I will do anything to mend it."

Perita's eyes widened, and for a moment, it seemed as if she might speak.

But no sooner had she parted her lips, than she snatched her hand back and covered her mouth. She turned away and dashed for the privy.

Cassia hesitated. Did Perita want her to follow? The sound of her friend heaving made her wince. That settled it. No one wanted to be sick alone.

She joined Perita in the privy and soaked one of the Hesperines' soft cotton cloths in warm water before kneeling beside her friend. Perita hunched over the waste bench, her face turned aside. But when Cassia put the cloth to her friend's forehead, Perita did not push her away.

When Perita was done, she took the cloth from Cassia and washed her face. "Thank you, my lady."

"Oh, Perita. On the voyage from Waystar to Selas, you weren't really seasick, were you?"

"Never been seasick in my life. I've been on the choppy waters of Hadria plenty of times."

"I've only seen you like this once before. When Callen was in prison. You had just visited him, and it was his suffering that sickened you. But before I knew that...before we knew each other...I questioned you rather awfully about what I thought must be the cause of your illness."

Perita swallowed. "You were trying to help."

"Well, I hope I do better at it this time." Cassia brushed a strand of damp hair back from her friend's forehead. "May I ask if some very happy news is the reason you're not feeling well?"

Perita nodded, then promptly burst into tears.

Cassia's congratulations died in her throat. She pulled her friend close. "How long have you known?"

"About since we got here."

"It's your decision when to tell me, of course, but if I'd known, I could have made your duties easier for you."

"Oh, my lady, I wanted so much to say something, but I've been too afraid to say it out loud. What if the Hesperines hear? They mustn't find out."

"No, no, don't be afraid. You are perfectly safe, I promise."

"You know how they are about increasing their numbers," Perita whispered. "What am I to do?"

"What a terrible fear to live under every night we've been here. Let me banish it for you right now. No harm will come to you in Orthros. I swear it."

"Always standing up for me, my lady. I thank you for that."

Cassia could tell her friend believed in her intention, but not her ability to protect the child. What could she do? She had to make Perita see she need feel no distress over her pregnancy, only happiness. "Have you told Callen?"

"I managed to make it clear without saying. He's beside himself. It's hard on a man when there's a threat to his family he has no power against. He feels he's to blame. You see, we were trying, before we found out we would be coming to Orthros. It seemed like such a good time, with all our prospects so bright, thanks to you, my lady. As soon as we learned where we were headed, of course, we changed our plans. But it was too late."

Cassia stroked her friend's back. "I am so deeply sorry I have put you through this."

"There you go, blaming yourself, just like Callen. It's no one's fault. It's just…"

"The way of things, Perita? You know my answer to that."

Her friend pulled back and smiled for the first time in a long while. "When the way of things doesn't satisfy you, you do away with it."

"As I shall do now." Cassia took her friend's hands again. "I am going to tell you something you must not ever share with anyone, except Callen, of course. It could be very dangerous for us if any other members of the embassy found out. But I am telling you, because this knowledge will help you see that you are safe from the Hesperines."

Perita frowned in thought. "Are you into some sort of magic I don't know about, my lady? If your Kyrian friends have given you some charms they have to keep off the books, I'll be the last one to tell the menfolk."

"I'm afraid my secret is more shocking than that. I hope you will understand. I have only ever wanted to protect us."

"Of course. You know how much I trust you."

"I'm grateful for that. I need all of your trust now." Cassia took a deep breath. "You know that last winter, we were the first to find out that the supposedly Tenebran royal mage was actually the Cordian war mage Dalos in disguise. I have you and Callen to thank for alerting me."

Perita nodded, her frown deepening.

"When the two of you told me," Cassia went on, "I was very afraid for us. No good could come of a Cordian mage deceiving everyone."

"And right you were!"

"I set out to discover his intentions. I shall not tell you how, but I learned of his assassination plan before he attempted it."

Perita gasped. "You knew?"

"I did. And I can tell you with certainty the Hesperines were not his only targets. Cordium sent him to sabotage the Equinox Summit by assassinating the Hesperine embassy, but also to eliminate the free lords who are hostile to Tenebra's alliance with the Mage Orders."

The color drained from Perita's face. "I wouldn't put it past Cordium, but...to know that matters are so far gone..."

Cassia held her friend's shoulders. "I know these are heavy secrets. I know you wish you had nothing to do with them. So do I. But the time has come when it is no longer safer to not know."

Perita put a hand to her belly. "Tell me the rest."

"I knew I couldn't stop Dalos, not without help. I enlisted aid." Cassia's heart was pounding so hard, she could feel her pulse in her head. She was really going to say it. It was time. "I knew who had the power to stop him, to protect all of us from him."

"You," Perita breathed. "You told the Hesperines."

Cassia waited, frozen, for the judgment to fall.

Slowly, an expression dawned upon Perita's face. Wonder. She smiled. "By Anthros's Sword. You aren't to be trifled with."

Cassia breathed. "You understand. I told them what Dalos was going to do so they would be prepared to counter his spell—so they would save us. And it worked."

"It sure as Hypnos did."

Relief and joy made tears rise in Cassia's eyes. "I was so afraid you would think me a traitor and a heretic."

Perita snorted. "Everybody's a traitor and a heretic sometimes, my lady."

Cassia embraced her friend, then pulled back and ran her hand over her eyes. "You have nothing to fear from the Hesperines. They know you and Callen were the source of my information. They know you helped me save the Hesperine embassy's lives."

Perita wrapped both arms around her middle. "The Hesperines owe a life debt to us."

"They will not repay what you did for them by endangering your family."

"Whatever else they may be capable of, I can believe that. Everyone looks out for their own kind, even Hesperines. Seven lives we gave back to them. They'll not take ours."

"You and Callen can safely have quintuplets and still be under the protection of the life debt."

"Oh gods. I hope not. At least not my first time."

"I'm so sorry. I never meant to inflict that much fertility on you when I tossed Kyria's blessed sheaves your way on the Autumn Greeting."

They laughed together.

The tension drained out of Perita, and her shoulders slumped. "Gods. I've been so frightened."

"It's time we stopped living in fear. I shall free all of Tenebra from its grip, mark my words."

"If I do say so myself, you'll need my help."

"Oh, I will. I am so grateful you are with me."

THE HESPERINE PATH

L IO WAS ON THE verge of pacing by the time he sensed Perita's aura recede from Cassia's rooms. Cassia peered out of the curtains, her eyes searching the darkness.

Shifting his veil to make himself visible to no one but her, Lio stood and held out his hands to Cassia. She darted outside, and Knight trotted in her wake with a wag of his tail.

She slid into Lio's arms. "I'm sorry for the extra delay, but Perita and I had to talk. It was important, and it couldn't wait."

"No need for you to apologize." He hugged her close to him, trying to let go of his frustration. "Is everything all right?"

"I had to convince Perita she is safe from your people. You see…"

"Goddess bless, of course she would be frightened, if she believes all those stories about Hesperines kidnapping pregnant women."

Cassia blinked at him. "You already know she is with child?"

"We can all hear the heartbeat."

Cassia sighed, shaking her head. "After all the effort she's gone to not to say it aloud, in case the walls are listening. She didn't breathe a word of it to me until tonight."

"I'm so sorry. We'll do everything we can to help her feel safe."

"Could you have some decent food brought to her and Callen's room each night? I don't want her poisoning herself with those rations from Tenebra. I think I've managed to convince her your food is safe to eat, for her, at least."

"I'll make sure the initiates see to it right away, along with some extra blankets, stockings, and an even warmer cloak. If any dangers arise, we will find a way to convince her to let our healers help her. I promise we'll take good care of her."

"Thank you. She says the Semna is mixing tonics for her in secret, but I know your healers could do much more. I wish she would realize this is the safest place in the world for her to be with child. I wish..." Cassia shook her head again.

"You clearly managed to reassure her a great deal tonight. She already feels safer."

Cassia took a deep breath. "I had to tell her another piece of the truth about what happened at the Equinox Summit. Now she knows I warned your embassy about Dalos, and that your people know the role she and Callen played. I know it was a risk to bring her deeper into our plot, but I had to make it clear that Orthros knows she saved seven Hesperine lives."

"She took it so well?"

Cassia smiled, her aura bright with relief. "Yes."

Lio let out a breath, considering the implications. "She is a friend and ally beyond compare. In fact, after you, she is Orthros's best ally in the Tenebran embassy."

"The Dexion will regret underestimating the strategic value of handmaidens."

Lio's arms tightened around Cassia. "To Hypnos with the Dexion. You don't know how close I came to—"

"Ohh, I was afraid of that. You must have been sorely tempted. I'm sorry you had to stand by and do nothing."

"You were clearly in command of the situation. But I shall not forget how he threatened you."

Her gaze on his fangs, she smiled wickedly. "He'd best watch his back, then."

"And the opponent in front of him, for she is clearly winning the game."

"I do believe we have him surrounded."

"You are dauntless. You certainly showed that in the face of the ugly truths tonight's circle brought to light." Lio rested his hands on her shoulders. "I think we're overdue for a walk on the grounds and a question-and-answer session about Hesperines."

At his mention of how they had first gotten to know each other, she smiled. "When we met, our ramblings at Solorum were the greatest solace I had ever known. But now I know the grounds of House Komnena."

Underneath her fond expression and talk of comfort, he still sensed a heavy gloom, which had only deepened since Hypatia's circle. It was time for a respite at home, where Lio could finally discover what weighed so on his Grace's heart.

When massive evergreens and frosty, verdant air surrounded them suddenly, she blinked as if she had barely felt Lio step them to the grounds.

He did not let her go. "I'm sorry you had to contend with Hypatia and Konstantina tonight."

"They are the gargoyles at the gates of Sanctuary. I respect that. They have wrestled with Anthros's dragons and still bear the burn scars."

"The same is true of you. Chrysanthos is on guard against you. He has made it clear there will be consequences if you continue to usurp his authority over the embassy."

Cassia slid out of his embrace, but kept hold of his hand. She set off along the nearest deer path. "Yes, he was rather obvious about that, wasn't he? Have you noticed how heavy-handed he's been ever since we arrived?"

Lio levitated them both over a fallen log covered in frost and lichens. "In true war mage form."

Cassia shook her head. "He is of the Aithourian Circle, yes—but he's the Dexion. How does a man achieve one of the highest offices in Corona?"

"Hm. You do well to remind me. He is a war mage, but also a politician."

"His princess mother probably taught him flattery and manipulation in the cradle. And yet all he has done since he arrived is launch bald insults at every Hesperine within range."

"I admit, I attributed his behavior to the insurmountable hostilities between Aithourians and Hesperines."

Cassia watched Knight charge off into the underbrush. "I thought he would at least be cleverer about expressing his loathing. I credited him with greater subtlety than he has so far displayed. I am disappointed in Corona's golden boy. More than that, I am puzzled as to what has thrown him off-balance."

"Was he like this before he arrived in Orthros?" Lio asked.

Cassia paused. "Yes. There were cracks in his armor even then.

When he…provided that demonstration of war magic for the king that I mentioned—"

"The one on the palace grounds that you risked your life to witness?" Lio scowled. But as soon as he felt the echoes of her fear, he regretted betraying his own. He pulled her closer and held her in the shelter of his arm as they walked on.

Cassia put a hand to her pendant. "As you know, the Sanctuary ward covered my escape. That morning, I could think only of avoiding capture, but now I've had more time to consider the event and Chrysanthos's general character. It was almost as if he was taking out his anger on the… demonstration."

"Then there are his barbs at the Blood Errant," Lio observed. "Every time he aims at them, he deals wounds close to the heart. Do you think his grudge is more personal than his Order's long-standing prejudice?"

"I wonder. What I am certain of is that he is not at his best, and he is outnumbered. I have the advantage."

"He still has Tychon and Skleros at his back."

"I have you."

Cassia detained Lio in the shadow of the tall garden wall and pressed her mouth to his. Her attempt to silence his worry, however tender, would not succeed. He deepened their kiss, letting his magic sink into her mind. Even as her determination rose, she lowered her defenses for him bit by bit.

Lio Willed the high garden gate open. The iron moaned in welcome, and the mosses that clung to it shivered. He drew Cassia out of the wild woods and into the overgrown garden.

She called out to Knight, breaking the spell. Her hound abandoned his unsuccessful chase to follow her. Lio had thought them past her using her dog to evade topics she didn't wish to speak about. He had his work cut out for him.

Lio guided Cassia around a thorn bush taller than her. "Hypatia's circle was not how I wanted you to find out about the Phaedric Terror."

"So that's what you're worried about, besides Chrysanthos."

"Can you forgive me for not telling you about Phaedros?"

"What is there to forgive? I do not wonder why the subject never came up between us. We were too focused on the Hesperines errant who have saved more lives than he ever took."

"Your faith in our people never ceases to move me." Lio drew a deep breath, then sighed. "But he took a great many lives, Cassia. If there is anything more you feel you need to know about him, it is only right that I withhold nothing."

She drew to a halt amid bushes heavy with blood-red berries and star-bright icicles. She rested her hand upon Lio's heart. "What I said at the circle was no diplomatic maneuver. I meant every word. How can any mortal hold a grudge against Phaedros, when we commit crimes like his each day as a matter of course?"

Lio sank down onto a stone bench, taking Cassia's hands, and looked up at her. "I cannot tell you what your words of forgiveness meant to every Hesperine in the room. When one of us stumbles, we all do. Hypatia may say Phaedros is not one of our own, but there is no severing the Union."

"I will not stand for mortal hypocrisy. Hypatia is right in this—there can be no peace unless all of us are willing to admit our mistakes and apologize to one another."

"And yet I have not looked forward to the moment when you would learn we are not without blood on our hands." He looked down at their joined hands.

"You told me when we met the Hesperine path is not easy. That you try and fall short. Do you remember what else you said that night? In the striving, you still achieve much. All I have to do is look around us to see how true that is. As far as I'm concerned, Hesperines have fulfilled the Goddess's calling to create Sanctuary in the world. We are living in it now."

He bowed his head and kissed her palms. "If that is how you feel about Orthros, then I consider my calling fulfilled."

"Your words are surely destined to convince many more humans of Hesperines' true nature."

"No mortal's good opinion matters to me as yours does."

"You have had mine as long as you have had my Oath. Phaedros cannot shake a promise such as ours. I will not allow him or anyone else that power."

Lio drank down her words, and his thirst for her promises eased for the time being. "Then we have nothing to fear."

"I promise not to fear the truth, if you will not fear to give it to me."

"By our Oath, we will continue to face the truth together, with courage. Ask me what you will."

"Phaedros was the only survivor of Hagia Notia, as Kia said?"

"Your first question regards what he suffered, not the suffering he caused."

"It has always been my way to seek to understand people rather than to judge them. In the past, morality was irrelevant to me, even counter-productive to my quest to see through others. I sought only to predict what goal a person would pursue against me or discover how I could use their motivations to my advantage. Now I hope I am willing to attempt understanding and withhold judgment for kinder reasons."

"I do not disagree that Phaedros deserves our compassion. In his time, no one imagined conflict of opinion would erupt into violent conflict. Hagia Notia was the first temple to fall. The war mages descended on them without warning. It was the opening strike of the Last War. Because of Phaedros's status and connections, the Aithourian Circle spared his life on the Akron's orders. But Aithouros made Phaedros watch."

Cassia sank down next to Lio on the bench. "I can only imagine what he endured."

"Don't imagine. What you have endured is enough for your mind and heart."

"People who have suffered less than Phaedros have committed greater crimes with fewer scruples." Cassia wrapped her arms around herself. "Did Phaedros really believe in what he was doing? Was he earnest in his desire to create a better world?"

"Yes, he was a genuine devout of his mad dream. He sought to liberate everyone from the dominance of the cult of Anthros by ensuring Hespera's victory. He envisioned a future in which everyone was a Hesperine."

"Who can deny the logic in his plan? He would let the Gift cure the world's ills for him. Everyone living in Blood Union? I can imagine what life would be like, if all of us had such empathy."

"Forcing the Gift on anyone defeats the purpose. Violating their Will violates everything Hespera stands for. By subjecting terrified mortals to the Gifting, Phaedros caused the very suffering he claimed he wanted to prevent."

Cassia looked around them at the garden, her eyes haunted. "And thus he cost himself his place in the Sanctuary he sought to build."

Lio nodded. "He could have been a founder of Orthros alongside my father, my aunt and uncle, and all the elder firstbloods. The Queens have given him every opportunity to rejoin our people, but he rejects their efforts at reconciliation. He has made it clear he is still a danger to humankind."

"I cannot imagine any other reason why the Queens would subject one of their children to such a horrible fate as spending Orthros's entire history apart from everyone."

"It is a wound on their hearts that will never heal. We all know that, because we feel it too. All of us are complicit in Phaedros's suffering. His time in exile has only broken his already fractured being. Perhaps that is the foremost reason why Hesperines cannot bear the thought of him. We cannot save him."

"Do you really believe anyone is beyond saving?"

"I don't want to. But everything about Phaedros challenges my dearest convictions."

"Phaedros must have been a good person once. He survived his Gifting, after all."

Lio started. "As to the…consequences that can occur when the Gift is given in the wrong way, or to the wrong people…"

"That's what the mages of Anthros don't understand, isn't it? Phaedros didn't intentionally commit murder, he simply gave the Gift, and those whose consciences could not endure the transformation did not survive."

Lio hung his head. Goddess have Mercy, they were going to confront this truth in the context of Phaedros! "We had no idea it was possible for the Gifting to be fatal, until the Phaedric Terror."

"So there was no trickery in Phaedros's promises of immortality. He didn't know he might kill someone."

"When he made that discovery, it only aggrandized his vision of purging evil from the world."

"While the rest of your people were heartbroken."

"You have drawn the truth out of tonight's discussion." Lio put his head in his hands. "That was *not* how I wanted you to learn such a thing is possible."

Cassia lifted his face to her. "Actually, your mother and I happened upon the subject of the Gifting last night. She acquainted me with the facts in a much gentler way than Hypatia's circle, I assure you."

Right after confessing she longed for a taste of his blood, she had talked to his mother about the Gifting? Lio's worry gave way to relief, and he could see elation on the horizon. "You just…happened upon the subject, did you?"

"Just as you said she would be, she was happy to tell me about how she came to Orthros. She is very easy to talk with."

"I'm glad you feel at ease with her."

Cassia's smile did not reach her eyes. "I learned so much I didn't know."

Lio leaned his elbows on his knees, meeting her gaze. "Cassia, the tragedies Phaedros's victims suffered are far from the normal experience of new Hesperines. I wish I were qualified to describe it. Nodora could tell you more about it."

"Nodora is very kind."

Lio still sensed the weight on her heart. He held her gaze. "Cassia, do you think my mother would have submitted to the Gifting while pregnant with me, if she had believed for a moment it would cost us our lives?"

Cassia let out a long breath. "Of course not."

"A Gifting is a time of happy anticipation. Family and friends begin the evening with a celebration and welcome gifts for their new loved one. I've often attended Gift Nights among our Ritual tributaries to offer the well-wishes of Blood Komnena."

"So on your very first Gift Night, you receive presents."

"That's right. Everyone gives with confidence. We wouldn't have such a party if mortality rates were high."

That roused a chuckle from her.

"After gifts," he went on, "the newcomer may announce his or her Hesperine name, if moved to choose a new name for a new life. Then friends and family withdraw to pray for an easy and joyful transformation, and the newcomer goes into seclusion with those who will perform the Gifting."

"You explained to me once that the only way to receive the Gift is to drink a Hesperine's blood in considerable quantity." She took a little breath that soughed in her throat. "Who actually provides this blood?"

Lio's heart beat faster. So she had not left it to his mother to explain the finer points. It would still be his task—his pleasure—to fill in the details.

"Sometimes," he said, "an adult receives the Gift from his or her Ritual parents."

Disappointment sank her aura. "I see."

He leaned closer, brushing her hair back from her neck to fetch her gaze to him. "However, if you choose to stay in Orthros with someone who cares for you, it is your lover's blood that welcomes you into eternal night."

She swallowed. The first stirrings of desire perfumed her scent.

Lio smiled slowly. "Your Gifting is your first feast. When your hunger overtakes you for the very first time, your lover is there to sate you with blood and pleasure. You transform in your lover's arms, with your bodies joined."

"There can be no death in such an act of love," she breathed.

He shook his head, lowering his mouth to her throat. He buried his hand in her hair, ready to ease her face against his own vein.

The bleat of a goat reached his ears.

Cassia sat back, flushed but grinning. He gave her a rueful look, rubbing his mouth, and limited himself to holding her hand.

An instant later Zoe came around a bend in the path. All Lio could see of his sister and her two pets were their faces, peeping out of her silk mantle.

"Zoe," Cassia exclaimed. "We were just coming to see you."

Zoe cast an uncertain glance at the sky, then joined them in the shelter of the bearberry bushes. The quiet suckling hopped up on the bench between Lio and Cassia. They settled their arms behind her, still holding hands. The goats scrambled down to lay by the bench with Knight.

Lio smiled at Cassia over Zoe's head. "I was just telling Cassia how Giftings work. Why don't you tell her about yours?"

Cassia appeared apprehensive. "Only if you want to, Zoe."

Zoe smiled. "Everyone brought me so many wonderful presents. That's when Mama and Papa gave me my goats."

Cassia's smile returned. "What did Lio give you?"

Zoe pulled out the spyglass he had made her. It was collapsible to a size that fit easily in a suckling's pocket, but the magic on it was big enough for her to grow into. She extended the instrument to its full length and held it out to show Cassia. "Lio crafted this for me. It's not just any spyglass. He asked Mak and Lyros to make the metal parts and came up with the lenses himself. But he also put a spell on it, so when I look into it, it won't just show me what's up ahead. It will show me the way to whatever I'm looking for."

Cassia cast a wondering glance from the spyglass to Lio. "This is a powerful artifact."

"Well," Lio said, "it did require quite a combination of mind, blood, and light magics."

"That's how I could find where you were in the garden just now," Zoe explained.

"A truly special gift," Cassia said, her voice softening, "just for you."

Lio nodded. After Zoe's human family had left to get provisions for her and the other children, never to return, it was no wonder she was struck with fear every time someone she loved walked out the door, even if they were only going as far as the next room. He wanted her to know her family was always within reach now and that she had the power to reach for them.

"Some children are scared of the Gifting, but not me," Zoe said with a hint of pride. "When Mama, Papa, and Lio explained how it works, I knew I wanted to be a Hesperine so I would be strong enough to take care of everyone. I told them I was ready for the Gift, and they mustn't talk me out of it."

"Zoe was very mature about her decision," Lio praised her.

"I don't know why anyone would be scared," Zoe said. "Mama and Papa gave me my first Drink, and Lio stayed with us the whole night."

"What did your Gifting feel like?" Cassia finally ventured to ask.

Zoe became solemn with thought. "I didn't feel hungry anymore. I felt full for the first time, well, ever."

Lio pulled his little sister and his Grace close. Cassia rested her face on the top of Zoe's head, looking at him. He saw no fear in her eyes now, only the solace of the present overtaking the shadows of the past.

THE IMMORTAL WORLD

CASSIA'S EXPRESSION MADE LIO smile. He could remember when she never showed her true emotions on her face, much less spoke of them aloud. He remembered when she had allowed herself no emotion. Now that she had flung open the floodgates of her heart, it seemed she had a hard time shutting them again, even when she wanted to.

She planted a kiss upon Zoe's hair. Zoe swung her feet, happiness peeking through her aura.

Lio sat back and fished in his scroll case. On the end of the bench, he set out a quill, ink, and some scraps of paper. He sketched a simple glyph in the shape of a moonflower, then scrawled the time under it.

Cassia peered over Zoe and around Lio's shoulder. "What is your brother up to?"

"He's writing to his Trial circle in code." Zoe crossed her arms. "Bosko and I are going to come up with a code, too."

Lio grinned to himself and paused to make a rough sketch of a goat, which he handed to Zoe. She giggled. He drew two more little goats dancing around the moonflower, then folded the note and addressed it to Mak and Lyros, Telemakhos Residence, House Argyros. He jotted the same note three more times for Kia, Nodora, and Xandra.

Cassia watched with the utmost curiosity as he tossed a red-and-white, flashing spell light above the bench. A mere moment later, a barefoot Hesperine youth appeared before them in a simple runner's tunic with a red-and-white sash.

"Cassia, may I introduce you to the Queens' Couriers," Lio said, "an honorable circle of uninitiated Hesperines who serve Orthros while completing their educations."

The courier drew herself up. "How can I help you, Firstgift Komnenos?"

He handed her the notes. "Please deliver these within a quarter of an hour."

An impish smile appeared on her face. "It'll be eight minutes, Firstgift, for I aim to beat my best speed from last week."

"Five notes in eight minutes! You are fast." Lio tossed her a tin of gumsweets.

She caught them, bowed, then stepped out of sight.

"I told Bosko he should become a courier," Zoe said. "He learned stepping so fast. He would get to go all over the city helping people. But all he likes is fighting. He says he hopes he gets warding magic like Mak."

"You learned stepping fast, too," Lio reminded her. "It won't be long before you can travel farther than from room to room in our House. If you ever wanted to be a courier, you would make an excellent one."

Wistfulness uncoiled in Zoe's aura, but she shook her head, pulling her mantle closer around her head. "I won't have time to be a courier. I'll be too busy learning my magic with animals, when it comes in."

"Well, I will tip you with gumsweets for being an excellent sister. Come on, there's a new tin for you on my desk."

Zoe's frown disappeared, and she hopped off the bench. Lio and Cassia each took one of her hands and set off through the garden, followed by the goats and Knight.

A vision stole over Lio of many future nights here with children's hands in his and Cassia's. Young laughter and voices filling the silent garden. A home full of their younger siblings—and their own children.

When Cassia was ready to think about it, he would ask her if she ever saw that same vision, if she longed for it as he did.

Whatever shape their future took, he would not let Tenebra rob them of it before it began. He would not let the mortal world pull her back in.

They arrived at the door of his tower to find the courier waiting for them. She bowed again and handed Lio five replies.

"Did you beat your record?" he asked with a smile.

She beamed. "Seven and a half minutes!"

"Well done!"

"Good veil, Firstgift. I've got another summons." She disappeared once more.

Lio took Cassia and Zoe inside and spread the replies on the coffee table. His sister gnawed on a huge wad of her new gumsweets while she opened his notes for him. He put Cassia's dinner and a treat for Zoe on the geomagical warming plate, then started brewing the coffee in the glass coffee service he had crafted for his residence.

Cassia studied the notes. "Hmm, I see a scroll—that must be from Kia."

Lio nodded. "As children, we had a fierce argument over who should be the scroll. Finally I chose the moonflower instead."

"A diplomatic move." Cassia smiled. "Here is a shamisen—Nodora, of course. Xandra is undoubtedly the moth. The entwined speires are Mak and Lyros." She looked over at Zoe. "But why did they draw two goats, too?"

Lio handed Cassia a mug of warm vegetable stew. "Everyone is on their way."

She wrapped her hands around the mug, raising her eyebrows. "They are?"

"They'll be here on the hour, and they're bringing Bosko and Thenie to see Zoe. That's what the goats meant."

"You mean you put us in your code?" Zoe smiled at him over the rim of her warm milk.

"Of course. I thought we all needed some time to relax among friends."

The tension drained from Cassia's aura, and she cast a glow of ease and contentment upon the Blood Union. That contentment sank deep into Lio. He needn't have worried about the time she had spent with the Tenebrans.

When the bells of House Kitharos signaled the hour, the tones of a flute drifted into Lio's library, mimicking the chimes.

Lio chuckled and called, "Come in!"

Nodora stepped in, laden with her flute, a lyre, her shamisen, and a lute. "As I suspected, I am the first one here. We of Blood Kitharos pride ourselves on punctuality."

"Living right under the bells, you must never be late," Cassia said. "But it's a good thing Hesperines don't have trouble sleeping."

They laughed together, and Nodora took the chair she preferred for its acoustical position, setting her instruments within easy reach. "Last one here is a rotten egg and misses out on my first tune. What do you think, Zoe? What shall I play?"

"Um," Zoe answered, "'The Happy Herder's Reel'?"

"With pleasure." Nodora put her flute to her lips.

None of them could resist tapping their feet to the energetic dance. Halfway through the song, Mak and Lyros bustled in with the other children. Mak started dancing with Thenie in his arms, and she beamed and cooed in delight. Lyros watched his Grace with a besotted expression that Lio finally understood.

When Nodora finished, she said, "All right, Bosko. Your turn to pick the song."

Bosko hung back behind Lyros. "That's all right."

Lyros looked down at him. "What's Thenie's favorite song?"

"Well…her eyes light up whenever she hears that one about the baby star." Bosko looked at Nodora and cleared his throat. "I guess you could play that one. For Thenie." He cast a glance at Lyros. "Please."

Lyros patted Bosko on the back.

Nodora exchanged her flute for the lyre. "'The Little Dreaming Star.'"

By the time the song was over, Bosko was sitting with Zoe and sharing her gumsweets, and Thenie was bouncing happily in Mak's lap. Lyros lounged beside Mak on one of the benches. When Lio finished passing around coffee, he joined Cassia on the other bench in the place she had left open beside her. He put an arm around her shoulders, and she leaned into him, her contentment deepening into happiness.

Nodora was just about to start her third song when Kia burst in, her arms full of scrolls.

Beside her, Xandra cast the scrolls a long-suffering look. "Sorry we're late."

"Before you ask, yes, we do need them all," Kia announced.

"Whatever for?" Nodora asked.

Xandra held up a single scroll that was tied with silver-and-white silk cord—the Summit itinerary. "I thought sometime tonight, we'd get around to conspiring—together. From now on, we should all coordinate whatever we're planning for the Summit."

Cassia looked around her at their room full of allies, her aura swelling with emotion. She met Xandra's gaze. "Thank you."

Xandra smiled and joined them around the coffee table, taking the chair next to Nodora. Kia deposited her haul of scrolls in another chair, then pulled up a seat for herself.

Zoe stared wide-eyed at the pile of scrolls. "I thought we were done with lessons for tonight."

"We certainly are," Kia reassured her. "These are your brother's assignment. He has to help me squeeze every one of these topics into the brief time dedicated to scholarship during the Summit."

"Challenge accepted," Lio declared. "We got through Hephaestion and Phaedros without any Hesperines and humans killing each other. I'm feeling encouraged."

"So am I," said Cassia. "Our conspiracies are sure to succeed. But they must wait until after coffee, music, and some fun."

Lyros rubbed his hands together. "I insist on a game of Prince and Diplomat. Mak and I didn't get to play at Xandra's."

"Prince and Diplomat is boring." Bosko pulled a bag out of the pocket of his play robe and held it up for Zoe.

"You brought the marbles!" she said.

They took their game, the gumsweets, and the goats under Lio's desk. Thenie showed no sign she wished to leave Mak's lap.

Mak plucked a scroll playing piece out of her hands before she could put it in her mouth. "Let's play. Lio needs a chance to win at something in front of Cassia. Otherwise his pride won't survive the first time she sees him fight us in the gymnasium."

"That challenge accepted too!" Lio began arranging the carved stone playing pieces on the polished marble board.

Cassia helped him set out the liegehound pieces. "I'll enjoy watching you at the gymnasium, whether you win or not."

He kissed her hand. "Will you be my second at the board?"

"I shall gladly come to the defense of your pride. No one stands a chance."

"My father crafted this board for me, but as you've heard, I first learned to play from my uncle."

"Made by a warrior, taught by a diplomat," Cassia said with relish. "Formidable indeed."

Lio laughed evilly at his Trial brothers, using his magic to enhance the sound. From under his desk, Zoe giggled, and even Bosko half grinned.

28

nights until

WINTER SOLSTICE

THE GREATEST ARTISTS

LIO'S LATEST WINDOW WAS finished. There was nothing to gain from polishing the panes further. He set aside the cleaning cloth with a sigh. It was a miracle the cement had dried in time. It was madness that he had performed the final cleaning the same night the work was to go on display. But he had done it. He stood back from his worktable and eyed the completed panel.

Cassia and Zoe sat on the floor nearby amid barrels and sacks of sand, plant ash, and minerals. They glanced up from the dictionary they huddled over together.

Cassia gave him a puzzled look. "You never told me Orthros means 'morning.'"

"I didn't know that either," Zoe said, "but I'm getting better at spelling it."

"Why would you name Hespera's Sanctuary after the time of day when the sun rises?" Cassia asked.

Lio smiled. "Because morning brings rest."

"Now I understand." Cassia smiled back.

He observed with satisfaction that nothing remained of her breakfast but crumbs on her plate and coffee grounds in the bottom of her cup. Thankfully, the goats had given up their quest to breakfast on Lio's pigments. They had settled down with Knight next to one of Lio's geomagical furnaces to nap in the warmth.

At the sound of the moon hours bells, Cassia's smile faded. Their Union twinged. The respite was over for tonight.

"Have a look at my window before you go," Lio said.

"Is it ready?" Zoe asked.

"As ready as it will ever be." Lio tried to muster some confidence. He wanted his sister to be happy with how he had executed the design she had chosen.

Zoe scrambled to her feet, not even bringing her mantle with her. He was glad she was so comfortable here in his workshop in the cellar of the tower. She hopped over remnants of sawdust he had used to absorb excess cement from the panes, and Cassia navigated around sudsy puddles that had splashed on the floor during the cleaning. They made it across the messy floor and gathered beside him at the worktable.

"The brushwork still leaves something to be desired," he said. "I wish I'd had more time to fill in greater detail with my paints. It's a good thing I did the glassblowing, staining, and cutting before the embassy started. At least the pieces went together well."

Cassia caught his hand and twined her fingers in his. She looked at him with a perfectly straight face and an aura overflowing with affection and amusement. "Lay down your worries. It is a masterpiece."

Lio glanced at Zoe.

His usually still, shy sister was bouncing on her feet. "It's perfect! Mama and Papa will love it."

For the first time, Lio looked upon his project with a smile. The nanny goat of russet stained glass looked back, and he supposed he had managed to give her a rather charming expression. He wondered if it was a good likeness of the meal Mother had offered to Father upon their first meeting. The animal she had left with a neighbor in Tenebra would now live forever in the art of Orthros. The frame surrounded the goat in celestial bodies that shone their glorious light upon her and symbolized day giving way to night.

"What shall we call it?" Lio asked.

A moment of silence ensued.

"Mama's Last Goat?" Zoe suggested.

"The Goat of Destiny," Lio managed without laughing.

"The Grace Goat," said Cassia.

At that, Zoe nodded.

"The Grace Goat it is," Lio agreed.

"It will be the pride of tonight's event, I am certain," Cassia said. "Surely no one else in Orthros will bring a tribute to caprines to House Timarete's Fair for Artists and Crafters."

Lio cast one more glance at his drafting table, where he had abandoned the sketches of the project he had intended to complete for tonight. Every stately figure in the ensemble exchanging goods and scrolls would have been an artistic parallel or parody upon real historical figures, and the floral motifs around the frame held philosophical symbolism. It would have been the perfect statement to make during the Summit, a compliment to his diplomatic work and quite possibly a worthy submission for his promotion from initiate to glassmaker.

Cassia squeezed his hand. "Don't worry about the other project you had in mind. How could you have found time to finish an entirely new work on that scale while keeping up with the events of the Summit?"

"Yes, I suppose I rather tapped more than I could swallow, didn't I? At least I've managed to finish our parents' Solstice present. Although it ruined the surprise, they are very proud that Zoe's and my gift to them will be on display at the Fair."

"A goat is better than a bunch of people standing around," Zoe said.

"And what you've been doing in your spare time is better than lonely hours in the workshop." Cassia stood on tiptoe and gave him a kiss on the cheek.

On second thought, Lio did not regret tapping more than he could swallow. Not at all.

Cassia hugged Zoe. "Have fun with the dictionary while we're gone."

Zoe clung to her for a moment. "I wish I could go to the fair."

"A bunch of people standing around are boring, just like you said," Cassia replied.

Zoe nodded, but did not smile. "We'll have more fun helping Lio put the window in for Mama and Papa at Solstice."

"So we shall," Cassia said. "I'm looking forward to Solstice so much."

In contrast to the cloud that goodbyes always cast over Zoe, Cassia's brightening aura was contagious. Zoe smiled tentatively, and Lio found himself smiling, too.

Cassia didn't talk about Solstice like it meant goodbyes.

Once Lio had dropped Cassia and Knight off at Rose House, he returned home long enough to get the sawdust out of his hair and wrap the stained glass panel securely. He stepped to the grounds of House Timarete and landed amid the bustle of preparations. Perhaps it was the good mood he had just caught from Cassia, but he quickly got into the spirit of the fair.

Spell lights made Lyros's family's grounds seem like a walk among the stars. Silk pavilions and awnings would offer warmth to the mortals. Delicious smells wafted from the booths of the culinary crafters, and everywhere one looked, Hesperine works of art offered a feast for the eyes.

Exchanging greetings with everyone along the busy paths, Lio made his way to the glassmakers' pavilion. Only when he spotted Master Theophilos there did his good mood falter.

Lio was about to show a smiling nanny goat to the greatest master of stained glass in the history of Orthros.

"Lio!" His crafting mentor clasped his free hand.

"Master Philo, how are you? I have scarcely seen you since the First-blood Circle."

"Not to worry, lad, you've been crafting with a medium even more fragile than glass." Theophilos rubbed a stout hand over the bald top of his head. He had added yet another long braid to the collection that ringed his pate.

Lio lifted his eyebrows with a smile. "It appears you have some news I have not heard. Perhaps I should ask how your Grace is?"

Theophilos beamed, resting his hands on his round middle. "She is at home with the sixth, ravenous addition to our family."

Lio gave his mentor another wrist clasp. "My most heartfelt congratulations, Master Philo."

"You must come by and meet the little one. Now then, let's see what you've brought me. I've prepared a display for you right here at the front."

Lio swallowed and set his wrapped piece on the easel. Master Philo looked at him with anticipation.

Lio cleared his throat. "Does your new suckling have a favorite animal?"

Master Philo chuckled. "He's too young to speak his mind as yet, although his lungs do get the point across when he's hungry."

"Ah." Lio gave a nervous laugh. "Have I told you how much my sister loves goats?"

Master Philo appeared puzzled. "Why, no, but now that I think of it, I did hear something about your parents selecting caprine familiars for her."

Lio nodded. "Did I mention Cassia named this piece?"

"Ahh, love. I know how it is. You have found your true inspiration."

Thorns. There was no more delaying. He couldn't meet Master Philo's eyes as he pulled the wrappings from his window.

Master Philo let out a laugh that drew gazes from every neighboring pavilion. "Those two young ladies are a good influence on you."

Lio let out a hesitant sigh of relief.

The ancient glassmaker patted Lio on the shoulder. "The greatest artists know not to take themselves too seriously. You will excel in our craft, my lad. You will excel."

Lio left his contribution in the glassmakers' pavilion and returned to the entrance of the fair grounds. He joined those who would welcome the embassy under a banner depicting a Tenebran blacksmith's hammer crossed with a Hesperine paintbrush. Spell lights enhanced by the geomagi made the area bright and warm.

Lyros's mother and father waited at the head of the gathering. Timarete might easily be mistaken for an initiate, with her large eyes and delicate, heart-shaped face, but her heavy braids and even heavier aura of power marked her as an elder firstblood. So did the bandolier of art supplies she wore, the very same one portrayed in her founder's statue in the harbor. She and Astrapas smiled at Lio as he went to stand by their son and Grace-son.

"This is my favorite event so far," Mak said.

"Why?" Lyros gave him a sly smile. "Because we're going to go into a dark room and look at my—"

"If that's what you were putting on display, the embassy wouldn't be invited." Mak gave him a squeeze. "I was going to say it's nice to see everyone in their work robes for a change, instead of formal silks."

Lyros nodded. "Mother and all the other mentors heartily approve of practical attire for the crafters' events."

"I wish Cassia had more confidence in our humble attire," Lio said. "I explained to her we hoped to appeal to the Tenebrans' pragmatism by putting away our formal robes this week. But she believes it won't work."

"Why not?" Lyros asked.

"She says," Lio quoted, "'You could sooner take the shine off a god than make a Hesperine appear plain.'"

Mak chuckled. "Say, do you think she might be in love with you?"

Lio didn't answer. His braid, thin as it was, seemed to weigh on him.

Lyros gave him a look and lowered his voice. "You haven't told her yet?"

"Still waiting for the right time. I don't want to ask her until I'm sure what her answer will be."

"How can she be sure of her answer before she knows the question?" Lyros asked.

"You're both sure," Mak said. "Just tell her so we can start celebrating already."

The embassy arrived at that moment, sparing Lio from replying. As the mortals came within reach of the warm lights, they put back their hoods and cloaks. At the sight of Cassia's gardening dress, Lio swallowed and shut his lips. Focus. Her attire was not an invitation to him this time, but a political statement.

It seemed her part of tonight's plan was a success so far, for the Kyrians wore their temple work robes, and Cassia's supporters among the lords were dressed in sturdy homespun as if for a day in the fields.

When Chrysanthos approached Timarete, Lio's satisfaction vanished. It was no surprise the mages of Anthros were in their full regalia, and Skleros appeared dressed for a bloodbath as usual. Lio took it as a warning that the Cordians did not let Cassia anywhere near the front of the group. It was the Dexion who exchanged courteous remarks with Lyros's parents as if compliments were instruments of torture.

Lio knew this posturing would not be the worst consequence of Cassia's triumph at the scholars' circles. They must be ready for whatever Chrysanthos might do to assert his authority over her.

"Our House and grounds are open to you, honored guests," Timarete announced. "Wander where you please, taste what you will, test the works of our hands, and discover for yourself the meanings in our art. Enjoy the fair."

She unleashed the dazed mortals upon the sensuous pageant before them, and the spell-lit pathways and silken grottoes drew them in.

THE GEM OF ORTHROS

WHENEVER CASSIA CHOSE TO conceal her expression, no one could tell she was hiding anything. Lio knew that the deliberate, thoughtful look she gave him under the glassmakers' pavilion was like a laugh out loud by her standards. His mouth twitched.

Standing on opposite sides of *The Grace Goat*, they watched the Tenebrans stare into the nanny's eyes and contemplate the mysteries of her smile.

Lord Severin furrowed his brows. Lord Adrogan tilted his head to one side. Lord Gaius crossed his arms.

"Perhaps," Benedict suggested, "goats hold some symbolism for Hesperines that we have yet to learn."

Lord Adrogan hooked his thumbs in his belt. "Well, you're the expert, aren't you? I saw all those notes you were taking at every library the Hesperines dragged us through."

"I am keeping a written record of our journey," Benedict replied. "I am expected to return with a report for my liege."

"Oh," said Lord Adrogan, "I thought you'd changed your mind about becoming a temple scroll pusher. I expected you to start praying over your scribbles any moment."

Master Gorgos signed a glyph of Anthros at the nanny goat. "Anthros sees your loyalty, Sir Benedict. You do well to remain diligent in your prayers. Unholy symbols are everywhere."

"I assure you, honored guests," Lio said, "there is no hidden meaning in the goat."

Master Gorgos frowned at Lio. "Goats and heresy have a long, shared history."

Benedict's shoulders twitched in his goatskin vest.

"So do goats and every belly in Tenebra," said Lord Adrogan. "That window is making me hungry."

Master Gorgos expounded, "Goats are the choice sacrifice of heretics, who disdain the sacred bulls of Anthros."

"As our scholars discussed at length," Lio replied patiently, "one of the founding principles of the cult of Hespera was to cease animal sacrifice and instead offer ourselves as sacrifices to our goddess and all people. The only blood we shed in worship or magic is our own."

Master Gorgos's eyes narrowed. "One of the formative experiences of my apprenticeship was my participation in a raid upon a hidden site where heretics performed profane rituals. There were decapitated goats everywhere. The walls ran with blood. Amputated hooves dangled from the ceiling, spreading the effusions of their foul charms—"

Lio's stomach soured, but he put on a conciliatory smile. "That was certainly not a Hesperine site, estimable Master."

Master Gorgos sniffed. "Heresy is heresy. But it was an Eriphite site."

Lio clenched his fangs shut. He heard Cassia's wool skirt crush in her fists. A growl hovered in Knight's throat.

Lio looked Master Gorgos in the eye. The mage took a step back.

"The Eriphites never slaughtered their goats," Lio said. "They believed their animal companions belonged to their god, who had bestowed upon them a sacred stewardship of his herds. The people who slaughtered the Eriphites' herds were their countrymen. They would often dismember the goats and put them on display as a warning—or a trophy from the humans they had slaughtered alongside the animals." All Lio's training told him it was time to stop, but so much louder were Zoe's silent cries in the Blood Union whenever she battled her fearful memories. "Congratulations, Master Gorgos. You arrived after the Eriphites' nearest neighbors had already done your work for you. Did you earn your mastery by cleaning up the carcasses?"

The mage's face flushed dark red. He shook a finger in Lio's face. "You seem to know a great deal about these killings you claim your cult does not commit. Heresy is heresy."

"Look there, Master Gorgos." Cassia pointed across the path between the pavilions. "The culinary crafters have fine spirits on display. The fire god's spirits you brew at the Sun Temple must make you an expert. Will you not come along with me and give me a lesson in sacred libations?"

Lio bit his tongue and watched in misery as Cassia cleaned up the mess he had just made. Within moments, she smoothed the mage's feathers and sent his pride aloft, and she succeeded in coaxing the Tenebrans away from a confrontation with Lio. Knight, with his hackles up, stalked Master Gorgos.

None of Lio's colleagues said anything. He bowed to the other glassmakers and headed for the back exit of the pavilion.

Master Philo stopped him with a hand on his arm. "I am glad to see your devotion to diplomacy has not made you forget your higher duties."

Lio hesitated, then clasped his teacher's wrist once more. "Thank you, Master. I needed to be reminded."

Master Philo nodded and let him go.

Lio escaped. He took side paths to the back of the smith's pavilion and sat down outside on a stone bench. He leaned back against one of Laskara's statues. He banged his head on the scroll poking out of the long-dead philosopher's hand. Lio rubbed the back of his skull. He had read that scroll during his studies with his uncle, and it had had a similar effect his brain.

Mak poked his head out of the back of the pavilion, frowned, and joined Lio. "You're supposed to come through the front with the embassy so I can impress them with my least-offensive wrought iron dressing stool."

"Yes, I was supposed to stay with the embassy after their stop at the glassmakers' pavilion and be touring the rest of the fair with them even now. But I'd best give them time to cool off first, then discover if I can rejoin them, make up for lost time, and somehow get back on the script Cassia and I rehearsed."

Mak winced. "What did Chrysanthos say?"

"The Cordians are all lurking at the calligraphers' pavilion as if they can spy our magical secrets in the ink pots."

"With Kia and Aunt Komnena to keep an eye on them, what's the worry?"

Lio sighed. "I offended Master Gorgos."

Mak sat down next to him. "You're off your game tonight."

"A whimsical portrait of a goat is enough to cause disaster! If we don't want to lose the ground we gained by apologizing for Phaedros, we have to try harder. I have to do better."

"The mage got his robes in a twist over your window?"

"No, he got angry when I insulted him to his face, after Zoe's window reminded him of the time he raided an Eriphite refuge."

Mak started from his seat. "Did that mage actually—"

"No. The coward was not responsible for the violence. But he boasted about discovering the remains of one of their sacred herds."

"You couldn't let that pass."

Lio shook his head.

"If Master Gorgos did have Eriphite blood on his hands," Mak asked, "what would you have done tonight?"

"I don't know." Lio put his head in his hands. "We are here to roll out the welcome carpet for the Tenebrans, not to let them trample all we cherish. There is a time for giving ground and a time for standing our ground. I just wish I always knew which was which."

Mak sighed. "In the Stand, we always know. You chose an uncertain service, Cousin."

Lio lifted his head. "But I'm not navigating alone." He pointed between the pavilions.

Mak smiled. "Cassia's got them back on schedule, and it looks like they've lost Master Gorgos along the way. Let's go show them that silly dressing stool I made for Nodora's brother."

"Let me guess. She commissioned it as a Solstice gift for Epodos."

"He'll wear it out sitting in front of the mirror and thank her when she gives him the same thing again next year."

Lio huffed a laugh and joined his Trial brother in the smiths' pavilion.

Cassia stood admiring a bin of pitchforks. "Steward Telemakhos, I had no idea your craft is smithing. What a fitting occupation for a warrior. It must require both physical strength and studied skill."

"Hesperine smithing demands the utmost expertise," Mak replied, "if I do say so myself. Geomagical forges allow precise temperature regulation, which provides greater control and produces more consistent results, but they require careful attention."

Lord Adrogan sat on the wrought iron dressing stool, bouncing a little to test its strength. He smoothed his hair.

Lord Gaius turned a kitchen knife over in his hand. "You work in steel as well."

Mak nodded. "And bronze."

"But you do not make weapons?" Lord Gaius asked.

"Certainly not, honored guest. As you know, those are forbidden in Orthros beyond the fortress of Waystar."

"You do not supply Hesperines errant with arms?"

Lio prepared to assist Mak in stifling mortal speculation. "As a warrior and a smith of Orthros, Steward Telemakhos is the first line of defense for the Queens' laws against weapons."

Mak's aura shifted with discomfort. "Only a very few Hesperines errant have ever wielded blades Abroad, in any case."

"Those are not made here?" Lord Gaius pressed.

Lio shrugged. "The origins of the Blood Errant's famous weapons are as mysterious to us as they are to you. They have never revealed the source of their arms, but whatever mortal smith from ancient times forged them, he is certainly long dead by now."

Mak took a file to the rough edge of a tankard handle.

Lord Gaius shook his head and dropped the knife back on Mak's display table. "Warriors without weapons."

"That's what comes of females running things," Lord Adrogan muttered.

"Yes, Lord Adrogan," Lio said. "Sixteen hundred years of peace and prosperity."

"Sixteen hundred years of apron strings!" the man scoffed. "That's all my mother ever did. Wring her hands and beg my father not to go to war. That's how men end up poor."

"If deprivation inspires him to battle," Lio replied, "might not prosperity endear any man to peace?"

"Oh, aye, I'll be right endeared to peace, once I can afford it. But you don't become prosperous without a sword."

"On the contrary, if prosperity were already at hand, you would not need a sword to procure it."

"You'd still need one to keep the next greedy lout from taking all that fine peace and prosperity from you."

"But if he too were prosperous—"

"Well, he would want to become more so, wouldn't he?"

Anger stirred in Cassia's aura. "For some men, there is no such thing as enough. They never stop."

"I do not doubt it, Lady Cassia," Lio said, "but as a devotee of peace, I must hold there is another way than the sword to stop them."

Lord Severin shook his head. "You have seen for yourself what talk of peace means to heart hunters. How is a man to meet them, if not with a sword?"

"Hmm." Lio raised his eyebrows in Mak's direction. "Perhaps you could rely on the Stand to intervene with magic—and fists."

"A Tenebran warrior relies on no one but himself and his sword," Lord Gaius said.

Cassia turned away. "Perhaps if all of you had listened to your mothers, none of you would have ended up on the battlefield."

"Are you taking the Hesperines' side?" Lord Adrogan demanded.

"I am taking the side of my sex." Cassia ran her finger around a bronze circlet. "Imagine what Tenebra might have one day become under the gentle hand of a queen."

Benedict set down one of Mak's knives a little too hard.

"Well, that concludes our visit to the smithing pavilion." Lio made for the exit. "Thank you for the demonstration, Cousin. Won't you join us on our way through the fair?"

Mak had filed right through the handle of the tankard. He cast his work aside and stood up. "By all means."

Lio and Mak hastened Cassia and the embassy away from the scene of the debate. They wound deeper into the grounds and nearer House Timarete, whose elusive halls peeked at them from the distance between glades and groves.

When fire glimmered at them through the night, Lio no longer needed to lead the Tenebrans. They followed the flame to Xandra's pavilion. Braziers flanked the entrance and burned within, where she waited in a cocoon of heat. She gestured at the table before her. One tray held silkworm eggs, another squirming larvae laying waste to mulberry leaves, a third a happy crew of adult moths frantically mating with one another. Benedict blushed and looked away.

"Welcome to the Sericulturalists' Circle," Xandra said. "We will give you a tour of the silk trade, starting with the egg and ending with the fabric. Allow me to demonstrate Orthros's innovations in silk making, which make it possible for the worms to become moths and live out their natural lives, rather than be killed for their cocoons."

Their journey through metamorphosis, spinning, dyeing, and weaving ended at the grand pavilion of Lio's Ritual mother. Kassandra had brought her great loom, an embodiment of her role in her craft and Orthros itself, all the way from her house. She sat on a cushion at the ancient loom, her locked hair trailing down her back and around her on the carpet. Her dark russet hands moved with such grace and speed that the delicate threads of silk seemed to transform by magic. The fabric came into being before her.

Upon their approach, she did not pause her work, only looked up and smiled in welcome. "Come, my dears. Bring your guests to join me."

Lio and Xandra bent to kiss their Ritual mother on the cheek and, together with Mak, seated themselves around Kassandra on silk cushions. The mortals sank onto the other pillows scattered about, gazing as if mesmerized at her hands working the loom.

But Cassia looked across the pavilion. Lio followed her gaze and shared in her surprise. The Cheran mages were already here. They sat silently together on the perimeter of the pavilion, watching Kassandra.

The knights and lords had hardly sat down when Lord Adrogan leapt to his feet again. "I've seen enough." He stared at the loom for an instant longer, then turned on his heel and departed the pavilion.

Cassia watched him go, her aura betraying the dismay that did not show on her face. "We crave your pardon, Elder Firstblood Kassandra. Please forgive Lord Adrogan's rudeness."

"He is responsible for his own deeds, and you are not obligated to make excuses for him." Kassandra looked around the gathering. "You are all free to wander the fair as you desire. My silk threads do not shackle you in my company."

Benedict tore his gaze from the loom. "Thank you for the demonstration, Elder Firstblood. If you will excuse me, I..." He cleared his throat and stood, offering his arm to Cassia.

Cassia shook her head slightly. "I wish to see how the fabric is made."

Benedict did not withdraw his arm. "Lady Cassia, if you will please leave with me."

Kassandra smiled at Cassia. "Men fear the weaving room, don't they, Lady Cassia? But you and I know better."

Lord Gaius got to his feet and bowed deeply to Kassandra. "Indeed, a wise man knows the power of the loom. I believe it is time for the embassy to proceed."

The men behind Lio kept whispering about unnatural weavings and seductive hands. Then Lio caught the word "witch." He and Cassia rose to their feet at the same moment.

"Ritual Mother," Lio said, "I will remove the embassy from your presence. We will impose upon you no longer."

"That's fine, Lio. They will see me again soon enough."

"Thank you for your hospitality," Cassia said. "We are leaving now, Benedict."

As they departed her pavilion, the Cherans' veils turned to follow them, but the mages did not rise to leave.

While Lio and his Trial circle guided the embassy past the last few sericulturalists' awnings, he noticed Cassia making extra effort to attract the Tenebrans' attention. She eased them right past the booths of silks, and Knight moved in tandem with her as if herding sheep. The smooth surface of her aura shattered into the frustration of someone who knows she has been cheated.

Lio tried not to frown at the stragglers he hastened after her. When their attention was on Cassia, Lio cast a glance in the direction she wasn't looking, and he saw what she didn't want the rest of the embassy to see.

Half hidden by a silk screen, Callen and Perita browsed the ribbon makers' booth. Their auras mingled in a haze of fun and affection. He had draped his forearm in silk ribbons of various colors and was trying them in her hair one by one. She turned around for him, stifling her laughter behind her hand.

Lio helped Cassia hurry the embassy along until they were back on the main avenue of the fair. They joined Nodora at the instrument crafters' display.

"We string all our sacred lyres with cattlegut, my dear," the Semna was saying to her. "The cord is made from the intestines of the sacrificial cattle. It has been so for generations."

Lio sent his Trial sister silent support through their Union.

Nodora smiled, although she looked a little green. "Naturally, we had to adopt an alternative that does not require killing animals. I craft my strings exclusively from the product of Princess Alexandra's silkworms."

"Silk is lovely," the Semna replied, "but it simply does not sound the same as cattlegut."

Nodora ran her plectrum over the strings of her lyre, releasing a cascade of delicate notes. "It has its own magic, don't you think?"

"But it is a different goddess's magic." The Semna sighed.

Her aura filled with a pining Lio recognized from his time in Tenebra. Homesickness.

Her now-silent lyre in tow, Nodora joined him, Xandra, and Mak in the avenue. The Semna and her attendants fell into step with Cassia, and they all moved on together. On their way, Ariadne excused herself with the Semna's blessing and found Eudias under the calligraphers' pavilion. The girl settled down across from him at a table, and their heads bent near over a pile of scrolls. Lio exchanged a significant glance with Cassia.

At last they made it through the forest of pavilions and awnings to the terrace where Lyros waited. The long wings of House Timarete stretched out behind him, open to the night.

"Welcome, honored guests," he said. "As a son of Blood Timarete, allow me to say what a pleasure it is to have your company here at our home. I hope you have enjoyed what you have seen so far."

He ushered them inside, holding the door open until the last mortal had passed into the room beyond. Lio came in after them, and Lyros gave him a nod. Lio worked the light spell he had prepared according to Lyros's specifications. At the same moment, Lyros let the door fall shut.

Utter darkness engulfed them all, and the mortals gasped.

"How are we supposed to see art in the dark?" Lord Adrogan asked.

"The fact is," Lyros answered, "I am the only person in my family who is not an artist."

"You are an artist," Mak said. "Every move you make in the training ring is pure art."

"Thank you, My Grace. But you know I cannot craft a likeness to save my life. Making a lump of marble look like someone recognizable? Not a chance. What was I to do with my education in the principles of art and the properties of minerals?"

Lyros clapped, and his warding magic resounded. Countless brilliant gleams flared to life all around them. At the sight of the precious gems glittering in the darkness, the mortals' wordless utterances of awe filled the room. Lyros's creations provided ample light for Hesperine sight, but the humans would be lost in a dreamland of darkness and jewels.

Lyros drifted through the room, a shadow who disappeared behind his craft. "Jewels have an inner light of their own. All they need is a touch of magic to bring out what is already there. Every gem has its own magical receptivity. It is endlessly fascinating to infuse different stones with my warding magic and discover the results. Let me show you the unique properties of each stone and how they respond to or enhance spells."

Lyros led the mortals on a tour from one glass case to the next, identifying the materials he had used for each of his works and explaining the magical techniques for enhancing them. The Semna and Pakhne enjoyed the display with the uncovetous delight of people happy with their lot, but Lord Adrogan's gaze burned with greed and bitterness. Lio was surprised to see Benedict linger with a wistful expression over a delicate anklet of copper set with tiger's eye. The knight's thoughts focused so powerfully on one person, Lio could not help but catch a glimpse of her in the man's mind. A cascade of chestnut curls, laughing eyes, and lips with a natural upturn at the corners.

Would the lure of riches accomplish what art had not tonight? The Tenebrans gazed upon beauty with suspicion and peaceful crafts with disdain. In new sights and sounds, they found no excitement, only estrangement. Lyros's display might prove the only act of tonight's drama of the forbidden that they understood. Perhaps the price of the Oath would prove to be mundane diamonds and gold, after centuries of conflict that had cost lives.

The crowd milled through the dark with the light of Lyros's works to guide them. Lio and Mak herded them away from breaking anything. In the quiet, slow shuffle, Lio felt Cassia's hand seize his. He wrapped his veil of darkness closer around them. She brought his hand to her lips and pressed a long kiss to his knuckles.

"Look at this, Your Ladyship," Benedict called.

Lio had to make himself let her go. She slid out of his veil and rejoined Benedict in the light of the displays.

She peered inside, folding her hands as if she dare not touch the precious contents within, the picture of the natural daughter who knew the crown jewels were not for her. Lio gazed upon his Grace in the light of Hesperine magic. If her countrymen would really look at her, they would see the truth—a woman who had no love for the gems and precious metals her unwanted suitors piled upon her, who had once given up all the riches she might ever possess to save a human life.

Her face was devoid of expression, but her aura filled with unmistakable longing. Lio drew nearer to see what held her attention.

The glass cover of the display case showed him his own reflection.

CONSPIRATORS

CASSIA COULD NOT ENDURE another moment in front of the toymaker's awning with the lords and knights.

"The evidence is right there before our eyes," hissed a devotee of Master Gorgos.

"How can we encounter such things and do nothing?" one of Benedict's fellow knights muttered back.

"Aye," said a third noble, "the proof is right here. They must use these profane charms to capture innocent children."

The Hesperine who was embroidering eyes on a silk doll focused on her work and did not dignify the comments with an answer.

"My lords, good sirs," Cassia reminded them again, "we have lost the rest of our party. Come now, we ought to reunite with the Kyrian mages before we proceed any further through the fair."

"She might bewitch a child with that very doll," the knight whispered. "We shouldn't let her finish it."

"If we stop her," said Master Gorgos's crony, "she will only make another. When you cut off the snake's head, more grow in its place."

The toymaker blinked hard, her eyes glistening.

Cassia hooked her arm in Benedict's. "I am going to find the Semna. Are you coming or not?"

"Of course, Your Ladyship. We would do well to keep close to Mother Kyria's power in this place."

Now Benedict hurried her away! The other men, who had ignored her pleas, followed his lead.

Cassia buried her free hand in Knight's ruff and looked through the crowd. Lio was still nowhere to be seen. It felt like much longer than half an hour since Kia had pulled him and their friends away to deliver some urgent news. Suspense made the moments creep by. When would they find a way to tell Cassia what had happened?

Cassia focused on finding the Kyrians. Her last hope to rescue the debacle at the toymaker's was for the Semna to dispel the suspicions about the dolls.

She kept a firm hold on Benedict and pressed on through the fair, trying to spot the Semna's white robes. Here and there amid the strolling attendees and the busy crafters in the pavilions were Hesperines who stood still. Their gazes missed nothing. Then there were the Hesperines who seemed to proceed aimlessly from awning to awning, while never getting out of sight of Cassia. The Charge was everywhere. Whatever trouble brewed, she could rely on them.

The shadows between the two nearest pavilions seemed to beckon her. She slowed her steps to a stroll. The alley there drew her gaze, and she saw Lio's eyes reflecting at her out of the darkness. His face appeared, and he put a finger to his lips. She felt his magic on her skin like a caress from light itself. A shiver thrilled over her. He beckoned again.

She drew to a halt as if pausing to look about for the Kyrians. She whispered a stay command to Knight and disentangled herself from Benedict's arm. The sight of her arm still in his startled her. She backed away toward Lio. A perfect image of her remained behind with Benedict. He glanced all around, apparently absorbed in their search for the Semna. Cassia hurried to join Lio in the alley.

He pulled her close. "Allow us to remove you."

Two nearby shadows manifested into the Queens' Master Envoys. As the illusion dispelled, light magic faded at Kumeta's fingertips, a bright gleam upon her night-dark skin. Basir smiled, his fangs white against his own deep black complexion.

"Master Envoys," Cassia said, "well met. I rejoice to see you are fully recovered from Martyr's Pass."

"Good moon, Cassia," Kumeta replied. "Yes, my Grace's fangs are in top form. If not his pride."

Basir bared his teeth further. "The ordeal of regrowing my canines has me in an especially ungenerous frame of mind where mages of Hypnos are concerned."

"Have you learned anything more about the mage of dreams we encountered in the pass?" Cassia asked.

"I'm afraid not," Basir answered. "We envoys have made no more progress than the Prince's Charge. Yet. Rest assured we will lay the matter to rest soon."

Cassia had to admit, she found comfort in the finality of Basir's choice of words.

She looked between Lio and the envoys. "What is happening? It must be important, for the Queens' spymasters to be here tonight instead of Abroad in the field."

"You are aware this type of event is especially vulnerable to sabotage," said Basir.

Cassia nodded. "The Charge and the Stand are out in force to ensure everyone's safety."

"So is the envoy service," Kumeta said.

"The Gift Collector appears to be making a move." There was a hint of a threat under Basir's factual tone.

Lio ran a hand down Cassia's back. "Don't be alarmed. Skleros has been tracking you through the fair, which is why it's time for you to come with me."

Cassia's chest tightened. "Do you think he'll try something like he did with my wine?"

"Whatever he tries," Kumeta assured her, "we have the situation well in hand. While you remain safe with Lio, Basir and I will maintain the necessary thelemancy and illusions to make the mortals believe you are still with them. If Skleros makes an attempt upon the illusion of you, we will catch him red-handed."

Cassia resisted the urge to rub her breastbone. "Perhaps I can help. Knight's presence would make it easier for you to distract the others."

"Yes," Lio agreed, "why don't you try your idea about sending him after Benedict?"

Basir studied Cassia. "You have a ready stock of diversion tactics, I see."

"I make a habit of keeping my escape routes open," Cassia replied. "I don't use it much outside of training because I always need Knight close, but the command to tail prey should make him follow anything anywhere."

"This sounds rather dangerous for Sir Benedict," Kumeta observed.

"Knight knows to hold off unless I command him to attack," Cassia said. Basir chuckled.

Cassia unwrapped Benedict's scarf from around her neck. "Benedict did not hesitate to loan this to me after I appealed to his chivalry in the cold. I am sorry to use his generosity against him."

"He'll live," Lio muttered.

Cassia stood at the front of the aisle between the pavilions. Knight fixed his attention on her. She patted her knees, and he came to her. Benedict didn't look their way.

Cassia held Benedict's scarf before Knight's nose. *"Ckada!"*

Knight darted out of the shadows and back onto the avenue. As he drew alongside Benedict, the knight glanced down and smiled at the dog.

Kumeta took the scarf from Cassia. "We will have your illusion return this to him."

"You may leave the rest to us," Basir said. "We will apprehend Skleros if he provides us with a justification. It would present us with an extraordinary opportunity to question a Gift Collector, then turn him over to the First Prince's justice. Everyone would go home from the fair with their desired prizes."

Kumeta wound her arm in Basir's. "While we're at it, we must make time for a stop at the confectioners for some festival ice."

He looked at her with a startled expression.

"They have your favorite flavor," she said.

"No, they don't." Basir's tone didn't change, but there was a warmth in his gaze Cassia had never glimpsed there before.

Kumeta's mouth twitched. "Second favorite flavor, perhaps."

"I don't need festival ice," Basir said.

Lio rubbed a hand over his mouth as if hiding a smile. "Cassia and I had best be off. Thank you for your aid tonight."

"You have my gratitude," Cassia told them.

"And you know you have ours." Kumeta gave a rare smile. "You know the Departure would mean withdrawing the entire envoy service from the field. As the one helping us prevent that, you need not call us 'Master Envoys,' you know."

Cassia smiled back. "Thank you, Kumeta. And you, Basir. I am glad to see you safe."

Basir's expression softened. "Away with you, now."

Cassia escaped with Lio out the other end of the alley. As soon as they were alone in a back grotto, he stopped and wrapped his arms around her. She tried to muster a jest about Hesperines absconding with maidens, but all she could do was hold him. With her heart beating against him, the painful tightness in her chest eased.

He ran a hand over her hair. "I know."

"The toy booth was a complete disaster. Somehow, the more truth we speak, the more stubbornly everyone ignores the evidence before their eyes. I'm so sorry, I tried everything—"

"It isn't your fault."

"I must return there without the embassy and make amends with the toymaker."

"She would consider it an honor if you chose the works of her hands as gifts for those you love. Might I suggest you take dolls home for Zoe, Bosko, and Thenie? Such a gesture would mean a great deal to the toymaker."

"In Orthros, male children play with dolls?"

"They don't in Tenebra? Even though fatherhood is so important to mortal men?"

"Boys play with swords."

"*Children* are given weapons?"

"It *is* horrifying, isn't it?" Cassia shook her head. "Well, I will pick out dolls for the sucklings and show my support for the toymaker."

Lio sighed into her hair. "It all might have been easier if I hadn't gotten us off on the wrong foot the moment everyone arrived."

"Master Gorgos deserved what you said."

"But I should have known better than to resort to insults to make my point."

Cassia truly should have known better than to breathe a word about a Tenebran queen. She could thank Lio's delicacy about her grief for Solia that he had not remarked on her slip. "I ought to have resisted the urge to debate with the lords over their warmongering. We can't afford to antagonize Lord Adrogan and Lord Severin. I cannot deny the sword is a necessary means of survival in the mortal world."

"They also cannot deny that women like you have proposed less harmful solutions to conflicts."

"I feel for the mothers of Tenebra. Their cries for peace fall on deaf ears."

Cassia sensed Lio's magic in her mind, felt *him* within her, as if he were reaching for her sinking heart and catching it before it drowned.

"Ohh." She relaxed against him. "You've never done it quite like this when we aren't feasting."

"Is it all right with you?"

"Mmm." Her eyelids slid half-closed. She turned inward, reaching for him with her thoughts. "I had no idea we could come this close any time."

He held her close, mind and body. "Our nearness knows no borders, my rose. Nothing can come between us."

She slid her arms around his neck. "You must be careful when you do this, though. For even in the absence of the Feast, it is very arousing."

Chuckling, he eased deeper into her thoughts. She let out a little moan and parted her lips.

"Oh, that is a sweet invitation." He took it and kissed her.

The embassy and Tenebra and everything else disappeared from her thoughts. There was only Lio's tongue sliding between her lips and his warm, gentle mouth caressing hers. The happy sounds of the fair carried on nearby, and the spell lights twinkled beyond her eyelids, while the sensations of his kiss dazzled her.

Too soon, he parted his mouth from hers and untangled their minds. "I'm afraid that is all the tide over we can manage at present. I have some news for you, and what we've just learned is not encouraging."

Cassia drew back. "There's more to it than Skleros following me?"

"I should have become a juggler instead of a glassmaker. We have a few different crises on our hands. We're trying to sort them out at the architects' pavilion."

But when Lio took her hand, he did not step them right to the council of war. He led her through the fair. No mortals even glanced at them, while most Hesperines smiled or waved. Cassia returned every kind expression and gesture, although she knew she could not erase every insult and blunder the embassy had made tonight.

Lio showed her to the other side of the grounds, where the architects' and sculptors' pavilions faced one another on opposite sides of a flagstone terrace. When Cassia saw who was there, she suddenly felt more able to bear the disasters of the night. The Queens sat together, talking with everyone who came by to see them.

"Let's pay our respects to the Annassa first," Lio said.

"Certainly. I'd like a moment with the Queens."

The greeting line wound around a table covered in an exquisitely detailed miniature model of the entire city of Selas. Cassia stared at it, studying the perfect, tiny buildings and miniature statues.

Lio smiled over the model of House Komnena. "The Circle of Architects and Circle of Sculptors collaborated on this as their Solstice gift for the Annassa. They got it ready early so they could bring it to the fair."

Cassia reached out to point to Zoe's goat barn. Her hand met a solid barrier, and light flashed under her palm. A sense of safety wrapped around her, and warmth emanated from her pendant.

"We love the gift so much," said Queen Alea, "that we contributed a model of the ward."

They had reached the Queens. Cassia made the heart bow. "It is so good to see you, Annassa."

"And you, Cassia." Queen Soteira smiled.

"It makes me happy to feel your Sanctuary ward drifting through the fair," Queen Alea said.

"I am glad that I can bring you some small joy, Annassa."

"It is not small."

Cassia put her hand on the model ward again to feel her pendant respond. Queen Alea's face shone.

"I understand." Cassia looked from one Queen to the other. "Orthros itself is your craft, Annassa."

"And our service," Queen Soteira said, "and our magic, and our Ritual. But most of all, our joy."

"I believe your father is waiting for you inside," Queen Alea said to Lio.

"Thank you, Annassa." Lio made the heart bow.

Cassia went with him into the architects' pavilion. They passed through a group of Hesperines he introduced as his father's students. A flap at the back of the pavilion led them into a smaller room.

Apollon sat on a stool with his arm around Komnena. Lio's Trial circle surrounded them.

Komnena sighed. "Oh, good. You managed to get Cassia away."

"I'm sorry it took me so long," Lio said dryly. "I thought Skleros was a challenge until I had to tear her away from Benedict."

Cassia rubbed her forehead. "I'll burn those notes of Benedict's if I find he records my nightly choice of stockings to report back to Flavian."

Lio gave her a hint of a smile.

"Kia," Mak said, "tell Cassia what you told us."

Kia scowled. "I held down the mages at the calligraphers' for as long as I could. Skleros just lurked, but Chrysanthos and Tychon love to argue—well, actually, they love to be right. Since they are never right and I keep telling them so, their battle to win our debate is everlasting, and I was sure they wouldn't get away from me. But then Chrysanthos sneaked off with Skleros. I knew I had to warn all of you."

"Mak and I shadowed them," Lyros said. "As soon as the Dexion and the Gift Collector left the calligraphy pavilion, they parted company. We reported it to Grace-Mother."

Mak nodded. "Mother decided it would be fun to follow Chrysanthos around the fair. Whatever mischief he has in mind, she'll nip it in the bud—or give him just enough rope to hang himself."

Lio squeezed Cassia's hand. "As you've seen, the envoys are handling Skleros."

Komnena propped her fist on her hip. "I'm afraid the mages aren't the only ones in the wind, otherwise I would have helped Kia keep them occupied. It came to my attention that Konstantina left the rosarians' pavilion shortly after the fair began."

Cassia grinned at Lio's mother. "Komnena, have you been spying on the Second Princess?"

"Well." Komnena tossed her braids over her shoulder. "I have been known to assist the Blood Errant with dangerous endeavors. In light of

Konstantina's recent disagreement with Ioustin, I feel honor bound, as her fellow mind healer, to take advantage of all the insight our professional association has to offer. When Apollon told me who was missing from his part of the fair, I realized something was amiss."

Apollon hugged Komnena around the waist. "One would expect Laskara to be highly visible across the terrace from us, as befits Firstgift Timarete and the greatest master of the Circle of Sculptors. But my former initiate masterminded their impressive display, only to leave it in the hands of her students. I have not seen her one time tonight."

Lyros shook his head. "If it came down to a contest between her reputation as an artist and helping her Trial sister, Laskara would choose her loyalty to Konstantina in a heartbeat. But this is our family's fair. Family always comes first."

"I see," said Cassia. "Laskara is one of Konstantina's partisans."

"Thick as thieves," Xandra said. "As you know, Rudhira, Methu, and Nike were the first Trial circle. Konstantina decided to carry on their tradition with Laskara, Epodos, and Baltasar when they went through Trial together."

"Epodos is my eldest brother," Nodora said. "The epic of Firstgift Kitharos's life is as grand as Orthros—according to him."

Kia crossed her arms. "Of course you saw quite a bit of my eldest brother, Baltasar, at the scholars' circles last week."

Cassia nodded. Although he had participated as a partisan of Hypatia's, he had done so with Khaldaios's moderation of character.

"It's a good thing Baltasar manages to talk sense into all of them," Kia grumbled, "most of the time. Tonight he never joined us in the calligraphy pavilion. I dared the mages into going with me to Mother's pavilion, in case Baltasar was attending her lecture on astrolabes, but he wasn't there."

"Epodos hasn't been at our display all night, either," Nodora said. "I thought he was wandering the fair as research. I was surprised when he announced he's writing a ballad about the Summit."

Cassia looked around their gathering. "So while we've been conspiring, so have Konstantina and her Trial circle, and it must be about Rudhira."

"This doesn't make sense," said Lio. "They spend as much time together as we do. If they wish to discuss a clandestine plan for getting

Rudhira home, they need not do it in the middle of the fair, when everyone will notice their absence. Oh, thorns." He pinched the bridge of his nose.

"They want everyone to notice their absence," Cassia concluded. It had taken her long enough to see it. She was certainly not at her best tonight.

Nodora's face fell. "Epodos is an expert on the music and literature of the Great Temple Epoch. He could have been rallying the Tenebran mages with their own songs."

"I'm ashamed of Baltasar," Kia said. "He's usually the voice of reason among them. He promised me he was going to give a demonstration of the advantages of paper over vellum. I know that doesn't sound like something that would matter very much to the Tenebrans, but Imperial paper-making techniques could advance learning by leaps if we can persuade the embassy to take that knowledge back home with them."

Xandra became very calm. Too calm. "I actually believed Konstantina was at the rosarians' pavilion, striking fear into the mortals' hearts with her flowers."

Lyros jabbed a hand in the direction of the sculptors' pavilion. "I can't believe Laskara is using our fair for this!"

Mak flushed. "Your entire family has been working so hard to make this a success."

Lyros paced in the small area. "I don't know how Laskara can do this. After everything Mother said to us about reviving the Tenebrans' lost arts before their very eyes. Did you see her face when she gave the tour through the hall of frescoes?"

Mak put a hand on his shoulder. "We have to tell her."

Lyros drew to a halt. "I know. She has to know Laskara won't be there for the walk through the statuary garden. That's supposed to be the grand finale of the fair."

"Laskara will be here for the statuary walk," said Apollon.

Lyros's shoulders relaxed. "Thank you."

Apollon nodded. "I did not teach her to dishonor her craft and her family."

"Tonight will not reflect on your family's honor," Lio reassured Lyros. "No one will doubt House Timarete fulfilled their commitment to the fair."

Lyros gave Lio a wrist clasp. "I wish I could say the same for your Summit."

Kia shook her head. "Their lack of support will make many wonder whether the Summit is worth supporting at all."

Nodora's eyes were full of regret. "And it won't end there. I don't think Epodos claimed he's writing a ballad just to cover his absence. That was a threat. He's going to tell Konstantina's interpretation of events."

"Yes," Lio said, "I think this is the moment when I am supposed to feel their slap in my face."

"Don't let it sting." Cassia caressed his cheek and spoke with far more confidence than she felt. "It's not over yet, and we aren't finished telling our version of the Summit."

HEDGE MAZE

I F Laskara felt an ounce of shame, it was not apparent. Cassia did not know how any person could come through a persuasion by Apollon and still appear so composed, especially when he was prowling the gardens a step behind her. But Lyros's eldest sister was all graciousness before the crowd of Hesperines and mortals who attended the sculpture walk. Timarete walked alongside her daughter with every appearance of approval, regardless of what her private reaction had been when Lyros had told her about Laskara's plans.

Laskara guided the embassy through manicured gardens she had populated with legends, heroes, and embodied virtues. Her comments were erudite, but understandable. Her modesty was no affectation. She looked on every sculpture with pride and pointed out half a dozen features of it she wished she had done better. Her arms were muscular and strong from working stone; her face did not conform to the standards of beauty, and neither did her works. Cassia found the renowned sculptor unbearable, because she longed to admire her, but they must be opponents.

Lyros spent the entire walk constantly on the move through the crowd, engaging Tenebrans in discussion, explaining anything that didn't make sense, and helping those who fell behind to keep up. Cassia's heart went out to him. He was working so hard to make up for a dishonor committed by someone of his own blood.

When the fair's finale was finally at an end, Hesperines gathered round to continue the discussion with Laskara and Timarete, Komnena and Apollon among them. The Tenebrans began to drift away. Cassia should go to the front and drag as many Tenebrans as she could along with her. She must not allow the Hesperine and mortal crowds to split.

Lio took her arm. Benedict wandered off with her illusion again, Knight at his heels, while Lio drew her away into the garden.

"Is Skleros still following me?" she asked.

Basir and Kumeta stood on either side of an arbor that led into a hedge maze.

"Never mind Skleros," said Kumeta.

Basir's mouth twitched. "As one who recently had occasion to appreciate the value of leave, I suggest you and Lio take some now."

"You've done enough," Lio said. "We've all done enough for tonight."

She let her thanks fill the Blood Union and left her protests behind. Clutching her cloak about her with one hand, she took off with Lio between the hedges that towered above their heads.

He looked back over his shoulder. For the first time in hours, she saw a smile on his face.

Veils and wards must cover the maze, for no other voices reached her ears through the garden. She could only hear Lio's and her shoes rushing over the gravel paths and her own breathing and his laughter. They passed through stretches of deep shadow, but with Lio to guide her, she did not become lost. Every time, he led her through into another alcove lit with spell light or an aisle that let in the light of the moons and stars.

"You must know your way through the maze well," she panted.

He gave her a half smile. "I grew up with Lyros, but I still have no idea how to get through the labyrinth. It's bespelled to change every time you enter."

"What?" She let out a reckless laugh.

He halted, and she ran into his chest.

"Don't worry." His deep voice seemed to fill the twists and turns of the maze. "If we get lost, I'll levitate us out."

"The spells don't prevent levitation? That makes it rather easy to escape."

"The point isn't to escape from the maze," he said. "It's to escape into it."

"Take me away, Lio."

They raced together through the labyrinth, she cared not where. They came to a ring of hedges with a statue at the center. Cassia's face flushed, and she was sure her heartbeat sounded thunderous in the silence, especially to a Hesperine's ears.

"This statue wasn't on the tour," she said.

"The passionate silkworms had already worn out our guests' tolerance," Lio replied.

Cassia stopped glancing at the statue and let herself really look at it. At the muscles rippling down the male's back, at his bare buttocks and his powerful legs braced on the pedestal. At the tenderness of his embrace around the female he held, at the expression on his face as he looked at her, which said he wanted nothing more than to have his stone gaze locked on her forever. She had her arms around his neck. Her legs around his waist. Her fangs were inches from his neck, poised to grasp him, frozen just out of reach of what she longed for.

Lio's mouth touched Cassia's neck. A whimper caught in her throat. She shivered and leaned back against him.

"I got you something at the fair," he said.

She turned to look at him. From a pocket of his work robes, Lio pulled a narrow silk gift box. He held it out to her.

She took it in her hands. "The box is so beautiful, I feel like you've given me a gift already."

He smiled. "Go ahead and open it. I can't wait to put it on you."

Returning his smile, she lifted the lid. Inside was a silk hair ribbon the color of her gardening dress. A lump rose in her throat. "Oh, Lio."

"You were very kind to cover for your friends when they sneaked off. Especially when all you wanted to do was sneak off yourself."

"You noticed."

"I always notice."

She lifted the treasure from the box and placed it in his hands.

He drew out her hair to let it drape down the front of her cloak. "I wish you didn't have to cover you hair."

"I wish I didn't need this cloak."

He drew a breath. "Cassia..."

She caught his hand. "Why don't you braid it?"

He went still. "Do you mean that?"

Cassia drew breath to tell him exactly what she meant. She stood there with his mouth close enough to kiss and the words close enough to say.

He brought his face a little nearer to her, and the spell light gleamed in his eyes. As if a veil had been drawn away, she saw the truth there. Hope. So much hope, it hurt to behold.

He wanted her to stay. As much as she wanted to be able to.

She closed her lips on all the words she needed to say. She must hold herself to her resolution that she would not announce her decision to stay until she could promise him it would actually happen. After all the progress they had lost with the embassy tonight, she was not in a position to promise anything.

If the Solstice Summit failed, unspoken promises would be easier to break.

But she could not bear to break his hope. Or hers. It was all she had.

She lowered her gaze from the revelation in his and brought his hand to her hair. "I do mean it."

She watched his long, elegant fingers slide between the sections of her hair and felt his gentle tugs as he wove the strands together. He braided her hair from the nape of her neck, over her shoulder, down her breast.

He knelt before her to weave the braid to the end. As he completed his working with the green ribbon, the motion of his fingers caressed her through her gardening dress. Looking up at her, he pressed the end of her braid to his mouth, as if making her a promise in return—or holding her to her own.

27

nights until

WINTER SOLSTICE

SPOILS OF PEACE

THE CURTAINS OF CASSIA'S guest room fluttered in the draft from the courtyard. A shimmer of light veiled by sheer silk caught her eye. Lio hadn't long taken his leave of her, but now he stood in the courtyard once again.

Cassia rose from her dressing table, and Knight removed himself from her feet. "I need to take Knight out before we go to the nightly conference."

Perita put the unused hairbrush down with a sigh. "Don't bother. Let him do his business on Honored Master Prettyface's shoes."

Cassia laughed. "We'll only be a moment. You go ahead and meet Callen."

"We'll just be in the gallery, my lady, keeping an eye on Sir Segetian."

As soon as Perita shut the door behind her, Cassia hurried out into the courtyard with Knight. She reached for the wraith of spell light and shadow who awaited her. He manifested fully in her arms.

"Is everything all right, Lio? I didn't leave a stocking in your workshop, did I?"

He shook his head, his gaze fixed on her hair. "You didn't let Perita disturb the braid."

"Of course not. The embassy is too superstitious about gifts from the fair for me to wear my green silk ribbon in front of them, but no one can stop me from wearing the braid."

He ran a hand down the length of her braid, his eyes agleam. She was so glad she had encouraged his hopes last night by the statue. Ever since, it seemed the failures of the fair had no power to dampen his spirits. She felt as if he fed his hopes to her and kept hers alive in return.

"I just relieved Basir and Kumeta," Lio said. "They reassured me that Skleros made no attempt to approach the illusion of you last night."

"So we are no closer to understanding what he wants with me."

"He is also no closer to achieving it. Tonight's Summit events will not provide him with any opportunities to threaten you, unlike the confusion of the fair. Of course, I'll shadow you during Chrysanthos's conference as usual."

Cassia let out a breath. "Did you get a chance to speak with Kassandra?"

Lio pulled her closer, tucking a scroll into her belt. "Your revised copy of tonight's itinerary."

"She agreed to the changes?"

"Yes, she supports our decision not to save her lesson on the economy of Orthros for after the negotiations. As much as we hoped to use the embassy's visit with her to talk trade deals once a truce had been secured, she is ready to change her tactics and hold up commerce as a temptation instead. After the way everyone reacted to Lyros's display last night, she agrees this will be effective."

Cassia nodded. "I'll do my best to put them in a receptive frame of mind."

"When I patrolled through Chrysanthos's study just now, I discovered something that may help. I believe we can take advantage of this to regain some of the ground we lost at the fair. Could you contrive a reason to pay the Dexion a visit in his study some time tonight and take witnesses with you?"

"Me, trespass on his territory? My pleasure. What are we to witness?"

"The spoils of his tour through the fair. It turns out that what he and Tychon were doing last night was visiting every pavilion to collect all the fair gifts the artists and crafters were offering our guests."

"This, after the mages expressly forbade the embassy to accept anything. It was much too generous of the artists and crafters to oblige him."

"Aunt Lyta advised them to play along so she could watch what Chrysanthos does with his plunder and perhaps catch him in wrongdoing."

"I regret the waste of fine Hesperine works. What in the world can he mean to do with them?"

"Unravel all our mysteries, apparently. I knew the culinary crafters shouldn't have hidden the secret of immortality in the gumsweets."

Cassia laughed. "Does Chrysanthos really think this will come to anything?"

"Regardless, Aunt Lyta instructed me to keep a close eye on his activities tonight. He has yet to do anything that gives us a justification to intervene, but I think you will agree this still presents a valuable opportunity for us to encourage the Tenebrans' disinclination toward the Cordians."

"Chrysanthos has a room full of all the luxuries the men were drooling over last night."

"Precisely."

"We must use this rope to give him a little choke."

Lio rested his hands on her arms. "But not right now."

"There is no time to waste. We must go now and do our best to discredit him before the conference."

Lio shook his head. "Skleros is there with him."

Cassia hesitated. "It will only benefit us that Skleros is there to incriminate himself."

"It is too dangerous to antagonize the mages with Skleros in the room."

"What would the necromancer dare try to do to me with the whole embassy watching?" she asked Lio and her fears.

"The whole embassy was watching when he put a potion in your wine."

"It was only teething tonic," she reasoned. "If we hesitate, Chrysanthos may have time to clean up after himself before the others see him in the act. We can't afford to waste any opportunities to recover from the fair."

"We are doing everything we can to ensure the necromancer keeps his distance from you."

"I must be in his presence in any case at the conference and the events tonight."

"With me at your side."

"You will be at my side during my raid on Chrysanthos's study, as well."

Lio's expression was grave. "I am glad you trust me so completely to keep you safe in Skleros's presence."

"Of course I do." She sighed. "But if it puts you in a difficult position to bait Skleros, then we will try this another time."

Lio shook his head. "If you are not afraid to take this risk upon you, I certainly shall not stand down."

Cassia gave him a kiss, then turned to go. "I'll see you at the New Guest House."

Lio caught her hand and pulled her back to him. "One more thing. It wasn't a stocking you forgot after we made great art together on my worktable." He dangled her underlinens in front of her nose.

With a blush and a grin, she snatched them from him. "I'd best hide the evidence of our inspired endeavors in my room this instant."

Cassia didn't manage to stop smiling until several minutes later, when she entered the gallery. She found Eudias waiting with Perita, Callen, and Benedict. Cassia held out the itinerary scroll. "Apprentice Eudias, how glad I am you are already here and that we have a few moments to spare before the conference. I need a word with the Honored Master about the sudden change in tonight's plans. Would you be so kind as to direct us to your master's study?"

The apprentice's eyes widened. "It is hardly my place to ask, Basilis, but perhaps this matter could wait until the conference?"

"It would ill behoove us to discuss such things before the entire embassy. Good leadership comes from presenting clear and united guidance to others."

"Well, I suppose it would not be objectionable, given that you have your handmaiden and your protectors with you. I will discover whether or not the master is accepting visitors."

"We are not visitors, we are his fellow ambassadors, and he will see us. Benedict, I believe Lord Gaius should be present for this, do you not agree? We would not wish to give him the impression Segetia is conspiring."

"I admire your delicacy, Your Ladyship. I will make our visit known to him, and he and I will join you at the mage's chambers."

"I am sure Perita and I would also be reassured if there were a few more ladies present." Cassia gave her friend a significant look. She need not mention what had happened last time the Semna had come to her rescue.

Perita nodded emphatically. "Aye, my lady, that's wise."

"Of course, Your Ladyship. I'll ask the Kyrian mages to join us."

They proceeded together to the end of the gallery and into the courtyard, where Benedict departed through a side gate. Eudias, saying nothing, gave the door of the busy common room a wide berth, leading Cassia and her friends discreetly behind a juniper toward a more secluded gate.

Cassia refrained from telling Knight to heel. Within moments, he obliged her by wading into a garden bed. He jostled a low-growing juniper, and the courtyard echoed with a cacophony of wind chimes. Eudias, Callen, and Perita winced.

"Lady Cassia?" Lord Severin appeared around the stand of junipers. "Is everything all right?"

An instant later, Lord Adrogan followed at his heels. "Say, what are you plotting back here? If it has to do with extra rations and you don't want anyone to know about it, I'm your man."

By the time they entered the mages' wing of the guest house, Cassia had accumulated Lord Gaius and a satisfactory retinue of uninvited guests, and Benedict had rejoined them.

At a door halfway down an elegant corridor, one spell light gleamed brighter in its iron sconce than the others. Cassia looked closer and caught a glimpse of Lio standing sentinel there.

Eudias walked right past him and halted at the door. The apprentice cast a forlorn look upon the invasion he must announce to his master. Cassia stopped within arm's reach of Lio. She gave the apprentice an apologetic smile. Eudias licked his hand and tidied his hair under his cap before disappearing into Chrysanthos's rooms.

A moment later, Eudias reemerged. "I'm afraid the matter will have to wait until the conference, Basilis."

Lord Gaius crossed his arms. Benedict frowned. Lio smiled in anticipation.

"As I said, it cannot wait," Cassia told Eudias, "and it will not do for us to have an audience."

The apprentice cast another glance at the audience behind her.

"I must object to a colleague turning away a brother in Anthros," Master Gorgos puffed.

Lord Adrogan cast a sour glance at the Dexion's door. "He expects us to be at his beck and call, but the first time we knock at his door, he dismisses us?"

"Apprentice Eudias," Lord Severin said, "Lady Cassia's sense of urgency is justified, and her discretion is to be applauded. Your master has certainly seen the itinerary and understands this."

"The royal representative is here to see him," Benedict insisted. "He must see her."

Eudias swallowed. "So I said to him, my lords, but you have heard his answer."

Lord Gaius smiled and put a finger to his lips, then clapped the young man on the back. Eudias skittered out of his way.

Lord Gaius grasped the door handle, and his knuckles tightened. Locked. He raised his eyebrows at Cassia. She nodded. Benedict and Lord Gaius exchanged a long look. Then they both put their shoulders to the door. The spell light flared, and the door gave way.

"Easiest siege I've ever led," Lord Gaius muttered.

Benedict half smiled. "Neither of us ever thought Hadria and Segetia would man a battering ram together, did we?"

Lio smiled and bowed to Cassia as she led the charge into the room.

Chrysanthos, his expression clouded with outrage, looked up from the spacious desk that furnished the study. Tychon was on his feet, his hands fisted.

Skleros sat across from the Dexion with his boots propped on the desk. The necromancer did not bestir himself from his chair, but his teeth clenched around his smoke.

Cassia paused for effect in the center of the room, and Knight stood just in front of her in a challenge stance. She turned all around, sweeping her gaze over the objects that covered the desk and every cabinet, chair, or cloak hook in the room. From glassware to silks, metalwork to pottery, she saw every fair display represented in the hoard. Skleros used a coffee tasting cup as an ash tray. One of the toymaker's silk dolls lay dissected on a side table amid wads of stuffing and the lingering buzz of Anthrian magic.

"What is the meaning of this?" Cassia demanded.

Skleros spat out his smoke, then pulled another from his robes. "Boy," he growled in Eudias's direction.

"Oh. Yes, Master." Eudias dug in his pockets, then handed his own flint and steel to the necromancer.

Skleros lit his smoke and settled back in his chair. Apparently he had decided to be a spectator, rather than rise to the defense of his brother-in-magic. Nonetheless, Lio loomed over the Gift Collector's shoulder with a silk handkerchief over his mouth and nose. The verdurous fog coiling around them all must smell awful to a Hesperine. Knight snorted and growled, pressing back against Cassia's legs.

"We are working," Chrysanthos said. "We will arrive at the conference at the appointed time. Until then, I will thank you all not to disrupt my research."

"Research?" Cassia shot back. Vandalism, she wanted to accuse. She took a deep breath to calm herself, then regretted the noseful of smoke. "Kindly explain how all this came to be here, and for what purpose."

Chrysanthos's eyes narrowed, and he skewered her with one of his smiles. "I must have misheard you, Basilis, for I am certain a lady such as yourself would never ask a mage of Anthros to explain himself."

She took a step toward him, although Knight resisted her effort to approach the threat. "I am indeed concerned for the health of your ears, Honored Master. Allow me to assist you by speaking more clearly. The royal representative of Tenebra is demanding an explanation from the embassy's spiritual guide as to why you make yourself inaccessible to those in your care in order to dabble in blood magic."

Lio's eyes gleamed with amusement. She was glad he was enjoying their display.

Chrysanthos rose to his feet and propped his hands on the desk. Did he think that scared Cassia? The king had worn out that trick over the years.

"I," said the Dexion, "do not 'dabble.' My colleagues and I are conducting vital experiments on heretical artifacts. This is an invaluable opportunity to discover what the Hesperines have been hiding from us." He seemed to realize he was giving Cassia exactly what she wanted—an explanation. He straightened, regaining his composure, and turned a more fawning smile upon the other Tenebrans. "It is my duty to keep all of you safe. That is precisely what I am doing."

"Artifacts these may be," Cassia said, "but they are luxuries—all the gifts the Hesperines offered us last night, which you forbade us to accept."

Lord Adrogan reached to pick up a beaded silk shoe. Tychon caught the lord's wrist and tightened his grip.

Lord Adrogan had no difficulty wresting his hand free. "If I didn't know better, I'd say you're keeping all the spoils of this journey for yourselves."

"Honored Master..." Lord Severin hesitated over one of Lyros's jeweled necklaces. "Are you certain there is malign magic on these items? My tenants live under the constant threat of starvation. One gem from this necklace is all I would need to change that."

"Perhaps I would be able to answer your question if my studies had not been interrupted," Chrysanthos replied.

Cassia could not let Chrysanthos turn that accusation back upon her. "Why did you say nothing to Master Gorgos? As our future royal mage, he should have been informed."

Master Gorgos marched to the desk. "Indeed, why was I not consulted? Why was my expertise not called upon?"

"Our realms of expertise are somewhat different," the Dexion said.

"Oh?" Cassia prodded. "How is your agricultural magic different from Master Gorgos's?"

Master Gorgos's eyes narrowed. "You *are* relying entirely on your, ahem, agricultural magic, aren't you, Honored Master?"

"Good gods, man." Lord Gaius faced Chrysanthos. "If you are testing these artifacts to the full extent of your ability, you are putting the tolerance of our hosts to the utmost test and endangering the lives of every man and woman in this embassy. I will not have it."

"What are you thinking?" Benedict demanded.

To further rattle Chrysanthos, Cassia brought up his rival. "Need we remind you how tenuous our situation is since Dalos antagonized the Hesperines during the last Summit?"

Tychon started forward, but Chrysanthos put a hand on his shoulder to hold him back. Or perhaps hold him up. The apprentice was swaying on his feet, his face pallid and sweating.

Tychon was obviously suffering the ill effects of acting as his master's channel. It was clear how much magic the Dexion had been pulling through his apprentice so he could use the power Skleros had stored for him in a vessel. Back in Tenebra, that poor man they had dragged out of the king's prison and placed under the guard of Chrysanthos's war circle must be suffering far worse than Tychon. Skleros, apparently satisfied with his work, remained a silent onlooker and smoked like a forest fire.

Knight pushed against Cassia's legs again. But she could not heed his protective urges, not now, even if it meant pushing the mages too far. She had not pushed them far enough. She wrapped her arm around Knight's neck. He shook his head vigorously.

In the tense silence, Cassia tried to enjoy watching Chrysanthos bear the brunt of everyone's stares. But the rush of the confrontation was deserting her. Her heart no longer raced. Drowsiness dragged at her. Perhaps she had underestimated the consequences of living on pleasure and coffee.

The moment of weariness wasted her reaction time. Chrysanthos got in a word. "Do not speak the name Dalos within my hearing. He was…" The Dexion paused. Took a breath. "…the most blundering, incautious excuse for an Anthrian mage who ever dared try his clumsy hand at dealing with Hesperines. No one could be more undeserving of the opportunities granted to him." The Dexion skewered Cassia with a look. "May I also remind you he was a Cordian interloper, and I am as Tenebran as all of you."

Cassia made no apologies for dancing close to the limits of his disguise.

"You'd best remember it," Lord Gaius threatened the mage.

Chrysanthos composed himself. "No potentially antagonizing spells have been attempted here. Our explorations have occurred well within reasonable limits and involved nothing to which our hosts might object. There are nondestructive methods that still provide a useful degree of information."

Cassia raised her eyebrows at the remains of the doll.

One of the men who had nearly made the toymaker cry sifted through the scattered stuffing. "It's just a toy!"

"Is it?" Chrysanthos returned. "Do you not think you have the right to know if there are any curses on the temptations the Hesperines paraded before you last night?"

Behind Tychon's back, Lord Adrogan sidled over to a chest under a window. He threw open the lid, and it banged against the wall. Everyone in the room looked toward the sound.

"Gold!" Lord Adrogan lifted out a heavy chain that had been on display at the goldsmiths' pavilion at the fair. "What else have you been hoarding in here?"

Chrysanthos's voice turned cold. "Do you imagine yourself entitled to some kind of reward for bravery because you attached yourself to the embassy? You cannot possibly imagine what the Hesperines owe my brethren. If I eke some compensation from this journey, it will be a drop in an ocean that no amount of riches can ever fill."

"You do not deny you kept these for their value alone?" Lord Gaius asked.

"I did not say that." Chrysanthos's smooth smile was back. "I may study anything I wish while I am here. It is both my duty and my right."

"Your duty," said Lord Gaius, "is to keep this embassy safe, and your privilege is to represent Tenebra. Do you forget where your loyalties are supposed to lie?"

Chrysanthos's hands fisted on the desk. "Do you forget to whom you are speaking?"

"What authority do you have here?" Lord Gaius challenged.

"Let him play with dolls," Cassia declared. "Let him leave the real work of the Summit to those of us who know our duty."

With that, she turned on her heel and swept out of the room. Despite her wobbly knees, she achieved a graceful and dramatic departure. Lio never left her side.

She must not lean on the wall of the corridor. Someone would notice. If only she could reach out and take Lio's arm. He felt awfully far away. For that matter, the carpet felt farther and farther away. Cassia's eyelids drooped.

Spell lights and metal sconces danced and intertwined on her vision, as if Lio were crafting a glass window before her very eyes. But the heavy fog over her mind obscured his working.

She reached for a decorative table right under her hand and discovered it was out of reach. Her knees buckled. She clutched at Knight as she went down, but then his fur slipped through her fingers.

Her mind fixed on only one fact. She had lost control. She clung to her anger to keep the fear at bay, but then she lost the strength to cling to anything.

THE SICKROOM

CASSIA OPENED HER EYES. She peered up through dust motes and wan shreds of sunlight at the gray stone ceiling over her. She recognized every rock, seam, and groove, although she had not seen them since she was fourteen. She had spent hours staring up at that ceiling, too sick to get out of bed, while her garden outside died from neglect and she wondered if she would follow.

No. No, this couldn't be happening.

Her gaze darted around her. Small windows. Casements shut tight. No light. No air. No way out.

No. She could not be back in Tenebra.

Knight wasn't with her. She couldn't feel the glyph shard around her neck. She was alone. Defenseless. Just like Martyr's Pass. Just like when she was fourteen.

Cassia made to spring off the bed. She couldn't move her legs. The blankets bound her. She stared at herself. No, not blankets. Straps. She strained against the bonds. Leather cuffs jerked at her wrists.

Cassia let out a howl of rage.

Orthros. Lio.

What had the mages done? How had they taken her away?

"Don't cry, child. You're not out of my reach."

The beauty of that voice defied the sickroom.

"Annassa Soteira?" Cassia gasped.

She took Cassia's hand. "I'm right here. All of us are right here. Just look around you."

Holding fast to the Annassa's hand, Cassia turned her head. Queen

Soteira sat on the edge of the bed, as if the night sky had descended into this little, squalid chamber. Behind her, the door of the room hung off its hinges. In the doorway stood a short figure with a long curtain of white hair.

"Annassa Alea," Cassia cried.

"She will make sure no one disturbs us," said Queen Soteira.

Beyond the door, a crowd of people struggled and shouldered and shouted to get through to Cassia. She spotted her old nurse, the crone who had pretended to comfort her the night Solia had died. There was the king's old healer, holding up a jar of leeches and extolling his qualifications. Perita shoved past him, her face streaked with tears. Callen was right behind her. Lord Gaius and Benedict were locked in a scuffle, too busy wrestling one another to get near the door. The Semna and her attendants stood on the threshold in grim conference. But none could get past Queen Alea.

"This can't be," Cassia said. "My nurse succumbed to old age just as I recovered from my illness. The king replaced his old healer that year with a new mage from the Order of Akesios. I didn't even know Perita then. The Semna wasn't there. But Knight was. He never left my side. Where is he now?"

"Do not be afraid. You are not alone."

Cassia looked from the sunlight creeping through the casements to the Hesperine Queen who was her lifeline.

Annassa Soteira smoothed Cassia's hair back from her clammy forehead. "The memory of sunlight cannot keep me from those who need my healing."

"These must be my memories and thoughts. You are in my mind."

"We are here together, and we will set you to rights in no time. Meanwhile, Alea and I are sitting on our terrace, and you are in your guest bed at Rose House."

Tears spilled from Cassia's eyes, and her breath shuddered in her chest. "I thought it was real. I thought I had lost Orthros. I can't—I cannot. Never again."

"You need never leave Orthros, unless you wish to."

Cassia met the Annassa's eyes. She saw the truth there, the secret one she knew and treasured. "I don't ever want to go back to Tenebra. I want to stay in Orthros forever."

"Then you will."

"Is it too late?" A hacking cough interrupted Cassia. Heave after heave, it burst from her chest and left agony in its wake. "If this is the end—I want—the Gift."

The uproar outside the door went quiet. The room faded into shadow. The space around Cassia seemed to fill with the silent music of joy and glimmers of unseen starlight that she could feel. Annassa Alea turned from the crowd at the door and together, the Queens of Orthros smiled at Cassia.

Annassa Soteira touched the top of Cassia's head. "That is a sacred request. We will honor it."

"If it must be now, I am not sorry. I can hardly wait. I want it so much."

"You shall have your Gifting under happier circumstances than this. Your life is not in danger."

Disappointment made tears cloud Cassia's vision again. When relief dried them, she could see the desolate sickroom around her again and smell the sweaty bedclothes on which she lay. "What happened to me?" she rasped. "I collapsed…after I left the Dexion's study. What did the mages do to me?"

"Your body is running over with Apprentice's Toddy."

"Only that, again!" Cassia cleared her throat, but that only made the pain worse. "I feel as if he poisoned me."

Queen Soteira put her hand over Cassia's heart, her face grave. "There is the scar of necromancy here. The Gift Collector turned medicine into malady. In normal doses, the tonic is merely relaxing, but this dose was so high, you fell unconscious. It entered through your lungs."

"I breathed it. Skleros dosed me with his smoke."

"This horrifies you in a personal way," Queen Soteira observed.

Cassia looked away from her benevolent gaze. "Can you see all my thoughts, Annassa?"

"I could, but I do not. I am not here to slay the monsters in your mind. If you choose to introduce me to them, though, I will help you tame them to be your liegehounds."

"The monster of which we speak cannot be changed."

"They can all be changed."

"This one is what it is—but I have yet to become it. I hope I will never have to." Cassia coughed again. "Is everyone else all right? Only Lio could have escaped inhaling Skleros's smoke."

"The necromancer crafted a dose that would affect only you, targeting your life force. I am cleansing every vestige of his magic from you as we speak."

"Rudhira has told me of your great powers against necromancy."

"The mind healers who passed their teachings down to me understood the ways of evil before people ever settled in the lands that are now Cordium and Tenebra."

Warmth and strength filled the hollowness in Cassia's chest and emanated through her entire body. The pain vanished. She felt like a cup that had been empty all along, but was now full for the first time and running over. If only she could feel this way all the time.

"You are using your magic from all the way across Selas," Cassia marveled.

"That is no distance at all. I would reach much farther for you."

Cassia glanced at the crowd Queen Alea held at bay.

Queen Soteira shook her head. "Do not fear that the mages will suspect I have come to your aid. Alea and I have discovered many creative combinations of Sanctuary magic and theramancy over the years. With her collaboration, I am healing you without anyone the wiser, right under the noses of some very attentive mages."

"Thank you, Annassa. You have come to rescue me, even though my life is not in danger."

"I heard you cry out. I would never leave you to face this nightmare alone."

Cassia looked around her again. On the bedside table sat her spade and her gardening satchel, much less stained and battered than they were now. They had been the only hope she'd had to cling to. "I don't know why I'm here. I never think about that year."

"What happened to you then?"

"I had a wretched fever that lasted a fortnight, and it looked bleak, but I recovered. My health was weakened for some time after that, though. I was sickly off and on all year."

"The connections that form in our dreams sometimes seem strange to us, but after some thought, we often realize our minds know what they are doing. You will discover why tonight's events reminded you of this time, I am sure."

"I did mention that fever to Lio at Waystar. But he was more upset to learn of it than I was to remember."

There came a sudden bang at the window, and Cassia jumped. The casement shuddered.

"Cassia!" Lio shouted.

"Lio!" she called out.

The casement crashed open, and light flooded the room. Lio stood outside the window, straining toward her. His father held him back.

Annassa Soteira smiled. "Lio is not content with his role as a diplomat presently."

"I'm all right! The Annassa are with me." Cassia started from the bed again, only for the straps to halt her.

Queen Soteira's hands eased her back. "He knows. But he must let us finish our work here."

"I want out of these straps, Annassa. They frighten me. They make me so angry."

"Do not be afraid." The Queen held fast to her hand. "Tell me how you came to be bound. That could help us discover how to free you."

"I don't know. This isn't a memory, but a dream. No one bound me to the bed when I was ill. That doesn't even make sense. But these straps feel so real. They won't give."

"Yes, they will. No matter what you have suffered, no matter what the people in your past have done to you, you are strong enough to break free."

Cassia drew a deep breath, then tried again. The leather creaked. "Everything is always so hard. Why can't it be easy for once? Why this, after everything else?"

"You have faced all those challenges and succeeded. After everything you have accomplished, you can do this, too."

Cassia gritted her teeth and pushed against the bed. "Dealing with the king is easier than this."

"How do you deal with him?"

Cassia lay back, catching her breath. "Brute force is no use against him. You have to outsmart him."

"You have maneuvered brilliantly at every turn."

"I couldn't have done it alone. I have met with so much kindness to help me forward."

"But it was your choice how to respond to that kindness."

Cassia felt two shapes against her chest that hadn't been there before. She glanced down. Solia's pendant and the glyph shard hung together at her neck.

"Ebah," Cassia breathed.

The leather shackle on one of her wrists fell away.

Cassia closed her free hand around the glyph stone. Its pulse reassured her the rhythm of the world had not changed. She worked the stone in her hand, and its broken edge drew blood.

Her other shackle slid off.

"You're almost there." Queen Soteira helped her sit up.

Cassia looked at the straps that bound her legs. Six thick leather bands with iron buckles secured her to the bedstead. As if a scrawny thing like her was dangerous and strong enough to require such precautions.

Well, if someone had bound her like this, that must mean she was dangerous. And strong.

"I knew that already, didn't I?" Cassia said.

She reached over and picked up her spade. She set the sharp edge to one of the straps and began to saw away at it.

The sunlight in the room faded. Gentle darkness wrapped around her, touched with the light that emanated from Queen Alea. A chill evening breeze breathed in through the window, and Cassia caught Lio's scent.

Cassia worried at the strap until her hands and arms were sore. She would not stop for anything. She had worked when she was tired before, and she had won. As her cut in the strap widened, the other five began to crease and crack. The buckles began to rust.

"You are no match for me!" Cassia cried.

The buckles crumbled, and the straps broke apart.

MEDITATION GLASS

L IO HAD TO STRAIN to hear her heartbeat.

A glass door was all that separated him from her. He could shatter it with a thought. Every political victory for which they had risked their lives demanded he keep his distance. He could destroy all of that with a single act.

The glass door hummed in warning.

His father's hand tightened on his shoulder. "Wait. Trust the Annassa."

Only the flow of the Queens' magic, concentrated on Cassia's still form, warded off Lio's despair. He watched Perita and the Kyrians hover over his Grace. The vultures of Chera waited on the edge of the room.

"If this is to be Cassia's Gifting, Father, I—"

"If it is not, you will still need secrecy."

"Politics don't matter if she is—"

Cassia's door and windows and every pane in the glass roof of the courtyard began to whine.

"I don't want to have to cast stone feet on my own son," Father warned.

Lio gritted his teeth and flattened his hands upon the fragile door. The glass stilled under his touch.

His father drew him away from the door and sat him down on a bench. "If she needs you, Annassa Soteira will tell you."

Lio held his power latent and prayed.

Father took a seat beside him. "When we realized glassmaking brings out a slight affinity between you and minerals, you told me you wanted to pursue that craft because you were happy to discover at least one small way you took after me."

"That's true."

"But you also chose to work with something fragile to prove to yourself you would not break it."

"I knew that if I could cast powerful spells without breaking glass, I was truly in control of my magic."

The windowpanes rattled.

"I have seen you succeed at those very spells," his father reminded him, "in your workshop, surrounded by the most breakable new glass. When we had the doors and windows here at Rose House spell-tempered against the elements, accidents, and wear, I did not think our planning would need to account for the threat of rogue diplomats."

Lio let out a pained laugh and forced his fingers to relax, trying to release his taut magic as he did so. "I have not been this angry since Martyr's Pass."

"You did not lose control then, either."

"I was sanctioned to do anything I deemed necessary to the heart hunters. There was an outlet for my power. Now I must sit out of sight and leave Skleros untouched, the man who—"

The glass's crystalline tones filled the courtyard. Lio's power made his heart pound, as if he could pump blood for Cassia. But he could not. That was denied him.

But if it was the only way to save her tonight, he would not let anything stop him from bleeding for her.

Lio's father wrapped one strong hand around his own. "You will get your chance. Just not tonight."

"I cannot let him continue to be a danger to her. I must ensure he does not have the power to threaten her again."

"You must also make sure the mortals never suspect Cassia is under our protection. The worst danger she could face is for the mages to suspect she is one of our own."

"You're giving me a lesson in diplomacy, Father."

"There are times when parents have the opportunity to share what they have learned from their children."

Lio bowed his head, and the glass quieted again. "Thank you for helping me not do anything rash."

"It's the least I can do. For many years, your mother and I breathed a sigh of relief, safe in the belief you did not inherit my temper. It appears I afflicted you with it after all."

"I try to wield its power only for just cause."

"How could protecting your Grace not overcome every other instinct?"

Cassia's heartbeat grew louder and stronger. Lio's own pulse leapt, and he jerked his head up. The women in the room stirred. The blankets rustled. He watched Cassia sit up.

The roof pane above Lio's head shattered. He heaved a sigh of relief and shook off shards of glass to put his face in his hands.

WING OF DARKNESS

CASSIA OPENED HER EYES to the sight of ribbed vaults. Knight lay against her. The room was bright with spell light and fragrant of roses. The open curtains revealed the thriving garden in the courtyard.

She scanned the whole view through the glass door and windows. No sign of Lio. Not even a glimmer of his veil. She sat up to get a better look.

Out in the courtyard, a high note shattered into countless chimes. A flurry of glass slivers and shards twirled down over one of the benches, parting and cascading and outlining Lio's invisible silhouette.

In spite of everything, she smiled. Silk bedclothes whispered around her, unresistant. She could move. She could breathe. She felt weak with relief, but stronger in body than she could ever remember.

She had not lost her chance. A breath of poison was not to be her end. The fair had dealt a blow to the Summit, the necromancer had ambushed her, but by the glyph stone, she would not give up now.

"My lady!" Perita hid her tear-streaked face against Cassia's hand.

Cassia touched her friend's shoulder. "Oh, Perita, do not cry for me. All is well."

"So it is." The Semna mopped Cassia's brow with a damp cloth. "I can only conclude you are in the peak of health."

Knight's tail wreaked havoc on the bedclothes.

Cassia held him to her. If only she had heeded his warnings when he had tried to herd her away from the mages. "*Oedann*, my good Knight."

Pakhne put a supportive hand behind Cassia's back. "Bless Mother Kyria. You gave us a scare."

"Your pulse was so weak," Ariadne fretted. "We feared the worst."

"I feel perfectly fine now," Cassia said.

"Nothing more than a fainting spell," the Semna concluded. "You are not adjusted to the strange climate and nocturnal schedule. You need less chill and more sleep."

"It was Master Skleros's smoke that made me ill."

"Is that so?" the Semna asked. "Well, I do not wonder. Those foul vapors are disastrous to the constitution."

"What a barbarian," Pakhne said. "A chivalrous man would never subject ladies to such habits, especially when the cold has rendered our lungs vulnerable."

"What does a necromancer smoke in such a thing?" Cassia pressed.

"The same vile weeds as any other man, my dear," the Semna answered. "He may tout his fearsome reputation, but he too puts on his robes one sleeve at a time. There is nothing magical about his vices."

It seemed only an ancient Imperial theramancer could fully understand his vices. Cassia said no more. She must think before she made accusations the Semna could not corroborate.

"Now then," the Semna said, "you are not to touch your feet to the floor for the rest of the night. Whatever the cause of your swoon, you need rest."

"Come, Semna." Ariadne took her hand. "You need a moment to rest yourself after such use of your magic."

The Semna sat back in her chair with a shaky breath. "I suppose a little nap wouldn't be amiss."

"Thank you for your care, Semna," said Cassia. "I am sorry to have cost you so much effort."

"Nonsense. That's what I'm here for. I will return to check on you later."

Men's voices rumbled outside Cassia's door. Only she saw Perita shoot a vicious glance in that direction. But then her friend smiled at the Kyrian mages and said nothing.

The panes rattled again. Everyone but Cassia jumped.

"These northern winds pierce my bones." The Semna let her attendants help her out.

When the door opened, Cassia caught a glimpse of Callen standing guard in her sitting room. Benedict broke away from an argument with

Lord Gaius. The door shut on his interrogation of the Semna as to Cassia's condition.

Perita's scowl returned. "A fainting spell, my arse. Not my lady! You don't fall unless someone knocks you down."

"I agree it is no coincidence I collapsed two steps from the mages."

"Wisdom is just a fancy word for a suspicious mind, my grandmama always says."

"There was something in the necromancer's smoke, Perita. I mean it."

Perita's hand tightened on hers. "That corpsefly! He wanted to stop you causing trouble for Honored Master Prettyface."

"Where are they now? I have to get up. The Hesperines are expecting us."

Perita grimaced. "The mages already left to meet Elder Firstblood Kassandra at the docks. If their plan was to leave you on your back and the free lords in disarray so they can take charge, it's working."

"Then we must catch up with them." Cassia threw aside the blankets. Light fabric. No straps. She had never felt so grateful to be able to simply move her legs and stand on her own two feet.

"Are you sure the Semna's not right, my lady? Oughtn't you to rest?" Perita reached to help her.

But Cassia had already snatched up her cloak and made it halfway to the door.

The moment she set foot in the sitting room, the men mobbed her as the crowd had tried to do in her vision.

Master Gorgos signed a glyph of Anthros over her. "Basilis, we lift up praises to the gods for your swift recovery. Thanks to the Semna's intervention, the Hesperine artifacts' influence upon you was short-lived."

Cassia winced at the sting of Anthrian magic. "What can you mean? The fair gifts had nothing to do with why I fainted."

"Your mind is understandably confused by your ordeal," Master Gorgos replied. "It is miraculous you are not experiencing even direr aftereffects of the heretical curses that overcame you in that room."

Cassia bit her tongue before she made an outraged defense of the Hesperines' innocent gifts.

They actually believed she was under the influence of Hesperine magic. She must be very, very careful what she said.

"I'm afraid it's true, Your Ladyship. The D—" Benedict stopped himself. "Honored Master Adelphos confirmed it."

"He confirmed his own arguments, and nothing more," Lord Gaius returned. "We have nothing but his word."

Master Gorgos drew himself up. "And the consensus of the other experts in our party."

"The Semna said I caught a chill," Cassia protested.

"She is naturally trying to contain everyone's fears," Master Gorgos said. "But rest assured, my brethren and I will stand as Anthros's bastion against the darkness."

"Thank you, Master Gorgos," Callen snapped. "Now that my lady has received your glyph, I'm sure your presence is needed elsewhere."

"I ought to make sure—"

Callen stared the mage down. "My lady needs rest. Now."

The mage blustered out of the room with Callen breathing down his neck. Her bodyguard shut the door firmly.

"Thank you, Callen." Cassia rounded on Benedict. "You cannot actually believe this nonsense."

The knight fingered his amulet of Andragathos. "We cannot deny the potency of the Hesperine magic to which we are exposed every moment we are here."

"And after all these nights, it chose that particular moment in the mage's study to strike me down?"

"There is no telling when that influence might build up enough to show its affects."

"Don't tell me you are feeling faint from Hesperine magic!"

"Your Ladyship, this is no laughing matter. It is a known fact that women are more susceptible to Hespera's influence than men. I am afraid for you."

She stared at him, her anger ringing in her ears. How dare he. Benedict, her friend.

If even Benedict now feared Cassia had been touched by Hesperine sorcery…what must the other men think?

While she had been watching Chrysanthos dash his pieces across the board, his second had crept up behind her and laid waste to her tokens.

Cassia looked to Lord Gaius. "I rejoice to see I am not the only one here unwilling to swallow what the 'Honored Master' serves us. Do you believe this?"

"No." Lord Gaius glared at Benedict. "It is clear the mages are making use of an insignificant event for their own purposes."

"I must rejoin the embassy at once so they can see I am well and there is no cause for concern."

Lord Gaius held up a hand. "That, I cannot advise. While your illness is mundane, we should not disregard the danger. Please follow the Semna's advice and return to your bed."

Cassia tried not to scowl at Lord Gaius's paternal tone. "Hadria's protection is duly noted, my lord. I will now catch up with the mages at the docks."

Callen and Perita flanked Cassia as she started for the outer door, Knight close at her side. Lord Gaius and Benedict both hesitated, then followed, dueling in their attempts to dissuade her all the way through the halls of Rose House.

When they reached the main hall, her heart leapt at the sight of Lio's grand rose window that adorned the building over the front doors. Shining in from outside, the Harbor Light gleamed through the multi-paned crimson petals of Hespera's Rose. That light illumined the words in the flower's center, and one by one, they became clear to Cassia. For the first time, she not only saw them, but was able to read them for herself.

> *Come unto me,*
> *to my certain embrace*
> *under my wing of darkness,*
> *where you shall find shelter,*
> *against my heart,*
> *where you shall find strength,*
> *in the light of my eyes,*
> *which shine with joy*
> *in my endless sky,*
> *where you shall be free.*

I will, she promised silently. *I Will.*

EYES ON THE UNSEEABLE

ASSIA AND HER RETINUE were almost to the front doors when a figure came into view around a pale granite column. She had to stop herself from looking twice. Apollon circled the pillar, a travel desk strapped to his shoulders. He had not even bothered to veil himself. The Lion of Orthros was a visible threat, wearing work robes and whistling while he examined the structure and jotted notes to himself.

The men gave him nervous glances and walked on the other side of the hall. She stopped trying not to notice him and urged Knight into an alert stance to keep up appearances.

As she and the others walked past him, the surety of his power wrapped her senses. He was here to keep her safe. She did not, could not meet his gaze. That she was glad for the excuse stung her with guilt. But that was not what she wanted him to feel in the Blood Union. She focused on her sense of gratitude.

She and her companions donned their cloaks before hastening out the main doors of Rose House and down the front steps. She spotted their goal right away.

Chrysanthos's red-gold robes stuck out like a sore thumb under the spell lights that reflected on the dark waters of the harbor. He stood with Tychon, Skleros, and Eudias at the end of a dock, where one of the Hesperines' pale, lithe ships lay at anchor. The mages of Chera had beaten Cassia there and waited near their brethren.

Frowning, Cassia approached the lords and knights who stood arguing at the mages' backs. With Knight's help, she pushed her way through.

"What does the witch want with us?" whispered one lord.

"Leave the experts to deal with her, I say." A knight nodded toward the mages.

Lord Severin looked at Lord Adrogan askance. "Where did you find such eagerness to visit Elder Firstblood Kassandra?"

"Folded up in the silk in the mage's study," Lord Adrogan answered under his breath. "When that cloth shines, don't you see the gleam of coin? The mages are men, too, and want it all for themselves."

"Lady Cassia." Lord Severin halted her, speaking softly, but with surprise in his tone. "Is your condition improved?"

The lords and knights fell silent. Everyone stared at her. Their fingers moved under the cloaks. Signing glyphs, of course. The cursed one had arrived.

Cassia was ready to howl with the same rage she had unleashed in her dream.

She would not put down her spade.

"The Semna has pronounced me perfectly hale," she announced.

"Why don't we return to the guest house?" Benedict asked in the low tones of the sickroom, trying to take her arm. "The Semna said you should rest."

Cassia evaded him and forged through the group. Holding her cloak close, she headed for the end of the dock. The ship's scarlet sails ruffled and snapped in the gusting wind. The vessel's figurehead was a graceful, horned gargoyle with the wings of a silk moth. The creature appeared ready to fly over the open sea and take the ship with her. A crew of Hesperines Cassia had not met were active in the rigging. On deck, a number of others busied themselves rearranging cargo that looked perfectly well organized, and Cassia spotted faces she knew from the Charge.

At the bottom of the gangplank, the Cordian mages stood like supplicants. Kassandra looked down upon them from up on deck. She appeared ready for an active night, wearing a knee-length robe over a pair of flowing trousers.

"Basilis is too ill to leave her bed tonight," Chrysanthos insisted.

"The entire embassy is invited to join me aboard," Kassandra said. "I will not insult any of my guests by leaving without them."

"You are prepared to set sail without the Kyrian mages."

"The Semna excused herself via Apprentice Ariadne. Until Lady Cassia or a member of her household relates to me her excuses, we do not lift anchor."

Kassandra gave Cassia an amused smile. At last Chrysanthos caught on and followed her gaze. His eyes narrowed at Cassia, then he flicked a glance at Skleros. The Gift Collector's scarred face betrayed nothing, but Cassia was grateful for the wind, which would make lighting anything impossible and shred any hint of smoke. Eudias did his best to become invisible behind the others, but Tychon, despite his green complexion, looked ready to pick her up and deposit her anywhere his master asked.

"Good moon, Lady Cassia," Kassandra called down. "I am so glad you can join us."

"Thank you, Elder Firstblood Kassandra," Cassia replied.

"Basilis," Chrysanthos said, "you should fear for your health. You must return to the heat in the guest house at once."

"I have a much stronger constitution than you imagine, Honored Master."

The mages stood between her and the gangplank. Cassia showed them her impassive face and her posture stiff enough to crack bones.

"Are you not eager to board?" Cassia prompted. "I will keep you waiting no longer."

Lord Gaius eyed the ship. "Where are we going?"

"An evening's tour of the coast," Kassandra answered. "You hail from coastal Hadria, I understand, known for strong ships and even stronger sailors. Would you like to stand on a vessel that has been to the Empire and back?"

Lord Gaius did not answer. The other lords and knights hung back, their wariness writ large on their faces. Benedict hovered between Cassia and the men, as if he did not know which side to choose.

Kassandra laughed. She turned to the nearest crate on deck. She picked up an iron crowbar, tossed it in her hand, then pried the lid off the crate. She lifted out a bolt of vivid green silk and tossed it into the crowd of mortals.

It landed in Lord Adrogan's arms. Other men inched away from him, but he examined the fabric with the eye of an old horse trader on market day.

Kassandra opened a barrel next. She pulled out a canvas sack and sent it overboard in Lord Severin's direction. He caught it, landing it safely on the dock before him. He hesitated, then opened it, only to stare at its contents. He reached inside, then lifted his hand, letting golden grain spill through his fingers.

"I can continue to deliver my gifts to you thus," Kassandra said. "But it may be more comfortable for you to receive them on deck."

"Heed not temptation!" Master Gorgos whispered loudly to the men. "Remain steadfast! Consider what unnatural power reveals to her the innermost lusts and longings of mortals."

A female voice rose above the gusts. "There is nothing unnatural about her power."

Cassia and the others looked all around them for the speaker. Cassia realized the unfamiliar voice had emerged from one of the woman-shaped shrouds who served Chera. Cassia wondered if any of them had exchanged more than five words with the mourning goddess's handmaidens in all these long fortnights.

The Cheran mage's veil turned as she took them all in with her hidden gaze. "Kassandra has already given her gift to my sister and me. A consultation. She is Orthros's seer."

The revelation met with utterances of astonishment. Kassandra's secret was now in the wind, and Cassia could do nothing to snatch it back. Cassia would never again underestimate the mages of Chera. Now she understood their strange attachment to Kassandra. But what was their intent?

"Well met, Sisters," Kassandra said to the Cherans.

The two shrouded mages bowed to Kassandra, who nodded in return.

"There is no mistaking it," said the Cheran who had first spoken. "We may never have had the privilege of a pilgrimage to the temple of our own oracle in Cordium, but we who are devoted to Chera know such power when we encounter it, and so too do our brothers who serve Hypnos."

The other Cheran swiveled her concealed face toward Skleros. "Did you not sense her manteia, Brother, when we met her at the welcoming ceremony? Elder Firstblood Kassandra has eyes on the unseeable."

"That's why I've kept my eye on her." Skleros looked up at her.

"You're looking the wrong way," Kassandra warned him.

Suddenly Knight let out a cacophony of warning barks. A sweat broke out on Cassia's skin. On instinct she glanced at Skleros and Chrysanthos. But Knight was facing the opposite direction.

Cassia spun around. A column of smoke rose from the guest houses.

DAMAGES

MAK AND LYROS HALTED the embassy at the front doors of the New Guest House. A bastion of soft shadow behind them revealed their Hesperine warding magic at work. The unruly men crowded behind Cassia, but with Knight's help, she kept her position at the head of the pack.

"Stewards, what has happened?" she asked.

Despite Mak's stern expression, a hint of amusement flashed in his eyes. "We have the situation well in hand."

Lyros stood with his arms crossed. "We cannot allow any of you to enter the building until we ensure it is once more safe for mortals."

Chrysanthos finally managed to join Cassia at the front of the throng. Skleros was the beast at his side who caused the other men to make way.

"I demand to know why we are locked out of our own quarters," Chrysanthos said.

"You may thank your comrade." Lyros leveled a glare at Skleros. "Your resident alchemist failed to properly extinguish his smoke."

"In one of my father's coffee cups," Mak added. "Now I have to explain this to him and to my uncle, whose guest house you nearly burned down."

"Half your wing went up in flames before we could contain the"— Lyros cleared his throat—"accident."

"Was anyone hurt?" Cassia asked. A few puffs of one smoke had felled her. Now all the Gift Collector's herbs had gone up in a bonfire. What if there was a medicine-turned-malady that could harm Hesperines?

"There were no casualties," Mak assured her. "Thank you for your concern, Lady Cassia."

"Orthros's defenders are experts at dealing with hostile fire." Lio emerged from the guest house and walked through his Trial brothers' ward to join them at the top of the steps.

Cassia breathed again. "Ambassador, I cannot express my relief that we have not injured you, our hosts."

He met her gaze, his own intense. "I am only grateful you, our guests, are safe and sound."

There were politic murmurs of relief all around her. She could almost taste the lords' fear of what the Hesperine retaliation might be should the mages go so far as to incite violence.

Mak loomed over Skleros. "Surrender any other smokes, tinderboxes, or alchemical materials you are carrying on your person."

Skleros planted his boot on the next step up. "I will surrender nothing. Accuse me of the worst deeds you can imagine. I have committed them all. But one thing I am not is careless. I have never made such a thoughtless error as letting a smoke set fire to a building on accident."

"Master Skleros," Lio replied, "if you wish to propose any other possible explanation for a fire in the middle of a Hesperine city, please do."

"It is the Stand who confiscated my tinderbox," Skleros retorted. "Explain yourselves."

Lio gave an unperturbed laugh. "Hesperines, use a tinderbox? Goddess have Mercy, even mundane fire strikes terror in our hearts."

"Your princess seems comfortable enough with fire," Chrysanthos said.

Lio's amusement vanished, and Mak and Lyros bristled.

Lyros warned, "The Stand will do whatever is necessary to defend the royal family."

"That means their honor, as well as their safety," Mak added.

"Princess Alexandra is in the guest house as we speak," Lio said. "It is she who has put out the blaze and done her best to save as many of your possessions from destruction as she can. You are fortunate to have the aid of the only Hesperine in our history with an affinity for fire."

"Then we owe her our thanks," Cassia spoke up. "How much was destroyed in the fire?"

"I am glad to report we succeeded in preventing the fire from spreading beyond the mages' wing," Lio replied. "Unfortunately, the chambers of Honored Master Adelphos, Master Skleros, and Apprentice Tychon were completely consumed. Apprentice Eudias's rooms escaped damage, being nearer to the gallery to facilitate his role as your arcane bodyguard. The common room and the lords and knights' lodgings were unaffected."

Eudias stood on tiptoe and leaned around Tychon's bulk. "Stewards, my affinity for water could be of some service in extinguishing the blaze, if you would allow me."

Lio bowed again. "Thank you. We sincerely appreciate your eagerness to assist. However, Muse Menodora is already within, using her water magic in partnership with Princess Alexandra's fire magic."

Chrysanthos's face was flushed. "This is an outrage. You expect us to tolerate the loss of the precious few belongings we were able to bring with us all the way to Orthros, then listen to your accusations that we are to blame for the damage? You treat my colleague like a criminal?"

"We are not making any accusations, Honored Master," said Lio. "If we were treating your colleague like a criminal, he would be expected to offer a gift to those affected by the destruction. As the guest houses are under the auspices of the Queens' Chamberlain, that would be my mother. As Firstgift Komnenos, I can speak for her and assure you she will overlook this unpleasant occurrence."

Skleros laughed. "No Hesperine will get a gift out of me. That's not the nature of my profession."

Lio looked at him. "Considering everything you have done, you are very fortunate that I am not demanding justice tonight."

"We will now remove your smokes," Mak informed the Gift Collector, "as well as any vials, plant matter, or tools capable of starting a fire."

"We will not tolerate this insult," Chrysanthos said.

Mak and Lyros drew closer to the necromancer. The surrounding Tenebrans backed away.

Skleros laughed softly, as if to himself. That laugh worried Cassia more than anything else.

He held out his arms, as if taunting the Stewards. Mak and Lyros's ward deepened. Lio's eyes dilated, and in her mind, she felt the magic he held ready.

Mak and Lyros methodically searched Skleros's person, pulling out a bundle of a dozen smokes. The tinderbox he had taken from Eudias was next. They proceeded to divest the Gift Collector of vials and packets until they had found all his tonics and smoking herbs. They deposited the lot in a bag like the one Rudhira had used to secure the suspicious wine goblet.

"We are thankful for your timely intervention," Benedict said to Mak and Lyros. "This could have been much worse."

"Thank all the gods there wasn't anyone inside," said Lord Gaius. "We are deeply sorry for the damage to your guest house. It does not sit well with my conscience that no reparation is to be made."

"Reparation is not *your* responsibility," Lio replied. "My family's only concern is that your stay in Selas is safe and enjoyable. Let us all simply be grateful no one was harmed. By comparison, the far lesser loss of possessions is not worth considering."

"I must recover what I can from my rooms," Chrysanthos insisted. "You must allow me inside."

Mak shook his head. "Out of the question."

"For your safety." Lyros's smile did not reach his eyes.

"The Stand has spoken," Lio said. "I'm afraid you'll have to wait. Until the Eighth Princess and Muse Menodora are completely finished, my father has inspected the structure to ensure the fire did not compromise its integrity, the Stand has declared the guest house safe for mortals, and my mother has arranged new rooms for you in an undamaged wing, I cannot allow you to pass. In the meantime, may I suggest you accept my Ritual mother's invitation to a pleasant sailing adventure up the coast?"

"Thank you, Ambassador," Cassia said. "We shall take your suggestion and seek refuge on the sea until the coast is clear."

GIFTS FOR THE FUTURE

CASSIA HAD OBSERVED THAT stranding men in Orthros, far from the king's listening ears, loosened their tongues. So too did stranding them on Kassandra's ship, away from the Dexion's rule over the guest house.

Men roamed the deck and with them, whispers that must soon reach the ears of the Cordian mages, who stood isolated amid a group of Charge-turned-deckhands.

Cassia drifted among the embassy, keeping Knight closely heeled in the confines of the gathering on deck. She added her own whispers to the storm and read busy lips when the murmurs were too low to understand. She listened to the tones that told her more than words and measured the Tenebrans' hearts.

"...what was that graveshit thinking?"

"...if a Hesperine had come to harm..."

"...could have gotten us all killed!"

"I don't buy the ambassador's pretty excuses...what if it was the Hesperines who..."

"Nonsense. Hesperines wouldn't touch fire."

"A necromancer, using fire? Golden boy must have helped him."

"How else could the mages destroy the artifacts without arousing suspicion...trying to protect us..."

"Trying to hide their lies, more like. Now I'm certain there were no curses on the artifacts at all."

"Well, that puts an end to their experiments, eh?"

"Serves the meddlers right..."

Lord Severin shook his head. "All those fair gifts, gone. Now they'll have no chance to benefit anyone."

"What a waste," Cassia lamented.

Lord Adrogan narrowed his eyes. "This is all too convenient for the mages. If they think we can't be bitter about what's not around anymore, they are very much mistaken."

Cassia nodded. "We know what we saw."

"That's right. The only thing we don't know is how much plunder they hid somewhere safe before they started the fire."

"I should have been consulted, I say," Master Gorgos repeated.

"Of course, Master," Cassia agreed. "Your wisdom and prudence would have moderated your colleagues."

"Indeed, indeed. None of this would have happened, had I been there."

"That's precisely the problem. The other Masters are not"—Benedict cleared his throat—"possessed of good Tenebran sense."

"They have gone too far," said Lord Gaius. "We can no longer tolerate their blatant determination to act on their own and erode our influence over our embassy."

"Wouldn't you say they have gone too far again?" Cassia asked. "We must not forget Martyr's Pass."

"Never," Lord Severin vowed.

The right words in the right ears were working their magic once more. Cassia would make sure the mages regretted this.

While the embassy conferred under their breaths, Kassandra strolled the deck. She paused to speak with the lady Hesperine at the helm, who appeared to be the vessel's captain. The captain called out orders to her crew in a language Cassia didn't recognize. The other Hesperines answered in efficient tones and went about their tasks with the energy of those who enjoyed their work.

When Kassandra faced the embassy, the murmurs hushed.

"Welcome aboard," she announced in Vulgus. "It is a pleasure to have you as my guests here on the *Far-Seer*, the flagship of Orthros's trading fleet."

"Elder Firstblood Kassandra," Cassia asked, "do you mean to say this ship is your own?"

The captain smiled as the polar wind tried to tug her locked hair out of the grip of her scarlet headwrap. "The whole fleet is hers. Blood Kassandra keeps all of Orthros's trading ships afloat. The Queens' Master Economist is the admiral of the mercantile fleet and the chief administrator of all economic relationships with our Imperial allies."

Kassandra gestured around her at her crew. "And I rely on the talents of everyone in my service, from our captains to our cabin sucklings, from our negotiators to our initiate bookkeepers."

The ship took flight, gliding through the glittering waters of Harbor. The captain guided the vessel so smoothly, Cassia scarcely needed to lean on Knight for balance. She looked back at the statue of Hespera, whose gaze promised surprises. The ship made for the gap between the arms of the bay.

Cassia found suddenly that she had no interest in seeing what lay beyond, even if it was a tour of Orthros's coast. Not if it meant standing on a ship that was carrying her away from Selas.

"Well." Lord Gaius lifted his gaze to the sails above. "This will certainly be a tale to carry home to my grandchildren. A ship that has sailed to the Empire and back."

"A ship owned by a lady, with a lady captain." Cassia turned once more to watch the crew at work. They were in the best of hands, she reminded herself.

Lord Gaius frowned. "On second thought, perhaps I shouldn't let on about this to my granddaughters. Next thing I know, they'll take a notion to go to sea."

"Too late, my lord," Cassia said. "We have seen the images of the goddess Angara in golden armor, bearing a sword. We are already full of dangerous ideas."

He laughed as if it were the most endearing jest.

"Your Ladyship," Benedict put in, "the iconic depiction of Angara in a warrior's attire is entirely symbolic. She never actually fights in the battles of the gods. It is her divine task to inspire the morale of fighting men."

How unaware they were of the very real danger of the woman next to them.

But Cassia must not stray from the Hesperine path she had chosen.

She would continue striving to be as kind as she was dangerous, to nurture her compassion with her power. She would be the sure hand steering the embassy into safe harbor. She would rally the fighting men to lay down their swords.

As the *Far-Seer* carried them into the open waters, Kassandra launched into a lesson on trade and economy. Cassia realized they were about to receive an entire education in a matter of hours. Her head spun, but she drank up all the information.

The dazed eyes the men had turned upon Kassandra's loom now sharpened with interest. They soon dared to ask questions, and the lessons turned into a dialogue, sometimes a debate. Kassandra's eyes sparked with enjoyment as she prowled the deck among her guests. Every question they fired her way, she met with an answer, another question, or a challenge.

The *Far-Seer* flew along, and Cassia breathed a sigh of relief that the shores of Orthros were never out of sight. When she could spare her attention from the proceedings, she stole away to the rail for a better look. Wrapping an arm around Knight's furry neck, she took in the view of the snowy coast.

She felt the soft certainty of a Hesperine veil wrap around her.

"You can keep looking at it," Kassandra said beside her, "but it will not change. It is all ice and snow, ice and snow, as far as the eyes can see."

Cassia looked at her. "As far as your eyes can see?"

"Yes." Kassandra's gaze was full of love for the land they beheld.

"Then everything will be all right."

"People have the power to change anything."

"Not an inch of Orthros will alter. The world may go up in flames, but this remains, frozen and eternal. That is the promise of Orthros, is it not? Constancy."

"Orthros is what we make it." Kassandra stepped back from the rail. "Come. It is time for me to present the rest of my welcome gifts."

Cassia feared taking her eyes off the shore, but she followed Kassandra to the center of the deck.

Kassandra opened a large trunk. "For Sir Benedict, a gift befitting a warrior and a scholar." She presented him with a metal box.

Benedict opened it to reveal fine paper and what appeared to be a set of drawing and measuring tools. A look of surprise passed over his features. "With instruments this accurate, a Prismos could draft the plans for a new temple to withstand the ages. Yet I am only a knight who was almost a temple scribe."

"You will put them to good use."

He stepped back, as if to make way for the other men, but Cassia saw in his steps a man fleeing. From what? Why did the oracle's harmless gift alarm him?

"For Callen, born to farm but made to protect." Kassandra reached into the trunk again.

The ship's spell lights gleamed along a curve of razor-sharp steel. Cassia and the others gasped. Kassandra held out a scythe.

Callen came forward, looking with unmistakable eagerness upon the blade. "Begging your pardon, Elder Firstblood. It's my understanding we're not to wield weapons here."

"This is not a weapon. It is the tool of honest, hard-working farmers like your father. You have the skill to use it and the heart to use it for good. Nowhere in Selas will anyone question why you wear a gift from the Queens' Ritual sister at your belt."

Cassia could scarcely believe it. Kassandra had just found a way to arm the one man in the embassy Cassia could rely on to protect her.

"You have done me a great service, Lady." Callen accepted the gift and bowed deeply to Kassandra over the blade. He fastened it where his sword usually hung.

Kassandra ignored the other Tenebrans' mutinous grumbles and the Cordians' affronted expressions. "For Perita, whose insight and courage are never to be doubted."

Cassia turned to her friend and urged her forward. Perita hesitated, but went to stand at her husband's side.

Kassandra handed her a cloth pouch. "I think this is what you're missing."

Perita loosened the drawstring and peered inside, sniffing. She lifted her head quickly, then tied the bag shut again. "Elder Firstblood, I can't fathom why you'd do yourself such a disservice."

"To prove my good intentions. Just be gentle."

"Aye. I'd never be otherwise."

"What is it?" Benedict spoke up.

"A female matter," Perita replied pertly.

Callen glared at the knight.

"Apprentice Eudias," Kassandra called.

"Me?" he stammered from behind the crowd.

Everyone waited while he wound his way from the back of the ship to Kassandra. Cassia made a point not to stare at him like the others. With so many gazes upon him, he straightened his hair and cap several times.

When Kassandra reached for his hands, he jumped. She pressed a small object into his hold. Cassia could not make out what it was, even from her position.

"Always remember who you are," Kassandra told Eudias.

He stared at the gift, cupping it in his palms. "How—how—how did you know? Well, of course, you would know, considering your affinity. That is, thank you."

"Thank you."

He glanced up at her, looking confused. "Thank me? For what?"

"For what you have yet to do."

His eyes widened, but then a look of determination came over his face. "You are most welcome."

Chrysanthos swept up beside Eudias. "I cannot allow my apprentice to be exposed to Hesperine artifacts." He reached for the gift Eudias held.

Kassandra caught the Dexion's wrist midair.

The mage flinched as if burned by her touch. She held his gaze, calm and unrelenting, while his lip curled.

"Unhand me!" He yanked his hand back.

He met with no resistance. Kassandra simply let him go, and he stumbled backward with the force of his own movement. Eudias tucked his gift into his robes and sought refuge in the crowd near Cassia and her retinue, as far as he could get from Tychon. Chrysanthos glanced after him with a scowl that promised he was not done with the matter.

The Dexion straightened and smoothed his robes. "Somehow I have the impression I am not welcome here."

"You are not. But you have more to learn from this voyage than any other man here."

"No doubt you do have an inkling as to my purpose."

"The lesson I have in mind for you is not the one you came for. For that reason, I tolerate your presence."

"Rest assured, what diplomacy demands of us tonight is mutually excruciating."

"There can be no diplomacy between us, Mage of Anthros. No need for your pretty, transparent lies. You have looked forward to this meeting since your arrival. You could hardly wait for your opportunity to ferret out any hints you can about the fate of the Akron's Torch. How does your investigation progress?"

"You should be careful asking me for honesty. I might give you more than you're prepared for."

Kassandra laughed. "I have heard every word you can think of to say and every possible way this conversation might end. Your words have no power here. You have taken nothing from me, and you can take nothing from me."

"Noble words from Prometheus's grieving mother. Do you think I believe them?"

"The truth remains true, whether you believe it or not. You would do well to confront the truth now, so it does not take you by surprise later."

"Your tactics will not work on me. My colleague warned me about your affinity the moment he detected it. I have known you would try to use prophecy to twist our thoughts. I will not heed you."

She reached into her pocket, and the mage tensed. But all she withdrew was a heavy iron key. She held it out to Chrysanthos.

"What is this?" he scoffed.

"Something you will need in the future."

"You think I would accept a gift from you?"

"That is up to you, but if you do not, you will regret it."

"Is that a threat?"

"Why don't you find out?" She held up the key.

His eyes narrowed at her. The fizz of an Anthrian spell made the hair on Cassia's arms stand on end. Kassandra gave the mage a cold smile, but did not so much as flinch.

"An utterly unmagical, harmless trifle," the Dexion declared. "What is it even a key to?"

"That is for you to discover on your own. Don't you want to know?"

"I do want to know what game you are playing with me. Do not doubt for a moment I will find out." He snatched the key from her hand.

Cassia had the distinct feeling the mage had just taken bait Kassandra had carefully placed for him. Cassia could only wonder at what long game an oracle might play, and she longed to know.

"Tychon," Kassandra said.

The apprentice's only answer was to cross his arms and maintain his post at his master's elbow.

Kassandra reached for a nearby pitchfork and tossed it to Tychon. He caught it in both hands to prevent it from braining him. He flushed the deep red of humiliation from forehead to collar.

"You don't want to need that, do you?" Kassandra asked. "But you will, if you do not learn to help others dig their way out alongside you, rather than burying them to raise yourself up."

"I will not listen to your poison words." Tychon threw the pitchfork down onto the deck with a clang.

"But you have heard them," said Kassandra.

"Do tell me you have something for me." Skleros's rasping voice oozed mockery.

"Not a thing," Kassandra replied. "You are beyond help."

He laughed. "And I worked hard to get here."

"You are unfit to receive the gift of my prophecy. You would not heed it, and even if you did, nothing will spare you in the end."

Skleros smiled. "No one will be spared in the end."

"Thorns remain in the desert, and roses rise from the ash." Kassandra turned from him. "Now, for Lady Cassia. I have something very special to give the royal representative."

Cassia stepped closer to Kassandra. "That is very kind of you, Elder Firstblood."

Kassandra bent and opened a different trunk. There was only one object inside. It appeared to be a length of fabric of some kind, rolled around a wooden pole. Kassandra lifted it in both hands and unfurled it.

Cassia took a step back. She wanted to look away. But she was the royal representative. She had to pretend she was glad to see a banner depicting the Tenebran royal coat of arms.

"What a tribute to my father's kingdom," she forced herself to say. "How generous of the crafters of Orthros to devote their time to such a thing."

"We did not make it," Kassandra said. "Look closer."

Because it was Kassandra who asked, Cassia tried to see past the glare of the king's sun in her eyes. Her heart still pounded, and she still had to hide her fists in her skirts. But she wondered how she could have missed the details she now noticed.

The banner was no new creation of Orthros silk. It was tough Tenebran weave, and old. She could see that its tattered edges had been mended many times with meticulous care and its stains thoroughly cleaned. But there remained the faint mark of dirt—and blood.

Knight was sniffing the air in the banner's direction, his ears and tail alert with eagerness. Whatever he smelled, he did not consider it a threat. Perhaps the scent of the blood excited old instincts.

"This has seen battle." Cassia studied the emblem, and a thrill of surprise traveled through her. "This is a different version of the royal arms— perhaps an older rendition from an earlier era? This must be a historical artifact."

"Have you really never seen it before?" Kassandra asked.

Cassia shook her head. "How strange. The fire is not behind the sword's hilt, and the sword isn't pointing downward. The flame and the sword are flanking the sun."

"The original royal arms of the Tenebrae, the Mage King's own design." Kassandra rolled it up with care and handed it to Cassia. "You will need it."

Those words struck Cassia like nails in her coffin. She didn't want it. She didn't want to need it.

She never wanted to go back to Tenebra. Queen Soteira had promised her she could stay. How could Kassandra present her with this vision of her future? "I can't accept this."

"Your Ladyship," Benedict broke in, "this is an honor beyond compare! No one could be a better bearer than you."

"Take it, my lady," said Perita. "It does you justice."

"It does you proud, my lady," Callen echoed.

"A fitting gift," Lord Gaius agreed. "But your modesty befits you as well. A true lady of Tenebra, you are."

All Cassia's allies pushed her closer to the precipice, and she could not make herself reach out and take the gift.

"A relic of a dead age," came Chrysanthos's voice, "and a forbidden one. When the Mage King's successors made the sacrifice for Anthros and gave up magic, they changed the coat of arms. The sword was repositioned to signal an end to conflict, the fire placed behind it to symbolize that the Orders back the King of Tenebra's rule. The drawn sword and wielded flame as depicted here are forbidden to be flown anywhere the Orders prevail."

Cassia rounded on him. "Excellent. I have no plans to visit Cordium. I shall display this proudly in Orthros and Tenebra."

Orthros was what they made of it. So was this gift, Cassia decided. She wouldn't fly it for Tenebra, but for peace, and to wipe that smile off of Chrysanthos's face.

This was nothing like the coat of arms she had seen over Lucis's desk in his solar her whole life. Here was no sword pointed downward in submission, no flame of the Orders looming behind. This banner showed the fire and sword held high for the cause of the Mage King, who had united Tenebra under his sun and let the Hesperines escape its rays.

Cassia took the banner from Kassandra, and every Tenebran on deck cheered.

"As a mage of Anthros," Chrysanthos said, "I feel it is my responsibility to express my concern for you, Basilis. That banner may not be so kindly tolerated by others of my cult, once we are no longer in these far-flung parts."

"A lady such as myself is well accustomed to the censure of small minds," Cassia replied. "I must be brave and act according to the demands of my honor, no matter what opposition I face."

DRAMATIC ALTERATIONS

ASSIA WATCHED ONE MAN lift another on his shoulders to hang the historical Tenebran banner over the front doors of Rose House. Applause filled the main hall. Cassia stomped and cheered with everyone else, while she lifted her gaze past the banner to Lio's rose window. She knew what she was fighting for.

Lord Gaius gave the banner a warrior's salute. "We'd best keep this here...out of the mages' reach."

"Certainly, Lord Gaius," Cassia agreed. "All of you may consider Rose House a refuge."

Eudias leaned in the shadow of a pillar away from the gathering, worrying his mysterious gift in his hands, but a hint of a smile crossed his face.

Lord Adrogan ran a hand over the silk Kassandra had given him. "I dare the mages to try to steal from me. I'm keeping this where I can see it."

Lord Severin hoisted the bag of grain onto the sideboard. "As much as I want to take this home to my people, I think we'd best make porridge of it here, given the state of our provisions." He looked around at everyone. "Are we all satisfied by now that Hesperine food won't harm us?"

Master Gorgos peered at the grain and sniffed it.

"Oh, come now. I've eaten their food," Lord Adrogan confessed. "Try to tell me I'm enchanted."

"No one would make the mistake of believing that," said Benedict.

"You ought to try their fare," Lord Adrogan retorted. "It might sweeten your disposition."

Cassia went to a wine rack that had remained untouched since the ceremony welcoming the embassy to Orthros. "What do you say? While the Honored Master and his colleague are settling into their new quarters, shall we drink to the loss of the fine Cordian wine?"

Laughter went up through the hall. Cassia broke out the cups.

The lords were quite tipsy, and they had made no few toasts to Cassia's health and Tenebra's future, by the time they staggered into the gallery to return to the New Guest House. She managed to persuade sober Benedict and Eudias to accompany the others.

But there was no convincing Callen and Perita to leave her on her own, not when they knew what Skleros had done. At last Cassia surrendered and went to bed, while Perita settled down to spend the night on the couch in the sitting room, and Callen posted himself beyond the outer door.

Cassia rolled over, nose to nose with Knight. "Guarding the courtyard front is all on you, dearest."

"Guarding you on all sides is entirely my responsibility." Lio suddenly stood silhouetted against the closed glass door. With the low light of the courtyard shining in behind him, he was a deep, dark shadow between her and the rest of the world.

Cassia tumbled out of bed and went to him.

He wrapped her up in his embrace, bringing her face to rest against his chest, sheltering her in his arms. "I thought I was going to lose you."

"You are not going to lose me." She held on to him as she had the night at Waystar when they had finally been reunited. Except this time, she did not weep. She smiled against him.

His breath was warm upon her hair, his voice ragged. "Are you feeling all right?"

"I feel…restored. I have experienced Annassa Soteira's healing for myself."

He framed her face with his hands, lifting her gaze to his. "I am so sorry for what happened tonight. I promised you would be safe here in Selas."

"Queen Soteira worked her magic from the other side of the city without batting an eye, just to save me from an overdose of Teething Tonic. I was never in real danger."

"Don't make light of what Skleros did. It could have been—"

"No, it couldn't. Javed confiscated all his dangerous poisons."

"But *I* should have protected you tonight. I should have predicted the threat. I should have realized there was alchemy in the smoke. Your *dog* knew you were in danger before I did."

"I could say the same about myself. I know better than to ignore Knight's warnings, and yet I did. Skleros caught both of us by surprise."

"I failed you."

Cassia put a hand over his mouth. "Enough of that. You have stood between Hypnos and me more times than anyone else."

"He managed to lay a finger on you tonight. Please, forgive me. Perhaps then I can forgive myself."

"There is nothing to forgive. Let me share some wisdom with you, which I learned thanks to the patient efforts of the strongest person I have ever known. It is all right to need help sometimes."

"Did your sister teach you that?" he asked, his voice softening.

"No, Lio. You did."

He sucked in a breath. "Thank you, Cassia."

She pulled his face down to her and joined their lips. She filled her mouth with the taste of him and let the sensation of his nearness and his kiss fill her body.

Her return to Tenebra had only been a dream. Her close call had been a false alarm. Lio would not lose her, and she would not lose him.

He kissed her with exquisite gentleness, but oh, so deeply. He ran a careful hand down her braid and eased his other palm down her spine. Through the fine linen of her tunica, the warmth of his hand sent shivers of heat through her.

The door to the sitting room whispered shut, and she felt his veil spell wrap tighter around them. She parted her mouth from his to gasp a breath and stepped back, pulling her tunica over her head and tossing it aside. His silhouette shifted, and when she moved close to him again, his bare body met hers. His skin was silken against her, the slight hair on his chest and torso striking sensation across her tight nipples and along her belly.

She wrapped her arms around his neck to pull herself up closer to him. The next thing she knew, her feet left the floor. He levitated her higher, supporting her with his magic, and buried his face against her neck. His stubble scraped the sensitive skin between her neck and shoulder, and desire burned down into her.

It was always there, this hunger, and it took only the slightest invitation from him to awaken it, the barest touch to make it run wild. But everything she craved was right here in her arms. Like the statue in the garden, she held all she desired. But she and Lio were not locked in stone.

She put her lips to his neck and kissed him there, mirroring where his lips touched her. Opening her mouth, she licked and sucked at his throat. He gave a deep sigh and laved her neck with his tongue, giving pleasure for pleasure. She suckled harder, nipping at him, driven by the pulse under her tongue and the pulse pounding through her. When she bit down on him, he cried out.

She snapped her head up. "Was that too hard? Did I hurt you?"

His laugh was gentle and low in his throat and seemed to descend into the lowest reaches of her. "Oh, no, my rose. I hope you will bite me much harder than that."

With that, he sank his fangs into her throat. She keened and fastened her teeth at his neck with all the force of the pleasure that tore through her. As he began to draw the blood from her in firm, rhythmic sucks, she whimpered, opening and closing her teeth on him.

She threw her legs around him. She felt him alter his stance, bracing himself. Then his long, sure hands were gripping her hips. Borne on his levitation and guided by his touch, she rubbed the wet entrance of her krana over the head of his rhabdos. His fangs plunged deeper into her. Locking her ankles behind him, she tightened her legs and pulled herself onto him, pressing him deep inside her.

His hips jerked as he thrust into her with a guttural sigh against her throat. She sucked in a breath, then tightened her teeth again. She felt his rhabdos throb inside her. A low moan escaped her. She tried to think through her daze of hunger. Deliberately, she matched her bites to his sucks at her neck and his thrusts between her legs.

He drove into her more urgently. She ground against him, needing the overpowering sensation in her kalux and the pressure of his flesh in her channel. She gripped him tighter between her thighs, dizzy as she floated on his levitation. Her hunger roared higher, until she blazed on the edge of satiation. Her head fell back, and she begged him in wordless cries.

Suddenly the weightless sensation left her. He held her securely in his arms and released her from his levitation. She hung heavily on the hard column of his rhabdos. He penetrated her deep and delivered her feast. Her back bowed, her hips arched, and she anchored herself on his neck by her teeth. They moaned together with every deep, gratifying course of her pleasure.

As she undulated in his arms, his body went rigid against her, and his jaw locked on her neck. He drove up into her hard, then harder, then closed his hands around her buttocks and pulsed inside her. She pleasured him with her bites and rode his climax with him.

His levitation supported her again just as she began to tremble. The next thing she knew, he was laying them down on her bed. They panted together in a tangle of limbs and blood.

He held her tenderly, tracing soothing caresses along her neck, her arm, her hip until their pulses calmed. But she did not feel the lure of sleep. She felt ready to challenge the world.

"I suppose it was wise to ask for help tonight," Lio mused. "Father was kind enough to cover my patrol while I took care of an issue that required diplomatic delicacy. Kassandra agreed to keep the mages occupied in the harbor to allow me time. My father and Ritual mother both appreciate it when a Hesperine dares to play with fire." His fingers glowing with spell light, Lio held up the tinderbox Kia and Mak had confiscated from Skleros at the library.

Cassia's mouth dropped open. "*You* started the fire?"

"The law of Orthros mandates I give Mother a gift. Perhaps I'll get her a new volume for the library."

"That was far too dangerous!"

Lio shook his head. "I enlisted Xandra and Nodora to contain the blaze. Before we started, Kia checked for magical traps and helped us remove Skleros's herbs. Mak and Lyros relished confiscating his remaining smokes and tonics once I contrived a justification. By now, Chargers have delivered the necromancer's entire stock of herbs, potions, and instruments to Rudhira. It's all gone."

"I never imagined diplomacy could be so destructive. I only wish I could have helped you."

"You were facing your own fire at sea, my rose."

"I thought I was turning the mages' own folly against them. But all along, I was making use of the plot you instigated for us, just like when you invited me to Orthros in the first place. You have become expert at making dramatic alterations to the status quo in order to keep me safe."

"The mages had best watch their backs. There's no telling what I'll come up with next."

21

nights until

WINTER SOLSTICE

THE BALLAD OF CASSIA

How Cassia's world had changed since the last time she and Lio had attended a dance. Not weapons, but garlands of roses decorated the Grand Ball of House Kitharos. There were no martial banners, only silken depictions of the constellation of Thelxinos, Ritual firstblood of Nodora's bloodline. It was the Tenebran embassy that stood in an uneasy knot on one side of the ballroom, while the Hesperines mingled and made merry. The dais was devoted to the Muses of Orthros.

There was no king on his throne, presiding over his macabre festival with watching eyes.

And yet Cassia and Lio still stood on opposite sides of the grand hall.

Well, she would not hold up the wall tonight. When Benedict paused to jot a note to himself, she seized the opportunity to slip away from him.

"Knight is restless in this crowd," Cassia muttered to Perita and Callen.

Perita shook her head at the multitude of Hesperines. "I should say he is."

"I'm going to walk him in the arcade and give him some space to calm him."

Callen nodded and imposed himself between her and Benedict.

Cassia gave them a smile and eased away from the embassy. She patted Knight in silent thanks for always being a wonderful excuse. They made their escape into the arcade that bordered the hall.

They strolled under the garlands, drifting through the music that filled the opulent chamber. Surely no one could keep from walking in time to the flutter of the drums. No one could resist the soft, teasing lyres, which promised the dance would soon begin.

The musicians' invitation rose up through the grand hall to fall asleep amid a profusion of roses in the triforium above, or to ascend past the clerestory and take flight amid the ribbed vaults of the high ceiling. The notes echoed under the archways, by turns chasing and guiding Cassia along the arcade, then receded into the gloom beyond the reach of the spell lights.

She spotted a figure ahead of her in the half-shadow of the arcade. His height gave him away. Cassia grinned and cast a glance around her. The embassy's backs were turned to her.

What a lovely opportunity to misbehave. She hastened toward her shadow lover. His reflective eyes and pale fangs invited her to join him.

Then his smile vanished. She perceived a quick shake of his head, and he was gone.

A sound reached her ears. She had almost missed it under the drums and lyres, the scuff of her shoes and the click of Knight's toes. Footsteps behind her. The rustle of a robe.

Cassia directed her gaze away from where Lio had stood and moderated her steps. She proceeded halfway along the arcade, as if nothing were amiss, then paused to pet Knight.

The footsteps and rustling paused.

She turned around and meandered back the way she had come, her face calm, her heart pounding. She let her gaze roam the arcade between her and the embassy. Empty.

She made it all the way back to Callen and Perita without catching a glimpse of her pursuer.

"Better?" Callen cast an affectionate glance at Knight.

"Yes, much," Cassia lied with a smile.

A cascade of notes summoned everyone's attention to the dais, where Nodora's fathers stood side by side. Elder Firstblood Kitharos, the Queens' Muse, held his famous lyre. He was as pale, slender, and youthful as his statue, but in living color, far more cheerful, with glossy dark curls and a grin that bespoke the uninhibited joy he took in his music. Elder Grace Dakarai, with the build of a dancer and the deep brown complexion of an Imperial, gave them all a composed smile, a drum in his hands.

"What a delight," said Kitharos. "It falls to our bloodline to mark the halfway point of this historic Summit, a milestone truly worthy of celebration."

"But what is this?" Dakarai frowned, tapping his fingers over the surface of his drum. "Guests of House Kitharos, standing still? The Muses of Orthros have failed in our duties tonight, to be sure."

Good-natured laughter went up among the Hesperines.

Kitharos winked. "Honored guests from Tenebra, tonight will be the most fitting of conclusions to this week dedicated to the arts, a true celebration of shared inspiration and evolving genius, a rare opportunity every musician must relish to immerse ourselves fully in a culture, a sound, a history—"

Dakarai gave his Grace an amused glance, his eyes warm with affection.

Kitharos cleared his throat. "Ah, yes. Not a lecture, though."

The Hesperines laughed again.

"I mean to say," Kitharos continued, "we will devote the entire evening to Tenebran songs and dances, just like you know from home."

The Hesperines clapped. Cassia stomped her feet and managed to rouse her supporters, at least, to approve their hosts' gesture. Even the Tenebrans who did not applaud breathed sighs of relief.

"Well, that's only right," said the Semna from a nearby bench. "If the young folk must dance, it had best be wholesome dances. Now, now, Pakhne dear, don't regret that your dancing days are over. Your music at dusk rites in the temple is far prettier than anything here."

Ariadne patted her fellow attendant's arm in sympathy, looking everywhere but at Eudias. Cassia did them the courtesy of behaving as if she had not noticed. Her heart twinged. A world of obstacles stood between Eudias and the hope of someone who truly appreciated him.

Had Cassia just felt more than pity for a mage of Anthros? Yes, she sympathized not only with Ariadne, but with Eudias as well.

So be it. Cassia had chosen the Hesperine path, the path of kindness. She really did have it in her to stay that course.

"Midnight approaches," Dakarai announced.

Booming tones shook the hall. Cassia looked up in delight toward where the bells of House Kitharos must reside out of sight. The tones of midnight reverberated through the air and the stone and her bones.

The rest of the embassy signed glyphs behind their backs, but for once, Cassia did not endeavor to hide her enthusiasm. Her crimson gown emboldened her to heresy. If the others wondered at her brazenness, their small minds would attribute it to some notion of females' thoughtless love for fancy dances and pretty flowers.

"Dances have sacred meanings." Dakarai's voice filled the silence between the tolls. "That is true in the Empire, Orthros, and Tenebra. They may have different steps and rhythms, but dances are how all of us honor our past, celebrate our present, and express our hopes for the future."

The house bells launched into a melody. Kitharos joined them on his lyre, and Dakarai took up a stately rhythm on his drum. Cassia recognized the traditional Tenebran processional.

Lord Gaius, the highest-ranking noble in the embassy, bowed to Cassia. She took his arm, and they led the other Tenebrans to line up on the dance floor. Cassia beheld who stood parallel to them at the head of the Hesperine line.

The Queens stood hand-in-hand, ready to lead their majestic people in Tenebra's little dance. Behind them, from Konstantina and Adwene to Xandra and Harkhuf, every royal firstblood in attendance adhered to their mothers' program. Next in line were all the elder firstbloods except Kitharos and Dakarai. Apollon and Komnena smiled at Cassia, and Argyros and Lyta gave her encouraging glances. Hypatia looked sour, Khaldaios disinterested. At least Lyros's parents looked happy to be here. Timarete's feet were already tapping under her robes. Astrapas kissed her hand.

Cassia had played Kyria in a dance, but never followed in the footsteps of the Queens. She gave them a curtsy as deep as she dared. She only hoped Konstantina and Hypatia would not hold this against her the way the Tenebran ladies had the Autumn Greeting.

Side by side but never meeting, the embassy and the Hesperines acted out the grand processional, and the old Tenebran formality became something more beautiful to Cassia than she had ever known it to be.

The opening procession seemed to establish a truce between the two halves of the ball. Although mortals only danced with mortals, most members of the embassy did venture to join Cassia on the floor through the following dances. The Hesperines honored the unspoken arrangement and danced with one another, never pressuring any of the embassy with invitations. Cassia did her duty with various lords in order of rank and watched Lio do the honors with his Trial sisters, his mother, and various Ritual tributaries of Blood Komnena.

Even now, she must not let on that she was watching. One stray glance, one gaze that lasted too long, might betray her. A circle dance carried her round and round, giving her a glimpse of Lio, then Chrysanthos, then Lio.

She could keep up appearances a little longer. This time she knew what reward awaited her. She would not pine, unrequited, as she had while Lio danced with the ladies of the Tenebran royal court. He was her partner, and every Hesperine in the room knew it.

Nodora had promised a reprise of her welcome gift to Cassia. Someone would have to break the ice between Hesperines and mortals. Of course that must be the ambassador and the royal representative.

Cassia stole a respite from the lords at the Semna's bench, where Perita had engrossed herself in a conversation with the Kyrians and Cherans about the fabric most suitable for veils. Callen wore a bored expression but did not budge from the bench beside his wife. Cassia suspected he would somehow thank Perita later, even if he wouldn't admit how much he appreciated her pretending she was too busy talking to dance.

Cassia's heart twinged again. Her lover had two good legs and always would. He would never have to worry about battle scars, or rheumatism, or...getting old.

Cassia looked at the faces of her friends. She had watched countless people, from the highest courtiers to the lowest palace servants, don mourning clothes. She, who had worn the mourning veil over her heart for her sister these fourteen and a half years, had seldom stopped to consider others' grief.

Those people hadn't been her friends. But they were all someone's Callens and Peritas, weren't they?

One day, Callen would lose Perita, or Perita would lose Callen. It might be childbirth that took her. It might be his leg that broke him.

Cassia would lose them both.

"My lady, are you feeling well?" Perita asked.

Cassia's throat ached. She cleared it and put on her most convincing smile. "Just fine. The music is beautiful, isn't it?"

"It's good to hear a bit of home," Callen agreed.

Cassia should get to her feet and dance onward. She found herself lingering on the bench, listening to Perita chat, watching the way Callen sat with his arm in his wife's as if it were his natural position. Such everyday matters had never before struck her as so precious, nor threatened to bring her to tears.

She looked away. Balls were always a good opportunity to observe others and glean useful information, especially about opponents. Konstantina and her partisans may have been glaringly absent at the fair, but tonight they were visible to the utmost. They dominated one area of the ballroom opposite.

The Second Princess held court beneath an arch of her roses, surrounded by her devotees, all of them smotheringly elegant. What a contrast to the Queens, who sat together in the triforium in a bower of roses and black-and-white banners, chatting so merrily with Mak and Lyros, one would never take Lio's Trial brothers for their honor guard.

Cassia observed that a musician from the dais joined Konstantina's party whenever he was not playing. He was extraordinarily handsome from head to toe, and his glamorous, oiled blond hair suggested he spent more time before a mirror than did all the princes of Cordium combined. He must be Nodora's oh-so-glorious brother, Epodos. The equally blond and pretty female fawning over him appeared to be his Grace, and well matched to him in temperament.

Konstantina laughed at everything they said. The only quiet one was Baltasar. As Khaldaios's son by birth, whom Hypatia had adopted as her own firstgift, he bore a family resemblance to his bronze-skinned Imperial father, but also seemed to share Khaldaios's moderate temperament.

Cassia stared without appearing to stare, unsure how much she could glean. Her Divine was so limited. Even so, she must start putting the sounds together with the lips sometime. Now seemed an excellent opportunity to start.

She focused on Konstantina and her partisans' display. Cassia watched the motion of their lips and let them suggest sounds to her. Sounds she knew from Vulgus came to her first, broken, imperfect suggestions as to the music of Divine. Every now and then she would seem to gain a flash of understanding, but as soon as she focused too hard, it escaped her.

She stopped thinking and trying to match and simply watched, as she was wont to do with any speakers. The music of the ball faded from her awareness, and the other voices around her blurred into an indistinct hum.

"I was going to put Lio's little Cassia in the ballad." Epodos's beautiful lips quivered with suppressed laughter. "Alas, I could not find any words that rhyme with liegehound."

Cassia put a hand in Knight's ruff and glared at them. Epodos's Grace was laughing too hard to notice, and he was too focused on himself.

Baltasar didn't smile. "You aren't creative enough."

"Oh, I thought of all kinds of creative ways to describe the smell," Epodos said. "Foul saliva anointed her hands! The beast's fur clung to her velvets like dew upon the grass of the lands of bloodshed, a testament to the prejudices of her ancestors, and left in her wake the fetid musk of barbarity!"

His Grace wiped her eyes, shaking with laughter. Konstantina hid her mouth behind a silk-gloved hand. Was she, too, laughing at the upstart weed wreaking havoc of her carefully cultivated garden?

Cassia kept watching. She had heard it all before. She had been here so many times before, sitting on the edge of the festival, enduring every little nick and cut from those around her. She must remember how not to bleed.

"This is beneath you," said Baltasar.

Epodos did not know when to stop. "Well, I couldn't write it to the standards of Blood Kitharos, could I? A Tenebran bumpkin wouldn't be able to understand it."

Cassia's heart pounded in the most alarming way. She must not allow her throat to ache like this.

"You underestimate her," Konstantina said.

"Ambition ill becomes the naïve and maladroit," Epodos waxed on. "These presumptuous young things, making a mess of millennia of politics like calves in the glass cabinet. What is Orthros coming to?"

His Grace shook her head. "I can scarcely believe it's been allowed to get so out of hand. Thank the Goddess for your leadership, Konstantina. I cannot bear to imagine how much worse matters would be if you did not stand between us and disaster."

"We have a responsibility to lead by example," the princess replied. "The young people need elders of character to look up to."

"Perhaps I should write an instructional hymn instead," Epodos drawled. "Shall I start by teaching her the alphabet? Or the basics of hygiene?"

Cassia got to her feet.

"My lady?" Perita asked.

"Knight is restless again."

Baltasar rapped Epodos on the shoulder. Kia's brother glanced right in Cassia's direction. Before Cassia made it to the arcade, Epodos followed Baltasar's gaze.

Oh, no, no, no. That godsforsaken poet had seen the first tears escape her.

Cassia fled into the shadows of the arcade and kept going, with Knight fretful at her heels. Would they follow her across the ballroom? Hadn't they done enough? When she stumbled upon an open archway that led out of the grand hall, she seized upon it, then upon the next escape, then the next.

She found herself in deserted side corridors lit only at distant intervals with mellow spell lights. She leaned against the wall, pressing a hand to her mouth, while Knight nuzzled her. She must be silent, lest every Hesperine in the building hear her.

The fragrance of moonflowers and sandalwood enveloped her. A gentle hand lifted a handkerchief to her face. Lio put his arm around her shoulders and held her close. The next thing she knew, he was leading her through a door into a small chamber with a thick carpet and heavy tapestries on the walls.

"There now, my rose." He sat down in a chair and pulled her onto his lap. "These practice rooms are bespelled against all sound. No one will cross the veil."

The most humiliating sobs erupted out of her. They simply wouldn't stop. She covered her face in his handkerchief and hid her tears upon his shoulder.

"You read Epodos's lips?" Lio asked.

Cassia nodded.

"That will teach him to insult your aptitude for Divine. Cassia, I am so sorry. Nodora and I were planning the next song, and I didn't hear his conversation until it was too late."

"What's wrong with me? I know better than this. I am immune."

"None of us are immune."

"I never—let it—hurt me. I've heard such nonsense all my life."

"From Tenebrans," he said gently, "from whom life has taught you to expect cruelty. Not from Hesperines, who have, against all odds, taught you to expect kindness. Epodos broke that precious trust. He has shamed our people."

"Cassia?"

At the sound of Nodora's soft voice, Cassia only wanted to keep her face hidden. But the kindness in that voice made her look up.

Nodora took a seat. "You understood what Epodos said?"

"Yes. I suppose—I'm learning—faster than I thought."

"Cassia, that is…astonishing progress. But what a wretched repayment! On behalf of Blood Kitharos, allow me to say that my brother's conduct was reprehensible. He has dishonored the gift of your presence and debased our fathers' hospitality. And on behalf of myself, let me say what a bloodless vulture Epodos is."

The door slammed open, then shut. Stepping in was too calm for Xandra, it seemed. Her pale cheeks were flushed with anger, and Cassia could feel magic latent in the air.

"I am going to file a formal complaint," Xandra said calmly. A spark popped at her fingertips. "We'll see how Konstantina likes having her own laws used against her."

"I'm going to slaughter them." Kia appeared and stood protectively over Cassia.

"That's our job." Lyros stepped in beside her. "I'd like to hear that flimsy poet recite his ballad in the fighting ring and see how hygienic he feels after we're done with him."

Mak's big hand came to rest on Cassia's back. "He's not worth crying over. He'll be worth even less when we've knocked all his teeth out and strangled him so he can't sing."

In spite of herself, a laugh escaped Cassia. She realized she was sitting surrounded by beautiful, fragrant Hesperines with her nose running all over Lio's silk handkerchief, and they were all looking at her like she was the dearest person in the world. Xandra plopped down on the rug to pet smelly, drooling Knight. Lio put Cassia's snotty handkerchief in his pocket and handed her a fresh one without even bothering with a cleaning spell in between.

"You are all—so— I will never stop expecting kindness, because I know you."

Lio kissed her hair. "That is the highest praise any Hesperine could hope for."

"We'll let the Queens know you're all right," Mak said. "They sent us two 'young things' to check on you."

"Please give my gratitude to the Annassa for their concern." Cassia sat up suddenly. "But the embassy—I was not careful enough when I left. Earlier—"

Lio hugged her closer. "Don't worry. We took care of covering your departure."

"We were planning a circle during the ball anyway," Mak said. "Time to conspire again."

"I'm not sure it's safe," Cassia cautioned. "When I was in the arcade earlier tonight, coming to meet Lio—"

"Tychon was following you," Lio said, "presumably on Chrysanthos's orders. We succeeded in deflecting him for this circle, although earlier I deemed it an unnecessary risk to exert the power required to kiss you under an attentive apprentice war mage's nose."

"I'll give you an extra kiss later, after I've washed my face."

His cleaning spell dried her tears and cleared her nose. She blushed, but could not resist giving him a quick kiss on the lips. She had seen Hesperines give one another such brief, tasteful gestures of affection in front of others. It was not inappropriate.

Their friends clapped. Cassia's cheeks got warmer.

Lio smiled at her tenderly. "That will tide me over the whole night."

"Now then," said Lyros, "the Stand has a report for you all. While Mak and I were on guard last night to make sure none of the mages tried to sneak back into their old rooms, one of the mages tried to sneak back into their old rooms."

"So predictable." Mak shook his head.

"Who was it?" Cassia asked.

"Chrysanthos," Lyros answered. "We did not make our presences known or attempt to prevent him, so we could discover his purpose there."

"Don't tell me he was that desperate to see if any of his wine survived," said Cassia.

Kia smiled wickedly. "He was probably looking for those spurred boots he got from the Gift Collector. As they melted, I enjoyed envisioning Chrysanthos's man tears."

Lyros shook his head. "He lost something more significant, it seems."

"He dug through the ashes for hours." Mak frowned. "Didn't care a bit about his pretty clothes, either. Got himself covered in soot, he was so frantic."

"What could be so important to him," Lio asked, "and did we destroy it?"

"Should we have destroyed it?" Nodora wondered.

"Surely it would be better to confiscate it for study," Kia said.

"Well," Lyros answered, "you know the inlaid box he kept next to the bed during veil hours and on his desk come first moon?"

Lio nodded. "I took note of it on my patrols."

"It was on his desk when you started the fire," Mak said. "He began his search right where it had been and spent the most time looking there. He went over his entire rooms, then returned to where he'd started to search again."

"That must be it," Lio said. "He scarcely let the box out of his reach, even when he slept."

"That was the only chest I couldn't open." Kia dusted her fingernails on her robes. "All his other spell locks popped easily enough."

"Do we have a theory about what the inlaid box might contain?" Cassia asked.

Lio nodded. "He would be a fool to come into enemy territory without a powerful artifact in reserve, or perhaps supplies for a devastating spell."

"We'll have to wait for Rudhira's verdict," Mak said. "The box is in the Charge's hands now."

Lio smiled at Cassia. "In the meantime, shall I return you to the ballroom so you and I can dance?"

"With that as an incentive, certainly." Cassia smiled.

"Wait a moment." Kia took a seat in front of Cassia. "Did Lio start teaching you Divine when you two were together back in Tenebra?"

Cassia shook her head. "We didn't have a chance till I came to Orthros."

"So you've been learning a new language in a different alphabet for exactly three weeks," the scholar said.

"Well, I'm not as good with the alphabet yet. It will take much more time before I can read and write fluently in Divine. But I spend a lot of time listening."

"I'm a teacher, Cassia," Kia said. "I know how long it takes students of various ages and levels of education to learn Divine. Listening does not suddenly enable you to understand complex conversations just by reading lips. At least, not most people. I have never seen anyone accomplish what you have in just three weeks."

Cassia shrugged. "Perhaps some of it rang a bell because I've heard Divine in temple all my life."

Lio shook his head, his gaze full of admiration. "You have a gift for languages."

Cassia snorted. "The last thing I am is a scholar."

"Your aptitude is more organic," Lio said. "You don't learn best from scrolls, but from, as you say, listening. Next thing you know, you'll be speaking."

Warmth suffused Cassia. "Well, perhaps I will."

Kia looked at her with great concentration. "How did you learn to read lips in the first place?"

"I bet Solia taught you," Lio guessed.

Cassia shook her head. "Actually, no. I just…picked it up along the way."

"You taught yourself to read lips that precisely?" Kia asked. "That must have taken practice."

"I don't remember teaching myself, or practicing, really. When I think about it, I suppose there was a time when I couldn't, a time when I could, and a time when I got better at it."

Kia's brows shot up. "People don't usually become so adept at it unless they're making an effort to learn, adapting to hearing loss, or both."

"What affinity does it sound like to you?" Lio asked.

"A lot of rare theoretical things occur to me," Kia answered. "No, it has to be something more practically applicable…"

"We have no reason to suspect me of being magical," Cassia protested. "We know now that Skleros didn't give me apprentice's toddy because of a mystery affinity, and we can lay our fears to rest that it related to some displacement he was planning. It was simply the only concoction available to him that would get me out of his way."

"I have laid no fears to rest where the necromancer is concerned," Lio said, "but regardless of Skleros's motives, you may have magic that never had an opportunity to manifest in Tenebra."

"I'd sooner have a gift for Hesperine language," Cassia confessed, "than all the affinities in the world."

"Mundane aptitudes often presage associated undiscovered affinities," Lio enthused.

"Tulips don't grow among the hedge nettle," Cassia said, "and I've always been happy to be a hedge nettle. Now I'd best take my prickles back into the ballroom. I owe you a dance."

"We aren't done with this topic," Kia said.

"Is that a threat?" Cassia teased.

"Oh, yes." Kia winked. "I'm determined to experiment on you. We will poke your magic until it gets annoyed and growls back at us."

"Your fingers will get tired, and I shall get very bruised," Cassia predicted.

"We'll nurture your sleeping tulips till they bloom," Lio amended.

"That sounds like something you don't need me for," Kia said.

Cassia wondered when she would run out of blood to blush with.

They all left the practice room together. Cassia couldn't help glancing up and down the hall, although she probably had six layers of veils around her.

Nodora touched a hand to Cassia's arm. "Wait here."

The musician disappeared. Moments passed in silence, and the Hesperines did not look surprised.

Then Nodora reappeared with Epodos in tow. His Grace hung stiffly on his arm, clearly wishing she were elsewhere. Baltasar stood behind them, a silent barricade to retreat.

"Cassia," said Nodora, "if you would be so generous as to spare my brother a moment of your time, he is here to tender his apologies."

Epodos wouldn't meet Cassia's eyes. "Which one of you was indelicate enough to repeat my conversation to your friend?"

Cassia must face him without a liegehound for intimidation. She lowered her hand, and Knight sat. She held her chin high and stepped forward to stand beside Nodora. Cassia opened her mouth to speak in Vulgus, but a fit of daring overtook her, and the words she needed came to her.

"I understood you," she said in Divine.

That made Epodos look at her. His startled expression was thoroughly gratifying. His Grace's eyes widened. Baltasar covered his face with one hand.

Cassia rubbed it in using the poet's own instrument, his beloved Divine. "In the three weeks since my arrival, I have picked up quite a bit of Divine. Oh, and I've known how to read lips since I was a child. It turns out Hesperines are just as easy to understand as mortals."

Epodos stood stiffly and smoothed the end of one of his braids. "I see. I did not realize a veil would have been in order."

Nodora threw up a hand at him. "Lack of discretion is not what you should apologize for!"

"Epodos?" Konstantina entered the hallway from the ballroom. When she saw Cassia, Lio, and their friends, she halted.

"Good moon, Second Princess," Cassia greeted her in Divine.

Konstantina raised her eyebrows. Then she smiled. "I did warn you, Epodos."

Seeing that smile, Cassia suddenly had the context for Konstantina's earlier remarks to Epodos. *You underestimate her...we have a responsibility...elders of character...* Konstantina had not been laughing behind her hand. She had been defending Cassia—and encouraging her Trial brother to be his better self.

For an instant, Cassia met Konstantina's gaze and saw approval there. Cassia looked away quickly. She had already refused the Second Princess's alliance and approval. She must best Epodos on her own. She tried not to appreciate how Konstantina stood back and let her do just that.

"I'm sure Lady Cassia can forgive a little courtly banter," Epodos wheedled, "which she has heard often enough in her father's house."

Cassia advanced on Epodos. "Yes, I have met people like you in the king's court, Firstgift Kitharos. Your pride will not allow you to offer a sincere apology, so you may keep it. I do not need your apology. I do not need your favor. I do not need your invitation. I belong here, because I fought to make it here." She took another step forward. "I risked my life for your people to earn my place among them. Then I arrived here and learned that I do not have to earn Orthros. It is a gift. Not from you. And not one you can take from me."

She took one more step. Epodos took a step back.

"Yes, I smell of liegehound. No, I can't recite Hesperine sonnets. Yes, I am young and mortal and, I assure you, entirely presumptuous. I wonder if the founders of Orthros smelled like fine soap when they made it over the mountains. Did the Hesperite villagers who fled to safety already know great literature, or did the temple mages of Hespera have to teach them? How many of the refugees were still mortal when they left Tenebra? How long had they been alive in this world when they chose the Gift and laid the foundation for Orthros's future? They are the most presumptuous people I have ever met, and I am proud to risk the ire of the king and the Orders for their sake. That is what you may write in my ballad."

Nodora linked arms with Cassia, and together they walked past Epodos. With Lio, Kia, Xandra, Mak, and Lyros at their sides, they marched between Konstantina and the poet's gaping Grace to return to the dance.

A TENEBRAN DANCE

ASSIA MINGLED BACK INTO the embassy just as the music paused for an announcement from Kitharos and Dakarai. With fatherly pride, they ceded the dais to their youngest daughter for a series of solos. Nodora took her fathers' place before the crowd with a blushing smile, holding only her lute.

When the spell lights softened, a few quiet gasps and murmurs could be heard among the mortals. The arcades faded into shadow, while the gentle glow in the hall seemed to draw everyone closer together. The vaulted ceiling disappeared into a darkness as complete as the night sky, while crystal clear light illumined Nodora.

She held her fingers against the silent strings of her lute. "From my mortal mother, I learned to play the bamboo flute and three-stringed shamisen that define the sound of the Archipelagos. From my Hesperine father Dakarai, I learned the sacred drums and dances of the high veld, where his mortal life began. From my Hesperine father Kitharos, I learned the lyre and the lute so dear to your Tenebran ears and hearts."

Nodora's voice was a music of its own, putting everyone at ease, yet enticing them to a mysterious thrill. Cassia watched in admiration. Nodora was truly a masterful performer. Her voice, her posture, her expression were all instruments, too, conjuring the desired effect on her audience.

And yet Cassia knew all this reflected the music of Nodora's heart, as genuine as could be. The Muse should have been a diplomat. Tonight the Summit would benefit from her skills and her conviction.

"In Orthros, I learned to love these musics," said Nodora, "and in these musics, I learned who I am. To love music is to love the people who make it, is that not so?"

Caressing the lute strings, she answered her own question with a cascade of notes that felt deeply familiar to Cassia, although she couldn't remember what song they were from.

"What songs do you miss from home?" Nodora asked, turning toward the embassy's side of the hall. "I will take any request!"

An awkward silence ensued. No one seemed bold enough to take Nodora's invitation.

Nodora spoke again. "What is your favorite, Apprentice Eudias? I could play a sailing song in honor of our mutual affinity for water."

Eudias shuffled on his feet, ducking his head. "I fear the fishermen's tunes I know are hardly appropriate this gathering."

"There is no such thing as lowly music," she replied. "All songs lift us up."

When the apprentice did not offer any suggestions, Nodora called out in a different direction. "What about you, Honored Master Adelphos? Name your favorite song."

Now that was clever. A subtle invitation to Chrysanthos to trip over his Cordian origins. Did he even bother to learn the names of the Tenebran songs he must regard as crude?

"Alas," he answered, "my time in Cordium as the King of Tenebra's emissary has spoiled me forever on the compositions of Aurelio. After hearing the golden bard's masterpieces, I am deaf to all other music."

"Aurelio it is, then!" Nodora plucked a string and tweaked a tuning peg. "How about 'Avior's Tryst'?"

"Oh, yes," Kia said from the Hesperine side. "I love that ballad. How intriguing that Aurelio never identifies the mysterious goddess who happens upon the woodland god Avior and cures his wounds."

"And his loneliness," said Xandra.

The Hesperine ladies' suggestive laughter seemed to daze all the men within earshot.

And then Nodora began to play. The tones of her lute conjured shadowed forests around them, summoned wind through their hair, lured them to tiptoe through cool streams and lay flat on their backs in sunny meadows. Her perfect, pure soprano was the voice of the goddess who beheld the woodland god and loved him. She made the rhythm of the ballad pulse with Avior's desire for his rescuer.

Cassia had never shed a tear over a song, but moisture came to her eyes when the nameless goddess had to bid Avior farewell and return to the stars. The closing strains of the ballad teased the mystery of their parting. A divine union consummated or eternally unrequited love?

Silence fell. The mortals seemed unable to awaken from their bewitchment, and Knight lay flat on his belly, staring at Nodora with his ears perked. When her lute strings at last stopped quivering, the humans stirred as if coming out of a dream. A few moments later, Knight's ears relaxed.

Menodora looked in Chrysanthos's direction. "Is that how they play it in Cordium, Honored Master?"

"Not hardly. Your Hesperine interpretation is unprecedented."

"Avior's sacred animal is a free-flying wren, not a starling adept only at mimicry. In honor of Aurelio's patron god, I will take your critique as a compliment."

Chrysanthos seemed to remember himself. He put his hands in his sleeves and gave a slight bow. "Well, I was only a visitor in Cordium. I am certainly not qualified for an extended discussion of musical theory."

"I believe the music speaks for itself. What shall I play now? Who would like to make the next request?"

Cassia spoke up. "Would you be so kind as to play us another dancing song?"

"Certainly, Lady Cassia." Nodora exchanged a conspiratorial smile with her. "I know just the one. I understand it's been beloved at the Tenebran court for generations and was quite popular during the most recent Equinox Summit."

She commenced the familiar notes of the chaste but lively Tenebran dance Cassia and Lio had shared at Solorum. But Nodora pulled from her instrument a beautiful variation of the introduction that transformed the song from courtship to seduction. Cassia couldn't wait a moment longer to see Lio move to this melody anew, to find this rhythm with him once more, to enjoy a dance here in Orthros to a friend's music.

"This event is going rather well," Cassia commented to Perita. "But I think we can do even better. Excuse me."

She put Knight in a sit-stay by her friends and strode through the embassy toward the open dance floor. Lio stood at the front of the Hesperine crowd. He watched her across the divide, but did not step forward. This move was hers.

She was just about to cross the distance when Chrysanthos stepped in front of her.

She halted in her tracks and lifted her chin. Half a dozen responses raged through her mind, all of them dangerous to her image with the embassy. If she spoke, she would err, so she gave the mage nothing more than an inquiring glance.

The Dexion held out his hand. "You have yet to dance with me."

The monster wanted to steal her dance with Lio.

"Honored Master, as a mage, you are beyond the order of rank. I did not think our duties required a dance."

"You would regard a dance with me as nothing more than a duty? You wound me, my lady. I assure you, it would be a pleasure."

Master Gorgos trundled over and imposed himself into their conversation. "I have to agree with Basilis."

Cassia had never thought he would be her rescuer. "Oh, Master Gorgos, do please advise us on the proper course of action in this delicate situation. While I am exceedingly flattered by the Honored Master's request, I cannot help but wonder if it is acceptable for a lady such as myself to join him in a dance while he serves in his capacity as a mage of Anthros."

"A lady such as yourself must surely have few opportunities to enjoy a dance partner such as I," the Dexion replied. "It would be a shame for you to have to miss it."

"Indeed, I have never received an invitation from a man of your character, much less accepted it."

"Your delicacy is to be commended." Master Gorgos nodded and smiled. "Adhere always to the path of retiring virtue! Lift yourself up upon the wings of humble resignation! The gods smile upon the young lady who forgoes worldly pleasures..." Master Gorgos eyed the Dexion. "...and upon the man who embraces the rigors of self-discipline."

"You've danced your feet off, my dear." The Semna patted the bench beside her. "Come sit awhile with me."

Nodora repeated the song's introduction in yet another variation, and the energetic melody heightened to tension. Lio watched the confrontation from among the Hesperines, his face perfectly composed into what Cassia knew was a mask of diplomacy reinforced by a veil spell or eight.

She let her regret fill her heart, a silent message to him. Even if she escaped a dance with Chrysanthos, there was no way she could dance with Lio now. The only way out of dancing with the Dexion was to revert to wallflower.

Cassia already knew she could never return to being that silent, passive girl.

Whatever the Dexion was planning for this dance, she would find out and turn it back upon him. She would make him regret standing between her and Lio.

"Come now," Chrysanthos cajoled. "Where in our vows does it say we may not dance?"

Master Gorgos frowned. "That surely falls under putting worldly pleasure to the scythe on the altar of Anthros."

"Oh, Honored Master," Cassia demurred, "I really couldn't…"

Chrysanthos extended his hand again. "You already know my opinion on your piety. I am sure we both understand precisely what this dance does and does not mean. You must weary of provincial partners. Come dance with a true expert who has studied the steps in the finest courts."

"Oh, dear. We are causing a scene." Cassia cast an indicative glance at the watching crowd, then turned a gaze that pled for rescue at Master Gorgos, even as she put her hand in Chrysanthos's. "Virtue demands discretion."

Before the other mages had further opportunity to protest, the Dexion gripped her hand and led her onto the floor. He was holding her hand, which only weeks ago she had scarred rescuing the glyph stone from the shrine of Hespera he had destroyed. A hand that had left behind bloody prints on the ruins, the evidence that had alerted him the heretic he hunted was a woman.

The dance forced him to release her. Safe a moment longer. She resisted the urge to scrub her hand on her clothes. They prowled around each other in the opening steps. Clap. Clap. The rest of the dancers assembled around them. Clap. Clap. Clap. Clap. Nodora launched into the main melody, every stroke of her strings a challenge.

Chrysanthos did not perform the steps. He worked them like a spell. When the dance brought them near, he lunged toward her. "It has taken me this long to corner you without your slavering liegehound to protect you, and I don't mean the Knight with four legs."

Cassia danced away before their shoulders could touch. "Corner me, Honored Master? That sounds rather like a threat."

He stalked around her again. "You're a better listener than I thought."

She matched him, watching him. "I hardly need my ears after you gave me a noseful of your intentions the other night. Where there is smoke, there is fire. But where is your chimney at present? Did Master Skleros stay home from the dance because he has two left feet?"

"The Hesperines insulted him by refusing to invite him to the Grand Ball. They gave a ridiculous excuse about not overcrowding the building and causing a fire hazard."

"It is a wonder they found room for a hazard like you."

"Watch your tongue." Chrysanthos clapped a warning in her ear. "I do not need my colleague's assistance to instruct a little girl."

"Do tell him to expect me later. I have yet to properly thank him for sharing his smoke with me."

Chrysanthos let out a haughty laugh. Too haughty. Too quick. "I don't know what you mean."

Was he denying it, or had she really caught him by surprise? "Of course not. You wouldn't know anything about your dear friend rolling a smoke of Apprentice's Toddy just for me and dosing me with enough for Eudias's entire mastery class. I'm sure you had no intention of sending me into the faint that had the Kyrians despairing of my life."

She paid careful attention to the Dexion's every minute reaction. The extra tension in his hands. The especially blank court face. She might have explained those away. But when the hair on the back of her arms stood on end, she knew she was dancing with an alarmed war mage.

Nothing could go wrong, she reassured herself. Unless she betrayed to him that he played on her fears.

Chrysanthos recovered his smile and accompanied her smoothly in a turn. "My lady, I know our previous conversations have not always been cordial, but you cannot really believe I would stoop to such a mean tactic against a defenseless woman."

"I am sure you are the last person who would be delighted for your dear friend to rid you both of my interference! You and Master Skleros must have thought I would have a long, harmless rest while the two of you set sail with Elder Firstblood Kassandra and hunted for the Akron's Torch in the scrimshaw."

"Basilis, you are a very clever woman. You should know better than to make such wild accusations."

"I get the impression you should know your colleague better. Did he take matters into his own hands? Is he, perhaps, a little out of control?"

"You may lay your fears to rest. Why would either of us do harm to you when we recognize your potential value to us? I invited you to dance so I can give you another opportunity to assist me in my endeavors."

"Go to Hypnos, and take the Gift Collector with you."

The music signaled a change of partners. She smiled at Chrysanthos as she danced away from him, and Kia seized him. Cassia went right into Lio's hands. She breathed a sigh of relief and held him as close as she dared.

"That bloodless vulture stole our dance," she said. "I'll make him pay."

"Cassia, he's seething. This is too dangerous. I'm afraid of how he'll retaliate."

"Remember when Lord Ferus threatened me at the dance in Tenebra?"

Lio's jaw clenched. "He was a brainless oaf. A violent, wicked one, but not a war mage!"

Cassia touched her shoulder to his. "I am capable of handling war mages, as well. Especially since this one is behaving like a brainless oaf. It's just as we said—the Dexion is off his game. He didn't know Skleros dosed me."

"What? You mean the necromancer is acting on his own? He might even have his own plot..."

"See how much information I'm extracting from Chrysanthos? I have him right where I want him."

"I want to amputate his hands for touching you."

"You must content yourself with burning up his rooms, and I with making him regret he ever asked to dance with me."

She withdrew her hands from Lio's. He watched her return to Chrysanthos with anything but acquiescence in his gaze.

Chrysanthos grasped her. "That was a very unwise answer."

"It is the only wise answer. I'm not fool enough to believe your pretty invitations and wait for you to betray me."

"I've been extraordinarily patient with you. I even gave you a second chance. You just ruined it. You are out of chances."

Cassia broke free of the Dexion and clapped, laughing. "What do you think you can do to me in front of all these people?"

"Frighten you." Chrysanthos dragged her into the next turn with a shake the dance disguised.

The Dexion was an exquisitely graceful dancer, the way the most skilled of swordsmen was an exquisitely graceful killer.

Cassia willed Lio not to intervene and hoped he would heed her thoughts, rather than act on her pounding heart and the sweat breaking out between her shoulder blades. If she could keep Chrysanthos blustering, he might let something else informative slip in his eagerness to intimidate her.

"You remind me of someone," she told him.

He leapt back. "I beg your pardon?"

"Someone my mother used to know."

He swept around her and turned his back. "I assure you, I have no connections with the sort of men your mother knew before the king elevated her."

"I know all about men like you, who use your bodies as weapons to make yourselves feel powerful." Cassia faced him. "I am not afraid of you."

"Then you are even more foolish than I thought."

"I am clever enough to see through you. You are too angry to be subtle and too driven to be careful. You are blundering through the game on brute strength while still believing you are a strategist, and everyone can tell these tactics do not suit you."

"You know nothing about me. You are playing at matters that are far above your head."

"I am in my element."

"Do you think the fact that you are female will keep you safe from me? Do you think your father will lift a finger to protect you if my Order turns on you?"

"As I said, I am not foolish."

Comprehension flashed in his eyes. "Who are you working for?"

He had to ask? That meant he didn't know. He had no inkling.

He was dancing with the so-called Hesperite sorceress and still befuddled over why the king's bastard was playing at politics.

"I already told you who I serve," Cassia answered. "Tenebra."

The Dexion gripped her waist painfully tight. "Who is protecting you?"

"I am."

Instead of trying to evade him as he expected, she kicked up her heels, leaving him to support her. Thrown off balance, he stumbled backwards, while murmurs erupted everywhere, the Hesperines' concerned, the Tenebrans' scandalized. Cassia landed on her feet without missing a step.

"You know..." For the first time, Chrysanthos sounded out of breath. "...at first I believed you were as simple as most women. Cleverer than average, perhaps, but ignorant—a combination that leads a female to ruin."

"I have heard Master Gorgos's sermons. Do spare me."

"I assumed you took this embassy to mean the king actually wanted peace with Orthros. I thought you insensible of the complexity of the situation. I considered the possibility that you were making your own clumsy, but well-meaning attempts to support your father's efforts and earn his favor."

"Do you always analyze your own thought processes this thoroughly? I'm sure it's fascinating to your apprentices, but you are outside the temple in the real world now. I'll give you a hint. A man who likes to hear himself talk is doomed to embarrass himself."

"Yes, you know all about the real world, don't you? You know that the quickest way to earn your father's favor is to earn mine. So that must not be what you want."

She need only keep him guessing and keep him talking. "It must be such a struggle for you to understand the desires of others, when you are so self-absorbed."

"A self-serving creature like you would think she sees that in others."

"Your own goals are so transparent and simple, the complexities of others' must bewilder you at every turn."

"Women. You always think yourselves so mysterious. I'm afraid I penetrated that territory a long time ago. You can stop pretending to be such a novice yourself."

"I have nothing to hide. Examine my conduct. Anyone in Tenebra will tell you I am a retiring, dutiful lady who prefers spending her time in Lady Hadrian's weaving room or the gardens at the Temple of Kyria."

"You keep trying to hide behind that masquerade. But you are no devout. Neither are you a simpleton."

"What do you know about women? You think because you've passed an hour with them at the Temple of Hedon so many times, that makes you an expert? I dare say those ladies could tell you more about yourself in five minutes than you have understood about our sex in your entire lifetime."

"Oh, I am far from insensible of your secret wiles."

"Men like you have tried all my life to tell me what I am. I do not form myself to your declarations."

He took her hands again, and this time yanked her close, closer than decency allowed, so close she could smell his expensive, fragrant mouth tonic when he spoke. She tried a pirouette to distance herself from him, but he held her fast, chasing her with a flawless elaboration on the dance that kept them turning, turning eye to eye.

"You are the worst monster a woman can become," he said. "A schemer."

She leaned close to him and whispered in his face. "Are you afraid yet?"

ENCORE

"WHAT CHRYSANTHOS BETRAYED DURING the dance was definitive," Cassia said to the shadows in Lio's library. "He is still ignorant of my true purpose. He does not suspect me of being the heretic he is hunting. That makes it well worth it, doesn't it?"

Lio could not find it in himself to answer right away. He raised the spell lights.

"It made a good bedtime story," Cassia went on. "Zoe was thrilled to hear of how I danced with a war mage and had the last laugh. Perhaps her nightmares about the Order of Anthros will be easier tonight."

Lio took her cloak, hanging it on the hook by hand.

"Lio?"

"You're right. You did learn valuable information. Chrysanthos is in the dark about you and his own comrade."

"Now that Chrysanthos knows Skleros dosed me, he may wonder what else the necromancer has done without his knowledge. He might even believe Skleros started the guest house fire. We can use this to drive a wedge between them."

"Yes. No."

She took his hands. "I'm sorry. I wanted to save our dance. But there was nothing we could do."

"There are so many times when there is nothing we can do."

"We knew that would be the case during the Summit. We accepted the difficulty, along with all the other challenges."

"Yes, of course. We must carry on."

Silence fell between them. Lio thought about offering to make coffee and changing the subject. But the words he was not saying boiled up in him like undisciplined magic.

Cassia looked up into his eyes and ran her hands down his arms. "You are truly unhappy about tonight. What can I do to make it right?"

"It is wrong of me to give in to these feelings. I will master myself."

"That isn't what I asked."

"I'll go make us some coffee."

She halted him. "I don't blame you for being angry."

Now she was coaxing him to admit his feelings, as he had so often done for her.

"Your anger is beautiful to me," she went on, "but only when I feel reassured I am not the cause of it."

It was her turn to tell him he was not immune. That it was all right to be angry.

"I could never be angry with you," he said. "Only at the situation."

She frowned. "You are unhappy with my decision."

"I weary of it!" His voice rose. "I don't know how much longer I can bear to stand by and watch when you're in danger. After what Skleros almost did—what he might have done—I watched you place yourself in the Dexion's hands. I got through the night, and I didn't stop you, and I respected your decision. But I'm not sure I can do that even one more time. It's too hard. I think that's wrong of me, but I am trying to stop holding myself to a standard I cannot achieve. This is one I can't achieve, Cassia. I can't watch you take that risk alone again and not be able to lift a finger to protect you."

He rubbed a hand over his mouth, as if that would put his fangs back in his head. The tense silence he had created made him second-guess his outburst.

Then Cassia said, "I'm glad you told me."

Lio let out a breath.

"I want to apologize," she said. "A better apology, now that I know why you are unhappy."

"I'm not sure you have anything to apologize for."

"I'm sorry I put you through that. Your feelings are more important to me than any information I might have learned." She hesitated. "There are times when I must face risks alone, and you must let me. You have done so every single time I needed you to. Next time, I will do what you need."

A relief more profound than he had imagined made him pull her into his arms. "Thank you, Cassia."

"I put you to the test, don't I? And you always pass. But you don't deserve to be tested, you who are the surest person in my life."

"Sure. I would much rather be that than perfect."

"Then you can stop trying, for you have achieved it."

"Cassia, there is something else I must confess. The danger to you was not the only reason for my anger." He sighed. "I am a diplomat, but I am also your lover. I am not in the least immune to getting cheated out of a dance with you by another. I am not immune to...you not fulfilling a commitment."

Had he really just said that? He was grateful to even have her here in his arms against all odds, and he was upset with her for not giving him a dance she had promised him? For not finding a way to overcome the obstacles that weren't her fault?

She drew back. "Would you rather I have sat it out than danced with Chrysanthos?"

"I'm sorry, Cassia."

"I don't think you have anything to apologize for, either."

He rubbed his face again. "Yes, I would rather you not dance at all than give our dance to someone else."

She swallowed. "It was *our* dance."

"The one we danced the night you asked me to become your lover. The steps we took while you made that declaration to me. It's sacred. How could you dance that with anyone else—with *him*? Why does every secret, precious thing that is *ours* get paraded around and debased by *politics!* My effort to bring you home to me was not a calf in a glass cabinet! Our dance is not a tool for interrogating the enemy!"

The windows rattled. Lio held Cassia's hands gently in his.

"I was afraid you would feel that way," Cassia said.

Lio frowned at her, his magic throbbing in his head. "You were?"

"It's the most natural feeling in the world. I realize now it would have been better if I hadn't gone through with the dance. But I thought it would be all right, as long as I make it up to you afterward."

The notes of an unseen lute crept into the tower with the fragrances of the garden.

"That's our dance," Lio said.

Cassia gave him a hesitant smile. "I asked Nodora if she would give us one more chance at her welcome gift."

The introduction to the song wrapped around them, a more sensual and compelling arrangement than could ever have been played within the hearing of the Tenebran embassy. The music beyond the windows waxed and became something transcendent.

"This isn't what we had in mind," Cassia said, "but it has its consolations, I hope. You can hold me much closer than you could in front of the embassy."

"And I can do this." Lio pulled her close and levitated them.

He carried her through the steps of their dance on his magic and in his embrace. They followed the pattern, but there were no partners to change, no onlookers to tell them their bodies were too close, no reason at all not to keep their hands joined.

When they were to touch their shoulders, he wrapped an arm around her waist and turned them. When she danced away and spun, he held her hands, flying round and round with her. When the dance brought them together again, he held her against him, felt her move, heard her feet dancing on air and a spell, knew how her blood would taste after this dance.

"I'm glad we're getting a chance to practice," he murmured to her.

"Practice? For what?"

"One entire night of the Winter Solstice celebration is devoted to a lovers' dance."

She gasped in delight as he spun her midair again.

"You'll dance every dance with me then, won't you?" he asked.

"Every dance, all night long, with no Tenebrans watching. No one to stop us. I promise, Lio."

Their kind, elusive siren gave them not one, but four repetitions of the song. They touched and danced and glided the height and breadth of the library. At long last, the notes trilled, thrummed, and faded into silence.

The Blood Union told Lio he had Cassia all to himself. He scooped her up in his arms and eased them downward toward their bed.

"You aren't going to feast on me midair?" she teased.

"Extended levitation with a human requires concentration. I might lose my control over my altitude. Unexpected ascent is exciting, but sudden descent would be an embarrassing interruption."

"Let's dance the next one to our own music in the window seat. I plan to help you forget what control is, without interruption, all night long."

20

nights until

WINTER SOLSTICE

HONOR AND VALOR

ASSIA SURVEYED HER WORK, still holding her arsenal of brushes and combs. Knight lay down on the privy's decorative tile floor, taking up most of the modest chamber. He gazed up at her with his tongue hanging out, amiable and clueless.

"What do you think, Perita?" Cassia asked. "Will he do?"

Standing right outside the open door, Perita put her hands on her hips, but her severe expression wavered, not quite hiding her smile. "I'd be out of work if you devoted half as much attention to your own hair as you have to that mat he's wearing."

Cassia sighed at the puddles of water and soggy towels scattered everywhere. Her entire guest chambers would be redolent of wet liegehound and herbal bath. "He's still a shaggy mess."

"Liegehounds aren't made to be groomed. You're taking him to a sparring match, not a royal procession, aren't you?"

"Elder Grace Hippolyta, the Guardian of Orthros herself, invited me to show Knight to her Stand. Orthros's warriors are accustomed to the heart hunters' mangy, vicious beasts. I want my Knight to make a better impression."

"I think Knight made all the impression he needs to when he killed a pack of the heart hunters' liegehounds in Martyr's Pass."

"Right you are." Cassia pulled at the masses of fur still clinging to her grooming tools, then gave up and set them aside. "He's out of his bandages, but everyone knows what he did during the battle. His beauty is in his deeds. *Ckuundat*, Knight."

He stood at attention.

"You must be a good ambassador tonight for your *kaetlii*."

His ears perked up.

"Dockk dockk. Hama."

Knight came to her and heeled, his posture perfect.

"Oedann, my brave Knight. You have already shown the Hesperines your good character. Let us give them no reason to doubt it tonight."

"Don't look so worried, my lady," said Perita. "He hasn't bitten off any body parts yet."

"It's true he gets on well with most Hesperines, but Hippolyta and Master Arkadia seem to awaken his sense of danger."

"At the welcoming ceremony," Perita reminded her, "the Guardian of Orthros put him on his belly with a look. I doubt he'll try anything with her again. Now then, my lady, you'd best have a quick bath yourself so you don't wear half your dog's fur to the Summit Games."

Cassia's hasty scrub at the wash stand was an injustice to the warm, running water that was a matter of course in Orthros but still felt like a luxury to her. She joined Perita at the dressing table so her handmaiden could set her to rights.

As Perita fished in the clothing trunk, Cassia cast a longing glance at a sapphire-blue, diamond-patterned gown. That would match Lio's eyes and his colors in the coming competition.

But Cassia must carefully follow the plan they had agreed upon for tonight. Crucial politics hinged on the most minute symbolism, and grave dangers lay in a moment of sentiment. She wanted to do her part in their conspiracies so she didn't let him and his Trial circle down.

"I shall wear gold tonight," Cassia announced.

"This velvet one, the color of ripe wheat?" Perita held it up.

Cassia nodded. "I must beg Callen's and your forbearance. I think it only appropriate that I wear Segetian colors to any tournament, regardless of who is or is not competing."

Perita sighed. "Aye, the way the embassy sees it, Lord Flavian's your champion, even if Sir Benedict is the only one around to stand in for him. I hate to admit it, but I suppose you'll have to wear gold until Lord Fancy Soap steps up and gives you better colors."

Cassia smiled at the epithet her friend had given her mystery lover in honor of the gift she had accepted from him. She had told Perita almost everything about him, except that he was the Hesperine ambassador.

While Perita attired her, Cassia studied her friend. "Why do *you* look so worried?"

"All the men are twitchy about this visit to Hippolyta's Gymnasium. None of them want to stand around and watch the Hesperines show off their prowess, least of all Callen. It grates on him enough that his leg sets him back against his own countrymen. Being no match for the enemy, and females at that, just rubs salt in his wounds."

"I would sooner trust my life to Callen on one good leg than to the king's entire able-bodied guard. Besides, according to the itinerary, tonight's athletic events are intended as 'a celebration of valor, a commitment to honor, and a tribute to the battle arts.' I think the Hesperines are trying to find common ground with our warriors, rather than alarm them with a show of strength."

Perita's frown deepened. "You don't suppose the Hesperines wrestle in the nude, do you, like our men do when they think we aren't looking?"

"Why?" Cassia arched her brows. "Are you worried our menfolk will remove us from the gymnasium before we get a peek at what's hidden under all those silk robes the Hesperines wear?"

"*I* will remove Callen before he gets to peek at Hesperine seductresses. There are women who are invisible when they turn sideways because that Arkadia got all the figure." Perita mumbled something else under her breath that sounded like, "Not all of us can afford to be an armful."

It was hard to fathom that pretty Perita would experience an instant of worry about how she compared to any fellow female. But Cassia had learned from her recent fears about Xandra just how unreasonable jealousy could be.

"Don't worry for a moment, my friend," Cassia reassured her. "Callen sees through the eyes of love, which grant true sight. His gaze won't stray from you."

Surprise flashed in Perita's eyes, and her expression lightened. "That's quite something for you to say, my lady. Did you learn that from the way Lord Fancy Soap looks at you?"

"Yes. Yes, I did."

They had just finished pinning a beribboned veil over Cassia's braid when a knock came at the outer door.

"My lady," Callen called, "we're ready when you are."

"Let Callen in and see if I'm not right," Cassia said.

With a smile, Perita headed for the sitting room. Cassia followed with Knight, pausing to pick up his training lure to take with them. Seeing that playtime was in store, he perked up his ears and wagged his tail.

Perita opened the outer door for her husband. The sight of King Lucis's coat of arms here in the middle of Orthros sent a shock through Cassia. Callen wore his leather breastplate embossed with the present-day king's heraldry over a blue and gold tunic, as befitted a special guard of the royal household.

Cassia strove to ignore the reminder of the king's power and focused on how proud Callen had been the first time he had donned his ceremonial attire.

Callen's gaze lingered on Perita. "Those are the blue ribbons you wore in your hair on tournament day back home."

"So they are." Perita patted Callen's breastplate.

By the looks on their faces, Cassia suspected those were the ribbons Callen had taken out of Perita's hair after the tournament, the night when she had promised to marry him.

Out in the corridor, Eudias cleared his throat. "Begging your pardon, Basilis, but the Hesperine escort is already waiting outside the New Guest House."

Cassia joined Eudias in the hall with Knight marching in his procession gait at her side, and Callen and Perita followed arm in arm.

At his usual post in the gallery, Benedict joined them and took Cassia's arm. He offered no comment on her Segetian colors. He must be distracted, indeed.

"You look well in your chain mail and Segetian tabard," Cassia said.

Benedict's troubled expression did not change. "I see little purpose in the Hesperines' invitation to attire ourselves as if we were attending one of our own tournaments."

"I think they are trying to show their respect for our traditions."

"Whatever their motivation, we must not leave our honor at the door.

Even when it comes to Hesperines." Benedict frowned. "Especially when it comes to them."

"You have been deep in thought since the week we visited Hypatia's library," Cassia murmured, "and even more preoccupied since our voyage aboard Kassandra's ship."

"I can identify his malady, Basilis." Eudias answered in a mordant tone she had never heard from him before. "Tenebrans in general suffer from a lack of knowledge, while apprentices such as myself suffer from too much. Sir Benedict has now met with my affliction. One glimpse inside a scroll, and we cannot unsee what we have beheld."

"Aithourians who disobey Anthros," Benedict muttered. "Hesperines who defend Aithourians. What's a man to make of it?"

"Perhaps," Cassia replied, "our time with the Stand tonight will shed further light on Steward Lysandros and his Grace, Steward Telemakhos."

On the docks in front of the New Guest House, Mak and Lyros waited on a pair of perfectly matched black warhorses. Their mounts sported no reins or saddles, only black accoutrements emblazoned with the constellation Aegis, which also appeared on their Stand regalia. Behind them, the docks were crowded with Hesperines and decorated with banners that matched the horses' barding.

Lord Severin gazed upon the equines with appreciation and envy in his eyes. "Those are the largest chargers I've ever seen, but they're as elegant as parade horses."

Mak patted his mount's shoulder. "Orthros Warmbloods, my mother's craft. No other horses like them in the world. She bred them from Imperial stock and her familiar, the mare she brought with her out of Tenebra sixteen hundred years ago."

At the mention of familiars, some of the lords stepped back. Benedict surprised Cassia by circling Mak to get a good look at the horse. Lord Severin was brave enough to get permission from Lyros to examine his mount more closely. Lord Severin and the Warmblood were soon blowing in one another's nostrils.

"I did not know the Stand uses mounts," Cassia said.

Mak leaned down over his horse's shoulders and grinned at her. "We know how to fight on foot or on horseback, in the snow or in a sandstorm, in Stand regalia or formal robes, with our eyes closed or our hands bound."

"But always without weapons," she observed.

Lyros gave one of his subtle smiles and lifted a hand. "The Goddess gave us the only weapons we need."

Lord Adrogan tried to examine the teeth of Mak's horse and nearly lost a finger. The Tenebran laughed. "I don't suppose your honorable mother trades these beauties?"

"She has been known to," Mak answered. "She breeds foals upon request—for the right buyer. Her chief requirement is a true appreciation for the animal."

"No one loves horses the way the men of Tenebra do," Lord Adrogan boasted.

"Then you'll enjoy the procession," Lyros promised.

Mak and Lyros escorted the embassy along the docks, past cheering crowds. Lio's Trial brothers kept their Warmbloods at a gentle walk, setting an easy pace for Cassia and the other mortals who followed on foot. Their procession left the harbor, and they made their way through Selas, where more enthusiasts lined the streets. Black pennants blew in the wind at every arch and on all the wrought-iron lampposts.

"It looks more like a funeral than a tournament parade," Callen muttered.

Lord Gaius studied the decorations with narrowed eyes. "Whose funeral?"

"I believe black is the Hesperine color of protection," Cassia said, "symbolizing the shelter of night."

Perita exchanged a look with her. "Not our funeral, then."

"Well, at least some of us came equipped for a festive procession," said the Semna from her litter. "Why didn't you ladies bring your fancy carriages?"

Perita and Cassia laughed with her attendants, and the knights carrying her smiled.

Cassia couldn't help feeling safe at the sight of the Stand banners hanging from windows all over the city. There were also colorful banners bearing the constellations of various bloodlines and other emblems whose meanings were still unknown to her. Those must be shows of support for the various athletes who would compete in this week's events.

"There is House Argyros, home of my bloodline." Mak pointed over the heads of the crowd at the silver edifice and the grounds beyond it.

Cassia knew Lio's parents were staying there with the children tonight, and she felt sorry for the sucklings, who must miss all the excitement. Then a shimmer at a high window caught her eye. Suddenly she could see faces there that hadn't been visible an instant before. None of the other Tenebrans around her seemed to notice.

From the window, Bosko watched the procession go by, his face alight, while Apollon said something to him, perhaps narrating a past adventure. Lio's mother held Thenie up, but the baby seemed more interested in playing with Komnena's braids. Zoe beamed right at Cassia and waved.

Cassia dare not draw attention to the child by waving back. Instead, she focused on her delight and let it fill her heart, hoping Zoe would feel her greeting through the Blood Union. Zoe pointed to the banners that hung together below the window—one for the Stand, the other jewel blue and embroidered with the constellation Anastasios. Lio's family might not be at the events, but they would be rooting for him.

The procession approached a triumphal arch. Scenes carved into its surface told a story. As an armed hoard descended upon a village, one young woman escaped alone on horseback. Cassia recognized her as Lio's Aunt Lyta. The Guardian of Orthros must have been young and mortal then. She rode through village after village, gathering followers under the shadow of her warding magic. At last she led the fleeing refugees to a Sanctuary where other Hespera worshipers awaited them.

Chrysanthos and Tychon exchanged scornful glances, recalling to Cassia's mind the Dexion's comments in the library about there being no victory in retreat. As Lyros had said that night, Chrysanthos really did need to look around him. If he did, he would see the banners that symbolized the lone rider's protection over her people. He would see the throngs of happy, thriving Hesperines she had led to safety. He would hear their cheers of pride for her favored sons, whose strength ensured the protection of Orthros would continue, and Hespera's people would never be in danger again.

The procession passed under the arch, and Lyros announced with unmistakable pride, "Welcome to Stewards' Ward, where we of the Stand work and train, and all Hesperine athletes are welcome to pursue excellence."

To one side of the avenue, a herd of Orthros Warmbloods of every color roamed in a snowy field, their breaths puffing clouds in the air before their noses. When the procession and the crowds' voices caught up to them, they sprang into motion, as if they had caught the Hesperines' excitement. Cassia was no horsewoman, but she watched in breathless wonder as the animals galloped over the snow, their hooves scarcely touching the ground. They were beauty and power in motion, their thick manes and the feathering on their legs like proud martial pennants.

The throngs left the sides of the road and followed in the embassy's wake. The procession passed stables and paddocks, spacious grounds and training yards, courts and smaller amphitheaters, heading for the landmark they could see ahead of them, a black stone gymnasium built in the round with traditional cornices and ribbed columns.

Cassia didn't realize just how large it was until they were standing at its entrance. The Stand might be few in number, but they had dramatic ways of showing their strength and their far-reaching impact on Orthros. Mak and Lyros turned their horses to face the embassy.

"On behalf of the Stand," said Mak, "we invite mortal Tenebrans to set foot in Hippolyta's Gymnasium for the first time in Orthros's history."

Lyros raised a hand to the two statues above them. "In the name of Valor and Honor, we ask that you join us in a celebration of the battle arts."

Cassia lifted her gaze to the statues. Valor was a strong figure in a breastplate and close-faced helmet, poised to charge into battle. Honor wore only a simple tunic like the Stand and knelt with a bowed head, hand on heart. Hair hung in the statue's eyes, obscuring the figure's face. It was impossible to tell if Valor and Honor were male or female, mortal or Hesperine.

Mak and Lyros pivoted their horses again and gestured for the embassy to proceed. With Lio's Trial brothers on either side, Cassia and the other Tenebrans entered the Stand's stronghold. The crowd dispersed into the stands, where a large ensemble of Muses were already seated. When Mak and Lyros took the Tenebrans right out onto the sandy floor of the gymnasium, marching music erupted all around them.

For a moment, Cassia thought she had suddenly joined the Hesperines in Blood Union. The song, the voices, the power that filled the gymnasium to its glass rotunda seemed to turn into pure emotion that reverberated through her from head to toe. She had never stood in a structure so vast. The Temple of Anthros at Solorum would look small dropped in the middle of the gymnasium. The sheer space above her head and the weight of stone around her both awed and reassured her.

A powerful instinct made her look to the first row of seats on the opposite side of the gymnasium. There was Lio. Other Hesperines who were also attired to compete filled the rows beside and behind him, but Cassia hardly saw them. She let herself glance down his body. His jewel-blue athletic tunic showed her a great deal, but the railing in front of him blocked her view of his long runner's legs. When she looked at his face again, he was smiling.

Mak and Lyros halted the embassy before a low dais at the center of the gymnasium, where Lyta and her daughter Arkadia stood waiting in their Stand regalia. Cassia hadn't seen much of Bosko and Thenie's mother lately, but looking at Kadi now, she could see what Javed had meant about his Grace enjoying the Summit. There was even more pride than usual in Kadi's military bearing, and her face was alight with eagerness. She might appear to be all soft, expansive curves, but the mortals now entering her home territory had seen her strength when she had fought for their lives in Martyr's Pass.

Benedict and Lord Gaius gave each other an uneasy glance, then positioned themselves at the front of the embassy. Cassia stood back, giving Tenebra's warriors room to dialogue with Orthros's. She put a hand on Knight's shoulders, but he halted beside her without her having to say a word, and he maintained his impeccable posture.

From the corner of her eye, she kept watch on the Cordian mages. Chrysanthos and Skleros appeared to disdain the proceedings. Cassia suspected they perceived the greatest value in watching the games like spies in the enemy camp. She could only hope the respect the Hesperines earned from the warriors this week would be worth the calculated risk of revealing some of the Stand's abilities to the mages.

Lyta smiled at the mortals with a challenge in her eyes. "All are welcome here who enter with valor and honor in their hearts. Within these walls, there is no rank. All stand as equals. Merit must be proved, respect must be earned, and authority can only be won through wisdom, strength, and compassion. All challengers must obey the same rules here, and those who violate any one of them will be cast from our company on the first offense."

Lord Gaius gave a slight bow. "Let the tournament rules be stated, and in accordance with Tenebran honor, we shall excuse ourselves if we cannot in good conscience agree."

Lyta gave a respectful nod. "Bow to your opponents when you begin and help them up when you finish. Deal no injury that is beyond healing. Fight only with your own strength, for these are unconditionally forbidden during a match: magic, weapons, and biting."

Lord Gaius lifted his brows. "I see no reason why we should not comply."

Benedict cleared his throat and glanced at the mages. "Those rules are amenable to warriors such as ourselves."

"Then we are agreed." Lyta swept a hand to indicate the seats behind them, across the gymnasium from the athletes. "We have prepared places of honor for our guests and designed this week's events with both Hesperines and Tenebrans in mind. You will have many opportunities to be not only observers, but participants."

Benedict's uncertainty was apparent under his polite expression. Lord Gaius barely hid his skepticism.

Lyta only smiled. "Let the Summit Games begin."

THE GIFT OF VICTORY

AUNT LYTA TURNED ROUND and round on the dais, eying the crowd. "Who will be the Stand's first challenger?"

That was Lio's cue. He took a deep breath and waited.

"Test your mettle against my Stewards," she dared the audience.

He gave the Tenebrans a moment to observe that none of the countless Hesperines in the gymnasium deemed themselves a match for even the youngest members of the Stand in hand-to-hand combat. When he thought Mak's and Lyros's fearsome reputations had sunk in sufficiently, and the silence had stretched on long enough, Lio rose to his feet and thrust his fist in the air.

The gymnasium erupted in applause and predictions of his doom. He looked across to where the embassy sat and sought Cassia's gaze again. Benedict held her in conversation, but her aura swelled with encouragement. Her silent cheer for Lio meant more to him than any other acclaim. She would support him, whatever his cause, however certain his defeat.

He had every confidence in tonight's conspiracy. He just hoped it made a sufficient impression on the Tenebrans, and that there was something left of him for Cassia to celebrate with when this was all over.

"Firstgift Komnenos!" Aunt Lyta beckoned to him. "Better known to our guests as Ambassador Deukalion—but to me as my dearest nephew. Join us and demonstrate your skill."

Chrysanthos's voice reached Lio's ears from across the gymnasium. "Well, well. The son of Apollon shows his hand at last."

"I warned you not to believe his diplomatic act," Skleros said.

"Well, he *is* just a light mage. You understand why I was predisposed to disregard him."

"You war mages get spell effects in your eyes and don't look further. You forget how many of your brilliant minds Apollon turned to jelly with nothing but a hammer."

"How thoughtful of you to remind me, my friend. But you may keep your 'I told you so' to yourself. I haven't made the mistake of underestimating Deukalion since I learned he is bloodborn. Prometheus was also 'just' a light mage."

To show off for the mortals, Lio levitated from his seat to the floor of the gymnasium, landing in a fighter's crouch. The Tenebrans' stoic expressions became less convincing. They might be surrounded by heretics and girded with the armor of their virtue, by they suffered a universal vulnerability: they loved a spectacle. They would fall for the Stand's display, yet.

"Here in Orthros," Aunt Lyta declared, "every fight is a gift to someone we hold dear, just as in Tenebra, champions carry into battle the tokens of the ones they love. Let us see to whom our challenger dedicates his fight. Who hopes to receive the gift of Deukalion's victory? Offer him your blood marks, that all may know he fights for you!"

Calls went up all over the gymnasium. Every tributary of Blood Komnena in attendance made an admirable effort to get Lio's attention. But Kia let out an ear-splitting whistle, and Nodora topped everyone by sounding a hand gong. Lio's Trial sisters jumped to their feet in the front row, unfurling his banner over the stands in front of them, and waved for him to pick them.

He swaggered over to Kia and Nodora and gave them his most elegant bow. He sensed Cassia's amusement. He was glad she had gotten into the spirit of their mischief when they had all agreed upon the plan together over coffee in his library. As she had suggested, Lio took not one, but both of his Trial sisters' hands.

Kia and Nodora preened. The entire Hesperine audience, who could not help being in on the joke, made good-natured noise. Someone in the crowd started a chant: "Son of Apollon! Son of Apollon!"

Lio heard Lord Adrogan say, "Popular with the ladies, that one."

"With a face like that, I don't doubt it," Lord Severin muttered.

Predictable Tenebrans. The ruse was working.

"It's not his face that's the subject of the rumors about him," Lord Adrogan said. "Have you heard what these Hesperines say about the bloodborn? His height isn't his greatest physical advantage."

"Adrogan, I don't spend time wondering what's in a Hesperine's loin-cloth, and neither should you."

"It doesn't seem fair that Hesperines should be naturally superior with the ladies. Why should a man have to submit himself to a profane goddess to get his sword reforged? Seems like Anthros's swords ought to be better from the start."

Lio could almost hear the blood rushing to Benedict's cheeks, and he could easily sense the silent laughter in Cassia's aura. She was also gloating to no small degree. How gratifying.

Nodora bit her hand, then clasped Lio's, leaving a mark of her blood on his palm. He gave her knuckles a courtly kiss. Then he and Kia repeated the gesture.

With both his palms marked in blood, Lio approached the dais, putting on a grim expression to keep from grinning at his Trial brothers. Lyros's face and aura were composed in concentration, but Mak just laughed. When he cracked his knuckles, Lio almost burst out laughing with him.

Aunt Lyta held out her hands toward Mak and Lyros on either side of her. "Which of Orthros's Stewards will you challenge?"

Lio looked from one to the other as if he were assessing their strength.

Mak needed no pretense to be the picture of relaxation and confi-dence. He flexed a few muscles, and the auras of his enthusiasts in the crowd melted. A group of initiates in the front row whistled and hoisted a Stand banner with Mak's name embroidered on it.

Lyros struck a pose and put a hand to his chin, studying Lio in return, as if he even needed to think of a strategy against the fighter he and Mak had taught. A rival group of initiates, Lyros's devotees, cheered his name and waved his banner.

Lyros lifted a hand to them. Their eyes and fangs gleamed with ado-ration. Mak smirked and performed a round of stretches, and his own devotees went wild.

A third group in the audience raised a banner that showed their heroes' two names intertwined. Those initiates chanted, "Telemakhos! Lysandros! Telemakhos! Lysandros!"

Well, at least Lio could be sure of one positive outcome from his defeat tonight. Mak and Lyros's young adorers would have a good time. His Trial brothers probably wouldn't make it home until veil hours were half over, there would be so many initiates lined up to beg them to shed a drop of blood on souvenirs.

"Those two are popular with *everyone*." Lord Adrogan's laughter was snide.

"Especially each other, I take it," Lord Gaius put in dryly.

"There's only one real man in the entire Stand." Lord Adrogan's tone dripped with condescension. "Which one do you suppose he is?"

Although the men's insults came as no surprise, they whipped up a wave of anger in Lio that had his fangs unsheathing and his blood pounding.

And had him all the more determined to make tonight's plan a success. This fury was not what his Trial brothers needed from him right now. It was Mak and Lyros who had taught Lio the dangers of anger in battle. He must make them proud today and fight better than he ever had before. To do that, he must keep a clear head.

As he and his Trial brothers had agreed, Lio turned to Lyros and bowed. "Steward Lysandros, would you be so generous as to answer my challenge?"

Lyros bowed in return. "It will be my honor."

Mak came to his Grace's side. He bit his palm and clasped Lyros's, pulling their joined hands close to his heart. Lyros touched a hand to Mak's face, then descended the dais to join Lio in the open space below the embassy's seats.

"Apollon's son versus one of the Stand," Chrysanthos said with relish. "This will be good."

"The Hephaestion defender comes from a family of artists, doesn't he?" Lord Adrogan asked. "My last venison jerky on the bloodborn."

Lio and Lyros exchanged wicked smiles. Lord Adrogan was about to lose his last venison jerky.

"Tenebrans have a taste for blood sport." Lio spoke low enough that only Lyros would hear. "Let's show them how real Hesperines fight."

"This is where our ruse ends," Lyros reminded him. "We have to make this real."

"My teachers prepared me for this night. I am ready."

"We are proud of you, Trial brother."

"That is a greater honor than any victory."

On the dais, Aunt Lyta bit her hand and held it high, cupping her blood in her palm. "This is a Glimpse of Mortality match. To win, trap your opponent in what would be a fatal position."

Lio and Lyros gave a nod, watching each other.

Cassia's heartbeat was a sound that reached Lio despite all the noise, a rhythm that transcended his surroundings. He attuned to her within the rhythm of his own blood, where he carried her, and his body relaxed into a ready stance. Whenever she had been stuck at the guest house, and he and his Trial brothers had found time for some sparring matches to prepare for tonight, he had realized what a difference it made in the ring to be empowered by his Grace's blood.

Lyros stood still, his gaze and aura sunk so deep in his discipline, he was impossible to read without the mind magic that was forbidden in the gymnasium. Lio let sight fade to only part of his awareness. He listened, although the audience was so loud, it would be difficult to hear his Trial brother's moves. He waited to feel a change in the air upon his skin or a vibration under his feet.

Aunt Lyta fisted her hand. Her blood plummeted. Lio heard the first drop hit the dais.

Suddenly Lyros was no longer there in front of him. Lyros's favorite opening moves ran through Lio's mind. Too many to predict. Lio waited on his senses.

He felt Lyros's ankle near the back of his own just in time to twist out of the way. Wisdom's Precipice as an opening strike?

This was going to be a real fight, indeed.

SILENT SPECTATOR

CASSIA MUST WEAR SEGETIAN colors. She could not give Lio her blood mark or even wave a banner bearing his name.

But her blood mark was in his veins. Her banner was her heart, and it was down there on the sand with him.

One moment, he and Lyros stood as still as only Hesperines could. The next instant, Lyros disappeared as surely as if he had conjured a veil around himself. Then Lio spun into a blur of motion. He and Lyros both flashed on Cassia's vision for the blink of an eye, before they were invisible again.

Hesperines needed no magic in the gymnasium. Their every motion was a spell.

The ring appeared empty for one, two, three heartbeats. Lio and Lyros came into sight again right below Cassia's seat and rolled onto the sand, locked in combat. The embassy started around her, and the Hesperine crowd let out a cheer. Lio and Lyros sprang to their feet again and into oblivion.

With bated breath, Cassia cast her glance back and forth around the ring, watching for every lightning strike of motion. Every time she caught a glimpse of the fight, her heart leapt. Each time they disappeared, it skipped a beat.

There is no art my people do not love… She recalled Lio's words, which she saw before her now.

Fangs flashed white. Jewel-blue fabric whirled. Muscle rippled down a long, pale leg. Lio was a disjointed dream playing out on the sand below.

…That includes the art of the body.

The Hesperines' gazes tracked across the sand with certainty. They must see all that mortal eyes were too slow to perceive. They must be able to hear the thunder before the lightning struck. Cassia followed their gazes, letting them guide her to where the battle now raged.

A few more glimpses rewarded her. But not enough to help her judge how well Lio was holding out against his Trial brother. The crowd was a powerful current around her, calling her into Blood Union. But if she closed her eyes, she would hear only noise.

Close your eyes, the voices seemed to chant.

But she dare not blink, lest she miss a glimpse of the battle.

Join us, the current summoned.

In the ocean of feeling and the crash of voices came a flash of awareness—of Lio. She felt his mind. It was his presence that called to her. Her lips parted, she caught a breath, and she shut her eyes, giving herself up to the lure.

"Don't close your eyes!" Perita's voice receded. "You'll miss something!"

"Too tense for you, eh, my lady?" Callen sounded far away.

All sound went silent, then the roar of the crowd burst on her hearing like a deafening crack of thunder.

"Watch the fight from down here," her mind mage whispered.

Sound and sight were so loud and bright as to mean nothing. Sensation took their place, silent and vivid. Sand caressed the bottoms of his feet. Air was a precise instrument that measured the changes in his opponent. Heat and cold were his allies, sounding the alarm of another body near or not where it had been an instant before.

Cotton was his weightless armor, his second skin. There was no blood to be smelled, only the blood inside him, his strength. There was no pain, only the instant responses of his supple, powerful body. There was no rage, no fire of battle. Only the satisfaction of a move well executed and the thrill of moving into the next.

As swiftly as she had flown down to him, she felt herself tossed back up and into her own vapid mortal frame. Her limbs felt weak. The enormous gymnasium felt smaller, the crowd quieter, the figures on the sand below too far out of reach.

All her mortal eyes showed her was a single set of heavy footprints across the sand. She fell forward, bracing herself on the railing, and followed the erratic path with her gaze from one end of the gymnasium to the other.

Lio came into view—because he was moving slower. He raised his arms to fend off a blow from his unseen opponent. Then he doubled over.

REAL WARRIORS

THE CONNECTION WITH CASSIA slipped from Lio's grasp. Their deep Union snapped. He gritted his teeth in frustration, but defending himself now demanded all his concentration.

He turned his blunder into a crouch and hooked his arm around Lyros's lower leg. The Weight of the World robbed Lyros of his balance as surely as he had intended to do to Lio in the first instant of the match.

Lyros went down on his back, but his heel shot up and dealt a Fang Breaker to Lio's chin. That move could leave Hesperine opponents regrowing their teeth and humans dead. The expertly controlled blow only tapped Lio's teeth together and tossed his head back, foiling him without causing him injury.

This was a real fight. Real skill was achieving victory without needless pain. Real strength was self-control. These were the tenets of the Hesperine battle arts, which Lyros taught in action, the warrior's language, as eloquent as words.

Lio shot to his feet. Still too slow. Lyros's right arm closed around Lio's throat from behind and choked him with a Mortal Vice. If Lyros tightened his grip a fraction, he could cut off the blood flow to Lio's head. Inconvenient, but not deadly to a Hesperine. Decapitation was fatal, though, and from this position, Lyros could do that with his bare hands.

Lio's heart pounded, counting off how much time he had before this move would make Lyros the victor. Lio jammed his chin into the crook of Lyros's arm to buy himself time. Tonight, it wasn't enough to stay on the defensive. He had to get on the offensive before it was too late, and stay there.

Lio made a Sun Strike in Lyros's eyes, then twisted to the right. He felt the Vice release. He kept moving, bringing Lyros's arm with him, and folded his Trial brother's wing back into a Crippled Dove. Lio spun the move into a Grounded Owl and put Lyros on the sand. Lio followed his Trial brother down and tried a choke-hold of his own.

But Lyros rolled before Lio could secure him in Hypnos's Grasp. Lyros found his feet with a parting blow to the side of Lio's head that befuddled his ears. Lio rolled to his feet and right into another Mortal Vice.

Lio brought both his hands around behind his head and tried to gain control of Lyros's wrists. It turned into a grappling match. But Lyros had built his strength through a lifetime of training. His grip was sure. Lio started counting again.

This time, when Lio twisted to his right, he swung his arm around behind Lyros. With a heave, he lifted his heavier Trial brother, leveraging his own height to swing Lyros up. He tossed his Trial brother to the ground. He followed through with a heel-strike at his Trial brother's sternum, Lyros's own favorite Stake Through the Heart.

Lyros's hands closed around Lio's ankle and twisted. Numbness started in Lio's joint and radiated outward. What move was *that*?

Lio stayed on the offensive, keeping the fight on the ground as much as he could, while Lyros's moves sought to force Lio onto his useless foot. Lio fought on one good foot, with his hands, and on his knees.

The noise of the crowd had become a massive heartbeat that pumped emotion through the gymnasium. Lio caught glimpses of the audience in flashes between the sand that flew in his eyes. The elders' dignified gazes gleamed with attention, while the youngbloods flushed with the thrill of the event. Both Hesperines and Tenebrans were on their feet, leaning out over the stands. Although not a drop of blood hit the ground, the mortals called out or pumped their fists at each feat of battle prowess. All of the Tenebrans but Cassia, who stood still as a statue and gripped the railing in front of her.

Her pulse raced inside Lio and fed his resolve. He kept up a frenzy of offensive moves, the only fragile barrier between him and certain defeat.

Lyros launched into a new set of moves. His precise strikes were unlike anything he had ever used on Lio before.

Lio had just survived to advance to the next level of training.

His familiar defensive tactics lasted him through exactly one set of Lyros's moves.

Lio landed flat on his back, not a puff of air in his lungs. Through a blur of sand and spell light, he saw his Trial brother's foot poised over his sternum.

Lio raised his hand and gave the salute of respect to the victor.

His ears still worked, because through the audience's cheers and moans of sympathy, he could hear the Tenebrans.

"Impossible!" Lord Adrogan had never sounded so incredulous. "He barely held his own for the entire fight!"

"Well, Skleros," Chrysanthos asked, "what's that you were saying about not underestimating him?"

"Perhaps he's better with a hammer," the necromancer quipped.

"How will he lift it with that wrist?" said the Dexion.

Lyros took hold of the hand Lio could still feel and helped him up. "Your wrist and ankle will regain sensation in approximately sixteen minutes."

Lio gave his Trial brother a rueful grin. "That's what I get for trying to use your favorite finisher against you."

"That was your best move, actually. Impressive choice for its meaning, not just tactics. Cultivate that strategy, and you could use it to manipulate your opponents."

"Huh. Maybe I should try a Mage's Supplication on Chrysanthos, then."

Lio let his Trial brother do the laughing and tried to catch his breath.

Lio limped back to his place in the stands just as Aunt Lyta ascended the dais again. She appeared to be enjoying her part in the drama. "Will our victor challenge his fellow Steward, his comrade in battle, his Grace?"

"I will," Lyros declared.

"It is my pleasure to accept," Mak replied.

Now Lyros put his fangs to his palm and clasped Mak's hand, and they faced each other on the sand bearing one another's blood marks.

When the screams of the nearby initiates lowered to mere yells, Lio managed to catch what the Tenebrans were saying.

Lord Adrogan snorted. "I'll win back my jerky yet. That Telemakhos is the size of a bull. I bet these velvet shoes the artist loses."

"The ambassador clearly isn't a warrior," Lord Gaius mused. "No wonder he lost. But in a contest against a professional soldier? Yes, I think we will see Lysandros lose this time."

Predictable Tenebrans.

Lyros left the men's arrogant predictions in the dust when he won the first round against Mak.

Lord Severin was the first to say it. "Lysandros is a real warrior."

"You don't sound surprised," Lord Gaius observed.

"He saved my life at Martyr's Pass. You should not be surprised, either."

"How do we know all this isn't staged for our benefit?" Lord Adrogan scoffed. "Maybe their skills aren't real, and all that was an act."

"Any real warrior," Lord Severin replied, "could not watch the battles we just witnessed without recognizing them for what they are and standing in awe."

Lio jumped to his feet to cheer. Victory was sweet. Pride filled his heart as he watched his Trial brothers. Mak took the second and third battle, then Lyros emerged the victor once more in the fourth. As their fifth match stretched on, all three groups of the initiates stood together in a crush as close to the fight as they could get, too enthralled to notice which of the banners they were helping each other wave.

When Mak and Lyros's stalemate had lasted eighty minutes, Aunt Lyta tossed a black handkerchief between the two blurs that were her Stewards. They came to a standstill and looked at her as if woken from a dream.

Their mentor's face and aura shone with pride. "Eighty minutes have passed, and you have yet to best each other. You have won the same number of rounds. I can only declare you equal in skill and equal in victory."

Mak and Lyros joined their bloodstained hands and held them up for the applauding crowd. The initiates levitated right out of their seats, pumping their fists in the air and embracing each other. But Lio cheered for his Trial brothers louder than anyone, joining his voice with Kia's and Nodora's.

Mak and Lyros rejoined Aunt Lyta and Kadi on the dais. The entire Stand faced the embassy.

"Honorable and courageous warriors from Tenebra," Aunt Lyta called, "tonight we have shown you a demonstration of the Hesperine battle arts. Now we invite you to show us your ancient and beloved traditions of war."

The Tenebrans were silent, but Lio and all his fellow Hesperines could sense their murmurs of surprise and wary grumbles in the Blood Union.

Aunt Lyta gestured to the sand. "We have made every effort to accommodate mortal warriors in the gymnasium tonight. Usually snow fills this ring. We have replaced it with sand. However, that is not our only means of placing ourselves on equal footing with you."

Kadi stepped forward. "My Grace, Master Healer Javed, has devised a potion that will reduce any Hesperine to mortal strength. Challenge us, and we shall meet you in battle as your physical equals, armed only with skill."

Unease skittered up Lio's spine, and he saw Cassia knot her hands in her lap. He wasn't the only one who still had misgivings about this part of the plan.

"Challenge us," Kadi dared them.

Cassia got to her feet. The lords looked at her in dismay, and some of them even laughed. Lio longed to drag them into the ring. He could handle those Tenebran clods, he was sure.

Cassia rested a hand on Knight. "You invited me to give you a demonstration of my liegehound's abilities. Knight and I will take this opportunity to accept."

That silenced the men's laughter, and her supporters applauded her by stamping their boots on the floor in the Tenebran way.

"Which of us will you challenge?" Aunt Lyta asked.

Cassia looked from one Steward to another. "Who among you has the greatest experience with liegehounds?"

Aunt Lyta held out a hand to Kadi. "That would be my daughter, Master Steward Arkadia. She is the Stand's expert at combating liegehounds. She teaches her techniques to all our trainees."

Cassia drew a deep breath. "Master Steward Arkadia, I challenge you to a match with Knight."

Kadi bowed. "It will be my honor to meet your challenge."

When Cassia turned to descend from the stands, Benedict halted her with a hand on her elbow and fretted over her. The whole audience watched while she stood her ground and tried to assuage his worries. In the end, he did not let her go. She and Knight simply walked past him.

"We welcome you," Aunt Lyta announced, "the first mortal Tenebran woman ever to compete here."

Cassia's aura colored with surprise, then swelled with pride. Had she not realized what honor would be hers tonight?

LAURELS

THE SAND SLID UNDER Cassia's shoes with each step she took out into the middle of the gymnasium. She kept a hand in Knight's ruff to steady herself. With all eyes on her, the force of the crowd felt even more powerful than before.

But she did not run the gauntlet of cruel spectators at the Tenebran royal court. She felt herself carried forward on the energy of the Hesperine enthusiasts, as if they passed her over the crowd on their shoulders. A strange exhilaration filled her as she had never felt before.

"*Dockk ckuundat!*" Cassia cried.

Knight launched into his parade gait at her side. She gathered her skirts and led him on a lap around the ring for all to see. Their display garnered resounding applause from Hesperine hands and Tenebran boots alike. She and her hound came to a halt before the dais.

Kadi strode to the stands, where her Grace sat next to her father in a section draped with the banners of the Stand and Blood Argyros. Kadi levitated before Javed, and he gave her his blood mark with a caress upon her palm, whispering something in her ear that made her smile. Argyros leaned forward and spoke to her, words of encouragement, by the pride on his face.

Kadi came to face Cassia. The Master Steward positioned herself slightly to the side of Knight and looked at Cassia instead of meeting the hound's eyes.

"May I propose the terms of our challenge?" As Cassia lifted her voice, the crowd quieted.

"Certainly, honored guest," Kadi answered. "We will hear your terms."

"Knight has the strength to face a Hesperine. You need not drink a potion to reduce your power."

"I deem that fair." Kadi turned around to include the mortal and Hesperine audience. "Do you?"

The Hesperines sent up a cheer for her strength, while the Tenebrans applauded Knight's ferocity. Everyone was ready to take sides and watch a bloody battle.

Time for Cassia to surprise them all. "I admit, my next suggestion is out of the ordinary, especially in a house of battle. I will not ask you to agree unless your honor allows it. Consider that my hound does not understand the difference between a friendly contest and a real fight. His instincts know no rules, and his only code of honor is the survival of his *loma kaetlii*, the person he lives to protect."

"Yes," Kadi mused, "I doubt we could persuade him to obey the 'no biting' rule."

The crowd laughed.

The spirit of the exhibition took hold of Cassia, and she lifted Knight's training lure for dramatic effect. "Even a liegehound's play is training for battle. That is the only arena he understands as a mock fight—his exercises with me. Therefore I propose that you, Master Arkadia, engage in a training exercise with him. You will not need your tactics, for I will teach you ours."

Kadi stood in a ready stance, a thoughtful expression on her face. "An unconventional suggestion indeed. Will he tolerate an exercise with me?"

"He will do anything I ask of him. In the spirit of our efforts to diffuse conflict between our peoples, I challenge you to do what no Hesperine has ever done before—meet a liegehound in battle not as his opponent, but as his partner."

"On my honor, I will not stand down from a challenge."

Kadi's devotees let out a roar, hoisting Stand banners bearing her name. The Hesperine elders, especially her father, just looked relieved. The Tenebrans looked warier than ever. Cassia suspected too many of them would view it as madness to reveal liegehound tactics to a Hesperine. She knew there would be Hypnos to pay when Chrysanthos took her to task for turning her opponent into an ally tonight. But she wasn't half done yet.

Cassia crossed the distance between herself and Kadi and offered

Knight's training lure to the Hesperine. Kadi's nostrils flared. Even Cassia could smell the lure's powerful odor of lanolin-rich wool, dead pheasant, and liegehound drool. But Kadi took the mangy thing in hand without a flinch. Cassia knew the Master Steward had faced far greater challenges to the Hesperine senses than this.

"You have managed to surprise me." Kadi spoke low, and the audience didn't appear to hear her. "I came here tonight prepared for a real fight with Knight."

"Did you really think I would agree to something that dangerous?"

"I am equal to it."

"I have no doubt of that. But Knight has been pitted against Hesperines for too much of his life already. I will suffer it no longer."

Kadi looked down at the lure. "I am glad for this opportunity. Do you know why I became the Stand's expert on liegehounds?"

"They are Tenebra's only weapon against Hesperines, and the heart hunters roam the border with packs of them, just on the other side of the ward you patrol."

"That threat is personal to me. Have you heard of the fate of the blood-born Atalanta?"

"Yes. I carry Orthros's grief for her in my veins."

"I was a suckling Bosko's age when Atalanta achieved her mastery. It was a glorious time for the Stand. I dreamed of serving with Atalanta and my sister Pherenike. Lanta and Nike guided me on my first steps as a warrior. But Lanta had been a Master Steward for less than a month when the heart hunters' liegehounds brought her down. I swore I would not lose another hero of mine."

And yet Kadi had lost her elder sister, too. Ever since Nike had gone missing in action in Tenebra, Kadi had lived with not knowing her beloved sister's fate.

"Are you certain you wish to do this?" Cassia asked.

Kadi glanced at Knight, still not meeting his gaze. "Yes. I think tonight will diffuse conflict in more personal ways than I expected. I am ready."

"Thank you for giving Knight a chance. Let us help him get to know you. Do you have an item with your scent on it?"

Kadi hesitated. Then she lifted her hands and untied her speires, letting her golden hair fall around her shoulders. She offered the ceremonial hair ties to Cassia.

The Hesperines gasped.

"You honor us, Master Arkadia!" Cassia gave a curtsy before accepting the speires.

"Let everyone see that I am not Knight's opponent tonight."

Leaving the lure in Kadi's hands, Cassia returned to Knight's side. She knelt beside her hound and held Kadi's speires before his muzzle. His nostrils flared, and his hackles rose.

"This is Arkadia *kaetlii*," Cassia told him.

Cassia whispered in his ear in the language they had cobbled together over the years, half her expressions of affection, half the iron commands the kennel masters had taught her. Knight understood both down to his bones. Together, they had tested their bond against every challenge, be it new friends or new foes.

"I have every confidence in you tonight, my Knight," Cassia assured him. "You are my *oedann*. Now *ckuundat!* Stand proud with Arkadia *kaetlii*."

Knight's devotion to Cassia was absolute. His bond with Lio was deepening. His urge to protect had overcome his instinct to destroy and made him a proud guardian of Zoe. Bosko and Thenie could spend time with him without fear. But would all that be powerful enough to teach him that their mother, a Master Steward of the Stand, was not his enemy?

Knight paraded toward Kadi. In the stands, Javed was on his feet, watching his Grace. Argyros sat frozen in his chair, a hand clasped to his mouth, while on the dais, Lyta was poised as if to go on the attack. But Mak and Lyros gave Cassia encouraging, confident glances.

Cassia caught a glimpse of fear in Arkadia's eyes. But all hint of it was gone when the Master Steward turned her face toward Knight. She met his gaze at last.

He halted at attention before her. He waited patiently and looked to her for command.

Cassia watched everything they had been through come together before her very eyes and listened to the crowd's murmurs of wonder.

She approached the two of them carefully, wary of breaking the spell. "Arkadia *kaetlii*," she reminded her hound.

He kept his eyes on Arkadia.

"*Oedann.*" Cassia halted at Kadi's side. "Master Arkadia, let us begin with a simple chase exercise that mimics a hound running down his prey. Throw the lure as far as you can. He will know what to do."

Arkadia pulled her arm back and gave the lure a mighty swing. Hesperine strength indeed. The lure became a blur Cassia couldn't even see, but Knight pirouetted in place and shot after it. The lure reappeared on the far end of the gymnasium. Knight streaked to it and lunged, pinning it to the ground.

"He never gets such a good run with me!" Cassia exclaimed to the laughter of the crowd. "A mortal's arm can scarcely provide him with a challenge. And yet everyone says Hesperines and liegehounds weren't meant to be partners."

A hint of a grin alleviated Kadi's concentration. "He appears to be waiting for orders, Lady Cassia."

"You can instruct him to abandon, hold, retrieve, or destroy his captive."

"Then by all means, let us call him back and give the lure quarter. It must last us through the match."

"He will bring it back so you can repeat the exercise if you command him, *dockk raat.*"

"*Dockk raat!*" Kadi barked in the voice of a field commander.

Knight pelted back across the gymnasium, halted before her, and dropped the lure at her feet, then stood at attention once more.

A few words at a time, Cassia passed the teachings of generations of kennel masters on to Orthros's resident Master Steward. Kadi took to the commands like the warrior she was. They came easier and easier to her tongue, and her determination gave way to obvious enthusiasm. It was not long before Cassia no longer supplied Kadi with commands.

The Steward and the liegehound worked their way from one end of the gymnasium to the other. She sicked him on his prey. She called him to her hand to attack the lure in her grasp. They wrestled his prey to the ground together and faced the enemy of their imagination in fighting formation.

With the crowd, Cassia watched the display of power and beauty in breathless silence.

The vision of fangs, fur, and black Stand regalia came to a standstill with Knight on his belly at Kadi's feet, gnawing the lure.

"*Oedann.*" She knelt beside him and rested a hand on his head.

Cassia thought the crowd's reaction would shake the granite walls.

"This night will live forever in history." Lyta's face was shining. "Let every competitor now stand with us on the dais."

Kadi, Mak, and Lyros stood shoulder to shoulder before their mentor. Lio descended from his seat, and he and Cassia took their places side by side. Knight heeled beautifully next to her, as if he took part in Hesperine tournaments every day.

Argyros and Javed joined them on the dais, and Javed took Kadi's arm. Argyros stood with Lyta with an air of ancient ritual and held a long box for her, which she opened.

She drew out an olive wreath and smiled at Cassia's hound. "For Knight, a transcendent symbol of peace."

Knight let her place the wreath around his neck like a collar.

Then Lyta lifted a laurel wreath from the box. "The Tenebran symbol of victory. For you, Lady Cassia."

Cassia gazed in astonishment upon the unprecedented prize. No woman had ever won the laurel wreath at a Tenebran tournament. She had never seen any female wear the crown of victory, except in symbolic temple frescoes of the goddess Angara.

Cassia bowed her head and let the Guardian of Orthros crown her with a laurel wreath before Hesperine and Tenebran warriors.

"Deukalion," Lyta continued fondly, "diplomat in spirit and warrior at heart, let both of us commend your dedication. For you, the rose foliage of effort."

Argyros handed her a stem of rose leaves, which she placed upon Lio's breast in a slit sewn into his athletic robes. He bowed, his expression as sanguine as if she had crowned him tonight's champion.

She took two pristine white rose blooms from the box and turned to Mak and Lyros. "Let all behold my pride in you. For my sons, the white roses of sustained excellence."

They puffed out their chests and let her place the flowers there.

At last she halted before Kadi. Argyros smiled expectantly as his Grace took their daughter's prize from his trove. When Kadi saw the branch of thorns in her mother's hands, her eyes widened.

Lyta placed the stem of rose thorns upon Arkadia's chest. "For you, Master of the Stand, the thorns of highest achievement."

"I have not received the thorns since I earned my mastery," Kadi said huskily.

"You have been at your peak," her mother praised her. "When your best is already perfect, I can only reward it with the white bloom. But tonight, you found a way to best perfection. You have surpassed your previous excellence and earned the thorns."

Cassia followed Lio's lead and turned with him and the others to face the embassy. The Hesperines bowed, and she gave a curtsy.

It seemed Tenebran pride got the better even of her detractors. The embassy almost unanimously applauded her, cheering as if they hoped to outdo the Hesperines. Only the Cordians were silent.

"Countrymen," Cassia called to them, "victory awaits you! Will you not show our hosts the honor and valor of Tenebra? Will you let me answer Orthros's challenge alone?"

CHALLENGE

Lio waited beside Cassia to see what the results of all this night's endeavors would be. He didn't breathe, listening to the lords and knights consult among themselves.

"Face the heretics in battle!" Master Gorgos urged.

"Not I." Lord Adrogan shook his head. "I won't let a female drag me around the gymnasium at the end of a lure!"

"You will let yourself be outdone by a girl and a dog?" puffed Master Gorgos.

"This could be a trap," Benedict cautioned. "What if the potion is a ruse? It's too dangerous."

Lio knew he wasn't the only one eavesdropping, for at the mention of the potion, Javed withdrew a vial from his robes and held it up for the Tenebrans to see.

"Esteemed guests," the healer invited, "allow me to recall to your minds that to ensure a fair fight, our warriors will drink this potion so that they match you in strength. This is Sunfire Poison, distilled from Anthros's fire and sunsword. Your own experts can verify the authenticity and potency of my mixture. Semna, Master Skleros, would you do the honors?"

Skleros gave a laugh. "I'll own to the title of expert in poisons. But I'll not lift a finger to prove a Hesperine right."

"Will you raise your fists to prove your skill?" Kadi called.

The necromancer's scars smiled at her. "I have already proved my skill against Hesperines."

It was all Lio could do not to charge to the front of the dais spouting diplomacy. He doubted any good could come of his bold cousin antagonizing the Gift Collector, but Kadi was master here.

"We have a challenger who taunts before battle!" Glancing around at the spectators, Kadi lifted a hand to indicate Skleros. "After a boast like that, you must back your words with action, Master Skleros. You heard the rules. In Hippolyta's Gymnasium, respect must be earned."

"I do not fight by any rules," said Skleros.

"Then I must disqualify you," Aunt Lyta announced. "No one who so blatantly disregards the rules of the tournament can be allowed to compete."

"Excellent." The necromancer sat back in his chair. "I have no patience with sportsmanship."

"You may take my word on the potion." Somehow the Semna's frail voice carried without difficulty through the gymnasium.

Lio felt a flash of magic in the air that reminded him of his visit to the Temple of Kyria.

"The potion is genuine," the Semna said. "Our boys will be safe if they enter the competition."

Javed bowed to her. "My gratitude, Semna."

She nodded, and the other Tenebrans continued to mutter amongst themselves. Until Lord Severin stood.

Lord Severin bowed in Lyros's direction. "Steward Lysandros, in the name of my life debt to you, I will answer your challenge. It will be an honor to meet in man-to-man combat the skills that spared me."

Lio could have raised a banner in his Trial brother's honor.

Lyros bowed to Lord Severin. "I have no doubt you would have fought bravely in that battle, had the heart hunters not robbed you of that opportunity with their dishonorable tactics. Let us make that right. I look forward to seeing your true skill."

Benedict was frowning so deeply in concentration, Lio thought the storm in the knight's aura must break at any moment. Suddenly it did. Benedict got to his feet.

"Let it never be said that I left Segetia's lady to defend our honor alone. Steward Telemakhos, I will answer your challenge."

That earned Benedict claps on the back. "Segetia versus the bull!"

called his comrades. Cassia stamped her feet with them, and Lio showed his support with a round of Hesperine applause.

Mak grinned and bowed to Benedict. "My respect. Let us both honor our families with a battle."

Worry crept up on Lio when he noticed Chrysanthos and Tychon exchanging glances. The muscular apprentice rose from his seat.

"Apprentice Tychon," Aunt Lyta said politely, "allow me to remind you no magic is allowed here."

"I don't need spells to prove my worth in a fight. I'll test my wrestling skills against any Hesperine. Master Arkadia, I believe you will find I put up more of a fight than a liegehound."

Goddess have Mercy, was Tychon that blindly arrogant?

With a long-suffering expression, Kadi bowed to Chrysanthos's lap-dog. "If it is a test you want, you shall have it."

Chrysanthos stood and folded back his sleeves one at a time with elegant precision. He eyed Aunt Lyta. As his gaze lingered on her, Lio realized what the mage intended, and he wasn't sure whether to laugh or beg his uncle to rescue the Summit.

"Guardian of Orthros," the Dexion said, "I will answer *your* challenge."

"I have issued no challenge," Aunt Lyta replied.

"Surely you will not back down from mine."

"I am the referee tonight. It would not be appropriate for me to enter battle."

"You mean to tell me you will let your children do your work for you?"

Lio gritted his teeth. Thorns, did the mage have a death wish?

"I do not fight with children," Aunt Lyta said. "I do teach them, how-ever. If you came here for a lesson, that I will give you."

"I already learned how to fight in a very different school," Chrysanthos retorted. "Of that, I assure you, I am a master."

"Then by all means, Honored Master Adelphos. Show us what you know. But you cannot do so with me. This is a cordial fight in honor of a diplomatic occasion. I think it would be in poor taste for me to meet any member of Aithouros's cult in battle, don't you?"

The Dexion's aura was afire. "Very well. It seems none of the real warriors are left to me. In honor of this 'diplomatic' occasion, I will teach the ambassador a lesson. Deukalion, will you accept my challenge?"

Before Lio could answer, Mak planted a hand on his chest and held him back.

"Hold your horses." Mak spoke at Hesperine volume, but his voice was implacable. "This isn't a good idea."

"This from my most reckless cousin?" Lio protested.

"I make sure never to be reckless at the same time you are. One of us has to keep a clear head to stop the other from being an ass."

"I cannot refuse."

"Yes, you can," Lyros returned. "We will contrive an honorable excuse."

"I will not refuse," Lio said. "Not *his* challenge."

Mak released him, albeit reluctantly. "Just remember what we've taught you."

"And remember the rules," Lyros warned.

Lio stepped forward and gave Chrysanthos an impeccably diplomatic bow. "It will be my pleasure to answer your challenge."

Lio sent up a silent prayer for self-discipline. He would have to work very hard indeed not to leave his own Summit in the dust of the gymnasium.

SUNFIRE

T HE WARDS ON STAND headquarters shut out all sound from the rest of the gymnasium, although the ring was right outside the door. Lio could still feel the crowd waiting on them. He wouldn't have been surprised if the furor of the mortals and Hesperines, combined in the Blood Union, had made the maps tremble on the walls and the documents shudder in the scroll racks.

Javed set his red fabric healer's satchel on Aunt Lyta's desk and passed out bottles of Sunfire.

Lio uncorked his blue bottle and sniffed the concoction. "This doesn't smell half as bad as thirst suppressant."

"I don't trust anything that smells like flowers." Mak peered into his brown bottle.

"You have nothing to fear," Javed assured them. "Sunfire is a truly deadly poison, but only in the hands of those with malign intent."

"Like Gift Collectors," Kadi supplied, "or heart hunters."

"Yes, as our guest Master Skleros could attest." Javed showed a rare scowl, his regret and protectiveness reverberating through the Union. "If I had been more thorough when I confiscated his supplies, he would not have been able to endanger Cassia. He has threatened our own by turning tonic into poison. Tonight, let me make amends by turning poison into an antidote to conflict."

"Thank you for doing this, Javed," Lio told him.

Javed nodded. "I have taken every possible precaution to ensure my Sunfire potion achieves the desired effect of guaranteeing fair matches, but without putting any of you in real danger. The concentration is only high enough to affect your capacities, and too low to prove fatal. I have also enhanced the solution with beneficial herbs and healing magic to buffer you from any unnecessary, unpleasant effects."

Worry wore at Lyros's determined aura, but he did not renew his attempts to persuade Lio there was still an honorable way to avoid Chrysanthos's challenge.

Mak voiced their fears. "The potion won't kill us, but it also won't protect Lio from a stray fireball of Chrysanthos's."

"Lio," Kadi instructed, "you know the code of the gymnasium. If Chrysanthos in any way violates the prohibition on magic in the ring, all rules are lifted, and safety is the only priority. Respond in any way you must to protect yourself."

"It must not come to that," Lyros told Lio. "If Chrysanthos shows any sign of disrespect toward the rules, call off the match. Stalemate, or even surrender, is a small price to pay for your safety."

"And avoiding diplomatic disaster. If I must forfeit to him to save the Summit, I will." But Lio would teach the bloodless vulture a lesson first.

"You cannot raise a ward," Lyros said, "and you are not trained to respond to surprise attacks from a war mage."

Mak put his hand on Lio's shoulder. "Don't take any chances."

Lio refrained from reminding them all that Aithourian battle wards couldn't protect the Dexion from thelemancy. Could Lio use his mind magic fast enough to protect his body from a fire spell? If Chrysanthos gave him an excuse, he wouldn't hesitate to find out.

Lyros uncapped his green bottle and clinked the vial against Mak's and Lio's. "No turning back now. To your health."

All three of them grimaced and tossed the potion back. It tasted like flowers laced with burnt spices. Lio shrugged and set the empty bottle on the desk by Javed's satchel. Mak and Lyros followed suit.

On the other side of the desk, Kadi hesitated with her yellow bottle in one hand and Javed's hand in her other. "You're sure you're equal to giving Bosko and Thenie their drink again tonight?"

"Don't worry for a moment," Javed reassured her. "I'll provide for them first so my blood will be untainted. Then we'll replenish each other."

"You're sure the poison will be completely out of my blood before the children thirst again? I must take my turn next. I won't let you wear yourself down."

"I will see to it your blood is cleansed before veil hours are through." He smiled. "And then you may cure your physician."

Kadi returned his smile and drank the Sunfire.

Lyros cleared his throat. "Javed, since both Mak and I have had the Sunfire, how long will it take us to cleanse each other's blood?"

"We'll figure it out without my Grace-brother's advice," Mak interjected.

Javed shot him an amused glance. "It will require multiple exchanges of one another's blood to achieve sufficient recirculation."

Mak coughed into his hand. "Challenge accepted."

Lyros grinned.

Javed turned to Lio. "As for you—"

"Cassia and I will figure it out," Lio said.

Javed continued, "It will be advantageous to you that you have a source of pure mortal blood to rely on. However, given your deprivation in recent months, it may require extra effort on Cassia's part to restore you."

Mak clapped Lio on the shoulder. "Cassia always goes the extra mile, doesn't she?"

At that moment, Nodora and Kia burst into the room, letting in a brief wave of noise before the door shut behind them. They went to Lio's side.

Kia made a face. "The mages are very much in the way, but we managed to confer with Cassia during this intermission."

Lio frowned at his Trial sisters. "Cassia shouldn't risk that here, now. It's too dangerous for her."

Nodora clasped her hands, her aura throbbing with concern. "It's your danger she's thinking of. Cassia is frantic with worry about your match with Chrysanthos. She gave us a message for you."

Kia cleared her throat. "I quote: 'This time I would not step outside the veil over the Font.' I trust you know what she means."

Few words could hold more meaning. The Font was an ancient monument of the Changing Queen on the grounds of Solorum, but also one of the greatest landmarks of Lio and Cassia's personal history. It was the place where they had first beheld one another, first spoken, first sworn their Oath of openness and honesty.

How well Lio recalled the occasion when Dalos had nearly discovered them there. Lio had concealed Cassia in a veil spell while he used diplomacy to throw the mage off the scent. But back then, she had still been loathe to trust her survival to anyone but herself. She had fled outside Lio's magic to make her own escape.

After that encounter with Dalos, Lio had confessed to Cassia how he had struggled to control his animosity in the presence of a mage of Anthros who questioned his honor and threatened all those he held dear.

Cassia was saying that tonight, she trusted Lio's protection. She had faith in his magic and his diplomacy. She trusted him to listen to his conscience.

Now, as then, he would not descend to the mage's level. He must remain the diplomat.

"Thank you," Lio said to his Trial sisters. "Tell Cassia I hold out hope no monster-slaying will be necessary."

"You should work on sounding as cryptic as she does," Kia advised.

"She'll understand what I'm saying. That's what matters."

"We'll deliver your reply," Nodora promised. "You and Cassia need a glyph code, don't you think?"

"One more thing." Kia turned to Mak. "Cassia says: 'Please leave some of Benedict intact to send home to his sweetheart.'"

Mak laughed. "Put Cassia's mind at ease. I'll aim away from the relevant parts."

Cassia had not mentioned to Lio that Benedict was attached. Was this about the girl with chestnut girls, to whom Benedict longed to give a tiger's eye anklet no knight could afford? Perhaps it was for her sake that Cassia treated Benedict so favorably. More favorably than a mere ally, like Lord Severin. More favorably than any emissary of Flavian's deserved.

When Kia and Nodora had departed, Javed said, "We'll just give the Sunfire a few more minutes to take effect."

Setting her empty bottle on the table, Kadi made a face.

"The flavor needs more work?" he asked.

414 Vela Roth

"No," she answered, "it is my opponent who leaves a bad taste in my mouth. Tychon! What a fool."

"His challenge is an insult to your skill," said Mak.

"I find myself honor-bound to embarrass a child," Kadi huffed. "Even if this potion reduced me to the strength of a suckling, I have lifetimes more training than any mortal. And this one is no Gift Collector—only an apprentice! The boy must know he has set himself up to fail. His circle has piles of records on my misbehavior." As she said that, her tone grew more cheerful.

Mak crossed his arms. "He's riding so high in Anthros's chariot, he doesn't see how far he has to fall."

"Perhaps he overestimates the effect of the poison," Lyros said.

Kadi shook her head. "He underestimates females."

Javed's shoulders shook with silent laughter. "I'm looking forward to this. Tychon is quite a boring opponent for you, but I shall enjoy seeing you teach him a lesson, regardless. How do you feel?"

"Nothing from your hands should be called a poison, my Grace," Kadi replied. "I've taken a heart hunter's poison arrow, and this isn't it."

Javed squeezed her hands, then looked around. "Is everyone else holding up?"

Mak yawned. "This reminds me of Stand drills right before dawn. This will be even easier than I thought."

"Is this what you felt like when you were human, Javed?" Lyros asked, his expression thoughtful.

"Yes," Javed answered, "until Kadi gave me her love. Then I felt immortal, even before my Gifting."

"Mm. He was just as charming before his Gifting, too." Kadi rested her head on Javed's shoulder. "Shall I play the helpless mortal tonight and let my strong Hesperine carry me home?"

Javed smiled slowly. "Be careful. I might take advantage of your situation."

"Turnabout is fair play," she said.

"By all means," Javed replied, "let us play."

Lyros looked at Lio with narrowed eyes. "Are you all right?"

"Fine," Lio answered.

He did not admit it was he who had underestimated the effect of the poison. The lethargy dragging down his limbs reminded him all too much of the Craving.

In his half year apart from Cassia, agony had been his perverse comfort. Pain meant he was still alive. He had constantly dreaded that moment when listlessness and apathy would arrive and with them, the dreadful certainty that it was too late for him.

"Did you give Lio the same dose?" Mak asked Javed.

"Every dose is tailored to the individual's affinity, age, fitness, and state of health," Javed answered. "Despite the magnitude of Lio's magic, I had to take into consideration his youth, his status as a trainee, and the fact that he is still in recovery from half a year of illness."

"I am quite recovered, I assure you," Lio insisted. The wait from breakfast to veil hours was much easier than before. As long as he didn't skip breakfast.

"Lio required the mildest dose," Javed concluded.

"See there?" Lio waved a hand. "I'll be fine, except for the blow to my pride."

How could those months without Cassia still affect him now?

Meaning, not just tactics. Lyros's words struck Lio anew.

Perhaps the pall creeping over Lio had nothing to do with the physical. Sunfire was just a potion. It would wear off within hours. But it showed him what it felt like to be mortal. What it felt like to face mortality.

Lio had experienced the very real threat of mortality far too recently.

He folded his hands behind his back to keep them from shaking. He could not let every little thing remind him of his close call and bring his fears back to life.

Fear was just as dangerous in the ring as anger, and one fed the other. He must, above all, keep a cool head when he faced Chrysanthos.

No monster-slaying necessary. Cassia trusted him.

"I am ready," said Lio.

"Very well." For the first time, Javed sounded reluctant. "Be careful, everyone."

When they exited the headquarters, Lio thought they had taken some of the wards with them, the crowd sounded so quiet. The step up onto the dais felt like a mountain. He lined up with Kadi, Mak, and Lyros on one side of Aunt Lyta, facing the mortal opponents who waited opposite, but Lio could not properly smell the humans to assess their state of anxiety. He tested the currents of the Blood Union.

He felt he put a goblet to his lips and swallowed, only to find the cup dry. His senses filled with nothing but his own alarm. Disoriented, he looked around him at the people whose auras he could not feel.

On instinct, he reached for Cassia in the Blood Union. Her presence filled him up and overflowed. He tasted her fear, her determination, and her confidence in him.

The vice around Lio's heart eased, and a familiar strength suffused him from within. Nothing could sever Grace Union.

He managed, barely, to resist the urge to look at Cassia. Instead, he kept his attention on the mortal challengers. Lord Severin and Benedict had unburdened themselves of their chain mail and other heavy gear and now stood ready to fight in only tunics and braccae. The mages had tucked their robes into belts.

Well, well. Chrysanthos was willing to take off his velvet shoes now and then. He was sun bronzed and muscular down to his toes. Lio had to admit the mage must have had some real training to achieve a physique like that. The man also probably sunbathed nude on the rooftops of Corona with willing maidens to mop his brow and feed him grapes.

I am expected to be a maiden, and willing.

Lio heard Cassia's war cries in his memories.

My father's god has no use for a whore's daughter.

How many concubines and their daughters had a man of the Dexion's privilege used?

You have not felt the weight of the gods, the mage had threatened.

The mage had threatened Cassia.

I would not step outside the veil over the Font.

But Cassia trusted Lio to drop hundreds of heart hunters unconscious at her feet—with their hearts still beating.

Chrysanthos stared all the daggers at Lio that were forbidden in the gymnasium. If the mage was hoping to evaluate his opponent with the silent feints, he was using the wrong tactics. Lio already knew Chrysanthos was expert at insulting glares. He would show the Dexion that a diplomat of Orthros did not stoop to such mean strategy.

Lio was not concerned about what hand-to-hand combat haughty princes learned in Corona. He only hoped Chrysanthos had no intention of breaking the rules and resorting to magic. He prayed the war between Hesperines and Aithourians would not begin tonight in the middle of the Summit dedicated to preventing it.

MAGE'S SUPPLICATION

LORD SEVERIN AND LYROS met in a mannerly and engaging fight. Mortals and Hesperines alike seemed to enjoy watching the two warriors test each other. With impeccable precision, Lyros walked a fine line, giving Lord Severin room to show his skill without ever condescending to the man.

More than once, a smile flashed across Lyros's face, as if he had just heard an unfamiliar poem in a beloved tongue he had studied for years. Lio's Trial brother was clearly enjoying himself, for he let the fight go on much longer than he might have before downing Lord Severin.

Lyros reached a hand out to Lord Severin. "I'm glad we met on sand instead of snow this time."

Lord Severin grasped the offered arm and let Lyros pull him to his feet, as the Steward had done in Martyr's Pass to save the mortal from an avalanche.

Lord Severin dusted himself off and bowed. "Perhaps we'll have time to do this again before the Summit ends."

"Name the night," Lyros replied.

Whatever came of Chrysanthos's challenge, Lio vowed, he would not let it taint the victory he now saw before him.

Mak was as good as his reassurances to Cassia and did not damage Benedict excessively, although their battle turned into a hard wrestling match in the sand. It appeared Benedict was accustomed to using his build against a lither opponent. Perhaps he was the draught horse...and Flavian the racing stallion, Lio thought with a glower.

Benedict's strategy prepared him well to withstand the way Mak used his bulk as an advantage. The knight was adaptable, too. As his defeat drew nearer, he transitioned into using Mak's size against him. So Benedict knew how to race when he needed to.

Benedict was a graceful loser. As he let Mak pick him up off the sand, there was a peace on the knight's face that came only from satisfying your own honor.

"That was fun," Mak said. "You must have had some fine brawls back home in Segetia."

"I learned to fight as soon as I learned to walk." Wistfulness crept into Benedict's tone.

"That's the only way to grow up."

"I did not realize any Hesperine received a warrior's upbringing. It seems we have both devoted all our strength to protecting our homes."

"It's a good night when the children can go to sleep without worrying about what's outside the gates."

Benedict bowed.

It was Tychon's turn. He strutted onto the sand barefoot. Facing Kadi, he fell into a threatening crouch, his arms out to his sides, ready to make a grab.

She stood and watched him, her face unreadable.

Tychon charged her. The only effect the potion seemed to have on Kadi was that her graceful sidestep was slow enough to be visible to the mortal eye. Tychon snarled, turned, and barreled at her again.

She tolerated his posturing for a few moments, evading his every attempt at contact. Finally she sighed and tapped him neatly at his neck, ribs, and groin. He fell at her feet and didn't move.

"Your apprentice seems to have lost consciousness," she said to Chrysanthos. "I'm afraid that concludes our match."

Chrysanthos came out onto the sand himself. He got his apprentice's limp body upright. None of the Tenebrans helped him.

"Be grateful he still breathes," the Dexion said through his teeth.

"Spare me your threats," Kadi replied. "I am too skilled and too conscionable to harm a child. I cannot say the same for your Order."

"Spare me your lies."

The Dexion delivered his apprentice to the seat next to the Gift Collector before returning to the ring.

"Ambassador," Chrysanthos called across the sand. "We have a score to settle."

Lio joined him in the ring. "Hesperines practice neither debts nor scores. But I believe repayment is a fundamental tenet of mortal honor where you come from. For the sake of cultural exchange, by all means, let us settle matters."

Chrysanthos seemed to have springs in the balls of his feet as he stood poised with his fists raised.

Lio tried to relax into his battle stance, but relaxation was dangerous. His body only wanted rest. He must fight tense, or give up and lie down. Tense it was to be.

Chrysanthos took a swing at him. One of the first dodges Lio had learned was sufficient to avoid the blow. But Lio's body responded so slowly to his effort that he felt the hair on the back of Chrysanthos's hand brush his chin.

Chrysanthos launched a series of swings. He was probing Lio's guard. Lio put only his most rudimentary parries on display and stayed on the defensive. The war mage was already convinced Lio was a poor fighter. Perhaps Lio could lure him into complacency, then take him by surprise.

"Diplomats!" the mage scoffed. "Always shrinking from a blow."

"As a mage, you swore to lay down the sword," Lio said. "You should know all about avoiding violence."

"Don't mistake a politician for a coward." Chrysanthos struck out twice more.

Lio managed a couple of basic evasions, but gave ground. "Does a politician always sit safely out of harm's way while the rest of his embassy is trapped in an avalanche and under attack by heart hunters?"

Something hard made impact with the side of Lio's head. Pain struck him dumb and spun him off balance. Starbursts on his vision dissolved his surroundings into a cascade of spell lights.

A weapon. Surely. Chrysanthos had broken the rules.

Lio raised his arms and retreated, squinting. His hazy vision revealed only the man's bleeding knuckles.

Goddess have Mercy. That had not been a weapon. That was what a fist felt like to a mortal. How had humans managed not to annihilate each other from the world long ago?

He was still reeling when the bones in his wrist ground and crunched and snapped. Chrysanthos had targeted the joint left vulnerable after Lio's last fight. His wrist was no longer numb. If only it was.

Lio fell back into fundamental defenses, avoiding blows by the skin of his teeth. Failing to avoid too many. He had only moments and the evidence before his eyes to learn and adapt to hundreds of years of Cordian boxing. Would less than a year of Stand training be enough to keep him in the match?

Meaning, not just tactics. Cultivate that strategy…manipulate your opponents.

Lio had one more arsenal at his disposal. His weapons of choice. Words.

He spat out a mouthful of blood and shook the shredded remnants of one sleeve off his shoulder. "You seem overly determined to convince me you are not a mere scroll-pusher like myself."

Chrysanthos kept up his volley of punches and insults. "For a self-described scholar, your comprehension is poor. I called you a devious coward, not a scroll-pusher."

As Lio had with Dalos that night at the Font, he now sought to mire Chrysanthos in discourse. "Such inconsistencies in your argument, Honored Master Politician. I am hard pressed to muster a response, for you keep changing your thesis. Which is it? You must declare your position. Say either that I am more scroll-pusher than warrior or that I am a devious coward who can fight."

Chrysanthos tossed his head, throwing a strand of hair out of his eyes. "Your performance in battle is laughable, and your father is the butt of the joke. Your silver tongue is the instrument of Hespera's deception, but I see through Argyros's ancient tricks. Do not think, however, that I underestimate your magic. You will not take me by surprise."

Lio laughed. "How flattering for my opponent to do me more credit than I deserve. Alas, that I must dispel your few remaining illusions of my ferocity and remind you I am but a light mage."

"You think I don't see through your pretty veil spells? I know exactly what you are capable of."

Lio dodged another blow and made a verbal feint. "Of course. You are well-informed regarding my performance at the Equinox Summit. As you have said before, I gave a few speeches and conjured some spell lights."

Chrysanthos slid right under Lio's guard. The mage's fist rammed into Lio's belly, and the man's other hand wrenched Lio's hair. Lio swallowed his gorge.

"You conjured the moons' light," Chrysanthos growled in Lio's ear. "Hippolyta and Arkadia built their ward on it. You powered the spell that ended the Equinox Summit."

"Dalos ended the Equinox Summit," Lio hissed. "I powered the spell that saved lives."

Chrysanthos twisted his hand again and drove his knee up into Lio's gut, robbing him of the breath to speak. The mage's foot came down, raking the inside of Lio's ankle and driving his foot sideways into the sand. Pain cracked open inside Lio's ankle joint.

Enduring the Craving had given him a higher tolerance for pain than he had known. His only outcry was a suppressed growl in his chest. He focused his thoughts.

No Union, no scent. He had only his flagging body to rely on. What could it tell him?

He could hear the anger in the man's tone of voice. He could feel the savage pleasure in the man's every blow.

Certainty emboldened Lio. Chrysanthos was angry.

Lio gritted his teeth against the pain in his ankle and pivoted toward Chrysanthos. Lio brought his hand down and hammered the man's forearm. Mortal strength was barely effectual, but Chrysanthos's hand loosened, and his elbow buckled. Lio pulled his good hand back and drove his fist straight into Chrysanthos's face.

Lio felt the man's nose break against his knuckles with a satisfying crunch. Thorns, that felt good. A few more beatings in the face would discipline the Dexion as befit a monster and bring the weight of the Goddess to bear upon him.

Lio reached for Chrysanthos's collar. Crimson poured from the mage's nose and over Lio's hand. Lio could barely smell the faint odor of Chrysanthos's blood, but the Hesperine spectators flinched and gasped.

The man staggered back and snarled. Lio let him go.

Lio shook his head, as if that could clear it. The anger had hold of him more powerfully than his opponent had.

Lio met Chrysanthos's gaze and beheld the pure rage in the man's eyes. In an instant, the rage disappeared behind the Dexion's haughty expression again, but his mask was stained with blood now.

Lio saw his opening. He could gain the advantage if his opponent was angry—but only if he was not.

Lio went still, favoring his broken ankle, and watched his enemy. He took a deep breath, then let it out. He pictured Zoe's face in his mind. What excited questions would she ask him about tonight's events? What answer would he be able to give her about his actions? How did he want the bedtime story about this battle to end?

His anger cooled.

He considered the weaknesses in Chrysanthos's guard. Lio had plenty to work with. The mage was chafing under the limitations of his role as a harmless Tenebran mage, just after his promotion to the office of Dexion.

He had only achieved that distinction because his competitor had died. He spoke of Dalos with such loathing that Lio could easily imagine the two war mages' rivalry. Lio need not reveal he knew Chrysanthos's identity to stir him up.

"Dalos was no match for seven Hesperines at full strength," Lio goaded Chrysanthos. "I begin to think you are no match for one weakened by Sunfire."

The mage's punches came faster, fiercer. Lio evaded with the fresh speed of confidence.

"But then," Lio mused, "it's not fair to make a comparison. All you have in common with Dalos is your god. He was a real war mage from Corona. You're just the King of Tenebra's emissary."

Chrysanthos tried to drive past Lio's guard again, but this time he failed. Lio could exploit that to go on the offensive. But he danced away. He hopped as lightly as he could on his injured joint. Chrysanthos pursued him. Lio, though the crippled fighter, led his enemy around the ring.

Lio was now in control of their battle.

He brought their fight right below the Tenebran embassy's seats.

"Where were you during the Equinox Summit? You, the great champion of the king's alliance with the Mage Orders? Why did Dalos face us in your place?"

Chrysanthos came at Lio like an enraged animal. The man threw himself into a flurry of attacks with manic speed and stunning force.

Lio was ready. The months he had spent in agony without Cassia had tempered him. His Trial brother's training on how to cope with battle injuries had honed his concentration and discipline. Despite the magefire in his damaged joints, he evaded and parried every attack with the intermediate defense moves he had held in reserve, adapting each tactic on the fly to the limitations of mortal reflexes and only two good limbs. Without hesitation, he transitioned into his best offensive sets.

Chrysanthos had no time to react. No presence of mind to realize he played right into Lio's hands. Until it was too late.

Lio brought Chrysanthos to his knees before him in a Mage's Supplication. Lio grasped the Dexion's head and neck with perfect control. One twitch, and he could snap the man's neck.

Chrysanthos went still. He shook from head to toe. Lio did not need the Blood Union to tell him Chrysanthos was drowning in his own anger and fear.

Lio took a breath, and the thrill of victory filled him. His ears throbbed with the cheers of his people. He looked up to the embassy's seats. The Tenebrans were silent. But they were smiling.

Cassia's gaze met his for the barest instant, and the triumph in her eyes braced Lio like a draught of her blood.

A black handkerchief fluttered to the ground before Lio and Chrysanthos. Aunt Lyta stood to one side, her wary gaze on the mage. With great care, Lio unhanded Chrysanthos and stepped back. Lio waved to show his gratitude to the crowd, then, as honor demanded, offered his hand to Chrysanthos.

The mage spat in Lio's direction and stumbled to his feet on his own, his face a mess of gore and hatred. "How dare you offer me your hand? You are no victor. Murderer!"

Lio composed his face. He replied only with a courteous bow.

Javed approached from the dais, but Chrysanthos did not wait to receive any offer of help from the healer. The Dexion limped off the sand to the nearest stairs and returned to his place in the stands. As he sank into his seat, a fresh outbreak of sweat beaded his brow. The war mage put on a stoic expression as Skleros looked him over.

"Alas." Aunt Lyta's voice rang throughout the gymnasium. "Mortal tradition proffers no reward for participation in the absence of victory. Would that Honored Master Adelphos would accept our rose foliage of effort."

Chrysanthos, too far away to spit upon Aunt Lyta's prize box, could do naught but subject her to one of his overused and unavailing glares.

"Deukalion," Aunt Lyta called, "join me on the dais."

Javed helped Lio limp onto the dais. For the second time that night, Lio took his place among the Stand. Kadi beamed with good humor and pride, and Mak and Lyros clapped him on his shoulders.

His uncle met his gaze over the prize box. In Uncle Argyros's dark eyes shone the sure gleam of admiration.

Until seeing it there, Lio had not realized how much he had missed it—and doubted it was still his.

Lio bowed his head to his uncle.

Uncle Argyros looked at Aunt Lyta and gestured at something in the box. She smiled in apparent agreement. He lifted a white bloom and offered it to her, and she took it from his hand to bring it to Lio.

"For maintaining your excellence in combat," Aunt Lyta announced, "and surpassing your previous achievements in diplomacy."

As she placed the white bloom upon his chest, he caught his breath. The thorns had not been removed from the rose.

BLOOD MARKS

As the musicians played the closing fanfare, Lyros slung Lio's arm across his shoulders. Before Lio knew it, Mak was supporting him under his other arm. Together, his Trial brothers levitated with him toward the nearest exit.

"Off to the baths with you," Lyros said. "A healer will be with you shortly."

"That's not on the itinerary," Lio protested. "I can't miss the closing ceremonies."

"You won't be the only one," Mak told him. "The initiates got a little overexcited and are hurrying out for snacks."

"Thanks to all the healthy snacks I've had lately," Lio reminded them, "I don't need a healer. My body will mend itself soon enough."

"You'll mend much sooner with a healer to counteract the Sunfire." Mak looked very amused indeed.

Lyros did not. "I don't want to give the mage the satisfaction of watching you sit in the stands and bleed."

Lio sighed. "If you insist. I do want to be in top condition for the footraces later this week."

They took Lio into the very chamber he least wanted to revisit. The baths were just one simple stone room after another with the same taps and steaming benches built into the walls. But Lio would never forget this one.

The steam vents were on, but the balmy warmth they released felt oppressive. Their gentle rushing sounded like a hiss of warning. He could almost smell the undigested deer blood he had vomited all over the floor.

A shudder moved through him, as if the Craving chills had reached out of his memories to take hold of him again.

"I use the bath on the north side now," he said.

"You're using this bath tonight." Lyros eased Lio down onto a bench.

"I left my things in the other one," Lio said, before he saw the bundle of his robes waiting for him in the corner.

"Take it easy. We'd better go say hello to the initiates before they follow us in here." Mak waved as he and Lyros departed.

Lio smiled after them, but he was soon alone with his injuries and his dire memories.

He should try to think of this as the place where he had first told Mak and Lyros about Cassia. That had been a joyful occasion, a deliverance. He wished he could disentangle those moments of solace from the blur of horror that was the half year he had spent without her.

He tried to focus on the present. He eyed his robes, which were out of reach at the end of the bench. Should he arrange them under his ankle while he waited for Javed? Was it worth the effort of moving? He was still debating when the door swung open.

"Please work fast, Javed," Lio said. "I can't be gone long. I don't want Cassia to worry about me."

"Then you can reassure me right now," Cassia replied.

Lio stared in the direction of her voice. The door shut on the seemingly empty room. Then she shimmered into sight as if a translucent cloth had been drawn away from her.

She smiled at him. "Surprise."

"Can you be here? How are you here?" he asked foolishly, even as he held out his good hand to her.

She came to him and, taking his hand, pressed a kiss to his sandy, bloodstained knuckles. "I plotted with your Trial circle."

Lio beamed at her. "If they'd told me which healer was going to tend my wounds, I wouldn't have resisted."

"We agreed to proceed under the strictest secrecy. Kia and Nodora used their veil spells to help me escape the embassy in the confusion of the intermission. Mak and Lyros delivered you into my care, eager to provide a consolation prize in honor of your sacrifice tonight."

Lio brought her wrist to his mouth and licked her vein. "You are no mere consolation, my rose."

With the utmost care, she eased his tunic off of him. Her smile disappeared. "Shouldn't these have healed already?"

"The Sunfire has slowed down my body's ability to repair itself, but it's only temporary."

She fashioned a cushion out of his tattered athletic tunic to elevate his ankle. "I expected the clean, elegant...*Hesperine* sort of fight you had with Lyros tonight. Not this."

"The mage didn't do anything to me that won't mend. And quickly, with your attentions."

"Just because you *can* withstand being broken into little pieces doesn't mean you *should*." She fetched his change of robes from the end of the bench and folded them behind his head, cushioning him from the wall. "I never understood the appeal of tournaments. I still don't. What pleasure is there in watching the one you love get hurt?"

Lio chuckled. "I think the pleasure is watching the one you love win. But alas, your champion is a diplomat. I do recall warning you upon our first meeting that I am no warrior."

"I wish you would keep it that way."

"I may use fists instead of words now and then, but my cause is the same."

The storm in her aura gentled, revealing the admiration beneath. "I know."

He smiled. "Didn't you enjoy the match? Just a little bit?"

An echo of excitement quivered through her aura. "Of course I enjoyed it. Before you got hurt."

He slid his hand down her neck to rest upon her pulse. "Your heart has not stopped racing since you entered the gymnasium."

She swallowed. "You are a sight to behold."

"Thank you for being with me."

"What you did during the fight...pulling me into your mind like that..."

She trailed off, her lips parted, her eyes full of emotion. Eyes he had once gazed through, entirely by accident, in the crowded great hall at Solorum. Tonight, in the deep withdrawal of battle, with all his power concentrated within himself, he had felt as close to her as he had that night, when they had still been strangers.

"I wasn't sure I would be able to do it," he tried to explain, "especially in the middle of battle. But in the tensest moments, you felt closest to me. It was easy to pull you closer. Until the fight disrupted my concentration. I'm sorry I couldn't keep it up."

"Those few moments of being under your skin were more powerful than the half a year when we were parted by the breadth of the world." Her aura glittered with the tears not to be seen in her eyes. "Half a year, I worried about you. I listened to the Dexion describe all the horrible things he wanted to do my Hesperines. I watched him destroy…" She shook her head. "And tonight I had to watch him hurt you."

"Cassia, my rose. I'm all right." Lio caressed her face with his uninjured hand.

"I just watched my share spit his own blood in the dirt, and that is not all right."

"I bit my tongue, that's all." He poked it out at her. "It will take time for it to turn to glass again. In the meantime, you may have to tell all the bedtime stories to Zoe."

That brought a hint of a smile to Cassia's face, but she shook her head. "I can do better. I can fix your tongue and the rest of you, too. I happen to know a draught of mortal blood will provide fuel for your body's natural regenerative properties, and I happen to know a mortal eager to be your draught, who is very fond of your natural properties indeed."

"A bit of your draught, and my natural properties will be at your service, and all without ruining your lovely gown."

"Please, ruin my gown as much as you like. I prefer blood red to Segetian gold." Cassia unwound her veil from around her neck and tossed it out of the way down her back. She yanked at the laces of her bodice and slid her gown down off her shoulders.

Lio watched, mesmerized, and pulled her closer. "Come here, oh Elixir of Life."

"I promise I'll be gentle."

Standing before him, she gave him the most delicate of kisses on his split lip. Her tenderness sent a shiver through him. With the utmost care, she cupped his head and eased her throat to his mouth.

Lio put his lips to the pulse that had sustained him during the fight.

The lingering furor of battle stirred once more within him, and his damaged body's need roared to life. With a growl, he sank his fangs into her throat and listened to her moan.

Hot, wet blood raced across his parched tongue and slaked his thirst. Her liquid warmth moved into him, at once soothing and rousing. Heat seared the sites of his wounds, and he gritted his teeth, biting down harder on her vein. He felt a little impact in the stone on either side of his head. Her hands on the wall.

He felt his crumpled ribs straighten and expand within his flesh. The pressure in his wrist eased. Pain retraced its path in his ankle, then faded to nothingness.

With two good hands, Lio pulled Cassia down to the bench beside him. Without parting his mouth from her vein, he traded places with her to kneel before her. He slid a hand behind her head and down her damp braid. His fingers ran afoul of that veil. He had just enough presence of mind to remember she must soon leave this room wearing her Tenebran entrapments. But they could still free her from them for a few moments.

He wrestled her skirts out of the way as she unwrapped his loincloth. He slid his body between her legs, and she yanked him to her. He took both her hips in his hands and buried himself inside her. She called out to him now, egging him on. He pumped inside her with all the energy her blood was giving his body.

Steam plastered her gown to her body and to his bare skin. She rubbed damply against him, even as his rhabdos slid through the wetness inside her and her blood flooded his mouth over and over. She parted her legs wider, and he heard her velvet shoes slide over the stone as she sought purchase. He smiled into the blood on her neck. Her feet didn't reach the floor from a bench built for Hesperine height.

When her hands clutched at his buttocks, he flinched with pleasure. She held him to her, kneading and massaging him into their rhythm. As he worked his muscles, she worked them in her hands. It felt wonderful to be in his own skin, to enjoy her, to feel her enjoy him.

Her krana rippled around his rhabdos, driving waves of pleasure through his entire body. Her fingernails dug into his buttocks, and her voice echoed off the walls of the bath chamber. He unleashed himself inside her, mind and body, magic and strength. They gripped each other, sharing their climax everywhere their bodies touched.

He dragged in a breath, filling his head with moist air that smelled of her blood and pleasure. He lifted his mouth from her. Her fingers released their grip on him.

She lifted a hand and cupped her palm under his chin. Her blood dripped from his mouth and into her hand. She flattened her wet palm on his chest and smeared her blood mark over his heart. The pure intimacy of it sent a shudder through Lio.

When he lifted his hand to his fangs, her eyes widened. He punctured his palm, then pressed his hand to her heart. His blood touched her skin for the first time. They both let out a gasp.

He caressed her, and a trail of his blood slipped between her breasts. Her krana quivered and tightened around him. A thrill slammed through him. His blood aroused her.

A memory flashed in his mind. The night in their shrine when she had first asked him to touch her, appointing him her guide on her journey into pleasure. She had sat before him just like this and dared only an exploration with his hand. Now here she was, in Orthros, with all of him locked between her thighs. With his blood on her skin. Their past and present blurred together, obscuring the unbearable time in between. He could reach out and touch their future.

"Cassia...the last time I was in this room..." No, he didn't wish to speak of it after all.

Her brow furrowed, and she ran her hands up and down his back. "You know you can tell me anything."

He could scarcely resist telling her anything she wished, when she asked so. "I fell ill while training. Mak and Lyros found me on the floor... just there...I was such a mess. I finally had to confess the true cause of my illness—hunger for you. It was the night I first told them about you."

"Lio!" She ran her hands over him, as if to reassure herself he was safe and hale. "You were that ill? I knew living on deer must have taken a horrible toll on you, but..."

"I hate to think of that time. I'm not sure I should even speak of it to you."

"As we've said, we must not keep such things from each other, even if it means worrying one another. We must both know when one of us in danger."

Soon she would understand it was not just deprivation, but Craving that had reduced him to that. Telling her a little at a time like this would pave the way for the truth. "I just want you to know how much it means to me for us to be together here like this."

She looked at him with her veil askew and the front of her golden gown stained dark crimson with blood. "It means that to me too."

He smiled and kissed her softly on her lips. But a stirring of sound from without made him lift his head and utter a curse. "I think the closing ceremonies are starting."

"Ugh. Time for me to go wave the Tenebran banners again."

He eased their bodies apart and worked a cleaning spell on them that left their blood marks untouched. He ran a finger over the bloodstain on her chest, drawing one last shiver from her, before he reluctantly turned to gather up his garments. He felt a blush in her aura and turned back to see her gazing at his backside with a rueful expression.

He grinned. "Yes, I incurred those scratches in our private wresting match."

"Well." She pulled her skirts down over her knees. "At least they're healing fast…ah. Gone already."

He sighed. "There are some marks I wish I could keep."

VICTORY PRIZES

A TOURNAMENT WAS NOT SUCH an ordeal after all, Cassia decided. At least, not a Hesperine tournament. She sat with her arm around Lio and his head on her shoulder, surrounded by friends and family in Mak and Lyros's residence at House Argyros.

"Are you going to fall asleep?" Cassia asked Lio with a smile.

"I just feasted on you," he muttered with his eyes closed. "I shouldn't be tired."

She touched her cheek to his hair. "You said, according to Javed, it would take me extra effort to set you completely to rights."

"Mmm. Why can't I enjoy a simple nap right here? If Sunfire must reduce me to this, it should allow me a little mortal pleasure and make it possible for me to sleep during polar night."

Cassia wanted to say he could expect his mortal pleasure as soon as they were alone again, and it would not be a little. But she could sense his veil slipping as his eyelids drooped. She glanced at the children and bit her lip.

Lio's eyes flew open. "On second thought, it's good I can't fall asleep."

"Sunfire doesn't seem to have dulled your mind magery at all," she observed.

He met her gaze, his eyes drowsy, but serious. "My Union with you is stronger than any poison."

A peal of the children's laughter fetched Lio and Cassia's attention back to the family gathering.

"The fool landed in a heap at my feet in three moves." Kadi stood gallantly in the middle of the sitting room. With Thenie in one arm, she mimed her winning attacks against Tychon with her free hand.

Lio's parents lounged together on a couch, having relinquished their young charges to the thrall of Kadi's story. Bosko sat on the rug at his mother's feet, swinging his fist in the air as if reliving the fight. Zoe watched with eager attention, sprawled on her stomach with her arm around Knight.

Mak appeared content to let his sister have the glory of recounting the Stand's victories. He had collapsed on a couch with his head on Lyros's lap, and neither of them looked like they ever wanted to move again. They murmured to each other, their voices unheard behind their veil. But they were apparently too sleepy to remember to conceal the motion of their lips. Cassia looked away with a smile, but couldn't help catching a glimpse of their conversation.

"Victor names the prize," Lyros said, "but we tied."

"You know I'll let you take command any time," Mak replied, "my beloved strategist."

Nodora shot Kia and Xandra a mischievous look and leaned around the coffee table, reaching out a hand toward Lyros's bare foot. Cassia stared. The composed musician tickled the bottom of the formidable warrior's foot.

Lyros made a choking sound, and his head snapped up off the back of the couch. His Trial sisters and Lio erupted into laughter.

"That's my move," Mak protested, but he was laughing with them.

"Try that again when I'm not poisoned," Lyros threatened. But his eyes slid shut, and his head fell back. He tucked his feet up out of harm's way.

"Shall I serve your guests in your stead, Grace-brothers?" Javed offered.

Mak waved a hand in silent thanks.

Javed went to the tall counter that bordered the sitting room. Beyond the bar, the room was open to a practice hall lined with padded mats, training dummies, and other equipment. Mak and Lyros kept a well-appointed, rather than luxurious residence. The wrought iron furniture had clean, strong lines, and the cushions and rugs were solid shades of green and brown. Cassia thought the simple, masculine elegance of their home suited them much better than Orthros's high opulence.

Javed poured coffee in everyone's cups, but to four, he added a potion from his healer's satchel. "All right, weary warriors. Drink up."

Mak, Lyros, and Lio groaned.

"It's a tonic. It will make you feel better, I promise." Three cups levitated in their directions, while Javed delivered the fourth to Kadi himself.

"I'll have whatever Kadi's already had," Mak grumbled. "How are you still on your feet?"

"Experience, Brother," Kadi replied.

Lio's aunt strolled into the room, another prize box under her arm. "If we could bottle it for you, we certainly would, but training is the best we can do."

Lio frowned and lifted his head just enough to look around. "Won't Uncle be joining us?"

"He is at our residence," Lyta answered, "changing out of his formal silks to accompany me on ward patrol."

Lio lay back again, his eyes full of disappointment.

"I cannot stay long either, I'm afraid. But I wanted to be here for this." Lyta set the prize box on the coffee table, exchanging expectant smiles with the rest of her Stand.

"You three are sleepier than sucklings," Javed said to his patients. "Drink your tonic so you can hold your heads up for a few minutes longer."

Cassia fetched the coffee cup hovering above Lio's nose and put it to his lips. He held his nose and obediently accepted her assistance. He shuddered, blinked, then sat up beside her, putting an arm around her. Mostly to support himself, she suspected.

"All right, we're ready." Mak rubbed his face and gave his head a shake.

Lyros crossed his legs to keep his bare feet protected, turning his attention on the prize box.

Lyta smiled and beckoned to Cassia. "Stand beside me and accept your real prizes."

Cassia looked around her. "The prize box is for me?"

Lyta nodded. "As meaningful as it was to award you a laurel wreath in the ring tonight, we regretted that we were not at liberty to offer you the Hesperine prizes you so rightfully won."

Kadi gave Cassia an encouraging smile. "We decided your first visit to the gymnasium would be a fine time for the Stand to present our welcome gifts."

"I get to give you mine first." Mak grinned. "I made the box."

Cassia ran her hands over the detailed ironwork, tracing the curls of thorny vines and the petals of roses. "It's exquisite. It shall not be only a keeper of treasures, but a treasure in itself."

"Go on," Lyros urged her.

Cassia got to her feet and stood at Lyta's side. Lyta lifted the lid of the box and withdrew a bundle of fabric. She let it unfold before Cassia. It was an athletic tunic the color of cassia spice that appeared to be just her size.

"From me," said Kadi, "the Stand's outfitter. Next time you and Knight join us in the ring, you'll have the proper attire."

Cassia found herself struggling for words.

Kadi laughed. "I bet you never guessed my craft is sewing."

"Kadi makes the best Stand dolls," Zoe piped up. "Bosko and I are collecting everyone—Aunt Lyta, Mak, Lyros... Kadi, you have to make you next."

That brought a smile to Cassia's face, and she found her tension draining away. "Thank you so much, Kadi. I'll look forward to training without having to fiddle with skirts and veils!"

"Why don't you try it on now?" Mak pointed past the bar, toward the training room. "We've got a place where you can change right there."

Cassia excused herself into the training room and went behind a dressing screen. She shucked her Segetian colors down to her underlinens, then pulled the tunic over her head and Lio's blood mark. She decided she wanted to wear cotton for the rest of her life.

Then she stared down at her bare calves, and her courage failed her. She tugged on the short sleeves, but they wouldn't reach over her elbows. Her breasts were too small to be noticeable, but *she* knew they were there.

She was about to parade herself in front of all Lio's family and friends in, well, next to nothing.

This wasn't public, she reminded herself. This was veil hours, the time of privacy and trust.

Oh, thorns. She was supposed to wear this in the middle of the gymnasium.

Cassia thought of big, gorgeous, powerful Kadi, who never hesitated to display her curves and the muscles beneath. Of Lyta, arriving in Orthros wearing a peasant's tunic and ragged footwraps.

Cassia stepped out from behind the screen and marched back into the common room.

Everyone clapped. No one stared. They just looked at her with contented faces. Except Lio. He stared at her knee freckles with a drowsy, besotted grin.

"It suits you," Lyta said. "Now you are ready for your rose of victory."

Cassia rejoined her by the prize box. Lyta lifted out a jeweled brooch, perfectly wrought in the shape of a life-sized white rose.

"Oh, Lyros, this must be your gift," Cassia said.

"White opals," he replied, "in a copper setting with just the right patina to give the stem and leaves a lifelike green color."

"It's beautiful," Cassia managed. "I shall wear it with the greatest pride."

Lyta pinned the rose to Cassia's tunic.

The box appeared empty, but Lyta reached inside once more. "And finally, my gift to you, because you have fought as hard as anyone I know for Orthros."

She held out her hand. On her palm was a set of speires.

Cassia thought of climbing through a murder hole in Solorum Fortress, of racing through the hidden passages in the palace, of clawing her way out of an avalanche.

She did not hesitate before the Guardian of Orthros. "I am honored to accept your gift."

Lyta gave a nod of approval and set the speires in Cassia's hands.

Cassia wound her braid into a knot at the nape of her neck and secured it with the speires.

The cheer that went up among their small gathering was more overpowering, and more precious, than all the roar of the crowd.

MORTAL PLEASURES

LIO GAZED AT THE window seat and wondered how much longer he could remain on his feet. "This is embarrassing."

Cassia laughed and got the rest of his robes off of him. He collapsed onto the bed with a groan. He just wanted to sleep forever, but this was worse than the drowsiness of approaching Dawn Slumber. Exhaustion held him in its grip, inside and out. Every inch of him hurt as if someone had beaten him with a blunt object. Oh. Chrysanthos had. With his fist.

While Cassia stood beside the bed and pulled off her athletic tunic, displaying her naked body and his blood mark, Lio actually had trouble keeping his eyes open.

"I *hate* this," he said.

"Well, I plan to enjoy it." She untied her speires and let her braid swing free. "Imagine, the Hesperine seducer at the mercy of the innocent maiden for a change."

"Your seducer can't move, much less seduce."

"Hmm. Perhaps I can show you the effect coffee has on mortals. A sip of me should demonstrate the effects nicely."

"Unfortunately that requires being able to reach your neck."

Cassia sat down on the bed beside him and caressed his forehead. "If you're too tired tonight, you can just drink from me and rest."

"We can try that the night I'm dead."

"It's nothing to be embarrassed about if you don't feel like feasting. You are always so considerate of me. You know if you need the same patience from me, you have it."

Lio blinked up at her and focused on a new thought. "This is how you feel all the time."

Cassia stroked his hair. "It probably feels worse to you than to me, because you're not used to it the way I am."

"I shudder to think of being used to this."

"You're right, you shouldn't only experience the downsides of mortality. You should get to enjoy some of the...well, I won't call them benefits. Consolations, perhaps." She slid into bed beside him, touching her bare body gently to his. She lifted his hand to her temple. "Let me show you. In here."

Thank the Goddess he was still capable of Union with Cassia. His thelemancy fixed on her thoughts, the music in his utter silence, and he was home, in the embrace of her mind.

"Spend a moment in this memory of mine," she said.

Lio felt soft ground under her knees and soil in her hands. Her back ached, and her limbs were weary, but a satisfied contentment filled her at the sight of the long rows of pea seedlings she had succeeded in planting. She was halfway there. She patted the soil down around the latest planting and straightened, stretching.

Together, they shut their eyes, relishing the warmth on her back. The gentle, sustaining heat seemed to sink into her bones and chase away the aches. She got to her feet and turned toward the warmth. Golden light shone beyond her eyelids.

Lio gasped and opened his eyes on stained glass and moonlight.

"That is a long afternoon in the garden," Cassia said. "Hard work, but good work."

"Is that what the sun feels like to you?"

"That's part of gardening."

Lio turned his head to look at her. "Do you...miss the sun, since you came to Orthros?"

She cuddled closer to him. "Not if you don't miss my freckles."

He studied her face. "They don't look a bit fainter to me. My magic is working."

"What?"

"The light spells I set up for our roses. They have the same effect on your freckles."

She laughed aloud and kissed him. "See there. I don't need the sun."

He breathed a sigh of relief and found the strength to hold her mouth to his.

She eased her body over him. "But I will be your sun, if you need one, my Hesperine."

"You are far better than a sun. You are my rose."

She bared her throat over his fangs. Her essence flowed into him, warmer and more life-giving than any sun.

He would fight as many rounds as the mages demanded. He would take as many hits as necessary to teach the lords the meaning of peace. Lio would do whatever he must so Cassia could bloom forever in the light of Orthros, right here in his arms.

Cassia and Lio's story continues in
Blood Grace Book 4, *Blood Sanctuary Part Two*.
Learn more at
vroth.co/sanctuary2

GLOSSARY

Abroad: Hesperine term for lands outside of Orthros where Hesperines errant roam, meaning Tenebra and Cordium. See **Orthros Abroad**

Adelphos: false name assumed by Chrysanthos to hide his identity as a war mage from the Hesperines.

Adrogan: ambitious young Tenebran lord, a second son who travels to Orthros to make his fortune. Once one of Cassia's unwanted suitors, now betrothed to Biata.

Adwene: Konstantina's Grace, a formidable Imperial scholar in his mortal life and now a thirteen-hundred-year-old intellectual of Orthros.

Aetos: winged messenger of the gods in the Tenebran and Cordian pantheon. First scion and eldest son of Kyria and Anthros, the most powerful among the lesser deities known as the Fourteen Scions.

affinity: the type of magic for which a person has an aptitude, such as light magic, warding, or healing.

Aithourian Circle: the war mages of the Order of Anthros, sworn enemies of the Hesperines, who have specialized spells for finding and destroying Hespera worshipers. Founded by Aithouros in ancient times, this circle was responsible for most of the destruction of Hespera's temples during the Last War. Oversees the training of all war mages from Tenebra and Cordium to ensure their lifelong loyalty to the Order.

Aithouros: fire mage of the Order of Anthros who personally led the persecution of Hespera worshipers during the Last War. Founder and namesake of the Aithourian Circle, who continue his teachings. Killed by Hippolyta.

Akanthia: the world comprising Tenebra, Cordium, Orthros, and the Empire.

Akesios: god of healing in the Tenebran and Cordian pantheon. The third scion, or third son, of Kyria and Anthros. A lesser deity alongside his brothers and sisters, the Fourteen Scions. Men with the affinity for healing magic become mages of Akesios.

Akron: highest-ranking mage in the Order of Anthros, who holds the ultimate authority in the Order that dominates all other mages.

Akron's Altar: the altar in Corona upon which the Order of Anthros executes heretics by immolation, where many Hesperines have met their deaths.

Akron's Torch: an artifact of the Order of Anthros, which holds great magical power and symbolizes their authority. Prometheus stole it from the Hagion of Anthros, enraging the Aithourian Circle. Its whereabouts have been unknown since his capture.

Alea: one of the two Queens of Orthros, who has ruled the Hesperines for nearly sixteen hundred years with her Grace, Queen Soteira. A mage of Hespera in her mortal life, she is the only Prisma of a temple of Hespera who survived the Ordering.

Alexandra: royal firstblood and Eighth Princess of Orthros, the youngest of the Queens' family. Solaced from Tenebra as a child. She raises silkworms for her craft. Lio's childhood sweetheart.

Amachos: false name assumed by Dalos while he was in disguise as the royal mage of Tenebra.

Anastasios: Ritual rirstblood who Gifted Apollon, founder of Lio's bloodline. He was a powerful healer and Prismos of Hagia Boreia, who sacrificed his life to help Alea protect their Great Temple from the Order of Anthros's onslaught.

Andragathos: god of male virtue and righteous warfare in the Tenebran and Cordian pantheon. The seventh scion and youngest son of Kyria and Anthros. A lesser deity alongside his brothers and sisters, the Fourteen Scions. See **Knightly Order of Andragathos**

Angara: goddess in the Tenebran and Cordian pantheon who blesses warriors with morale in battle. Often portrayed wearing golden armor and bearing a sword. The second scion and eldest daughter of Kyria and Anthros, a lesser deity alongside her brothers and sisters, the Fourteen Scions.

Annassa: honorific for the Queens of Orthros.

Anthros: god of war, order, and fire. Supreme deity of the Tenebran and Cordian pantheon and ruler of summer. The sun is said to be Anthros riding his chariot across the sky. According to myth, he is the husband of Kyria and brother of Hypnos and Hespera.

Anthros's fire: a flower commonly grown in Tenebra, used by humans in combination with the herb sunsword to ward off Hesperines.

Anthros's Hall: the god Anthros's great hall beyond the mortal world. Tenebrans and Cordians believe that those who please Anthros in life are rewarded with an afterlife in his Hall with his company of eternal warriors.

Anthros's pyre: Anthros's eternal, holy flames, where he punishes those who displease him.

Apollon: Lio's father, an elder firstblood and founder of Orthros. In his mortal life before the Ordering, he was a mage of Demergos. Transformed by Anastasios, he was the first Hesperine ever to receive the Gift from one of the Ritual firstbloods. Renowned for his powerful stone magic and prowess in battle, he once roamed Abroad as one of the Blood Errant. Known as the Lion of Orthros. Now retired to live peacefully in Orthros with his Grace, Komnena.

apostate: rogue mage who illegally practices magic outside of the Orders.

Apprentice's Toddy: an alchemical infusion for Hesperine sucklings or young mages whose magic has begun to manifest. Remedies the discomfort and anxiety that accompany blooms of power.

Archipelagos: land to the west of the Empire comprising a series of islands, which maintains strict isolation from the rest of the world. See **Nodora** and **Matsu**

Argyros: Lio's uncle and mentor in diplomacy and mind magic. Elder firstblood and founder of Orthros from Hagia Anatela, Gifted by Eidon. Graced to Lyta, father of Nike, Kadi, and Mak. An elder firstblood and founder of Orthros like Apollon, his brother by mortal birth. Attended the first Equinox Summit and every one since as the Queens' Master Ambassador. One of the most powerful thelemancers in history, known as Silvertongue for his legendary abilities as a negotiator.

Ariadne: an apprentice mage of Kyria who accompanies the Semna and Pakhne to Orthros. One of the mages who helped the Hesperine embassy take Zoe and the other Eriphite children to safety.

Arkadia: Lio's cousin, daughter of Argyros and Lyta. Solaced from Tenebra as a child. With her mother's affinity for warding and aptitude for the battle arts, she serves as a Master Steward in Hippolyta's Stand.

Astrapas: Timarete's Grace, Lyros's father.

Atalanta: bloodborn Master Steward of the Stand who used her running skills to rescue humans from heart hunter territory. Martyred when their liege-hounds hunted her down.

Athena: two-year-old Eriphite child Solaced by Javed and Kadi. Younger sister of Boskos by birth and blood. The severe case of frost fever she suffered as a mortal damaged her brain. While the Gift has healed her, she is still recovering lost development.

Aurelio: most famous minstrel in Tenebra and Cordium, whose songs are universally beloved.

Autumn Greeting: ancient courtship festival of Tenebra. When a woman shares this dance with a man, it is considered a promise of betrothal, after which their fathers will arrange their marriage.

Avior: woodland god in the Tenebran and Cordian pantheon.

avowal: Hesperine ceremony in which Graces profess their bond before their people; legally binding and an occasion of great celebration.

Baltasar: Hypatia's firstgift, birth son of her Grace, who joined her bloodline. From the Empire like his father, Khaldaios. A scholar and member of Konstantina's Trial circle.

Basilis: title of a non-royal female relative of the king, outside of the line of succession.

Basir: Hesperine thelemancer and one of the two spymasters of Orthros, alongside his Grace, Kumeta. From the Empire in his mortal life. His official title is "Queens' Master Envoy" to conceal the nature of their work.

Benedict: First Knight of Segetia, Flavian's best friend, who harbors unrequited love for Genie. Cassia trusts him and considers him a friend, despite his hostility toward Hesperines as a devotee of Andragathos. Travels to Orthros as Lord Titus's representative during the Solstice Summit.

Biata: young Tenebran lady who is one of Lady Hadrian's followers and frequents her weaving room. Prone to gossiping. Betrothed to Lord Tyran.

Blood Errant: group of four ancient and powerful Hesperine warriors who went errant together for eight centuries: Apollon, Nike, Rudhira, and Methu. The only Hesperines errant who have ever carried weapons, they performed legendary but controversial deeds in Hespera's name.

blood magic: type of magic practiced by worshipers of Hespera, from which the power of the Gift stems. All Hesperines possess innate blood magic.

Blood Moon: Hesperine name for one of the two moons, which appears red with a liquid texture to the naked eye. Believed to be an eye of the Goddess Hespera, potent with her blood magic.

Blood Union: magical empathic connection that allows Hesperines to sense the emotions of any living thing that has blood.

bloodborn: Hesperine born with the Gift because their mother was transformed during pregnancy.

bloodless: undead; a corpse reanimated by a necromancer, so called because blood no longer flows through its veins, although it has a semblance of life. Often used as an insult by Hesperines.

Bosko *or* **Boskos:** ten-year-old Eriphite child Solaced by Javed and Kadi. Elder brother of Athena by birth and blood. Harbors anger over what the children suffered and is struggling to adjust to life in Orthros.

Caelum: Solia and Cassia's thirteen-year-old half-brother, only son of King Lucis, crown prince of Tenebra.

Callen: Perita's loving husband. Once a guard in Lord Hadrian's service, he lost a promising military career due to a leg injury he suffered during his unjust imprisonment. Now serves the royal household of Tenebra as Cassia's trusted bodyguard.

Cassia: Tenebran lady, illegitimate daughter of King Lucis and his concubine, Thalia. Secretly a traitor working with the Hesperines from within the Tenebran embassy. Deeply in love with Lio, she hopes to secure peace so she can stay with him in Orthros forever.

Castra Justa: the stronghold of the First Prince and base of operations for the Prince's Charge.

Chalice of Stars: Nike's legendary round shield, which she uses along with the Stand's hand-to-hand combat techniques.

Changing Queen: Queen Hedera of Tenebra, the Mage King's wife and co-ruler during the Last War. As a Silvicultrix, she was a powerful mage in her own right. Her own people knew her as Ebah. Also known as the Hawk of the Lustra and associated with her plant symbol, ivy.

the Charge: see **Prince's Charge**

charm: physical object imbued with a mage's spell, usually crafted of botanicals or other materials with their own magical properties. Offers a mild beneficial effect to an area or the holder of the charm, even if that person is not a mage.

Chera: goddess of rain and spinning in the Tenebran and Cordian pantheon, known as the Mourning Goddess and the Widow. According to myth, she was the Bride of Spring before Anthros destroyed her god-husband, Demergos, for disobedience.

Chrysanthos: war mage from Cordium with an affinity for fire, rival of the late Dalos. As the Dexion of the Aithourian Circle, he is one of the highest-ranking elites in the Order of Anthros. An adroit politician born to an aristocratic family in Corona.

Cordium: land to the south of Tenebra where the Mage Orders hold sway. Its once-mighty principalities and city-states have now lost power to the magical and religious authorities. Wealthy and cultured, but prone to deadly politics. Also known as the Magelands.

Corona: capital city of Cordium and holy seat of the Mage Orders, where the main temples of each god are located, including the Hagion of Anthros.

the Craving: a Hesperine's addiction to their Grace's blood. When deprived of each other, Graces suffer agonizing withdrawal symptoms and fatal illness.

Daedala: Prisma of Hagia Zephyra. Ritual firstblood and Gifter of Timarete.

Dakarai: Grace of Kitharos, one of Nodora's fathers. A dancer and drummer from the high veld of the Empire.

Dalos: Aithourian war mage who disguised himself as a Tenebran and conspired with King Lucis to assassinate the attendees of the Equinox Summit. When the Hesperines' ward stopped him, his spell rebounded, killing him with his own magic.

Dawn Slumber: deep sleep Hesperines fall into when the sun rises. Although the sunlight causes them no harm, they're unable to awaken until nightfall, leaving them vulnerable during daylight hours.

Demergos: formerly the god of agriculture, now stricken from the Tenebran and Cordian pantheon. His worshipers were disbanded in ancient times when the mages of Anthros seized power. According to myth, he was the husband of Chera, but disobeyed Anthros and brought on his own death and her grief.

Demetrios: royal firstblood and Third Prince of Orthros, the Queens' second-eldest son.

Departure: contingency plan that dates from the founding of Orthros, when Hesperines feared the Last War might break out again at any time. If the Queens invoked the Departure, all Hesperines errant would return home, and the border between Orthros and Tenebra would be closed forever.

Deukalion: bloodborn firstgift of Apollon and Komnena, Ambassador in Orthros's diplomatic service who has devoted his career to improving relations between Orthros and Tenebra. While in Tenebra for the Equinox Summit, had a secret affair with Cassia and helped her stop Dalos's assassination attempt. Upon his return to Orthros, he discovered she is his Grace. He is determined to free her from her duties to Tenebra and persuade her to stay with him for all time.

Deutera: respected mage at the Temple of Kyria at Solorum, the Prisma's right hand and trusted confidant.

Dexion: second highest ranking mage in the Aithourian Circle, second in command to the Synthikos and destined to succeed him.

Discourses on Love: Orthros's canon of erotic texts.

Divine Tongue: language spoken by Hesperines and mages, used for spells, rituals, and magical texts. The common tongue of Orthros, spoken freely by all Hesperines. In Tenebra and Cordium, the mages keep it a secret and disallow non-mages from learning it.

the Drink: when a Hesperine drinks blood from a human or animal; a non-sexual act, considered sacred, which should be carried out with respect for the donor. It's forbidden to take the Drink from an unwilling person. *Or* Hesperine sacred tenet, the commitment to thriving without the death of other living things.

Ebah: see **Changing Queen**

Eidon: Prismos of Hagia Anatela. Ritual firstblood and Gifter of Argyros.

elder firstbloods: the ancient Hesperine founders of Orthros. Gifted by the Ritual firstbloods. See **Apollon**, **Argyros**, **Hypatia**, **Kassandra**, **Kitharos**, **Timarete**

elder Grace: the Grace of an elder firstblood.

the Empire: vast and prosperous human lands located far to the west, across an ocean from Tenebra. Comprises many different languages and cultures united under the Empress. Allied with Orthros and welcoming to Hesperines, many of whom began their mortal lives as Imperial citizens. Maintains a strict policy of isolation toward Tenebra an Cordium to guard against the Mage Orders.

the Empress: the ruler of the Empire, admired by her citizens. The Imperial throne has passed down through the female line for many generations.

envoy: according to common knowledge, a messenger attached to the Hesperine diplomatic service. In fact, envoys are the Queens' spies who gather information from the mortal world to protect Orthros and Hesperines errant. See **Basir**, **Kumeta**

Epodos: Kitharos and Dakarai's firstgift, Nodora's eldest brother. Solaced from Tenebra as a child, he is Orthros's leading bard and a member of Konstantina's Trial circle.

Equinox Oath: ancient treaty between Orthros and Tenebra, which prescribes the conduct of Hesperines errant and grants them protection from humans.

Equinox Summit: peace talks in which the Hesperines send ambassadors from Orthros to meet with the King of Tenebra and renew the Equinox Oath. Each mortal king is expected to convene it once upon his accession to the throne.

Ereba: elder firstblood from Hagia Notia who was martyred during the destruction of the temple and did not survive to become a founder of Orthros.

Eriphites: worshipers of the pastoral god Eriphon, branded heretics by the Order of Anthros. The last surviving members of their cult are twenty-four orphaned children recently brought to safety in Orthros thanks to Cassia and Lio. See **Zosime**, **Boskos**, **Athena**

Eriphon: lesser deity, pastoral god known as the Herder of Demergos, whose worship was also banned during the Ordering.

errant: a Hesperine who has left Orthros to travel through Tenebra doing good deeds for mortals.

essential displacement: process by which necromancers can transfer the magic of one person, the source, into another person, the vessel, through a third person called the channel. The vessel must die for the source to reclaim their power.

Eudias: young war mage from Cordium with an affinity for weather, including lightning. Compelled to join the Aithourian circle due to his magic, he does not relish their murderous plots. Apprenticed to Dalos, he reluctantly assisted his late master in Tenebra and now answers to Chrysanthos.

Eudokia: Hesperine youngblood, one of Lio's Trial sisters in Orthros. Solaced from Tenebra as a child. An initiate mathematician, calligrapher, and accomplished scholar. Daughter of Hypatia.

Eugenia: young Tenebran lady, believed to be Flavian's cousin and daughter of his late uncle, Lord Eugenius. In fact she is his sister, the daughter of Titus and his concubine Risara.

Evander: see **Evandrus the Younger**

Evandrus the Elder: Tenebran free lord who assisted Lord Bellator in Solia's kidnapping and joined forces with him inside Castra Roborra during their rebellion.

Evandrus the Younger: son and heir of Evandrus the Elder, who died with him at Castra Roborra during the Siege of Sovereigns.

familiar: the animal companion of a Hesperine, bound to them by blood.

the Fangs: Prometheus's famous twin swords.

the Feast: Hesperine term for drinking blood while making love.

Ferus: a Tenebran free lord, the most threatening of Cassia's unwanted suitors, until she exposed him as a traitor. Now in exile in the eastern Tenebrae.

fire charm: a charm created by a fire mage that those without the affinity for fire can use to light a flame. In Tenebra, they are rare and valuable because only a war mage of the Aithourian circle can make one.

First Prince: see **Rudhira**

firstblood: the first Hesperine in a bloodline, who founds the family and passes the Gift to their children.

Firstblood Circle: the governing body of Orthros. Every firstblood has a vote on behalf of their bloodline, while non-voting Hesperines can attempt to influence policy by displays of partisanship. The Queens retain veto power, but use it sparingly.

firstgift: the eldest child of a Hesperine bloodline, first to receive the gift from their parents.

flametongue: rare herb whose oil can be used to fireproof armor or clothing against mundane flame. Offers no protection against magefire, but still prized by the few royals and nobles who can afford it. The Order of Anthros forbids anyone but their mages to grow and prepare it.

Flavian: young Tenebran lord, son of Free Lord Titus and heir to Segetia's seat on the Council. Despite his family's feud with Hadria, he is admired by women on both sides of the conflict as a paragon of manhood.

fleeter: a person from the Archipelagos. See **Honorable Families**

Font of the Changing Queen: stone fountain on the grounds of Solorum Palace that dates from the time of the Changing Queen. This historical monument is a subject of legends, which say it ran with blood the day the Mage King died.

foregiver: a Hesperine's ancestor who gave the Gift to their bloodline in the past.

the Fourteen Scions: see **Scions**

free lord: highest noble rank in Tenebra. Has a seat on the Council of Free Lords and heredity authority to vote on whether a king should receive the nobility's mandate.

Gaius: aging Tenebran lord loyal to Free Lord Hadrian who travels to Orthros to represent him during the Solstice Summit.

Galanthian: Tenebran free lord with lands in the cold northern region of the kingdom. Father of Nivalis.

gargoyle: mythological creatures with fangs, horns, and wings, which are said to be Hespera's familiars, created from her blood. Hesperines believe they guard the gates of her divine Sanctuary to protect it from Anthros and the other gods.

Genie: see **Eugenia**

geomagus: mage with an affinity for geological forces, who can use their magic to conjure heat from the ground or create artifacts like warming plates for heating food and drink.

the Gift: Hesperines' immortality and magical abilities, which they regard as a blessing from the goddess Hespera. The practice of offering the Gift to all is a Hesperine sacred tenet.

Gift Collector: mage-assassin and bounty hunter who hunts down Hesperines for the Order of Hypnos using necromancy, alchemy, and fighting tactics. Known for adapting common items into weapons to skirt the Orders' religious laws against mages arming themselves.

Gift Night: the night of a person's transformation into a Hesperine, usually marked by great celebration.

Gifting: the transformation from human into Hesperine.

Glasstongue: see **Lio**

glyph: sacred symbol of a deity. Each god or goddess in the pantheon has a unique glyph. Often used as a pattern in spell casting or carved on shrines and temples.

glyph shard: a fragment of the glyph stone from the Shrine of Hespera where Lio and Cassia fell in love. Although Chrysanthos destroyed the sacred site, its Sanctuary ward lives on in the stone Cassia took from it.

glyph stone: the capstone of the doorway of a shrine, inscribed with the glyph of the deity worshiped there, where any spells over the structure are usually seated.

the Goddess's Eyes: the two moons, the red Blood Moon and the white Light Moon; associated with Hespera and regarded as her gaze by Hesperines.

Gorgos: master mage from the Sun Temple of Anthros at Solorum who aspires to become royal mage.

Grace: Hesperine sacred tenet, a magical bond between two Hesperine lovers. Frees them from the need for human blood and enables them to sustain each other, but comes at the cost of the Craving. A fated bond that happens when their love is true. It is believed every Hesperine has a Grace just waiting to be found. See **Craving**

Grace braids: thin braids of one another's hair that Graces exchange. They may wear them privately after professing their bond to one another, then exchange them publicly at their avowal and thereafter wear them for all to see to signify their commitment.

Grace-family (Grace-son, Grace-father, Grace-sister, etc.): the family members of a Hesperine's Grace; compare with human in-laws.

Grace Union: the particularly powerful and intimate Blood Union between two Hesperines who are Graced; enables them to communicate telepathically and empathically.

Great Temple Epoch: the historical period when the Great Temples of every cult flourished across Tenebra and Cordium, and all mages cooperated. Came to a cataclysmic end due to the Ordering and the Last War.

Great Temples of Hespera: powerful, thriving temples where mages of Hespera worshiped and worked their magic in peace, before they were branded heretics. Razed during the Last War.

Gregoria: royal firstblood and Fourth Princess of Orthros, the fourth child and second-eldest daughter of the Queens.

Guardian of Orthros: see **Hippolyta**

Hadria: domain of Free Lord Hadrian, located on Tenebra's rocky western coast, where they seas are treacherous.

Lady Hadrian: Lord Hadrian's wife, a mature lady above reproach in the court of Tenebra, admired for her graces and respected for her political acumen.

Lord Hadrian: one of the two most powerful free lords in Tenebra, who commands the fealty of many other free lords and lesser nobles. His family has been feuding with Segetia for generations. Known for his loyalty to the throne, but also for honor superior to the king's.

Hagia Anatela: one of the four Great Temples of Hespera that flourished during the Great Temple Epoch, located in the eastern part of the continent. See **Eidon, Ourania**

Hagia Boreia: one of the four Great Temples of Hespera that flourished during the Great Temple Epoch, located in the northern part of the continent. See **Alea, Anastatios**

Hagia Notia: the southernmost of the four Great Temples of Hespera that flourished during the Great Temple Epoch, located in Corona, where the mages of Hespera co-existed with the mages of Anthros and other gods.

Hagion of Anthros: the most powerful and sacred temple of Anthros in Corona, where the Akron presides over the Order of Anthros.

Hammer of the Sun: Apollon's famous battle hammer, which he wielded while Abroad with the Blood Errant. He left it in Tenebra when he brought Komnena to Orthros.

Harbor: bay in Orthros around which Selas was built. The founders landed here when they first escaped Tenebra and found refuge in the unsettled north.

Harkhuf Addaya Khemkare: Imperial human guest visiting Orthros to study theramancy, a cousin of the Empress. Xandra's share.

harlot's kiss: Tenebran and Cordian name for roses which, as Hespera's sacred flower, are forbidden to be grown there.

Healing Sanctuary: infirmary in Orthros founded and run by Queen Soteira, where humans are given care and Hesperines are trained in the healing arts.

heart bow: traditional gesture of devotion to the Queens of Orthros, a deep bow with one hand over the heart.

heart hunters: warbands of Tenebrans who hunt down Hesperines, regarded by their countrymen as protectors of humanity. They patrol the northern borders of Tenebra with packs of liegehounds, waiting to attack Hesperines who leave Orthros.

Hedon: god of pleasure and chance in the Tenebran and Cordian pantheon, patron of sexual acts and gambling. Styled as the god of fertility and prosperity by the Order of Anthros in their attempts to promote morality.

Helene: royal firstblood and Sixth Princess of Orthros, the Queens' sixth child and second-youngest daughter.

Hephaestion: a mage of the Aithourian Circle during the Last War, the war mages' most brilliant military strategist and inventor of magical siege engines. Because of his sexual relationship with another man, his fellow war mage Gladius, Aithouros expelled him from the Order, punished him for apostasy, and took credit for his ideas.

Hespera: goddess of night cast from the Tenebran and Cordian pantheon. The Mage Orders have declared her worship heresy punishable by death. Hesperines keep her cult alive and continue to revere her as the goddess of the moons, Sanctuary, and Mercy. Associated with roses, thorns, and fanged creatures. According to myth, she is the sister of Anthros and Hypnos.

Hespera's Rose: the most sacred symbol of the Hesperines, a rose with five petals and five thorns representing Hespera's sacred tenets. Frequently embroidered on clothing or represented on stained glass windows. Based on real roses, which are the Goddess's sacred flower and beloved by Hesperines. The mages uproot them wherever they're found in Tenebra or Cordium and punish those who grow them for heresy.

Hesperine: nocturnal immortal being with fangs who gains nourishment from drinking blood. Tenebrans and Cordians believe them to be monsters bent on humanity's destruction. In truth, they follow a strict moral code in the name of their goddess, Hespera, and wish only to ease humankind's suffering.

Hesperite: human worshiper of Hespera, persecuted as a heretic by the Orders.

Hippolyta: Lio's aunt, Graced to Argyros, mother of Nike, Kadi, and Mak. Greatest and most ancient Hesperine warrior, a founder of Orthros. Known as the Guardian of Orthros for her deeds in Tenebra during the Last War and for establishing the Stand.

Hippolyta's Gymnasium: gymnasium in Orthros founded by Hippolyta, where she trains the Stand and Orthros's athletes compete.

Hippolyta's Stand: Orthros's standing army, founded by Hippolyta. Under her leadership, they patrol the border with Tenebra as Stewards of the Queens' ward. So few of the peaceful Hesperines take up the battle arts that Nike, Kadi, Mak, and Lyros are the only Stewards.

hold lord: Tenebran lord who holds a homestead in the eastern Tenebrae.

Honorable Families: noble bloodlines that rule the Archipelagos from aboard their fleets of dynastic ships.

House Annassa: the residence of the Queens of Orthros, the Hesperine counterpart to a royal palace.

House Komnena: Lio's family home in Orthros, seat of his bloodline, named for his mother.

Hulaic Epochs: eras of pre-history before the Great Temple Epoch, known only through oral traditions.

the Hunger: a combination of sexual desire and the need for blood, which Hesperines experience with their lovers.

Hylonome: bloodborn from Orthros's history who starved herself to death on the top of Hypatia's Observatory after the death of her Grace.

Hypatia: elder firstblood and founder of Orthros from Hagia Anatela, Gifted by Ourania. Grace of Khaldaios and mother of Kia. Orthros's greatest astronomer, who invented the Hesperine calendar.

Hypatia's Observatory: tower in Orthros established by Hypatia, where Hesperine astronomers study the heavens and teach their students. Every Autumn Equinox, Orthros's diplomats watch for the Summit Beacon from here.

Hypnos: god of death and dreams in the Tenebran and Cordian pantheon. Winter is considered his season. Humans unworthy of going to Anthros's Hall are believed to spend the afterlife in Hypnos's realm of the dead. According to myth, he is the brother of Anthros and Hespera.

In Sanctuary: Hesperine term for the current historical era, marked from the date of Orthros's founding.

initiate: Hesperine who has achieved initiate rank in their craft or service, more advanced than a student but not yet of full rank. Attained after the young Hesperine completes a significant crafting project or research treatise that meets with their mentor's approval.

Initiation: see **Trial**

Ioustin *or* **Ioustinianos:** First Prince of the Hesperines, eldest child of the Queens of Orthros. Lio's Ritual father. Solaced from Tenebra as a child. Once a warrior in the Blood Errant known as the Blood-Red Prince, he now leads a force of Hesperines errant known as the Charge. Young Hesperines call him Rudhira, an affectionate name given to him by Methu.

Iulios: royal firstblood and seventh prince of Orthros, the seventh child and youngest son of the Queens.

ivy pendant: wooden pendant carved with a triquetra of ivy. Secretly passed down from one Tenebran queen to another and finally, from Solia to Cassia. Imbued with Lustra magic and connected to the Changing Queen in some way, it allowed Cassia to access secret passages inside Solorum Palace.

Javed: Lio's Grace-cousin, avowed to Kadi, father of Bosko and Thenie. From the Empire in his mortal life. Has an affinity for healing and now serves in Orthros's Healing Sanctuary.

Kadi: see **Arkadia**

kaetlii: word in the tongue used by Tenebrans to train liegehounds, meaning the person the dog is bonded to and will protect until death.

Kalos: the Charge's best scout who uses his tracking skills to find Hesperines errant who are missing in action.

kalux: Hesperine word in the Divine Tongue for clitoris.

Kassandra: Lio's Ritual mother, an elder firstblood and founder of Orthros. Ritual sister to the Queens, who Gifted her, and mother of Prometheus. An Imperial princess in her mortal life, she became the first Hesperine from the Empire and secured Orthros's alliance with their Imperial allies. Now the Queens' Master Economist who oversees Orthros's trade. Has the gift of foresight and as Orthros's oracle, guides the Hesperines with her prophecies.

Khaldaios: elder Grace, avowed to Hypatia, father of Kia. From the Empire in his mortal life.

Kia: see **Eudokia**

King of Tenebra: see **Lucis**

Kings and Mages: Tenebran and Cordian name for the game Hesperines call Prince and Diplomat.

Kitharos: elder firstblood and founder of Orthros from Hagia Zephyra, father to Nodora. One of the Hesperines' greatest musicians.

Kleos: royal firstblood and Fourth Prince of Orthros, fourth child and second-youngest son of the Queens.

Knight: Cassia's beloved liegehound. Solia gave him to Cassia as a puppy so Cassia would have protection and companionship.

Knightly Order of Andragathos: holy warriors who adhere to a strict moral code and persecute Hesperines in the name of their patron god. See **Andragathos**

Komnena: Lio's mother, still rather young by Hesperines standards. Fled a life of squalor as a Tenebran farmwife and ran away to Orthros with Apollon, who Gifted her while she was pregnant and raised her son as his own. Now a respected mind healer. As the Queens' Chamberlain, she is responsible for helping newcomers to Orthros settle and adjust.

Konstantina *or* **Kona:** royal firstblood, Second Princess of Orthros, the second child and eldest daughter of the Queens. From the Empire in her mortal life. As the Royal Master Magistrate, she is the author of Orthros's legal code and an influential politician who oversees the proceedings of the Firstblood Circle.

krana: Hesperine term in the Divine Tongue for vagina.

Kumeta: Hesperine light mage and one of the two spymasters of Orthros, alongside her Grace, Basir. From the Empire in her mortal life. Her official title is "Queens' Master Envoy" to conceal the nature of their work.

Kyria: goddess of weaving and the harvest in the Tenebran and Cordian pantheon, known as the Mother Goddess or the Wife. Her season is autumn. According to myth, she is married to Anthros.

Laskara: Timarete's firstgift, Lyros's elder sister. One of Orthros's most renowned sculptors, know for her contributions to art and mathematics.

the Last War: the cataclysmic violence sparked by the Ordering sixteen hundred years ago. When the Order of Anthros sought to suppress all resistance to their authority, magical and armed conflict ravaged Tenebra and Cordium, destroying the civilization of the Great Temple Epoch. Peace came at the cost of the Hesperines' exile and the Order of Anthros's victory, while the Mage King secured his rule in Tenebra.

Laurentius: favored warrior of the Mage King. Worshiped Anthros, but loved Hesperite mage Makaria. After the Orders martyred her, he sacrificed himself in battle. Went to his funeral pyre with his amulet of Anthros and her votive statue of Hespera.

liegehound: war dogs bred and trained by Tenebrans to track, hunt, and slay Hesperines. Veil spells do not throw them off the scent, and they can leap high enough to pull a levitating Hesperine from the air. The only animals that do not trust Hesperines. They live longer than other canines and can withstand poison and disease.

Lio: see **Deukalion Komnenos**

Lion of Orthros: see **Apollon**

Lucis: current King of Tenebra, who reigns with ruthlessness and brutality. Born a lord, he secured the crown by might and political schemes, and he upholds his authority by any means necessary. Cassia has never forgiven him for Solia's death.

Lysandros *or* **Lyros:** Lio's Trial brother and Grace-cousin, avowed to Mak, Solaced as a child from Tenebra. Also a warder and warrior serving in the Stand.

Lyta: see **Hippolyta**

Mage King: King Lucian of Tenebra, who reigned sixteen hundred years ago, widely considered by Hesperines and mortals alike to have been a great monarch. He and his wife, the Changing Queen, made the original Equinox Oath with the Queens of Orthros. A fire mage and warrior, he ruled before the Mage Orders mandated that men must choose between wielding spells or weapons.

mage of dreams: mage of Hypnos with an affinity for thelemancy.

Mage Orders: the magical and religious authorities in Cordium, which also dictate sacred law to Tenebran temples. Responsible for training and governing mages and punishing heretics.

Mak: see **Telemakhos**

Makaria: Hesperite Sanctuary mage martyred in the Ordering. Lover of Laurentius Centuries later, Lio and Cassia fell in love at the shrine of Hespera she once tended near Solorum.

manteia: paradigm of magic that includes praeternatural affinities such as mind magic, foresight, and necromancy.

Martyrs' Pass: the only known passage to Orthros through the Umbral Mountains. Site of Aithouros's last stand against the Hesperines when he and his war mages tried to pursue them into Orthros.

Matsu: Nodora's Ritual mother and the only other Hesperine from the Archipelagos. A beloved thespian and fashion leader in Orthros.

Menodora: Hesperine youngblood, one of Lio's Trial sisters. Daughter of Kitharos and Dakarai. An initiate musician, admired vocalist, and crafter of musical instruments. She is one of only two Hesperines from the Archipelagos and the immortal expert on the music of her mortal homeland.

Mercy: Hesperine sacred tenet, the practice of caring for dead or dying humans.

methodological deconstruction: an application of magic by which a scholar can use observation and deduction to reverse charms and spells by mages of other affinities.

Methu: see **Prometheus**

Midnight Moonbeam: black-and-white dwarf goat kid, one of Zoe's two familiars.

mind healer: see **theramancer**

mind mage: see **thelemancer**

moon hours: by the Hesperine clock, the hours corresponding to night, when Hesperines pursue public activities.

moskos: Hesperine term in the Divine Tongue meaning testicles.

Muse of Orthros: Hesperine whose service is music, dancing, or poetry.

Namenti: Tenebran coastal city on the southern border, near Cordium.

New Guest House: guest house for visiting mortals on the docks of Selas, built four hundred years ago.

newblood: Hesperine youth, no longer a suckling child but not yet an initiated youngblood.

Nike: see **Pherenike**

Nivalis: young Tenebran lady, one of Lady Hadrian's followers who frequents her weaving room. Daughter of Lord and Lady Galanthian. Her three younger siblings died in a past epidemic of frost fever. Betrothed to Deverran.

Nodora: see **Menodora**

the Oath: see **Equinox Oath**

Oracle of Chera: mage with the gift of foresight, appointed by the Orders to serve in Corona. The affinity is so rare that usually only one woman is born with it in each generation.

Order of Anthros: Mage Order dedicated to the god Anthros, which holds the ultimate religious and magical authority over all other Orders and temples. Bent on destroying Hesperines. War mages, light mages, and warders serve in this Order, as do agricultural and stone mages.

Order of Hypnos: Mage Order devoted to Hypnos, which holds authority over necromancers, mind mages, and illusionists. Oversees rites for the dead, purportedly to prevent Hesperine grave robbing, but in practice to stop rogue necromancers from raising the dead. The Order of Anthros's closest ally in their effort to destroy Hesperines.

Ordered Time: Tenbran and Cordian term for the current historical era, which they mark from the Ordering.

the Orders: see **Mage Orders**

Orthros: homeland of the Hesperines, ruled by the Queens. The Mage Orders describe it as a horrific place where no human can survive, but in reality, it is a land of peace, prosperity, and culture. Located north of Tenebra.

Orthros Abroad: the population of Hesperines who are errant in Tenebra at any given time. Under the jurisdiction of the First Prince, who is the Queens' regent outside their ward.

Orthros Boreou: Hesperine homeland in the northern hemisphere, located north of and sharing a border with Tenebra.

Orthros Notou: Hesperine homeland in the southern hemisphere, near the Empire.

Orthros Warmbloods: unique breed of horses originated by Hippolyta. Hesperine blood magic gives them intelligence, strength, and longevity superior to mundane horses.

Ourania: Prisma of Hagia Anatela. Ritual firstblood and Gifter of Hypatia.

Pakhne: eldest daughter of Free Lord Galanthian, sister to Nivalis. Happily left her life as a lady to become a mage of Kyria. Travels to Orthros as one of the Semna's attendants during the Solstice Summit.

Perita: Cassia's handmaiden and dearest friend. Wife of Callen. Has assisted Cassia in her schemes ever since Cassia helped her save Callen from prison, and she delivered crucial information that enabled Cassia to save the Hesperine embassy from Dalos's assassination attempt.

Phaedric Terror: historical event during the Last War, when Phaedros sought to cure the world's ills by turning all humans into Hesperines. His campaign of forced Giftings resulted in many deaths and inflamed the conflict between Hesperines and the Mage Orders.

Phaedros: mage of Hespera and brilliant scholar from Hagia Notia, who received the Gift from one of the Ritual firstbloods. The only survivor of the temple's destruction by the Aithourian Circle. After he perpetrated the Phaedric Terror, he lost his status as an elder firstblood. Now lives in eternal exile under the midnight sun.

Pherenike: Lio's cousin, a warder and warrior second only to her mother Lyta in strength, a thelemancer second only to her father Argyros in power. Solaced from Tenebra as a child. Known as the Victory Star, one of the Blood Errant alongside her uncle, Apollon, and her Trial brothers Rudhira and Methu. After the surviving Blood Errant's campaign to avenge Methu, she remained Abroad alone and has now been missing in action for over ninety years.

Philo: see **Theophilos**

Prince and Diplomat: board game and beloved Hesperine pastime; requires strategy and practice to master. See **Kings and Mages**

Prince's Charge: the force of Hesperines errant that serve under the First Prince.

Prisma: highest ranking female mage in a temple.

the Prisma of the Temple of Kyria at Solorum: powerful mage who leads the women of her temple with pragmatism and kindness.

Prismos: highest ranking male mage in a temple.

Prometheus: legendary Hesperine warrior and martyr. Bloodborn to Kassandra and descendant of Imperial royalty. Known as the Midnight Champion, he was a member of the Blood Errant with his comrades Nike, Rudhira, and Apollon. Captured by the Aithourian Circle before Lio's birth. Orthros still mourns his death.

the Queens: the Hesperine monarchs of Orthros. See **Alea**, **Soteira**

the Queens' Couriers: young Hesperines who serve Orthros as messengers, delivering correspondence and packages throughout Selas.

the Queens' Terrace: a terrace at House Annassa that fulfills the function of a throne room, although the Queens sit together on a modest bench, and their terrace is open to all.

the Queens' ward: the powerful Sanctuary ward cast by the Queens, which spans the borders of Orthros, protecting Hesperines from human threats.

Rainbow Aurora: brown-and-white dwarf goat kid, one of Zoe's two familiars.

rhabdos: Hesperine term in the Divine Tongue meaning penis.

Ritual: Hesperine sacred tenet. A ceremony in which Hesperines share blood, but in a broader sense, the whole of their religious beliefs.

Ritual circle: area where Hesperines gather to perform Ritual, usually marked with sacred symbols on the floor.

Ritual firstbloods: the eight blood mages who performed the Ritual that created Hesperines. As the leaders of the Great Temples of Hespera, all except Alea were martyred during the Ordering. See **Alea, Anastasios, Daedala, Eidon, Ourania, Thelxinos**

Ritual hall: central chamber in Hesperine homes where the bloodline's Ritual circle is located.

Ritual parents: Hesperines who attend a new suckling's first Ritual or who give the Gift to a mortal who becomes a Hesperine as an adult. They remain mentors and trusted guides for eternity. Comparable to Tenebran temple parents.

Ritual tributary: Hesperine who establishes their own bloodline rather than joining their Gifter's family.

Rose House: the newest guest house on the docks of Selas, built in recent years by Apollon and Lio for Komnena's use.

royal firstbloods: the Queens' children, who are to establish their own bloodlines in order to share the Annassa's power with their people.

Rudhira: see **Ioustinianos**

Sanctuary: Hesperine sacred tenet, the practice of offering refuge to anyone in need. *Or* Hesperine refuge in hostile territory, concealed and protected from humans by Sanctuary magic.

Sanctuary mage: a mage with a rare dual affinity for warding and light magic, who can create powerful protections that also conceal. Queen Alea of Orthros is the only mage with this affinity who survived the Orders' persecution of Hespera worshipers.

Sanctuary Rose: a variety of white rose that originated in the Great Temples of Hespera. The only vine that survived the Last War now grows in Princess Konstantina's greenhouse, and she has propagated it throughout Orthros. Traditionally, each person who requests Sanctuary is given one of these blooms in welcome.

Sanctuary ward: ward created by a Sanctuary mage, which can both protect and hide those within it. Strong Sanctuary wards require the caster to remain inside the boundaries of the spell. Should the mage die there, their sacrifice will increase the ward's power and sustain it indefinitely.

Scions: lesser deities in the Tenebran and Cordian pantheon, the fourteen children of Anthros and Kyria, comprising seven sons and seven daughters. Each has their own cult and mages.

Sea of Komne: the sea that separates mainland Orthros from the landmass where Tenebra and Cordium are located.

Segetia: domain of Free Lord Titus, landlocked and known for its gentle hills.

Selas: capital city of Orthros Boreou.

Semna: elderly former Prisma of the Temple of Kyria at Solorum, who travels to Orthros for the Equinox Summit to spread her goddess's teachings to the Hesperines.

Severinus *or* **Severin:** son and heir of Severinus the Elder, who tries to mitigate his father's abuses against their people.

shamisen: long-necked, three-stringed musical instrument from the Archipelagos favored by Nodora.

share: human or immortal with whom a Hesperine is romantically involved, sharing blood and intimacy.

Skleros: master necromancer and Gift Collector who holds the Order of Hypnos's record for completing the most bounties on Hesperines. Expert in essential displacement.

Slumber: see **Dawn Slumber**

Solace: Hesperine sacred tenet, the practice of rescuing and Gifting abandoned children.

Solia: late Princess of Tenebra, King Lucis's legitimate daughter and heir before the birth of his son. When she was seventeen, rebel lords kidnapped her. Lucis refused to ransom her or collect her remains and ensured all witnesses perished in the ensuing Siege of Sovereigns. Nobles and commoners alike still mourn her.

Solorum: ancestral capital of Tenebra, royal seat of the king.

Solorum Fortress: castle built for the defense of the capital by seven successive kings over the course of two hundred years. The Hesperine embassy lodged here during the Equinox Summit due to the humans' fears.

Solstice Summit: diplomatic negotiations between Tenebra and Orthros marking the first time a mortal embassy from Tenebra has ever entered Hesperine lands. An unprecedented event proposed by Lio in an effort to build on the tradition of the Equinox and rescue relations between Tenebra and Orthros.

sophia: title of a Hesperine whose service is teaching and scholarship.

Soteira: one of the two Queens of Orthros, who has ruled the Hesperines for nearly sixteen hundred years with her Grace, Alea. Originally from the Empire, she was a powerful mortal mage with an affinity for healing before leaving to found Orthros alongside Alea.

speires: symbolic hair ties Lyta gives to trainees when they begin learning the battle arts. Stewards wear them as part of their Stand regalia.

the Stand: see **Hippolyta's Stand**

starflake: evergreen tree that thrives in Orthros's climate. Its fruit, which it bears in winter, is sweet with a tart aftertaste, a beloved Hesperine delicacy.

stepping: innate Hesperine ability to teleport instantly from one place to another with little magical effort.

Steward: see **Hippolyta's Stand**

Summit Beacon: bonfire on the border between Tenebra and Orthros, which the King of Tenebra lights to announce to the Hesperines he wishes to convene the Equinox Summit.

Sun Temple: see **Temple of Anthros at Solorum**

sunbound: mild Hesperine curse word.

Sunfire Poison: alchemical poison concocted from sunsword and Anthros's fire. Lethal to Hesperines at the right dose, in smaller amounts it can reduce them to mortal strength and ability.

sunsword: herb commonly grown in Tenebra, used by humans in combination with the flower Anthros's fire to ward off Hesperines.

Telemakhos: Lio's cousin and best friend. Exposed as a child in Tenebra due to his club foot, Solaced by Argyros and Lyta. A warrior by profession and warder by affinity, he serves in the Stand. He and his Grace, Lyros, are newly avowed.

Temple of Anthros at Solorum: temple in Tenebra's capital, once an ancient site of outdoor Anthros worship that was later walled and roofed by kings. The temple of the royal mage, where the king and his court attend rites.

Temple of Hedon: any temple dedicated to the god Hedon, where the Orders allow prostitution and gambling in order to control and profit from such activities.

Temple of Kyria at Solorum: most influential and respected temple of Kyria in Tenebra, located near the royal palace. Houses orphans and provides healing services to the surrounding area. Due to their reputation and magical power, the women here enjoy a great degree of autonomy.

Tenebra: human kingdom south of Orthros and north of Cordium. Agrarian, feudal society ruled by a king, prone to instability due to rivalries between lords. Land of the Hesperines' origin, where they are now persecuted.

the Tenebrae: former name of Tenebra, a plural indicating the free lords' independent domains under the nominal rule of a king affirmed by the Council. King Lucis has since changed the name to Tenebra, singular, to symbolize how he has united the kingdom under his absolute power.

thelemancer: a mage with an affinity for thelemancy, or mind magic, which gives them the power to manipulate others' thoughts and control their Wills.

Thelxinos: Prismos of Hagia Zephyra. Ritual firstblood and Gifter of Kitharos.

Thenie: see **Athena**

Theophilos: ancient Hesperine, Orthros's greatest master crafter of stained glass, who mentored Lio in his craft.

theramancer: a person with an affinity for theramancy, or mind healing, who can use magic to treat mental illness.

Thorn: Rudhira's two-handed sword, which he carried as one of the Blood Errant and now wields as he leads the Charge.

Timarete: elder firstblood and founder of Orthros from Hagia Zephyra, Gifted by Daedala. Mother of Laskara and Lyros. One of the Hesperines' greatest painters.

Titus: free lord of Segetia, one of the most powerful men in Tenebra, who commands the fealty of many other free lords and lesser nobles. Segetia has been feuding with Hadria for generations.

Trial circle: age set of Hesperines who go through the Trial of Initiation together. They consider each other Trial sisters and brothers for the rest of their immortal lives. Although not related by birth or blood, they maintain strong bonds of loyalty and friendship for eternity.

Trial of Initiation *or* **Trial:** Hesperine rite of passage marking an immortal's transition into adulthood.

Tychon: young war mage with an affinity for fire, Chrysanthos's apprentice. Zealous in his devotion to his master and the Aithourian Circle's cause.

Union: Hesperine sacred tenet, the principle of living with empathy and compassion for all. See **Blood Union**

veil hours: by the Hesperine clock, the hours corresponding to day, when Hesperines Slumber or devote their private time to friends, family, and lovers.

veil spell: innate Hesperine ability to cast magical concealments that hide their presence and activities from humans or fellow immortals.

Vulgus *or* **the vulgar tongue:** common language of all non-mages in Tenebra and Cordium.

war mage: mage with an affinity for fire, lightning, or other type of magic that can be weaponized. The Order of Anthros compels them to dedicate their lives to the Aithourian Circle.

warder: mage with an affinity for warding, the power to create magical protections that block spells or physical attacks.

Waystar: Hesperine fortress, Orthros's first refuge for those crossing the border from Tenebra. Hesperines errant who use weapons must leave their armaments here before crossing the Sea of Komne to Selas.

Will: free will, willpower. *Or* Hesperine sacred tenet, the principle of guarding the sanctity of each person's freedom of choice.

Winter Solstice: the most sacred time of the Hesperine year, when they celebrate Hespera with the sacred Festival of the Rose and Vigil of Thorns.

Xandra: see **Alexandra**

youngblood: young adult Hesperine who has recently reached their majority by passing the Trial of Initiation.

Zoe *or* **Zosime:** Lio's little sister, a seven-year-old Eriphite child Solaced by Apollon and Komnena. Loves her new family and idolizes her brother for his role in saving her from Tenebra. Has yet to heal from the emotional wounds she suffered as a mortal.

PART TWO
BLOOD SANCTUARY
BLOOD GRACE BOOK IV

**When an ancient evil rises,
can they save the peace talks and their love?**

Lio and Cassia spend their nights in each other's arms, but sit on opposite sides of the negotiation table. Their clandestine partnership has brought his immortal kin and her fellow humans close to a treaty after generations of violence. Lives hang in the balance. Failure means war. Peace would bring the future they hope for, when their love will no longer be forbidden.

Just when success is within reach, they realize their plan has played into the enemy's hands. A threat lurks within the delegation, an old nemesis with magic unlike any they have ever faced. Together, are they strong enough to stop the destruction of everything they love?

Steamy romance meets classic fantasy worldbuilding in Blood Grace, now in a new edition with a map and glossary. Follow fated mates Lio and Cassia through their epic love story for a guaranteed series HEA.

Blood Sanctuary Parts One and Two were previously published as one ebook

Learn more at
vroth.co/sanctuary2

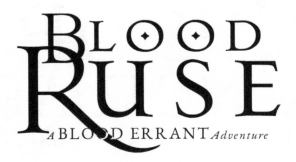

Saving damsels is all in a night's work for these four chivalrous Hesperines. Too bad the gutsy women believe they're the enemy.

The Blood Errant are famous heroes. Or infamous monsters, depending on who you ask. When they set out to save a roadside inn from bandits, they can't show their fangs to the charming locals.

In a daring trick, they pose as human guests with the help of Apollon's mortal lover. Alas, Methu cannot woo the vivacious innkeeper while impersonating a cleric. Or can he? Nike pretends to be a lady, but spars with a handsome soldier. Rudhira plays the role of holy knight even as the lovely barmaid stirs his forbidden desires.

If anyone sees through their disguises, their allies will be more dangerous than their enemies.

In this romantic fantasy, join the Blood Errant on their past adventures in battle and misadventures in love.

Get this book for free when you
sign up for my newsletter!
vroth.co/ruse

ACKNOWLEDGEMENTS

It's wonderful to be publishing books as part of the FaRoFeb community. With FaRoFeb 2022 having just finished, I want to thank all the authors, readers, bloggers, and other book lovers who helped those of us on the organizers team make this year's event such a huge success.

In particular, I want to give my gratitude to my fellow members of the team. Simply put, you are some of the best people I've ever had the privilege of knowing. Here's to many more FaRo events together!

Team FaRoFeb

HR Moore (founder)	Trish Heinrich	Elsie Winters
Lisette Marshall	S.L. Prater	MJ Faraldo
Colleen Cowley	Zoey Ellis	

I'm also thrilled and humbled by the reader community that has grown up around the Blood Grace series, not only in the years leading up to now, but in the two short months since the Blood Mercy launch.

I want to dedicate these acknowledgements to those of you who have become my Ambassadors for Orthros. Thank you for lending your incredible talents to helping Blood Grace succeed and for friendships that are about so much more than just my books.

Mak hugs to all of you!

Editor & Research Ambassador   **PA & Ambassadors Coordinator**
Brittany @brittany.wilson1764   Kaija @strictlybookish_kai

Ambassadors

Abi @words_and_dreams

Abigail @a_reads_alot

Ahana @tohearts_content

Alex

Alisha

Angela

Anshul @stories.buddy

Ashleigh

Aurora @AuroraLydia

Barbara

Brandy @better_0ff_read

Bridie

Brittany @bookwyvernlovestea

Carole

Cheyenne

Christine @
anxioustattooedandbookish

Deborah

Emily @thehamsterreads

Erika @theenchantedshelf

Haley @thecaffeinated.reader

Heather @_the_forgotten_books

Jessica @reddoorromance

Jessica @readbelievelove

Jordie @bookish.and.blonde

Julie @1bookmore

Kadie

Keshia @808bookdr

Kris @a_bookish_dream

Kristen

Kristin @madhattersfolly_reads

Leah @leahlovestoread

Madhu @mabookyard

Megan @bookish_megeen

Melissa

Nadine

Nancy

Nat

Nicole @starsbooksandtea

Nina

Patricia @myromancehasnolimits

Raley

Riley @paperroselibrary

Rishma @bookaddict__ril

Sahana @books_and_draws_
eclectic

Samantha @
bookobsessedandblonde

Sarah @books.and.tea.princess

Sarah @theheavycrownreads

Sharon

Sherri

Shreya @my_fair_fiction

Sonya

Stephanie

Tammy

Tara

Taylor @tmo_reads

Tia @tiaisreading

Whitney

ABOUT THE AUTHOR

VELA ROTH grew up with female-driven fantasy books and classic epics, then grew into romance novels. She set out to write stories that blend the rich worlds of fantasy with the passion of romance.

She has pursued a career in academia, worked as a web designer and book formatter, and stayed home as a full-time caregiver for her loved ones with severe illnesses. Writing through her own grief and trauma, she created the Blood Grace series, whtich now offers comfort to readers around the world.

She lives in a solar-powered writer's garret in the Southwestern United States, finding inspiration in the mountains and growing roses in the desert. Her feline familiar is a rescue cat named Milly with a missing fang and a big heart.

Vela loves hearing from readers and hopes you'll visit her at velaroth.com.

CPSIA information can be obtained
at www.ICGtesting.com
Printed in the USA
LVHW042343211222
735706LV00001B/41